GOING GREEN

OTHER TITLES BY NICK SPALDING

Logging Off
Dumped Actually
Dry Hard
Checking Out
Mad Love
Bricking It
Fat Chance
Buzzing Easter Bunnies
Blue Christmas Balls

Love . . . Series

Love . . . From Both Sides
Love . . . And Sleepless Nights
Love . . . Under Different Skies
Love . . . Among the Stars

Life . . . Series

Life . . . On a High
Life . . . With No Breaks

Cornerstone Series

The Cornerstone
Wordsmith

GOING GREEN

NICK SPALDING

LAKE UNION
PUBLISHING

Text copyright © 2020 by Nick Spalding
All rights reserved.

Published by Lake Union Publishing, Seattle

www.apub.com

Amazon, the Amazon logo, and Lake Union Publishing are trademarks of Amazon.com, Inc., or its affiliates.

ISBN-13: 9781542017503
ISBN-10: 1542017505

Cover design by Ghost Design

Printed in the United States of America

To everyone who is trying to do what they can.
Keep it up. It'll be worth it, trust me.

Chapter One

CLIMATE CHANGE

Glass . . . Glass . . . Glass . . .

Why do none of these sodding drinks ever come in something made of *glass*?

Hugh Burnley Fishingstool tells me I should be buying more of my drinks in glass bottles, instead of plastic ones, but how the hell am I supposed to do that when there are literally none on display here in the Meal Deal section of Boots?

I shouldn't even be spending this much time looking, though, because time is something I most definitely do not have today.

I'm already ten minutes late for work, and I simply don't have the precious minutes to waste peering at the refrigerator section, trying in vain to locate a smoothie that isn't contained within the dubious confines of a single-use plastic bottle.

Hugh Wormley Fittingshawl will just have to look down on me with disgust.

I have to get going, and I have to get going *now*!

I grab a bottle of Evian, and pile it on top of my chicken mayo sandwich, along with a slightly sweaty-looking millionaire's flap-jack. None of this looks all that appealing, if we're being perfectly honest here – but given that the sandwich person who used to come around the office at lunchtime has been let go thanks to all of the cutbacks, and because I have no time to prepare food myself, I am forced to grab this kind of bland culinary experience every day, or starve to death.

If it were only the sandwich person that had disappeared from work, then things wouldn't be in the dire straits that they are. But so much more has gone wrong, and it isn't over yet.

. . . which is the reason I can't be any later than I already am!

It's become hard enough to avoid getting the heave-ho from Stratagem PR recently – without turning up dishevelled, and ten minutes late.

I *have* to get to work!

The queue at the till is of course twice as long as it usually is.

When I eventually get to the girl on the till, I curse myself internally when I realise I have once again forgotten my bag-for-life.

There are now ten or twelve of the bloody things floating about in the cupboard under the stairs. Sadly, I don't also have one tucked away in my handbag, waiting for me to pull it out and do my bit for the polar bears.

I'll just buy another one. It'll be fine.

Hugh Turnley Wobblingschool will be turning in his grave. Or possibly his kitchen, as I'm pretty sure he's still alive.

But I don't have time for the guilt to suffuse every part of my being. That's just the way of things today.

Neither do I have time to exchange pleasantries with the till girl. As soon as she's idly beeped the Meal Deal across the scanner, I stuff it all into the hastily grabbed bag-for-'life', and head for the exit as fast as my late-for-work legs can carry me.

My idiotic Mercedes C-Class starts to clobberdy-bang before I've even driven it out of the car park. The clobberdy-bang usually doesn't begin until I've been driving for at least five minutes, but this morning it starts as soon as I turn the ignition key.

I have no idea what the clobberdy-bang is. It is a thing of purest mystery.

The clobberdy-bang has been going on for a few months now, but the car is still driving okay, and the noise really isn't all that loud – especially if you turn the radio up.

Okay, the occasional black smoke that emanates from the exhaust pipe when it happens isn't good, I will concede that. But again – and I can't stress this enough – the car is *still driving okay.*

I'll get the problem sorted out at the garage sooner or later, but it will not be today. I'm sure the car will get me the five miles down the road to work, clobberdy-bang or no clobberdy-bang. The Germans know how to build cars that can put up with things like clobberdy-bangs. They're famous for it.

I've said clobberdy-bang way too much. The phrase is now going around and around in my head like a strange, alien mantra.

God, I'm tired. I probably shouldn't have been up until 1 a.m. last night ordering stuff in the ASOS sale, but it was up to 70 per cent off, for crying out loud. I simply had no choice!

I'm riddled with buyer's remorse this morning, of course. In a couple of days I'm getting three dresses, two tops and a pair of leggings delivered to my door that I will probably feel a bit sick about taking from the delivery guy. Especially when I still have two pairs of jeans I have yet to wear that I bought in the *last* ASOS sale. Cream and burgundy seemed like a good idea at the time.

What can I say? I'm a sucker for an online bargain – and for browsing the internet at inappropriate times.

. . . which is why I have sandy eyes and a permanent yawn today.

Luckily for me, the traffic isn't too bad this morning, and I manage to make it to Stratagem in relatively good time – having made up a few minutes by breaking the speed limit to the extent that I'm lucky there are no coppers about.

As I pull frantically into the large car park that serves the whole ten-storey office block, I have to slam on my brakes so I don't crash straight into a tall man in a slightly ill-fitting suit as he crosses in front of me.

My fault entirely. I'm going way too fast – such is my desire to get up into the office as quickly as possible. He looks at me through the windscreen of the Mercedes in horror, backing away a few paces as I screech to a halt. I return the look with one of harassed apology. He's a good-looking guy, which makes this near collision even worse. The first attractive man I've been around in ages, and I nearly kill him.

It's at this moment that the car decides to give me the biggest clobberdy-bang of the day yet, accompanied by a billow of black smoke from the exhaust that travels straight over to the poor man I've nearly just shuffled off this mortal coil, enveloping him in its toxic miasma, forcing him to cough out loud.

Mouthing 'sorry' for all I'm worth, I drive slowly past him as he recovers from the gassing I've just delivered, and carry on deeper into the car park, my heart hammering.

I find a parking space right at the back, near the bins, and leap out of the car, grabbing my Boots Meal Deal as I do so.

It's only ten past nine by the time the elevator door pings open, and I hurry across the fifth-floor atrium towards the company's main doors.

That's not too bad, is it? Not a sackable offence, to be just ten minutes late? It was all the fault of the poor selection on offer at Boots.

As I walk into Stratagem PR's offices, the familiar blanket of gloom enshrouds me like an unwanted relative.

It's been like this for weeks now. If you've ever wanted to know what it's like to work in a coffin, pop by sometime.

Okay, I may be slightly exaggerating for effect, but not by much. My place of work has gone from one I thoroughly enjoyed, to somewhere I dread coming into each and every day.

It's a little hard not to feel that way, when you can see the place falling apart in front of your eyes, like a slow-motion car crash that just won't end.

It was a *tractor* crash that started it all, two years ago . . . but that was only the first in a long series of misfortunes that have plagued Stratagem PR.

Not least of which was when Pierre left Peter. That was the real turning point, I think. A company can't really survive the break-up of its founders. Not this one, anyway.

Peter and Pierre Rothman have been the beating heart of this PR firm since I joined five years ago – and when one half of that beating heart decided it didn't want to be with the other half any more, it stopped beating completely.

Poor old Peter has tried his best to keep going with Stratagem on his own, but it's been like watching a pining dog circling a gravestone. Without his partner by his side, Peter has been lost, distracted, and the whole business has suffered for it.

Clients started deserting us like rats leaving a sinking ship after Pierre was gone – the biggest rat being my ex-boyfriend Robert, of course. I pleaded with him not to take his property develop-ment company away from Stratagem, but he was having none of it – which meant I was having none of *him* from that moment on.

I broke up with him right in the middle of Stratagem's offices. It was highly embarrassing for everyone concerned. Except Robert – I doubt he has the capacity to be embarrassed about anything. There I was, all snotty and teary-eyed in front of all my colleagues, and he looked entirely unconcerned about the whole thing. Given that I'd made such a huge deal of dating him to everyone, he could have at least pretended to care that I was splitting up with him in such a histrionic manner, the utter bastard.

Sigh. Never mix business with pleasure, kids. That's the hard and painful lesson I learned with that relationship. Thank God it only lasted a few months.

The Christmas flood didn't help Stratagem's fortunes either. We all came in on 27 December to find that the whole office had turned into an aquatic fun park. So had the offices in two of the floors above us, and every single one below.

All because somebody had shoved a pair of knickers into something called a macerator. Quite how they'd managed this is anybody's guess. The plumbers were so nonplussed, one of them thought it could have been an act of God.

Given that the knickers were white, a bit baggy, and emblazoned with Santa Claus penetrating one of his reindeer, I'm more inclined to think it was an act of Drunk.

The water penetration took weeks to sort out. We all had to work from home, and as I'm sure you're aware, there's a vast difference between working in the office and 'working from home' for those who aren't used to the experience.

The whole episode cost Stratagem *thousands* – and added to Peter's mounting stress, of course. We've all been tiptoeing around him in the months since – hoping against hope that the company's fortunes would start to turn.

This has not yet happened.

Hence the pervading sense of gloom and doom that hits me like a depressed sledgehammer the second I walk on to the office floor.

I fight against it as I hurry my way over to my desk. If I can get to it, and keep my head down, then maybe no one will notice how tardy I am.

I get some fairly desultory glances from most of my work colleagues as I rush past them, trying not to make eye contact. This previously vibrant, happy bunch have been reduced to cold stares and shrugged shoulders. It really is quite a horrible thing to both witness and be a part of.

I know damn well that, in about twenty minutes, I will be exhibiting exactly the same kind of behaviour. The atmosphere in this place does it to you.

Still . . . this apathy does mean that nobody really gives a shit that I'm late for work, so I am able to reach my desk and set myself up for the day without anyone taking me to task.

I should be happy about this, but I'm comprehensively *not* – because any workplace that doesn't care whether you're late or not is probably a workplace that isn't long for this world.

The knickers are well and truly stuck in the macerator – figuratively speaking, anyway.

I fire up the PC and look at my inbox. This is free of new emails, save for a spam piece of marketing, asking me if I want to invest in gold bullion. I have about as much money in my bank account as there is hope in this office, so I delete the offer and sigh.

There was a time when my inbox would be full every day.

. . . is it possible to slit your wrists with a plastic bottle bought in Boots?

Just behind me I hear the sound of Peter's office door opening, and I turn to see him walk out. He has a tentative, nervous look on his face.

Oh dear.

Oh dear, oh dear, oh dear.

That is the face of someone who's about to impart dreadful knowledge.

I'm about to lose my job.

The cold certainty of it strikes me at my very core. Peter hasn't even opened his mouth yet, but I know what he's about to say.

He's going to stand there in front of the dozen of us that are left, out of the twenty plus who used to work here, and he's going to tell us that our jobs are going into the same macerator that chewed up the Xmas knickers.

My heart leaps into my throat.

I'm going to have to find another job. I'm going to have to go to job interviews. I'm going to have to – *gulp* – put myself *out there* again.

'Good morning, everyone,' Peter says to us, hesitantly. I instantly feel incredibly sorry for him. This must be so very difficult.

Pierre was always the stronger of the two when it came to this kind of stuff. He used to do all of the hiring and firing. Peter was always the creative driving force of Stratagem, and Pierre was the businessman.

'I have some . . . some news I need to impart to you.' Peter takes a deep breath, and unconsciously pulls at the front of his tailored powder-blue shirt.

This is like watching a small boy confess that he's just smashed the greenhouse window with his football.

'If you could all gather in the conference room at ten a.m., I'll tell you about it then.'

Oh, great. He's prolonging the agony.

Why not just throw our P45s at us now, and let us get out of here before lunchtime?

'What's this about, Peter?' asks Nadia from her desk next to mine, a distraught look on her face. My heart instantly goes out to her. I only have myself to worry about, but Nadia has a daughter, a husband and a mortgage. She's not been the same since Kate left Stratagem last year, and everything that's gone on since has probably hit her harder than it has the rest of us.

'It's . . . it's about the future of the company, Nadia,' Peter replies, in a very shaky voice.

'Are we losing our jobs?' Terry pipes up from his desk at the other end of the office.

Terry McClellan is in his late forties, and is probably dreading the prospect of having to find new work even more than I am. The marketing and PR business is cruel enough to people like me, in their early thirties – it's an absolute horror show for anyone around the age of fifty. The chances of Terry finding another job easily are slim to none.

Peter looks anguished. 'Please, Terry. Let's just all meet in the conference room shortly. I've been asked to wait until then to say anything more.'

'Asked?' Terry replies, confused. 'Asked by who?'

'Everything will be made clear shortly, Terry. Please just wait.'

Well, this is slightly bizarre. There's obviously someone else calling the shots here. Is it Pierre? Has he come back? Are things nowhere near as bad as they seem?

If that were the case, I doubt Peter would look so distraught.

As we all watch him slump back through the tinted glass door to his office, I start to chew on one fingernail, and wonder what's in store for us when we go into our small conference room in a few minutes.

I have to fight down another swell of panic when I realise that the most likely outcome is still the loss of my job – regardless of who is pulling the strings.

Oh God.

I don't want to lose my job. I *love* my fucking job!

Well . . . I did, up until the last few months anyway. Stratagem was a fun, exciting place to work. We had some great clients (with the large and obnoxious exception of my aforementioned ex-boyfriend, Robert Ainslie Blake), a strong portfolio and a happy work environment. My colleagues and I used to go out together for drinks on a Friday night, and we'd generally have a whale of a time. We got along so well that it was always something I really looked forward to.

I want that back again! I don't want it to all fall apart!

I don't want to have to update my bloody CV, and try to prove that I'm worthy of employment to anyone else. I want to stay here!

. . . I'm aware that I'm starting to sound like a spoiled little girl who doesn't want to go to Grandma's for tea, but fear and stress always tend to make me regress a bit. Sometimes the unfairness of the world just makes you want to retreat back to a time when things were simpler and easier to understand.

Also, little girls don't have to go out and find new jobs, do they? The lucky little sods.

At 9.59 a.m., my mouth goes incredibly dry. This always tends to happen to me when I'm extremely nervous. As the clock strikes ten, I take a big swig of water from my Evian bottle, and go to join my colleagues as we troop into the conference room.

If you've ever watched an episode of *The Walking Dead*, you'll recognise the short line of people that shamble their way in. Or possibly, a more accurate analogy would be a herd of particularly depressed cows going to slaughter.

I take a seat around the circular boardroom table with the other doomed cattle, and start to squeeze my half-empty bottle of water nervously. I can feel my heart jackhammering in my chest as the nerves ramp up.

As we all get about as settled as a group of people can be when they're terrified, in walks Peter, looking equally nervous. He knows he has some horrible information to impart to us, and he'd quite clearly rather be anywhere else than here – up to and including inside a macerator, next to a pair of dirty Xmas knickers.

And then . . . somebody else walks in behind Peter. A man I have seen only once before.

He's tall, quite thin, slightly awkward-looking, and wearing a dark-blue suit that's probably a size too big for him. The thick mop of black hair on top of his head is unruly, and the expression on his face is one of expectant anxiety. He looks to be about my age – though there's a youthful quality to his face that means he can probably pass for a lot younger in the right light. You might call him 'unconventionally handsome', if you were pressed to provide a description. There's a touch of Adam Driver about his looks.

And it's *him*.

The guy from the car park.

The one I nearly murdered with my malfunctioning Mercedes.

Oh, fucking hallelujah. This is going to be *wonderful*, isn't it?

Peter gets to the head of the table, with the other man standing next to him, offering us all one of those smiles people tend to plaster over their face when they have to greet a room full of complete strangers.

It's meant to convey warmth and friendliness, but rather comes across as someone who's hoping that they're not about to be assaulted.

'Thanks for gathering here, folks,' Peter begins. 'I'm going to try to keep my part in this meeting as quick as possible, before I hand over to Nolan here.' His eyes go wide. 'Oh, I'm sorry, everybody, please say hello to Nolan Reece.'

'Hi,' Nolan Reece says, waving a hand at us and broadening that smile a bit.

'Hi,' we all parrot back at him, returning the wave. The confusion plastered across our faces must be quite something to behold.

'So, this is how things are,' Peter continues, holding out his hands. He takes a deep breath. 'I have sold Stratagem PR, and will be stepping down immediately as its CEO.'

Gasps. Groans. Moans.

Make no mistake, Peter Rothman has been the best boss I've ever had. Kind, hard-working, honest and understanding.

'Please . . . it's okay. Honestly it is,' he tells us. 'This was the only way this was going to go. I simply couldn't keep Stratagem running any more in the state it's in.'

Well, that is a fair enough point, I suppose.

'It's right for me to leave, and start a new chapter in my life,' he says.

Can't disagree with that. And even as he speaks, I can see a transformation happening on the face of my (former) boss. It's a cliché to say that someone has a weight lifted from their shoulders, but it genuinely looks like that's what's happening to Peter Rothman right now. He grows about two inches right in front of me.

'But it's also right that Stratagem continues,' Peter carries on. 'And the only way for me to guarantee that was to sell it to someone who can bring it back from the brink.' He gestures towards the man standing next to him. 'And that someone is Nolan here.'

Slowly, inexorably, a dozen pairs of eyes turn to regard the tall, skinny man, with a mixture of curiosity, doubt and probably a little fear.

Nobody likes the unknown, do they?

Nolan Reece does the smile-and-wave thing again. 'Hello everyone, it's very nice to meet you all,' he says, and looks at Peter.

'Er . . . Nolan here is the new owner of the company,' my former boss tells us, before lapsing into an awkward silence.

Nolan stares at Peter for a moment, before realising that this is his time to speak. 'Oh! Yes! Yes, I am!' he says, clapping his hands together and looking back at us. 'And I'm very happy to have bought it!'

I'm not sure he looks it. In fact, he looks like someone suffering from the same kind of buyer's remorse I always get after my ASOS order has been delivered.

This, as you can imagine, I find *extremely* reassuring.

'I'm happy to have bought it, because it gives me a chance to both secure the future of such a renowned and respected PR company . . .'

Hmmm. Not sure we're all that renowned, to be honest, but I like his confidence in us.

' . . . and also because it gives me a chance to do something I've always wanted to do.'

Make your employees fight to the death for their jobs?

Nolan Reece seems to relax as he speaks. Now we're past that awkward introduction stage, he's warming to the crowd.

'I've been in the marketing and PR game for most of my working life,' he tells us, 'and have done okay out of it.'

'Nolan here was the man responsible for bringing Walker & Wright Pharmaceuticals back from the brink,' Peter interjects.

I blink a couple of times. That *is* bloody impressive. Walker & Wright Pharmaceuticals nearly went under a few years ago, because its CEO was caught molesting a pig on camera, while high as a kite on some of the company's own product.

Don't laugh.

It was *harrowing*.

Walker & Wright quickly became *Porker* & Wright, to anyone born with a sense of humour. Said CEO went slightly bonkers in the aftermath, and made some decisions before he was forced out that further ruined the company's reputation.

All seemed lost, but then a PR firm called Chantry Relations was hired to turn things around . . . and boy, did they. An aggressive campaign to change the company's branding and reputation began in earnest, and now W2 Pharma is one of the most respected businesses of its type in the UK. Nobody even mentions the pig thing any more – except at parties.

Nolan Reece looks humble. 'I did my part.'

'Did your part?' Peter exclaims. 'You designed the whole damn campaign!'

'Well, yes, I guess I did . . . and it was a very successful promotion for me.'

Yeah. I bet it was. Rumour has it that Chantry Relations built a performance-related bonus into its contract with the then-desperate Porker & Wright, which meant that when the pharma company's fortunes turned around, they were blessed with a massive dump of cash.

If Nolan here was part of that, no wonder he has the money to buy Peter out.

Mind you . . . given the way things have been, we were probably worth about £3.64 and a packet of AA batteries.

'Working for Chantry was great,' Nolan tells us, 'but I've always wanted to run my own PR company, so when the opportunity came up to buy Stratagem, I jumped at it. It'll give me the chance to do what I've always wanted to.'

'And what's that?' I blurt out, immediately going wide-eyed. It's not like me to speak up in such circumstances, but I'm currently suffering an intolerable level of confusion, doubt and worry, and my social skills have apparently been deeply affected by it.

Nolan Reece and Peter Rothman both look at me in surprise. As does everyone else in the room. I shrink into my chair a little. How decidedly embarrassing.

'I know you, don't I?' Nolan says, gently pointing a finger in my direction.

I elect for subterfuge. 'No! No, I don't think we've ever met.'

This is actually true, if you think about it. Nearly running somebody down in a car park can't really be classed as having 'met' them, can it?

Nolan nods a little uncertainly. I'm not sure he believes me. I certainly wouldn't.

'I've always wanted to run a PR company that emphasises working with environmentally friendly businesses,' he tells us – or rather *me*. He's still got a pleasant expression on his face, but the focus he's now putting just on me is a little bit disconcerting. Those eyes are quite piercing, when their attention is solely on you. I would be blushing like mad, because he is a handsome chap, but the worry about what's going to happen to Stratagem is keeping me very pale at the moment. With any luck, the two things might actually balance my complexion out, and I'll look normal. 'The environment and climate change are things I'm passionate about, and I'm at the stage in my career where I'd like to think I can help do something about them.'

He stops talking and gives me a smile.

Oh God. I think he wants me to *reply*.

My stupid intervention has focused all of his attention on me, and now I have to respond.

'That's . . . that's . . . *nice*?' I say, squirming in my seat and going red in the face.

What else am I supposed to add? It is *nice*. Being environmentally friendly is very *nice*. I don't know anyone who would think otherwise. I'd like to say something a bit more impressive than that, but Nolan Reece's focus on me has left me more than a little discombobulated.

'Yes, I guess it is,' Nolan says, still examining me, a little like someone examines a particularly strange and alien-looking creature they've just discovered hiding in their garden pond. He's still wondering whether he's actually met me before or not – I can tell.

'More than nice though, I hope!' he continues, returning (thankfully) to address the whole crowd. 'I want to run an ethical PR company that prides itself on its green credentials.' He holds out his hands expansively. 'And I want you all to be part of it!' He stops himself. 'Well . . . almost all of you. I'm afraid I don't quite have the money to keep you all on. I'm so sorry about that.'

The cold hand of fear runs down my back.

We're not all going to keep our jobs.

The mood in the room immediately turns dark.

Dark*er*, I should say. I don't think any of us were exactly turning somersaults about the company being bought out in the first place. But that pales alongside the knowledge that some of us might be heading out of the door.

Nolan immediately looks regretful, like he knows he probably should have broken that piece of news a little more *carefully*. 'We'll only have to let a couple of you go, though! Two or three at most. I'll be having a close look at all of Stratagem's finances, and coming to a decision after that. Rest assured that any of you we can't keep on will have solid redundancy packages in place!'

That's when Nolan looks right at me again, and my soul dies a little.

My hand also involuntarily squeezes the Evian bottle I'm holding, creating a loud, obnoxious scrunching noise and sending the remaining contents up and out, all over the conference table.

'Eeeek!' I squawk, and immediately start rubbing at it with my hand, as if my skin has suddenly turned sponge-like.

'Can somebody get Ellie some tissues to mop that up?' Peter asks, and my face flames even redder.

'Ellie?' Nolan Reece says.

Oh, great. Now he knows my name.

'Yes . . . it's Ellie,' I reply, still frantically massaging water across the desk with my hand for some reason. I look like I've developed some kind of problem with my motor functions. 'Ellie Cooke.' I then hold out my hand, which is now dripping with water, for him to shake.

He does not do this.

Of course he does not do this. Why the hell would he?

Nadia leans forward and hands me a wad of tissue that someone has kindly spirited from somewhere, and I soak up the water with it.

So, now I have a mound of unsightly wet tissue parked in front of me, to go next to the crushed water bottle. This is not turning out to be a good meeting for me, is it?

Nolan looks at me closely again, as I turn my attention back to him. 'Do you . . . do you drive a Mercedes?' he asks, the realisation dawning in his eyes.

I am saved from having to respond when Terry stands up from his seat at the back of the room. 'Mr Reece, when exactly will you be letting us know who's getting the sack?' he asks bluntly.

Thank you, Terry. Thank you for turning everyone's attention away from Ellie Cooke and her wodge of used tissue, and single-use plastic. You are a godsend, sir.

'It's going to take me a few days to go through it . . . er . . . ?'

'Terry.'

'Terry. But I promise I won't leave you all hanging for too long. I want us to get started on our new business portfolio as soon as possible. I already have many contacts I want to exploit, all of whom are committed to more environmentally friendly practices.'

'What kind of practices?' asks Amisha, our supremely talented social media manager. She won't be going anywhere, I wouldn't imagine. She's far too good at her job to be let go.

The same goes for Amisha's husband Joseph, our tech guy. The two of them come as a package, and if we lose one, we lose both.

'You know the kind of thing,' Nolan says to her. 'Companies that try to be carbon-neutral, ones that promote healthier living – vegetarian foods, for instance. Places that trade in technologies and products that will help the planet.'

'Like renewable energy,' Nadia pipes up from beside me.

'Exactly!' Nolan replies, looking pleased.

'Electric-vehicle manufacturers,' Terry adds.

'Precisely!' Nolan beams.

Oh, *fabulous*. This has become an inadvertent question-and-answer session, with everyone trying to impress the new boss with their environmental knowledge. I have to think of something to say!

This is going to be quite difficult as, I must confess, I am to environmentalism what Ann Widdecombe is to bikini modelling.

Think, Cooke! Think!

'Recycling companies,' Joseph mutters.

Damn! Why didn't I think of that?

'Sustainably produced clothing,' Peter remarks.

Oh, sod off, Peter! You're leaving*! I could have had that one!*

'Spot on!' Nolan replies, with a broad grin.

'Getting rid of single-use plastic bottles,' Sarky Marky says, from where he's sat next to Terry.

Bloody hell. Sarky Marky never contributes anything constructive to the conversation. He always just takes the piss, or has a moan. That's why we call him Sarky Marky. And yet, here he is, contributing something valuable. The pressure really is on to impress this guy, and remain employed by him.

'Absolutely!' Nolan says, clearly enjoying the to and fro. 'Plastic bottles are an absolute blight on our society. They're one of the single worst things in terms of environmental damage. Any business that is trying to replace them with a biodegradable equivalent should be top of our list.'

'Along with people trying to stop all that paper waste!' Nadia adds. 'I read the other day that we waste billions of tonnes of paper a year. It kills so many of the trees!'

'Yes, it does!' Nolan is super animated now. 'That's why I want this company to do all it can to increase the profile of businesses trying to combat climate change! We need to get rid of things like plastic bottles and paper waste . . . and the people that cause it.'

Everyone in the room goes silent as they digest this.

They don't look at my mound of tissues and crumpled-up Evian bottle all at once, but slowly, inexorably, all eyes are dragged down to them over a period of a few seconds – like asteroids pulled into the gravitational well of a large planet.

Nolan Reece looks particularly perturbed, as he stares down at my mess.

I also look down at it, and consider my next move . . . to the job centre.

That's probably where my next move is going to be, isn't it?

I lean forward and gently pick up the wodge of sodden tissue, and the bottle. 'I'll just go and put these in the bin, shall I?' I remark, in as calm a voice as possible, and stand up.

With all eyes upon me, I exit the conference room and walk over to where the nearest bin is, depositing the two offending items into it.

When I look back in, reassuringly things appear to have moved on, with Nolan and Peter now standing by the smartboard at the end of the conference room.

Is there any point in going back in?

Or should I just slope off and spend the rest of the day on Monster.com?

The thought of rewriting my CV and attending job interviews fills my head again, and I feel my legs go wobbly.

No. I can't go through that!

Get back in there! It's not too late!

Or is it?

Stratagem PR is apparently about to become a standard-bearer for all things environmental, according to its new Adam Driver–ish owner Nolan Reece. Do I have any place in a company like that?

After all, I drive a dreadfully polluting car, I order way too much fast fashion online, I can't even be bothered to find a drink in a glass bottle at Boots, and I used to date a man who ran a property business that built on pretty much every available green space it could gobble up.

I'm the anti-Nolan.

But you can't look for another job! It's hell out there!

Yes, yes, I know!

Then forget all of that! Just get back in there and try, Ellie! For the love of God!

Alright, alright!

I do as I'm told, by scuttling back into the conference room and sitting in my seat just as Nolan unveils the new name and logo for our company.

'Viridian PR,' he tells us triumphantly, as the logo flicks up to the smartboard. It's a very nice logo. Simple, but elegant.

I quite like the name too.

Stratagem PR has always been a pain to both write and say. It'll be nice to have something that trips off the tongue a little more easily.

Well . . . it'll be nice for all the people still working here, anyway. I've managed to nearly run over the new boss, choke him to death with car fumes, and show him that I apparently couldn't give two shits about plastic waste. I'm out on my arse, and there's no point in trying to think anything different.

Don't be such a defeatist! my brain says, trying its hardest to rally the troops. *Just get through the rest of this meeting without doing anything else stupid, and maybe we can think of a way to make up for the bad first impression.*

Yes, brain! I like your thinking.

Thank you. Now say something nice about the logo. That'll be a good start.

'The serif font is great,' I remark, nodding my head at the smartboard. 'Feels quite timeless, but with a hint of the modern.'

Nolan points an excited finger at me. 'Exactly! That's just what I was after. I told Andy the graphic designer that's what I wanted, and he definitely came up trumps.'

Oh, thank God for that. I've contributed something worthwhile at last.

I might not be in Nolan Reece's good books as yet, but at least I might have done something to start climbing out of the bad ones.

The meeting carries on for a little while longer, with Nolan continuing to sell us on the concept of Viridian PR. It all sounds lovely and quite exciting, but there's an ongoing tension in the room that can't quite be broken by all of this apparent good news.

The fact of the matter is that two of us will be losing our jobs very soon, and none of us knows who yet. It's a little hard to get super enthused about a company you might be thrown out of in the very near future.

Proceedings conclude with Nolan telling us he's going to be sending us all an extensive email proposal, outlining everything in detail.

'It will tell you everything you need to know,' he says. 'Everything I've probably missed out today, for definite.' He pauses for a second before continuing. 'Look, I know this has been difficult, and given how up in the air things are currently . . . I thought it might be nice for you all to have some time off. Starting now.'

A pleased murmur goes up. Nobody minds when they get told they have a surprise couple of days off, do they?

'You should all go home, read the Viridian PR proposals, and get back here on Monday, ready to start work with the new focus in your heads.' His smile fades a little. 'I'll also be able to say more on who will unfortunately be leaving us. I'm so sorry to leave you hanging, but we just need a little more time on it.'

'I'm sure they all understand,' Peter says, reminding us that he's still in the room. Our focus has been so lasered in on the man who will decide our futures that the man who used to no longer seems to matter. I find that very sad.

My mood is as bleak as a winter moor as the meeting concludes, and we all troop back out on to the main office floor. The general atmosphere appears to be one of supreme ambivalence as we all gather in small groups to discuss what's just happened. Everybody else feels pretty unsure about their future, but muggins here is convinced she'll be looking for new gainful employment by this time next week, given the performance she's put on today.

I get the feeling the other Stratagem – sorry, *Viridian PR* – employees agree with me, as I'm being treated with a lot of sympathy, like the axe has already fallen. I guess I can't blame them. If they think I'm a goner, then that at least improves their chances a bit.

'I'm sure everything will turn out okay,' Amisha remarks, ostensibly to the three other people standing with her, but I can tell she's talking to me more than anyone else.

'Absolutely,' Joseph agrees. 'Whoever has to leave, I'm sure they'll find work elsewhere quickly. We're a talented bunch here.'

Okay, Joseph, you don't have to look directly at me while you're saying that, you know.

'No doubt about it!' Nadia adds, in a slightly hectic voice. 'I'm sure it'll all be fine, like Amisha says.'

'Mmmm,' I half-heartedly respond.

Oh God, I do wish they'd stop looking at me like that. I feel like a dog that's going to be put down.

I can only take ten or so minutes of this before I decide it's time to leave for the day. The others seem happy to hang around for a bit and continue to indulge in a combination of speculation and navel-gazing, but I've decided that I need to go home and climb into a bottle of wine.

Day drinking is not a habit I want to get into, but I think – given today's events – I can be forgiven.

Back down in the car park, I hurry over to the Mercedes as fast as I can. I just want to get out of here for the day. Partially to get cosy with that bottle of Chardonnay, but also because I really do need to go and find my CV – wherever it's lurking on my laptop – and start the annoying and stressful process of sprucing it up.

The second I turn the ignition key, the car gives me an enormous clobberdy-bang. I'm a lot more worried about the implications of this now. It's one thing to have a faulty car when you have a job that can pay for repairs, but being unemployed with a clobberdy-bang brings a whole new level of terror.

I pull out of the car-parking space, my brain afire with dark and worrying thoughts.

As I hit the exit, I am forced to slam on my brakes once again, as I see a car appear to my left. It's a bloody Tesla – and those things are most definitely silent but deadly. They can creep up on you without you even knowing about it, thanks to their hushed battery-powered engines. I hate them with an absolute *passion*.

Guess who's driving it?

Go on . . .

It won't be hard.

Yes. That's *right*.

It's Hugh Firmly Blittingstool. He's come to bask in my misery.

I jest, of course. The man driving the Tesla is Nolan Reece.

He looks at me with alarm through his windscreen as he slams on his own brakes.

So, that's *twice* I've nearly managed to crash into him today. I'm doing so very, very well with my life.

I offer another one of my patented 'Ellie Cooke is sorry for being so Ellie Cooke today' apology smiles, and hold up a hand to acknowledge my driving error.

As if on cue, the Mercedes gives me a clobberdy-bang so huge and loud that it nearly shakes the fillings out of my teeth.

The black cloud of toxic emissions that blanket the car immediately afterwards smells so bad that I know I'm going to have to drive the stupid car straight to the nearest garage, instead of going home to open that bottle of wine.

Nolan Reece watches this happen from the confines of his ultra-clean, ultra-environmentally friendly car, with a look on his face that can only be described as 'perplexed'.

He should probably just jump out and hand me my P45 now. It'd save us all a great deal of time and effort.

Instead, he gives me a stilted wave, and accelerates silently out of the car park, causing the black cloud to disperse as his car passes mine.

The black cloud around my Mercedes, I should point out – not the one in my head.

I sit there for a few moments, gathering myself.

This could not have gone any worse if I'd just clubbed a baby seal to death in front of my new boss, and then set fire to his Tesla.

I don't see any way of pulling myself back from the brink here.

. . . but I'm going to bloody well try, anyway. That fear of the unknown will *make* me.

I will do *anything* to stay on at Viridian PR. Better the devil you know than the job interview you don't.

But first, it's time to sort out the clobberdy-bang, while I still have the money to do so.

That should make me feel a little better about myself.

And once the clobberdy-bang in my car is fixed, maybe I can come up with a plan to fix the clobberdy-bang in my life.

Yes.

That's the way to think about it. Be positive. Be hopeful. Be proactive. Be—

CLOBBERDY-BANG.

Oh, for the love of an environmentally conscious god . . .

Chapter Two

Dying to Make a Difference

Okay, I have to think of a plan now – a *good* one.

A way to keep my job at Viridian PR, and solve the second clobberdy-bang in my life.

The first cost £750 to fix . . . which was as painful as you'd imagine. I was assured by the mechanic that it had something to do with my gearbox synchromesh. Given my knowledge of cars, he could have said it was down to my bogbox winkywonk and I would still have forked out the cash. Car repairs generally have to be taken on trust, which is why they can be so stressful to sort out.

Still, at least I had a nice man to sort out the problem in the car for me. There's no one who can sort out the problem that is my job.

Nope. That task is solely down to me, and the only plan I can come up with to fix it is one I don't feel comfortable with in the slightest.

I'm going to have to butter up Nolan Reece as much as possible . . . as *fast* as possible. I literally have *days* before my goose is cooked, so I need to do something big, obvious and impressive to get on his good side, and wipe away the appalling first impression I gave of myself.

Now, I'm not going to lie. I did briefly think about trying to seduce him.

I can do sexy perfectly okay, thank you so very much – provided I have enough time to organise things properly. The knicker and bra set Robert bought me from Vicky's Secret is still in very good condition, and I'm pretty sure I can still get it on, if I only eat dust for a couple of weeks. And Nolan Reece is unconventionally handsome, as we've already noted. The consumption of dust could end up being *entirely* worth it.

But I dismissed that idea almost as soon as it came into my head. First, what kind of message would I be sending to womanhood if I debased myself like that? Not a good one, that's what.

And second – for all I know, Nolan Reece is in a happy relationship with another woman . . . or he's gay . . . or celibate . . . or he might have a knackered penis. I simply do not have the time to find any of these things out.

And who wants to force themselves into a pair of pants that feel like they're garrotting your undercarriage, and a bra that stops you breathing, if the target in question stays resolutely floppy throughout?

Not this lady, I can tell you.

With that line of attack firmly ruled out, I'm truly stumped. I just can't think of another way of improving my situation.

. . . actually, though, thinking about it, I *do* have a nice man who can help me with my second clobberdy-bang – my ever-so-reliable and sensible brother, Sean. He's a problem solver. And he's very good at it. I should know, he's been helping me with mine for decades.

'Hello, sis, what have you done now?' are the first words out of my brother's mouth when he answers my call.

'Um, excuse me . . . why would you think I've done something?'

'Because, Ellie, it's half ten in the evening. You only ever call at this time of night when you've done something, have thought about the problem for as long as you can on your own, have arrived at no decent solution, and therefore decide to give me a call about it.'

My brother is unwholesomely smart, as I'm sure you've probably noticed. He's also bang on the money, 90 per cent of the time.

It must be a nightmare for the kids in his class.

'Well, okay. You're right. But try not to be smug about it.'

'What's up?'

I take a deep breath, and fill Sean in on all the gory details.

I've been filling Sean in on all the gory details for the best part of my life. Out of the two of us, I'm always the one that creates the gory details, and he's always the one that suggests ways to clean them up. That's always been the dynamic of our relationship. I've been promising myself that I'll do something about it at some point, but life always seems to get in the way, and I never get around to it.

'Hmmm, tricky,' he says, when I've finished weaving my sorry tale.

'Any ideas?'

Sean pauses for a moment.

'Pot plants?' he suggests.

'Pardon me?'

'You say you need to impress your new environmentalist boss . . . how about some pot plants around the office?' he says. 'They're green – in both senses of the word.'

'I don't think that's going to cut it, Sean. Me waggling a rubber plant in Nolan's general direction isn't likely to do me that much good. I need something a little bigger, and more obvious, to get me on his good side.'

'Well, I don't know, sis. Maybe look him up on social media? Find out what he gets up to in his spare time? That might lead you to something.'

'Facebook-stalk him, you mean?'

'Yeah. I guess so. You'll get to know him a bit better, if nothing else. That couldn't hurt, could it?'

'No . . . it couldn't.'

It's a *great* idea, to be honest. I don't know why I didn't think of it myself.

Because it's sensible, Ellie. And Sean is the one that does sensible. You do silly. Hence the ridiculous idea of seducing a man you've only met once.

'Thanks, Sean, I'll give it a go. And I'll let you know how I get on.'

'Okay, sis. If you could see your way clear to not letting me know at ten thirty at night, when I'm still in the middle of marking English essays, that'd be favourite.'

'Agreed. Love you lots.'

'You too.'

I put the phone down on my clever brother, feeling ever so much better. I don't think I've ever put the phone down on my brother without feeling better – especially when he's given me some decent advice.

And I'm going to take the advice he's given me this time, by doing a bit of constructive online investigating . . .

I grab my laptop and spend a couple of hours on social media, stalking Nolan Reece like there's no tomorrow.

I'm not the biggest fan of Facebook or Instagram to be honest, but they are very useful ways to discover more about a person – and Nolan has recently been very active on both.

And what he's active about is the environment – as you'd expect.

Consistently and constantly.

What he told us in that meeting the other day really does seem to ring true. He is very environmentally conscious – to the exclusion of almost everything else.

If I *had* decided to seduce him, I could have just dressed up like a vegan sausage, and showed him that my boobs are 100 per cent plastic-free.

Nolan's Facebook feed is full of memes and comments about the planet, the environment, climate change, and sustainability. He doesn't appear to have that many friends or followers, but that means nothing in this day and age. Long gone are the days of people manically adding everyone they can to their friends list to appear popular. It almost seems like it's more a badge of honour to keep your friends list small these days.

It becomes more and more apparent as I continue the online stalking of my new boss that the only way I'm going to impress him is by persuading him that I am also an environmentally conscious person – despite the backfiring car and plastic-bottle squeezing. And I'm sure I'm not the only one in the office who thinks that way. Everyone will be wanting to prove their credentials. The question-and-answer session that I botched so magnificently proved that.

If I'm going to stand out from the crowd, I'm going to have to do something BIG. Something noticeable. Something *obvious*.

I have no idea what that might be, until I find a post on Nolan's Facebook feed from a week ago that gives me the answer . . .

Someone called Jill is asking Nolan if he'll be attending the event on Saturday 'at the shopping centre', to which Nolan has replied that yes, he most definitely is.

Aha!

There's nothing much more to go on than that in the actual post, but I then spend half an hour searching for environmental events in my local area, and discover that on Saturday, at Whitehaven Shopping Centre, an organisation called Warriors For The Planet will be staging a protest.

That must be it, right?

An environmental event 'at the shopping centre' on Saturday?

That's got to be it!

It's not an official event, of course. I doubt the owners of Whitehaven particularly want an environmental protest getting in the way of their consumerism, but there's enough buzz about it online to suggest it's going to be well attended by those of an environmentally conscious nature.

And maybe, just maybe, if I can get down there . . . and just happen to bump into Nolan, I can show him just how green I truly am! After all, I'd have to be, if I attended an event like that, wouldn't I?

Yes.

Yes, that's it.

I'll go down to the protest, find Nolan, impress the shit out of him with my heartfelt love of our planet, and make him see that keeping me on at Viridian PR is absolutely the right thing to do!

. . . stop looking at me like that.

No. *Stop it.*

I know it's a deeply cynical move, but can you really blame me? This is my livelihood we're talking about. And if keeping my job means pretending *just a little bit*, then so be it.

And it's either that or sling on the bloody Vicky's Secret underwear for my new Adam Driver–ish boss – and I still have half a bag of Minstrels in the cupboard which I do not intend to waste!

Not having a clue when the protest is meant to kick off, I figure I'd better get down to Whitehaven as early as possible. In my experience, public events tend to happen more in the mornings than the afternoons, so it's probably a good bet that things will start not that long after I arrive.

And if not, I can always get a Costa coffee and do some light shopping while I wait. There's a roll neck from FatFace I've had my eye on for a couple of weeks now, and I definitely need some new tops for sleeping in too.

Whitehaven Shopping Centre is a monument to Western consumption that sits just off the motorway, for maximum ease of access. Each and every one of the seventy or so stores is housed in massive, grey identikit buildings that are 100 per cent glass-fronted, and have about as much personality as a maths teacher's wardrobe.

They've tried to inject some character into the place by dotting a few trees and benches around the broad plazas in front of the monolithic grey shops, but it's a token gesture at best. The goal here is to get you into those shops and spending, not hanging about smelling the flowers and having a nice time outside.

I get to Whitehaven at just gone 9 a.m.

By half eleven I'm bored to tears, jazzed on coffee, and my car boot is full of several roll necks from FatFace, a myriad of sleep tops from Next, a particularly fluffy pair of slippers from M&S, and, for some reason, a kitchen utensil pot with a picture of a whale on it. I bought it in that weird Scandinavian shop – the one whose name no one can ever entirely remember once they've walked out of the doors. It sells thousands of different products, while at the same time being completely chock-a-block with nothing but memory foam cushions and kitchen utensil pots featuring pictures of aquatic mammals.

This protest had really better get going soon, before I end up spending the rest of my month's shopping allowance in one morning. There's only so long I can hold out before I just have to buy that fluffy green onesie in Primark.

Luckily for my bank balance (and sense of self-worth . . . mark my words, the wearing of a onesie puts you on a very slippery slope), at about eleven forty-five I start to see and hear a commotion coming from the main central plaza that sits right in the middle of Whitehaven, where two of the broad pedestrian streets intersect with one another.

Coming out of Primark, I see that a small crowd has started to form in front of about a dozen people. This group is an eclectic bunch. Half hippy, half middle-class ex-prep school – they aesthetically mix about as well as milk and olive oil.

Two of them are currently erecting a large banner, strung across two very heavy-looking metal stands. When the banner is taut enough to read, I can see that it says *Warriors For The Planet*. The a's in 'warrior' and 'planet' are stylised to look like the planet Earth. This means that the banner actually reads *Worriors For The Plonet*, which is a little unfortunate. Quite why they chose to convert the a's and not the o's is beyond me. Sounds like they need a good PR company to handle their branding.

I'm definitely in the right place, though. That much is certain.

The question is, where is Nolan?

I crane my head to look at the crowd that's fast gathering around the Worriors, but there's no sign of my new boss as yet. Perhaps he's only coming once the protest is officially underway.

Never mind, this gives me the chance to ingratiate myself with the protestors a little. That way, when Nolan does arrive, it'll look like I already know them. This will help cement my climate-friendly credentials.

I sidle my way up to one of the Worriors who is decidedly in the middle-class camp. Nobody else in the world could – or would want to – pull off a chunky-knit blue cardigan and a dark-green blazer. They both go well with the thick spectacles, wavy brown quiff and pinched expression.

'Morning!' I say brightly, affecting my most friendly of tones. I really want to get on this chap's good side.

He looks quite startled. 'Er . . . hello?'

'You're the Warriors For The Planet, then?'

'Er . . . yes. Why do you want to know?'

He's gone very cagey.

I'm not all that surprised. I doubt they get many ordinary members of the public chatting to them at these kinds of events. The inclination of the great British public is to stand and watch in curious amusement at protests, not actively engage with the participants.

Either that, or he thinks I'm an undercover police officer about to search him for cannabis.

'Because I'm very keen on being more environmentally conscious!' I lie through my teeth. I can hardly say I'm here to save my bloody job, can I?

'Oh, right. That's, er . . . that's super.'

Well, you could be a bit more enthusiastic about it, pal. I thought you'd be delighted that someone was actually taking an interest.

'What are you protesting about here today?' I ask him.

In return, he gives me a rather scared and unsure look. This is clearly not what he was expecting.

'Er . . . um . . . I don't usually talk to people.'

'Don't you?'

'No. Not after what happened at the petrol station.'

'What happened at the petrol station?'

'Um . . . I ended up telling a reporter where our old HQ was.'

'Oh dear.'

'Bandy was really mad at me.'

'Bandy?'

The middle-class chap holds out an arm and points at one of the hippy-looking Worriors – a woman in a tie-dye tank top who sports very muscular biceps and a fine head of white dreadlocks.

'That's Bandy,' he tells me. 'She does the talking.'

'Ah, right. I should probably go and have a chat with her then, yeah?'

'Er . . . yeah.'

I think that's just about all I'm going to get out of him. He looks like he'd rather be doing absolutely anything else than talking to me.

I take my hasty leave, and walk over to where Bandy is finishing off the erection of the banner. Still no sign of Nolan in the crowd, which is probably a good thing. I want it to look like I'm well ensconced with this lot before he arrives.

'Bandy?' I say as I approach her.

'Yeah? Can I help you?'

Well, she seems a little happier to talk – if no less suspicious, from the looks of her narrowed eyes.

'I hope so! I'm very interested in the protest and just wanted to have a chat.'

She nods her head. 'Oh right, are you from Padlo's bunch?'

'Padlo's bunch?'

'Yeah. He said he'd try to get a load of his lot down, to swell the numbers a bit.'

'Yes! That's right! I'm with Padlo's bunch. Most certainly. With Padlo. And his bunch.'

Oh good grief. What on earth am I doing?

'There any more of you coming?'

'Er . . .'

'Only he said he'd try and get at least ten of you down.'

'Oh . . . well . . . I don't really know. I'm a bit new to all of this. A bit new to being part of . . . *Padlo's bunch.*'

Bandy nods again. 'Oh well. Let's just hope more of you do turn up.' She looks me up and down. I'm not dressed as a hippy or a cast member from *Made in Chelsea*, so she's not too sure about me – I can tell. 'Have you done a die-in before?'

'A die-in?'

'Yeah. That's why we're here. Didn't you know that?'

'Er . . . yes! Of course I did! And of course I've done one before! Oh my, yes. I've done . . . two. Two die-ins.'

'Great! Looking forward to making a statement with you!'

'Absolutely!'

Again, what the bloody hell am I doing?

Seriously . . . anyone have any ideas? Because I'm all out.

I think I must have lost the plot.

Bandy looks around to see a group of about ten or so people making their way with purpose towards us. 'Ah! There you go! Padlo's bunch!' she says with some relief in her voice. 'Nice to see that some more of you have turned up!'

Oh *shit*.

Coming towards me are more Made-in-Chelseas, more hippies, and a couple of people combining both looks to create monstrous Hippies-in-Chelsea, wearing fashion choices that would make the entire staff of *Vogue* magazine spontaneously combust.

I'd better make myself scarce, before Padlo's bunch get closer. My brilliantly devised piece of subterfuge will be exposed otherwise.

But how do I get away from Bandy before they get here?

'Ellie Cooke?' a voice says from the crowd behind me.

Oh, lord. The timing is *perfect*.

I turn around to see Nolan Reece standing at the edge of the crowd, looking at me in disbelief. 'Are you . . . are you part of the *Warriors*?' he calls over, stepping forward a little.

I look back at my new dreadlocked friend. 'Sorry, Bandy. That's a friend of mine. Can I go and say hello?'

'Yeah, yeah,' she replies. 'I'll go and talk to the rest of your bunch. Make sure they're all happy about what's going on, like you are.'

'Great!' I respond, and walk swiftly in the direction of Nolan, letting Bandy go and greet Padlo's bunch, of which I am supposed to be a part.

'Hi, Nolan,' I say as I reach him. 'How are you?'

'I'm fine, thanks. Are you part of this? Are you part of the Warriors' protest?'

'Yes!' I lie. 'Yes I am! I'm one of Padlo's bunch.'

'Padlo's bunch?'

'Yes! Padlo's . . . *bunch.*' I laugh in a slightly hysterical manner. I've managed to weave a web of utter lies around myself in virtually no time at all. It's a little terrifying. 'So nice to see you here too!' I say, grinning for all I'm worth.

And I am genuinely happy, if I'm being honest. Everything is more or less going to plan. My new boss has just seen me chatting animatedly with one of the senior Worriors, and further, I've managed to convince him that I'm one of Padlo's bunch.

Whoever the hell they actually are.

Now all I have to do is stand here with Nolan Reece, watch the protest unfold, and keep maintaining the fiction that I know the Worriers Of The Plonet like they were my best friends. That should do it.

'Oi! You!' Bandy calls over to me, having said her hellos to Padlo's bunch.

'Yes?' I call back.

'We're about to start! Are you coming over?'

'Coming over?'

'Yes! To start the protest! All the rest of your lot are ready to go!' She waves a hand in the general direction of Padlo's bunch, who are now lined up behind Bandy, along with the rest of the Worriers For The Plonet.

Padlo's bunch are all looking at me with a great deal of confusion on their faces. And who can blame them? Bandy's probably just told them I'm part of their crew, and they've never seen me before in their lives.

'Come on!' Bandy insists again, beckoning me towards her.

Nolan gives me an expectant look.

Oh.

Oh, I *see.*

I may have painted myself into something of a corner here . . .

'Go on,' Nolan encourages. 'Good luck. I'm sure it will go very well.'

'Yes. Thank you,' I reply, in a stilted voice.

I'm now going to have to take part in an environmental protest in front of about a hundred shoppers, and my new boss. And I have no clue what I'm supposed to do.

I scuttle over to where Bandy and the rest of them are waiting in three rough lines of people. I'll just have to watch what they do, copy as best I can, and hope I come out of it all without actually looking like what I am – an interloper who has zero clue what the hell is going on here.

As I take my place just to Bandy's left, she stands up straight and adopts a pose obviously meant for some hardcore oratory.

'The world is dying!' she virtually screams to all here gathered. 'Our planet is doomed!'

Cheery start, then.

Bandy points an accusatory finger at the crowd. 'And you are to blame!'

Oh, well. At least she's trying to get the crowd onside early.

'*You*, with your consumerism! *You*, with your consumption!'

Around me, the rest of the Worriors are all nodding along with this diatribe. I don't feel like I can join in with them, as I have a kitchen utensil pot with a whale on it in my car.

Bandy waves her pointy, accusatory finger around Whitehaven Shopping Centre. 'And here, in this monument to consumption, we make a stand! A stand against you! A stand against the abuse of our world by corporations, who only exist to strip the planet of its resources, and sell pointless objects of desire to you!'

A few of the Worriors cheer at this.

Marvellous. I'm surrounded by raving nutters.

I look over at Nolan to see that he's listening to all of this with a mixture of concern and doubt on his face. It's a little hard to discern whether this concern is for the planet, or for his own personal safety in the face of this verbal onslaught.

'The waste we produce. The waste you create when you buy this garbage!' Bandy continues, now at the point where there's every chance she's about to start frothing at the mouth. 'All of the waste that surrounds us! It is killing our animals! It is killing our creatures!'

Well, no argument on that one.

'YOU are killing our creatures!' she screams at the crowd.

That's a bit harsh.

I doubt anyone who pops into Next to pick up a new cushion thinks they're murdering an elephant or a porpoise at the same time. Possibly poking a halibut until it swims off in a bad mood, but definitely not killing a porpoise.

'We are here to show you what that killing looks like!' Bandy wails.

Oh no. She's not going to start pulling out pictures of animals being murdered, is she? I don't think I can cope with that, and if she hasn't lost the crowd already, that's sure to do it.

'We will now re-enact what it looks like to be one of the majestic creatures being murdered by your consumerism! By YOUR own hand, every time you shop in one of these places! Listen to their screams!'

Re-enact? Screams?

What?

'Everybody!' Bandy screeches, turning around to look at the rest of us in her motley crew. 'Begin the die-in!'

And with that, the group of climate protestors around me simultaneously start to thrash around like their lives depend on it. As they do this, they all also start to grunt, scream and moan, in what I can only assume is a vague approximation of a bunch of dying animals.

There's a lot of roaring going on – which I take it is supposed to embody the big cats of the world in their death throes. There are quite a few people barking too, so the dog population is being represented very well, you'll be pleased to know.

A small man wearing a woollen beanie is making farting noises and hopping up and down on one leg. What animal that is meant to be, I have no fucking idea. I'll have to run it by David Attenborough the next time I see him.

Bandy is particularly animated up front. She's flailing her arms around above her head, and jumping from one foot to the other. She's also jerking about like someone's stuck a cattle prod up her arse, and is doing her very best impression of what I can only assume is a dying monkey, or possibly an ape – it's hard to tell which.

'*OOH-OOH AAAH-AAAAAAAAAHHH!!*' she cries to the heavens. '*OOH-AAH! OOH-AAH! OOK! OOK! OOK!*' she screams out to the firmament.

Is that what a dying monkey sounds like? You'd have thought a dying monkey would be a bit *quieter*, wouldn't you? What with all the dying going on, and everything. That just sounds like a really *pissed-off* monkey. The only dying that will happen will be from whoever is on the other end of it.

The rest of the Worriors are putting almost as much effort into their impressions, it has to be said. I'm surrounded by a group of people who wouldn't look out of place in a terrible amateur-dramatics production of *Life on Earth*.

The middle-class chap I first spoke to is apparently trying his best to recreate the death of a dolphin, as he's lying on the ground, making distressed clicking noises, and has popped an upturned, open hand on the back of his head, which I guess is meant to be a fin.

'*CLICKY WICKY CLICK-CLICK-CLICKETY*,' he goes.

Now, I've confessed that I don't know what a dying monkey sounds like, but I'm slightly more familiar with dolphins, and I'm pretty sure that, when they do die, they don't sound like someone's fucking a box of chopsticks.

Nevertheless, he's giving it his best of British, and I can hardly fault the enthusiasm.

Bandy breaks off from her ooking to look up at me. 'What are you doing?!' she hisses.

'Pardon me?'

'Die with us!' she demands.

Oh, crap badgers. I'm supposed to be doing this as well, aren't I?

But I can't! It looks so *embarrassing*.

I wasn't expecting all these amateur dramatics. I just can't put myself through it!

But then I look over at Nolan Reece, who is staring back at me with confusion. He's obviously expecting me to do my bit as well. And if I don't, I'm going to ruin whatever goodwill I may have built up since arriving here at this bizarre moment in my life.

Fuck it.

Let's just get this over with.

. . . but what dying animal should I do an impression of?

Another monkey?

Nope.

We've already established I have no idea what one of them sounds like when it's expiring, and I wouldn't want to be inaccurate.

A dolphin?

Again, no. Chopstick-fucking isn't really my thing.

What animal is it easy to do an impression of? I can't do a dog or a cat, they're already being well served.

Chicken?

Nah. That's no good. Everyone loves a KFC.

Cow?

Nope. McDonald's.

What animals do people love? I want to connect with my audience here, so have to go for the heartstrings . . .

I know! Pandas! Everyone fucking *loves* a panda, don't they? They're cute, fluffy, and most of all – *endangered*.

Right then. Excellent choice, Ellie.

Now . . . what the hell do pandas sound like? Especially when they're being murdered?

I saw that one video that went round of the panda sneezing, but that probably won't do the trick. Can you sneeze in agony? Can you convey the depths of human depravity towards our planet's natural fauna with a sneeze?

Probably not.

Fuck it, I'll just mime eating a bamboo shoot, and then start screaming for a bit.

I hold out both hands, clutching an imaginary thick sheaf of bamboo, and start to nibble at it. When I feel an appropriate amount of time has gone by, I let out a high-pitched scream of agony. Then, for some reason, I go back to nibbling the bamboo.

Look, it's all I fucking know about pandas, alright? They sit around and nibble bamboo. They're famous for it.

Nibble.

'Aaaargh!'

Nibble.

'Aaaaaaaaargh!'

Nibble.

'Aaaaaaaaaaaaaaaaaaaaaaargh!'

'What the fuck are you *doing*?'

This is Bandy, who has stopped her dying-monkey impression to berate me.

'I'm dying,' I reply, somewhat indignant that she's not appreciating my efforts. 'I'm being one of the planet's most noble creatures, being murdered in the middle of its favourite snack.'

Bandy looks nonplussed. 'You think a *squirrel* is one of the planet's most noble creatures?'

'Squirrel? What do you mean, *squirrel*?'

Bandy points at my invisible bamboo sheaf. 'You're miming eating a nut.'

'A nut?'

'Yes!'

I hold out my invisible bamboo sheaf for inspection. 'That's not a bloody nut, it's a load of bamboo!'

Can't she bloody see the difference? It's quite clear to me!

'I'm a fucking panda!' I assert, most adamantly.

'Well, you look like a squirrel! And you sound like one!'

'Do I?'

'Yes! I accidentally shot one once when I was at Granny's place in the country. Sounded just like you did, before Daddy . . . sorted it out.'

There are a whole series of issues going on in that sentence, but I don't have the time or the inclination to work through them right now.

'No! I'm not a squirrel! I'm a *panda*! I'm a nibbling, screaming, dying panda!' I insist, feeling that this whole thing is getting away from me.

'Dying pandas do NOT sound like that!' Bandy insists.

I point a finger over at the middle-class chap, who is continuing to do his impression of a dying dolphin. '*CLICKETY CLICKETY CLICK-CLICK WICKETY CLICK,*' he goes, waggling his hand about on the back of his head for all he's worth.

'Well, dying dolphins don't sound like someone shagging a Chinese restaurant, either!' I say, in what I believe is a very valid defence of my impression – even if I do say so myself.

'Are you mad?' Bandy exclaims.

'Am *I* mad?' I retort.

'Everything alright, ladies?' I hear Nolan Reece call over from his vantage point at the front of the crowd. A crowd, it has to be said, that has thinned out considerably since we started the actual die-in. Not surprising, really. Once it's been established that the people in front of you are stark raving loonies, it's probably best to get away from them as quickly as possible, and get on with your shopping.

'Er . . . yes! All fine!' I call back to him, plastering on a hectic, positive expression. Nolan cannot think I am not completely at one with my protesting brethren here. I look back at Bandy. 'I'll try a little harder, I promise!' I stage-whisper at her, so Nolan can't hear.

'Good! This a very serious thing we're doing here. There is no time for humour!'

My brow furrows.

I'm holding an invisible sheaf of bamboo, surrounded by people jerking about like someone's just put fifty thousand volts through Noah's Ark, and this woman doesn't think this is a time for *humour*? These green folk may have their hearts in the right places, but their funny bones are entirely absent.

'Alright, alright,' I say, trying to mollify her.

I thought my bamboo-nibbling was exceptional. There's no accounting for taste, is there?

Bandy nods, and returns to her own strange gyrations.

Another few minutes of thrashing and wailing go by around me, while I stand there like the spare prick at a wedding, until Bandy makes a particularly loud moaning noise, which seems to be the cue for everyone to bring their performances to a close. Thank the lord.

When the whole crew of Worriors have finally become as motionless as I've been for the past five minutes, Bandy gives it a couple of beats before coming out of her appalling monkey impression. The rest of them follow suit.

'We die here, so that you may see!' Bandy shouts at the vastly diminished crowd. 'To see how our animal friends are dying! We die for them!'

Bloody hell, love. Monkeying about on a bit of concrete for ten minutes is not *dying*. I'm sure if the average endangered species could see what's gone on here, and make a comment about it, they'd probably tell good old Bandy to do something a bit more practical about the situation – give a few quid to Greenpeace, for instance. Or lobby a few politicians.

Performing overwrought amateur dramatics in front of a load of bored shoppers probably isn't going to do much, other than reinforce the idea that environmental protestors are a right bunch of Padlos.

'We leave here now, hoping that you have seen us!' Bandy continues to enunciate, in a tone that suggests she's about to bust a gasket. 'Hoping that you see *them*! Hoping that you feel their pain! That you stop your endless consumerism here in this place, because it's *killing them*!'

I'm not convinced Bandy and chums have managed to persuade anyone that there's much of a link between popping into JD Sports for a new pair of flip-flops and the murder of our planet's fauna. By the looks on the faces of the small crowd left watching us, I'd say they're not convinced either.

Only Nolan appears to be agreeing, and nodding along to what Bandy is saying. It really does seem like he's taking all this environmental stuff to heart. Viridian PR is going to be a very different place from Stratagem – there's no doubt of that.

'Thank you all for watching!' Looks like Bandy is wrapping things up now. Probably for the best. I can see three Whitehaven security guards standing over by Topshop, giving us very dark looks. 'We will continue to fight for our planet!' she says, with obvious passion. 'We will continue to call out the injustices! We will continue to speak truth to power!' Bandy takes a deep breath, and thrusts a fist into the air. 'We will continue!' she cries, once more to the heavens.

'We will continue!' all of the other Worriors say in unison, also punching their fists upwards.

Oh shit, this is a thing, is it?

'We . . . we will continue!' I say, a bit half-heartedly, while gently shaking a loosely clenched fist at about head height.

As far as clarion calls go, I'm not sure 'we will continue' is quite up there with 'cry havoc, and let slip the dogs of war'. These people are clearly in dire need of some decent public relations.

With the mission statement proudly echoing around the glass-fronted shops, the Worriors For The Plonet protest comes to an end.

I'd better get my butt over to where Nolan is, and see what he thinks of my contribution. I have a lot riding on this.

I skip over to where he's now talking quite animatedly with one of the Worriors. I have to dodge Bandy and the middle-class chap as I do this, as they take down the banner with practised ease.

'Hi!' I say cheerily to Nolan, interrupting whatever conversation he was having with the Worrior – who is a very middle-class lady of about fifty, wearing a white denim jacket and a maroon pashmina that was probably made in a factory that eats sea lion cubs for breakfast. I seem to remember she was one of the barking dogs from the protest. Possibly a chihuahua.

'Hello, Ellie!' Nolan replies brightly, before looking back at his companion. 'Jill, do you know Ellie?' he asks her.

The lady standing with Nolan gives me a blank look. 'No . . . I don't think we've ever met.'

'Oh,' Nolan replies, a bit confused. 'Well, this is Ellie Cooke, one of the employees at the PR firm I just bought.'

'Er . . . hello,' Jill says. This must be the same Jill whose comment on Facebook led me here today. 'You were part of the protest?'

'Yes, I was!' I reply. 'I was doing a panda.'

Jill's eyes narrow a bit. 'I've never seen you at any of the meetings, or seen you in the Facebook group?'

I'm prepared for this.

'I'm part of Padlo's bunch!' I tell her confidently. This excuse has seen me right so far today, and I'm hoping this will continue. The one thing I've learned from being in public relations is that if you say or do something confidently enough, people tend to go along with you. Perception is reality, after all.

'Ah,' Jill replies, a bit unsure, and nods her head slowly.

Ha! Works like a charm, every time.

At some stage, I'll actually have to try to meet this Padlo person. They have become a vitally important part of today's subterfuge, and I probably owe them a drink.

'Well, it was nice to meet you, Ellie,' Jill adds, and looks back at Nolan. 'And wonderful to see you too, Nolan.'

'Yes! Absolutely!' Nolan replies. 'We'll definitely have to arrange a meeting for you guys to come in and discuss your needs going forward. I'm sure there's something we can do to help you raise the profile of the whole organisation.'

Jill beams at this. 'That would be *magnificent*. The more people that hear about us, the more we'll get them onside, I'm sure. I'll be in touch.'

Jill gives Nolan a warm hug, shakes my hand briefly, and then returns to where Bandy and co. are milling about, talking to one another in what I can only assume is some kind of post-protest debrief.

'Are we going to be doing PR for them?' I ask Nolan.

You'll note my cunning use of the word 'we' there.

'Yes, probably. They'd only be a small client, but the small ones often bring in the bigger fish, don't they?'

'Absolutely.'

He blinks a couple of times. 'So . . . you're an environmental protestor?' He sounds quite amazed.

'Yes! Well . . . this is my first time,' I confide. I figure I can admit as much. It's the fact that I'm here and taking part that matters. 'But I've been very concerned about our planet's wildlife for years now. You know, because of all the global warming and stuff.'

Look, I don't like lying – even when it's for a good cause. I know I sound incredibly awkward when I attempt to tell falsehoods, and I'd rather not have to do it, but we all know what the stakes are here.

If it troubles you morally, feel free to go and look at the Primark window display. They have a sale on.

'I thought I needed to do something. To show just how much I care . . . so I came down here today with Padlo's bunch to do my bit.'

Nolan nods his obvious approval. 'Well, I was quite surprised to see you, but I think what you're doing is *lovely*. And brave. Not sure I could do something like that in front of lots of people.'

'Me either! But when it comes to saving the world, what choice do we have?'

Oh God, I'm going to vomit. Throw up right here and now, if I'm not careful.

'Er . . . no! Exactly! There is no choice,' Nolan agrees. 'That's why I wanted to see if the Warriors For The Planet wanted any help with their public profile. They can't pay much, but I'm happy for us to take the work on anyway, as it's for such an important cause.'

Us.

He said *us*.

My Machiavellian grand master plan appears to be working!

Aha ha ha ha ha!

'Excuse me?'

I feel a finger lightly poke me in the shoulder.

I swing around to see a little mole-like man in a woollen beanie staring up at me. He was the hopping, farting thing from earlier, if you recall.

'Hello? Can I help you?' I ask.

'I don't know. My name is Padlo. Bandy seems to think you're part of my bunch?'

Oh *fuck*.

Oh fuck on toast.

I need to get out of this conversation before everything goes resolutely south.

'Aha! Padlo!' I exclaim as excitedly as possible. 'So nice to see you here!'

'Sorry? Who are you?'

'Aha! Come on Padlo! You know me!' I tell the little man, throwing an arm around his shoulders in the chummiest of fashions. I then whip my head back around to look at Nolan. 'Sorry, Nolan, have to chat with Padlo here. You know how it is!'

Nolan looks nonplussed.

Nonplussed is better than angry or upset, so we'll go with it.

'Oh, okay,' he says. 'I guess I'll see you at work on Monday then?'

'Yes! Yes, you absolutely will! At work! On Monday! You and me!'

I can feel Padlo starting to wriggle out of my grip, but I'm bigger than him, and have actually been using my gym membership properly for the past few months, so have no real trouble keeping him in place.

'Come on, Padlo!' I command, starting to drag him away.

I don't let him go again until we're back among the crowd of Worriors.

'Will you please let me go!' he insists, and manages to extricate himself from my grip.

I stare at him for a second, before affecting an expression of fabricated horror. 'Oh! I'm so sorry! I completely mistook you for somebody else!'

'You did *what*?'

'Or I mistook me for somebody else, one of the two.'

I've become aware that a whole sea of faces is now regarding me with a mixture of incomprehension and irritation. I think that my time among the Worriors For The Plonet may be coming to an end . . .

I glance back over to see that Nolan appears to have disappeared, and breathe a sigh of relief. My barely held-together subterfuge has worked.

Whether this will be enough for me to keep my job or not remains to be seen, but for today, I think we can safely chalk this one up as a victory.

Returning my attention to the unhappy Worriors, I notice that Padlo and Bandy have come together in front of me, both looking decidedly unhappy.

It's time I got out of here.

'Bandy! Padlo! Thank you so much for letting me join in with your excellent protest today!' I say to them both.

Effusive thanks always disarms people, I find. The more exaggerated you can be about it, the better. It's probably not something you could get away with in any other country, but it goes down a storm in Great Britain.

'Oh, well . . . that's okay,' Bandy replies.

'Yes, yes,' Padlo agrees.

'It really was a great experience!'

'I'm sorry – who are you again?' Padlo asks, a bit more about himself.

'I'm a person who has learned a valuable lesson!' I tell him. 'A valuable lesson about how our world needs us to do more!'

The crowd behind him actually nod approvingly at this.

'I've learned that we can't just sit back and do nothing!'

More nods – quite enthused this time.

'We've got to make a stand!'

Now there's some murmurs of agreement.

'Make a *difference*!'

The murmurs become cheers.

'Stop the rot!'

There's a couple of fist pumps now.

'Make the people see that something needs to *change*!'

Now even Bandy and Padlo are nodding along and looking inspired.

'And for me, that starts *now*!' I cry – channelling Mel Gibson in blue face-paint as hard as I can. 'I'm going to leave here now, and start fighting the good fight!'

More cheers and fist-pumping.

'Farewell, my friends! I go now to save our world!'

Oh God, a couple of them are actually clapping, bless 'em.

I thrust out one arm in front of me and stride off in the direction of the car park, with the raucous approval of the Worriors as my backing music.

All things considered, I think I got out of that quite well.

People with causes are always quite easy to get on the right side of. You just have to convince them that their cause is as important to you – if not more so – as it is to them. The rest is ethically produced gravy.

Highly manipulative, I know . . . but needs must, and all that.

My efforts here today should go some way to persuading Nolan to keep me on at Viridian PR. They certainly can't have done any harm.

I'd probably do a little more environmental protesting, if it weren't for all the bizarre amateur theatrics. I've never been one for the stage . . . I'd rather be in the audience.

Rest assured though – as soon as environmentalists swap monkeying about in shopping centres for eating cake and watching Netflix, I will be there like a bloody shot.

Chapter Three

Pot Plants, Pants and P45s

It's the following Monday morning, and only one thought suffuses my poor, sleep-deprived brain: *Have I done enough?*

Have I done enough to convince Nolan Reece to keep me on?

On Saturday, as I drove back from Whitehaven, I felt confident that I had – but you know what it's like . . . it doesn't take long for the worm of doubt to crawl back into your head and start rummaging around.

I gave Sean a call that evening to fill him in on all the gory details, and to get some kind of reassurance that my scheme had probably worked.

Sean is always good for reassurance. It's one of his greatest qualities.

He was in hysterics by the time I'd finished telling him all about my panda impression, but after he'd calmed down a bit, he did tell me he thought what I'd done would probably help my cause with Nolan, which was tremendously *reassuring*.

For about an hour, anyway.

By the time I went to bed that night, I'd managed to convince myself that my antics had done nothing to prevent the loss of my job, and that the only thing I'd accomplished was to wind up a load of hippies.

I spent Sunday trying to calm myself down a bit, and convince the brain worm that I had indeed managed to impress Nolan Reece.

But that wasn't enough to quieten my worries.

Not by a long chalk.

Have I done enough?

The thought still echoes around my worm-filled brain as I get to my desk on Monday, and fire up the computer.

Of Nolan Reece there is no physical sign this morning . . . but he has sent an email to us all.

In it, he apologises for his absence, and bids us to continue with whatever tasks we still have on hand. He also tells us that it will be Friday before we know for certain who will be staying on and who will be leaving the company.

He does not mention how much he enjoyed bumping into me at Whitehaven Shopping Centre, which is annoying. I would have liked some idea of whether my efforts have borne fruit, but I'll just have to remain worryingly in the dark for now.

Nolan concludes the email by telling us he'll be back in the office after lunch, and wishes us all a good morning.

A good morning is not all that likely, given that he's left us on tenterhooks again.

Furthermore, I don't actually have any work left to do myself, having wrapped up my last job the day before Nolan Reece came along. I was hoping to speak to Peter about the Hollington Stores contract, but given that he's nowhere to be seen today either, that's a complete dead end.

I simply have no work to do. You can't really be much of a publicist if you have absolutely nothing to publicise.

Now, this should be something to be celebrated – and in circumstances where my job wasn't up for the chop, it probably would be – but under present conditions, being sat here twiddling my thumbs is not going to help me stay employed at Viridian PR, is it?

As I look around the office, I can see that everybody else appears to be getting on with something constructive. In fact, I've not seen such a strong work ethic in this office for a long time. This is obviously down to the present circumstances as well. Everyone is trying to impress, aren't they? Given the paucity of work that we've had coming in over the past few months, I have no idea what they're all actually doing, but at least they *look* busy, which is more than can be said for yours truly.

I must find something to do!

But what?

I spend a few minutes chewing on my fingernails, until something occurs to me – when I remember the suggestion that my brother came up with on the phone the other day. The one I dismissed out of hand at the time as not being a big enough gesture, but which now sounds like something that might just do the trick: pot plants.

Nolan Reece said he wants to run an environmentally aware business – and part of that is having an environmentally friendly *office space*, yes?

The offices of Stratagem PR have always been quite modern and clean, but geared towards environmentalism they are most definitely not.

What if I went along with Sean's suggestion, and took it upon myself to make some changes that would accomplish this? Wouldn't that further endear me to my new boss?

Yes.

Yes, it probably would.

And if Nolan Reece associates Eleanor Cooke with something as environmentally friendly as a load of pot plants, then he can't possibly fire me!

Big rule of good PR: create strong subconscious links between your client and some relevant, positive imagery, and you've pretty much won the battle before it's even started. Nobody else in the office shows any signs of wanting to make it a greener place to work in. The idea is mine, and mine alone.

I guess Terry could be secretly working out how to recycle his farts into a renewable energy source to run the photocopier, but if he is, he's keeping a tight lid on it.

No. I think I'm actually the only one who's had this idea.

Pot plants – according to Google – are very good at improving air quality. And who doesn't like improved air quality, eh? Also, pot plants are very *visible*, aren't they? Very *obvious*. If I bring a load of them into our office, then they will definitely be noticed! And everyone – especially Nolan Reece – will know that it's *me* who bought them.

What a fantastic idea!

'Er . . . I'm just heading out for a while,' I say to no one in particular. 'Just have a client . . . a client to go and see.'

Nadia looks up at me and offers me a small smile, before getting her head back down again.

Nobody else seems to care what I'm up to, so I shrug my shoulders and make a beeline for the exit. If I'm about myself, I can get to B&Q, buy a load of pot plants, and get them back here before Nolan comes in after lunch.

Yes, yes!

Off we go then!

◆　◆　◆

Do you have any idea how fucking *expensive* pot plants are?!

No, neither did I. Not until I got to B&Q.

By the time I left again about half an hour later with my car boot full to bursting, I was a good hundred and fifty quid lighter in the purse.

But it'll all be worth it. I'm sure of it. Just as soon as I get these bloody expensive things situated around the office – looking all green and leafy, and improving our environment.

If my leaving the office barely registered on anyone's radar, then the same cannot be said when I re-enter it. Awkwardly carrying a four-foot rubber plant will do that.

'That's a nice plant you've got there, Ellie,' Joseph remarks, as I pass the desk he and Amisha are sat at. They're both working on the new website at the moment, so are probably the only ones having no problem keeping busy.

'Yes, yes it is,' I reply, somewhat non-committally.

'Any reason for bringing it in here?' Amisha says, the smile trying its hardest to stay off her face.

Joseph and Amisha are unwholesomely clever.

They can see what I'm up to. They can see it quite clearly.

'Just thought I'd brighten the place up a bit,' I reply, in a light, breezy tone. 'Just trying to . . . you know . . . do my bit for team morale.'

'Ah . . .' Amisha says. 'Well, that's . . . that's very good of you.'

'Yes. Yes it is,' Joseph adds.

'Indeed. Indeed it is,' I say, looking in every direction but at them. 'I'll just go pop it by the photocopier,' I tell them, and scuttle away, muttering under my breath. I know when I'm being teased.

The rubber plant goes over in the corner next to the photocopier, where it looks quite lovely.

On my next trip back up from the car – still avoiding Joseph and Amisha's gaze for all I'm worth – I position several succulents along the windowsills, in what I hope is a pleasing manner. As I do this, Nadia comes over.

'What you up to, Ellie?' she asks, all curious.

Oh God. Not her too. Everyone is taking far more interest in my exploits than I'd like. 'Oh, you know . . . just trying to spruce the place up a bit,' I tell her in a light voice. 'Thought the office could do with a little greenery.'

Nadia's eyes have gone understandably narrow. Before this, my only perceived interest in our office space was how quickly I could get out of it at 5.30 p.m. Much like Joseph and Amisha, she's finding my new-found interest in pot plants rather suspicious.

'Hmmm,' Nadia says.

So as not to engage in further conversation with her about it, I pop the last succulent down and immediately turn around, rushing off to get some more of my green haul before Nadia has the chance to question me further.

I know I'm doing all this out of pure self-interest, and I'm sure most people in the office have deduced the same – but what choice do I have?

That's my life right now – doing things royally outside my comfort zone, just so I can stay working in this increasingly pot-plant-filled office.

On the next load up from the car, I bring ferns. Many leafy, bouncy ferns.

'I had a fern once,' Terry tells me, as I pass him in the kitchen. 'It died within a week. I think my cat took a shit in the pot.'

'You *think* your cat took a shit in the pot?' I reply, not really wanting to think too much about the cleanliness of someone who can't tell whether an animal has defecated in their pot or not.

'Yeah. Shame really. It was a lovely fern. Looked just like that one.'

'Ah . . . that's . . . that's lovely Terry,' I say to him, before backing away slowly.

I put the ferns in various strategic places that also please me aesthetically. I don't go quite so far as to plonk any of them on people's desks. That probably wouldn't go down all that well.

The final trip up from the car brings with it three hanging plants. All of which have strange and complicated names that sound like something from a Harry Potter book.

I hang the *Ceropegia linearis* up by the entrance to the kitchen, where it dangles pleasingly. The *Hedera helix* gets strung up in the hallway leading to the toilets, and the *Wingardium leviosa* takes pride of place just outside the entrance to Nolan Reece's private office.

And with that, my pot-planting efforts are complete. With satisfied hands placed on satisfied hips, I survey my work with a satisfied look on my face.

Nadia sidles up to me while I'm basking in my own cleverness.

'Have you considered,' she says, with a sly smile on her face, 'that you're going to be the one watering all of these? You know that, don't you?'

My face falls. 'Oh shit.'

'Yep.'

'Er . . . how often will I have to do that?'

Nadia cocks her head. 'Oh, *every day* Ellie. Every single day.'

'Balls.'

'Probably twice.'

'Crap.'

She gives me a look, and a pat on the shoulder. 'Hope it was worth it,' she says, before sidling away again, back to her desk.

We're about to find out – as Nolan Reece has just walked in.

I'm half tempted to go running up to him to point out my pot-planting efforts, but that might come across as a little too eager. Better to just stand here and wait, while he takes in the environmental glory of it all. I'm sure he'll immediately want to know who had the great idea to brighten the office up and make it greener.

As he comes towards me, I plaster on a fake but wholly expectant smile. I also try to channel my inner earth goddess as much as I possibly can, by putting my clenched fists on my hips and tilting my chin up slightly, to really hammer home my efforts.

Nolan glances up at me, throws me a quick smile of his own, and powers past into his office. He doesn't look at the pot plants once – save for a quick glance at the *Wingardium leviosa* hanging just outside his door.

Bollocks, I remark in the vaults of my mind, as he closes his door behind him.

I look around at the rest of the office to see that most of my work colleagues have clocked Nolan's indifference to my endeavours, and are smirking like schoolchildren.

A couple of them are also sneezing, it should be noted. I probably should have checked with people about allergies.

Anyway, that appears to have been a complete waste of bloody time, doesn't it?

. . . no, no. I'm not leaving it at that. I'm £150 down here. I have to make it *worthwhile*.

Under the gaze of my highly amused co-workers, I beetle my way over to Nolan's door and knock.

'Come in,' I hear him say, and I do just that.

'Er, Nolan?'

He looks up from where he's sat at his desk with a concerned expression on his face. 'Oh, hello, Ellie. How are you?'

Glad you still remember my name, for starters.

'Fine thanks. Just wondering if you'd noticed the plants.'

Nothing like getting straight to the point, in my book. I learned that in my job. Sometimes, there's no point sodding around with subliminal messaging, when a bloody great big billboard will do the job.

'Plants?'

'Yeah . . . the new pot plants around the office?'

Nolan looks confused, but rises from his chair, walks around his desk and comes to join me at the entrance to the office. He pokes his head out and regards my efforts properly.

'Oh, that's very nice,' he says, but in a disturbingly distracted tone. He then turns and goes back to his desk, still with that furrowed brow and pinched look on his face.

'Everything alright?' I ask.

He stares at me for second. 'Um . . . sort of. The financial situation here is . . . very difficult.'

'Oh no.'

'Yes. It's all quite *tricky*. We're going to need to get clients signed up as fast as possible.'

'Oh dear.'

'It should all work itself out okay . . . with any luck. I've just been with the guys who run Hempawear, and they sound like they might be on board. That'd be really, really great if they are!'

'Hempawear?'

'Yeah.' Nolan looks a little flummoxed. 'I'm quite surprised you haven't heard of them. The Warriors For The Planet swear by their stuff. They wear them all the time.'

'Oh! *Hempawear!*' I exclaim, waving a hand. '*Of course* I know who they are!' I stick a finger in my ear. 'Sorry, hearing is playing up a bit. Might be having a reaction to one of the pot plants *I bought myself and put in the office to make it more environmentally friendly.*'

'Oh, okay,' Nolan replies. 'Thanks for that.'

'No problem!'

'You've got some Hempawear stuff then, have you?' he asks me.

'Of course!' I lie. 'Love . . . love their *stuff*.'

Quite what *stuff* this is, I have no idea. Wearable items, obviously. But whether that's clothing or jewellery or hats is anyone's guess. My clothes-buying habits are strictly ASOS, Primark – and FatFace, if I'm feeling a bit flush.

I think I'd better get out of this conversation as fast as possible.

'Well, I'll leave you to it,' I say in a hurry. 'You're obviously very busy.'

'Oh . . . well, yes. I guess I am.'

'And so am I!' I assure him.

'Okay.'

'Oh, yes. Extremely busy, that's what I am.'

'Okay,' Nolan repeats.

I open my arms expansively. 'Plenty of work to be getting on with, that's what I've got!'

'Great.'

'And I've got to water those pot plants as well! Aha ha ha ha . . .'

'Fine.'

This is not getting out of the conversation *at all*. What I am in fact doing is the exact *opposite* of that. If anything, it's Nolan who wants out of it far more than I do. I can tell from his expression.

'Well, off I go then!' I say cheerily.

'Okay.' Nolan nods and his eyes flick over to the doorway.

'Yes, yes. Off I go. To work . . . and to water pot plants!'

'Great,' Nolan repeats.

Just leave, Ellie.

I turn on my heel and scuttle out of Nolan's office, finally leaving him to his worries.

I have plenty of my own as I get back to my desk. The pot plants clearly haven't done the job I needed them to. Nolan is way too distracted with trying to bring in new clients to notice them.

That £150 has gone down the drain, and I'm still not entirely sure I won't be following it at the end of this week.

There must be something else I can do.

If pretending to be a dying panda and making the office a greener place hasn't done the trick, then what will?

Perhaps another call to Sean?

No! No, Ellie. Think of something on your own for a change!

My mind goes back to the company Nolan just mentioned in his office.

Hempawear.

Maybe there's something there I can use?

I google the company name, and find out that they are in fact an underwear manufacturer that makes pants out of hemp. And bras. And socks. And long johns. In fact, Hempawear seem to produce just about every item of underwear you can think of. All out of natural hemp fibres.

They also do next-day delivery.

Hmmm.

Interesting . . .

◆ ◆ ◆

So, now it's Thursday, and I'm wearing hemp knickers.

This may sound like the first lyrics of a particularly bad Ed Sheeran song, but I assure you that is *my* current status, as I ride in the elevator up to the office.

They're not the flashiest knickers you've ever laid eyes on, it has to be said. I haven't worn anything quite so plain and expansive since I was thirteen. They certainly do a good job of covering most of my bum. They're the biggest and most modest pants I've owned in decades. About as sexy as a sideboard.

They seem to fit very nicely though, which is good.

My thinking has been thus: Nolan seemed very keen on getting Hempawear's business, and as he thinks I actually already own
some of their product, I figured it could only help my cause to turn
up to work in some of Hempawear's finest undergarments. It'll help
to reinforce my green credentials even further.

The only issue I have now is letting Nolan Reece know that I
am in fact *wearing* said undergarments.

Do you know how hard it is to make another human being
aware of what underwear you have on, without coming across as a
lunatic sex monster?

Very hard, let me tell you.

I've tried to think of ways I can do it that appear natural and
normal, and I'm coming up blank. It's just impossible to do . . .
without coming across as a lunatic sex monster.

Now, I want to keep my job here at Viridian PR – that much
has been readily established. But do I want to keep that job having
earned a reputation as a lunatic sex monster?

Probably not.

All I can really do is get on with my working day, and hope
an opportunity arises to safely bring up the fact that I'm wearing
Hempawear products, without also bringing up the fact that I am
a lunatic sex monster.

As the lift gets to the floor Viridian PR is on, another small
issue arises.

The pants are getting a little . . . *itchy*.

Nothing too bad, you understand. But it is a little distracting. I put it down to the hempyness of the material. Apparently,
Hempawear use more hemp in their products than any other rival
hemp clothing company. It's something they are very proud of. I'm
sure my new pants just feel a little uncomfortable because they're
new. There's no way they'd sell underwear that wasn't naturally
comfy.

Thankfully there's no one else in the lift with me now, so I can have a sneaky little scratch of my backside before the door pings open.

I probably shouldn't have worn this trouser suit, to be honest. It's always been just a bit too tight around the thighs and butt. That might not be helping to make my large Hempawear knickers feel comfortable. But good impressions and all that. I look like a confident business executive in this suit. Having my buttocks hugged a little harder than I'd necessarily like is a price worth paying.

That's probably why the pants are itching a bit. I'm sure it'll pass as the day goes on.

Having had a brief but satisfying scratch, I make my way into Viridian PR, still pondering how I'm going to let on that I am a fan of Hempawear's product.

When I get to my desk, I have to let out a little chuckle, as I see a brand-new red watering can sat next to my in tray, with a little bow wrapped around the handle.

Somebody – probably Nadia – is having a little fun with me, it appears. I've spent the last couple of days using one of the old cups in the kitchen to ferry water to my pot plants, and I guess this present has been donated to make my life a little easier.

I'm actually quite touched.

'Morning, Ellie,' Nadia says as she appears from the kitchen. 'I see you've got our gift.' The grin on her face is enormous.

'Yes. Thanks very much,' I reply ruefully.

'We had a whip-round. Figured if you kept using that World's Best Mum cup with the chip in it, you'd probably end up killing half the plants. Who knows what horrific germs lurk in its stained porcelain?'

'You're probably right.'

I look up to see the same amused expression on the faces of everyone else – they're all looking at me with no small degree of joy. Amisha and Joseph are particularly pleased with themselves at the back there.

'Thanks, everyone,' I say to them. 'I'll put it to good use right now.'

I pick up the watering can, pull off the bow, and go through to fill it up at the kitchen tap. I can't help but smile to myself as I do so. I have now become the constant gardener of the office, so why wouldn't I have my own special little watering can, to help me with my daily task?

The smile starts to drop off my face as I stand at the sink though.

That's because the small and slightly distracting itch from a few minutes ago is now starting to get *worse*. It's gone from a little irritating to quite annoying, in no time at all. I would have another satisfying scratch, but there's no door into the kitchen, so several members of staff would get a right eyeful of me playing with my backside.

Instead, I'll just have to grin and bear it, until I can get to the toilet and sort it out – after I've finished watering the plants. I should be able to put up with it for at least that long.

With a full can of water, I make my way back out of the kitchen. I go over and water the rubber plant by the photocopier, and then move over to the succulents along the windowsill. By the time I've done them, the itch is becoming almost unbearable – partly because it's spread in an extremely disconcerting manner to areas beyond my backside.

Well. This is *marvellous*.

I hurriedly finish watering the rest of the pot plants, going over to do the *Wingardium leviosa* outside Nolan's private office last. It doesn't look like he's made it in today yet – this seems like the kind of guy who has no issue being out of the office for long periods. It's not all that easy to see through the tinted glass door, but I can see enough to know that his chair is empty.

I'll just get this last plant done, and then get to the toilet for a good rummage. I can only imagine it's the hemp pants that are causing me such distress. If I can just get them off and go commando for the rest of the day, I should be okay. Not wearing underwear isn't a situation I'm particularly happy with, but it's certainly better than having holly-bush vagina for the rest of the day.

Good. That's the *Wingardium* watered. Now to get these pants sorted.

I just about manage to get across the office floor and down the corridor to where our two toilet cubicles are, without having to scratch myself enthusiastically – but it's touch and go, to be honest.

Though I have to let out a small groan of dismay as I reach the toilets and find that they're both occupied.

Damn it.

What the hell do I do now?

There's nowhere else in Viridian PR's office space that has the privacy I need!

I could go back out and get in the lift, but I have no guarantee somebody won't be in it.

The prickling has now ramped up another notch. I have to get this bloody hemp material away from my private parts as soon as possible. God knows what level of damage is being done down there!

Then inspiration strikes.

Nolan's office is private – and empty right now. There's no lock on the door, so I should be able to get in there and do what's necessary without being seen by anyone.

Yes. That sounds like a plan!

I hurry back along the corridor and over to my desk, where I plonk the watering can down and pick up a random couple of bits of paper, which I carry over to Nolan's office, studying them carefully. I'm hoping this makes me look like I'm delivering highly important documents. People delivering highly important documents can go into other people's private offices with alacrity and confidence. This is the way of things.

Nobody's really paying much attention to what I'm doing anyway, to be honest. They're all hard at work trying to justify their continued employment.

I close the office door behind me, throw the bits of paper on Nolan's desk, and unzip my trousers. Yanking them down around my thighs, I shove my right hand into the gusset of the hemp pants, pulling the material away, and immediately breathe a deep sigh of relief as the prickling sensation stops.

With the other hand, I move my shirt aside to have an inspection of the area. I'm expecting to see a very red and sore lady garden, but I'm pleasantly surprised to see that it all looks fine down there. No damage has in fact been done. I haven't had a hideous allergic reaction or anything.

My bottom is still prickling like mad though, so I hastily move my right hand around the back, to push the hemp pants away from that as well. Again, the instant relief is palpable.

Good. This is good. As long as I can get to the toilets as soon as possible, and get these stupid pants off, I should be fine.

The crisis will be averted, with no real harm don—

'Yeah, I'll call you tomorrow once I know what's happening.' I hear Nolan's voice from behind me . . . and the blood instantly drains from my face.

I then hear the door swing open, and I know that my fate is sealed.

My hideous, hideous fate.

Because here I am: Eleanor Rose Cooke – thirty-four years old and in what should be the prime of her life – with her hand down the back of her arse and her trousers around her knees, presenting herself to her new boss like a horny street cat.

'Jesus!' Nolan screams, as I whip my hand out from the hemp pants.

O h g o d o h g o d o h g o d o h g o d . WhatdoIdowhatdoIdowhatdoIdowhatdoIdo?

How on earth can I even begin to salvage this? What possible good can come of this situation?

Nolan Reece is looking at me, bent over his desk, with my pants on display like a lunatic sex monster!

. . .

. . . pants.

Hemp pants.

I'm wearing hemp pants!

'Hey, Nolan!' I exclaim. 'I told you I have Hempawear pants, didn't I?!'

Look . . . I'm clearly and inextricably fucked here. There's no getting away from it. And there's no way I can possibly make this situation any *worse*, so I might as well do what I came here to do today anyway – let Nolan Reece know just how much I love wearing itchy hemp knickers.

'What?' Nolan cries, slamming the door behind him so no one else can see me presenting myself.

'Hempawear, Nolan! I love wearing Hempawear!'

And then, because I'm not sure my boss is clear enough on what I'm trying to get over to him, I thrust my bum in his direction, just so he can get a really good look at the marvellous Hempawear pants I obviously love so dearly.

'Bloody hell, Ellie!' Nolan wails, coming around his desk to face me. He's gone beetroot red with embarrassment.

This gives me the opportunity to yank my trousers up and zip them up again, finally covering what's left of my modesty.

. . . now it's time to talk my way out of this.

Ha!

'I'm so sorry, Nolan!' I gasp. 'I'm just so excited about us having Hempawear as a client that I got carried away!'

'Pardon me?!'

'I really wanted to show you how much I love my Hempawear pants!'

Jesus Christ, girl. What the hell are you doing?

'You did?'

'Yes!' I flap my hands about a bit. 'I just get too excited when I think about being environmentally friendly, and do silly things sometimes!'

'You do?'

'Absolutely! I'm just so keen to show others how important it is to be environmentally conscious!'

Nolan appears to *actually think about this for a moment* – to actually consider the words of a woman who was showing him her arse twenty seconds ago. He's either a saint, or clinically insane. 'Well, I guess you did do the protest the other day . . .'

'Yes!'

'And it's good to see you're enthusiastic about Hempawear.'

'It is!'

His reddened face crumples. 'But you really didn't need to show me the pants, Ellie. You could have just told me you like them.'

I nod feverishly. 'Yes. I know. I'm sorry, Nolan. I get caught up in the moment sometimes.'

'That's okay.'

'I'll . . . I'll leave you to it then, eh?' I ask him.

He blinks at me a couple of times, a flabbergasted look on his face. 'Yes. I guess so.' He swallows hard. 'Thanks for . . . thanks for coming in to see me.'

Oh dear. The poor man. I think I've broken him.

'No problem!'

I chuck Nolan a quick smile (it misses by about two feet), before throwing the door open and getting the hell out of Dodge. The horrendous prickling has already come back, and I need to do something about it.

One of the toilets is thankfully empty now, so I'm able to get these stupid bloody knickers off in short order.

As I'm pulling my trousers back up again – grateful that the prickle has been permanently banished – I have to wonder what additional damage I've done to my chances of keeping my job.

I'm forced to conclude that the damage must be *enormous*.

Even more enormous than my silly hemp pants.

Sigh.

Maybe I'll just stay here in the toilet for the rest of the day. I might have a hunt for the macerator while I'm in here. At least I'll have somewhere to stuff the pants.

◆ ◆ ◆

And so, we come at last to the day of reckoning – Friday.

I didn't stay in the toilet for the rest of the day. But I did keep my head down at my desk and not look anyone in the eye. Not that anyone else saw what happened in Nolan's office, but they must have heard a bit of a kerfuffle going on.

For his part, Nolan didn't speak to me, or even acknowledge my presence, for the remainder of the day. This was entirely understandable.

I threw the hemp knickers in the bin when I got home. I would have ritualistically burned them out in my postage stamp of a garden, but I developed an irrational fear that the hemp fumes might get me high if I did that. Spending the rest of the night on a pant high would have just about finished me off.

As it was, I slept fitfully – knowing full well what was coming today.

This is it.

This is the day I lose my job.

. . . yes, I know I'm being pessimistic, but what chance do you realistically give me of keeping it at this point? The man's seen me with my hand down my gusset.

Things really aren't looking good.

I'm not the only one with a pervading sense of gloom in the office this morning, though. At least half of my colleagues look equally unsure of their fate. And even those like Amisha and Joseph, who are guaranteed to be staying on, look a bit downcast. Nobody likes to see their work colleagues thrown under the bus.

I spend the first few minutes of this trying day watering the pot plants again. I'm wearing the comfiest pair of knickers I own, so there's no repeat of yesterday's shenanigans.

At just gone 10 a.m., Nolan appears from his office and calls us all to attention.

'Um . . . hello, everyone. Can you just look and listen my way for a moment, please?'

He really is dreadfully polite.

This will somehow make it worse when he shows me the door. I'd much rather be shouted and screamed at. It'd give me something I can get my teeth into. Having a placid, pleasant person like Nolan tell me I'm out of a job will be like being bitten by a puppy.

'I'm afraid I've come to a decision about who I have to let go,' Nolan continues. 'It's been a very hard choice to make, and I am hugely regretful that I'm having to downsize like this.' He does look regretful . . . and not a little stressed. I wonder whether that

Hempawear contract has come in or not. 'Could I please see both Terry and Mark in my office, one after the other. I'll speak to you first, Terry, if that's okay.'

From the back of the office, Terry stands up. 'Nolan . . . don't worry about it, mate. At least not on my account. I figured this was coming. You don't need to chat to me privately about it.' Terry's face screws up. 'In fact, I'd rather you didn't, please. Just let me know my end date and the details of my leaving package in an email. I'll get everything sorted out at my end.'

Nolan looks a little taken aback by this. 'Oh . . . alright, Terry. Thank you for being so understanding.'

Sarky Marky looks like he doesn't understand. Not in the slightest. He's gone grey.

Nolan looks over at him, that same regretful look on his face.

It's admirable he wants to do the firing face to face, but perhaps he could have picked a slightly less dramatic way of doing it? No wonder Terry wanted to avoid playing his part in this impromptu ritual. It all feels very clumsy and cack-handed.

I guess Nolan Reece has a little more to learn about being a boss. It's easy to forget that he's never done it before. I wish Peter had stuck around a little longer to show him the ropes.

'If you could come through, Mark,' Nolan says, and retreats back into his office. He holds the door open while the distraught-looking Sarky Marky walks over and goes in with him. Nolan then closes the door behind them both, sealing Sarky Marky's fate.

If I'm honest, I'm not too troubled about Mark leaving the company. He takes an unwholesome interest in my breasts every time I wear a low-cut top in the summer, and I'm pretty sure he's been stealing teabags for several years now. He offends me slightly, as both a woman and a British person.

But nobody deserves this kind of humiliation, the poor bugger.

Looking very much more on the bright side though – Nolan didn't say *my* name! He hasn't called *me* into his office! I think I might be keeping my job!

Yay!

I look over at Nadia, who looks similarly relieved.

As does everybody else – even those who were more or less guaranteed to be keeping their jobs anyway.

Of course, we all feel sorry for Sarky Marky, but it's only human nature to celebrate a little when you find out the hammer isn't falling on your head.

We all remain respectfully silent as the minutes tick by, with Sarky Marky being given his marching orders.

I even jump a little when the door to Nolan's office opens a few minutes later, and Mark comes back out.

Oddly, he doesn't look too traumatised any more.

He sees us all looking at him as he wanders out, and a smile crosses his lips. 'Don't worry, everybody. It's okay.' Mark jerks a thumb back at Nolan, who is just behind him, standing in the doorway to his office. 'Mr Reece here has offered me and Terry a generous severance package.'

'Has he?' Terry says, looking up from the box he's started filling on his desk.

'Yeah!' Sarky Marky assures him. 'It's not too bad at all, mate!'

And with that, Sarky Marky trots over to Terry's desk, and starts talking animatedly with him.

Oh well.

All's well that ends well, I suppose. At least Nolan is taking care of his now ex-employees properly, which is good of him.

And thank God this is over.

It looks like I did just about enough to keep my job here. I guess the disaster of yesterday's knicker-flashing must have been offset by the dying-panda impression and pot plants after all.

'Ellie?' Nolan says, looking over at me. 'Could you come into my office now, please?'

My heart plummets.

My soul blackens.

My bowels loosen.

My eyes water.

'Um . . . okay,' I reply, voice shaking.

I try to get out of my seat, but my legs won't hold me. I take a deep breath and try again, and this time they just about manage to function.

I catch sight of Nadia looking at me with abject pity. This only makes me want to cry even more.

No.

No, Eleanor Cooke. You will *not do that.*

That steadies me a little, and I'm able to plaster on a stoic expression as I turn to face Nolan and follow him into his office.

I can feel a dozen sets of eyes boring into my back as I go.

So, this is it then. I haven't escaped the chop. Nolan was just stringing things out a little, for maximum dramatic effect.

The bastard!

The towering, idiotic, ungrateful, nasty bastard!

Anger has utterly consumed my dread as I sit in the chair in front of Nolan's desk. If I weren't a girl who had been brought up in a decent, upstanding household, I might be about to launch into a tirade of swear words at the way I'm being treated.

Nolan sits down opposite, and regards me for a second with those piercing eyes of his, before speaking. 'Ellie, I need to talk to you about something.'

'Yes, I get that,' I reply, barely able to get the words out through my gritted teeth.

'Something very important. That's why I called you in here.'

'Okay. Well, you'd better get it over and done with then,' I tell him, hands gripping the arms of the chair in a way that will probably leave permanent marks.

Hah! No more Permanent Marks around this office any more!

And no more Permanent Ellies, either!

Nolan takes a deep breath.

Here it fucking comes.

'I'd like you to be my number two here at Viridian PR.'

You fucking *bastard*! You absolute fucking bas—

What?

'What?' I splutter.

'My number two.' Nolan smiles. 'You demonstrate a commitment to environmentalism that I greatly admire, and you're obviously very engaged with the subject.'

'I am?'

'Yes. Clearly.' He chuckles warmly. 'I've never known anyone so keen to show me that they wear sustainable pants before.'

This causes me to blush furiously.

'Really?'

I should probably be saying something more constructive, but Nolan's announcement has discombobulated me to such a degree that I simply cannot put the words together.

I thought I was coming in here to get fired, and instead I've been . . . *promoted*?

'Absolutely!' Nolan holds up his hands. 'Now, I can't pay you any more money as yet. Our finances won't allow it, but I still want to officially make you my second-in-command here at Viridian PR, so that we can move forward on the right foot. Your remuneration package will of course increase once we have the cash flow from new clients.' He beams. 'That should give you enough incentive to help me get them, I would imagine.'

'Yeah,' I say. 'Yeah . . .'

Nope, still unable to string a sentence together. Maybe I should start communicating with him by banging my hand on the table. Once for yes, twice for no, thrice for 'would you like to see my knickers again?'

'We'll pop out in a moment to officially announce your new status to the rest of the staff, but I obviously wanted to break the news to you in private first.'

'Great,' I say in a squeaky voice. 'Super.'

'So, you'll accept then?' Nolan asks me, eagerly.

Oh *Christ*.

Do I accept?

Do I say yes to this?

It sounds like an awful lot of responsibility, and a much bigger workload. I'm not sure I want that, if I'm being honest. I'm the type of person who just likes to get their work done and get out of the office at a reasonable time. That's why I love being a publicist. Okay, you're further down the pecking order, but at least you don't have to work all the hours God sends. It's better for your sense of well-being, I think.

You know . . . work to live and not live to work . . .

Find the right balance . . . that kind of thing.

But here I am being offered a new job that will see an end to being able to stick to that philosophy.

It appears that I have been far too clever by bloody half . . .

In my desire to keep my job, I have inadvertently made a rod for my own back.

Nolan Reece here thinks I'm his go-to girl for all things environmental, when the truth is I've been making it all up just to save my own hide! I'm not his go-to girl, even though I'd really like to be. I'm not really environmentally conscious in the *slightest*. I still drive that big polluting Mercedes. I still buy my clothes in Primark. I still use single-use plastic bottles, and I still once happily dated a man who would think nothing of levelling an entire deciduous forest to put up blocks of luxury flats.

I've been lying through my teeth, and done such a convincing job of it that it's got me a promotion I really don't deserve at all!

I have been hoisted by my own petard . . . whatever that actually means.

But I can't say no, can I? Not now. Not after all of this. It might expose my true colours!

I've backed myself into a corner so expertly that you could give me a job as a forklift driver.

Bloody hellfire.

'Yes, Nolan. Of course I accept!' I say, trying to sound as enthusiastic as he wants me to.

If anything, my grip on the arms of the chair has got even firmer.

'Excellent!' Nolan replies, actually bouncing up and down on his seat. 'I'm so pleased!'

Yeah? I'm not so sure everyone else will be!

All they're going to see is Little Miss Pot Plant brown-nosing her way into a cushy promotion. Thank God none of them saw me in here with my pants out and my trousers down. Tongues would wag harder than an excited dog's tail.

But that's it, isn't it?

I'm committed now. I've said yes to what amounts to a massive change of lifestyle, and I'm sorry to say that it *terrifies* me. Not least because my promotion is built on a tissue of lies that I cooked up just to avoid demotion to the ranks of the unemployed!

As Nolan starts to fill me in on what he's going to expect from me as his number two at Viridian PR, I can't help but feel a certain amount of internal whiplash.

I've gone from being scared to death about having to find a new job, to being even more scared to death at the prospect of staying in this one – all in the space of a few seconds.

What on earth am I going to do now?

. . . apart from water the bloody pot plants again this afternoon, I mean. I doubt being Nolan's second-in-command is going to stop me from having to do that.

Curse me and my Machiavellian levels of stupidity!

Chapter Four

Veganthropy for Beginners

There goes a joke:

How do you know if someone's a vegan?

Don't worry, they'll fucking tell you.

It's not a joke I've ever had much truck with, to be frank. The intimation is that vegans are all self-righteous, pompous idiots, who can't wait to pontificate at you about their healthy, animal-friendly lifestyles, while at the same time berating you for being a disgusting corpse-eater.

That's an image that is prevalent in the media, and across society in general. It has not, up until now, been my personal experience of them, though.

Of the vegans I have met in my life, I have found most, if not all, of them to be perfectly ordinary human beings, who just happen not to eat or wear animal products.

This is by and large how most people actually are – just getting on with their lives, having made choices for themselves that they have no huge desire to foist on to others.

Of course, there are a small minority of vegans who aren't as sensible as that – and do make it their job in life to annoy as many other people as possible, by lecturing them about the evils of eating animal products. But they are very few and far between, and are very much the exception, not the rule.

This, of course, holds true for most facets of our day-to-day lives: most people are decent, sensible and pragmatic – it's a small minority that are ruining it for the rest of us. See also: people in politics, the religious, nerds, and every third person on Twitter.

So, in my personal experience, those who adopt veganism are perfectly fine, and I haven't been annoyed or upset by any of them even once. I can even see the point they're trying to make, some of the time. Like most people, I've thought about cutting down on my meat consumption – but it always occurs to me to do so right after I've done a big shop, or right after I've eaten a large pepperoni pizza.

I'm going to have to meet with a couple of vegans when I take on my first big task as Viridian PR's new Head of Client Relations. I'm hoping they'll be ones I can successfully get along with.

Nolan gave me that grandiose title last week, which is certainly a step up, and a change of direction from being a plain old publicist.

The news of my promotion was met in much the way I feared. Most of the Viridian staff didn't seem all that impressed. There was no actual outcry at my behaviour leading up to the promotion, but I wouldn't say people were exactly effusive with their congratulations either.

Those who did seem happy for me were the three staff members I generally feel the closest to: Nadia, Joseph and Amisha. They could have been faking it of course (always best to stay on the right side of someone higher up the pecking order than you), but I think I know them well enough by now to believe that they were being honest.

'The pot plants definitely did the trick then,' Amisha says in a wry voice, as I spritz the succulent on the windowsill close to her desk.

'I seriously didn't think he'd bloody *promote* me, Mish,' I reply, in a stage whisper.

She actually laughs at this. 'No. I never figured you for the managerial type!'

'Exactly! But I did such a good job of coming across like one of his environmentalist friends that I've well and truly snookered myself!'

'Yes. Yes, you have.'

'You don't have to look *quite* so amused, you know.'

'Oh, but I do . . . *boss*. I really, really do.'

'Aaaargh! Don't call me that!'

This sends her off into another gale of laughter, drawing the attention of those around us.

'Shh!' I demand, putting a finger to my lips.

Amisha sobers up and flicks off a salute. 'Sorry, ma'am!'

'Oh, for God's sake,' I lament, spritzing water over the succulent again.

Amisha suddenly looks a little concerned. 'Have you . . . have you told Nolan about . . . about . . . *you know?*'

'You know?'

'Demonic Rab?'

My eyes instantly flatten. Amisha is referring to my ex Robert Ainslie Blake. The man I met because Stratagem used to represent his property firm, R.A.B. Developments. The nickname Demonic Rab was an obvious choice, given how Robert dumped us as fast as you like when Pierre left Peter.

'No,' I say in a dark tone. 'I haven't.'

'Are you . . . are you *going to?*'

'I don't know.'

'It might not be such a great idea. Demonic was famous for chopping down every tree in sight, wasn't he? You remember that newspaper article? The one we had to do all the counter-PR for?'

I look aghast. 'Yes, Mish . . . I wrote some of the bloody stuff, remember? When Kate needed the help?'

'What was the headline they used again?'

I moan, and pinch the bridge of my nose. '*Property Tycoon in Nature Reserve Destruction Scandal*,' I say in a dead voice. That headline is seared on to my memory for all time.

In fact, thinking about that entire campaign still makes me queasy. The effort we went to. The money we spent. The photo shoots we set up. Kate and I had Robert pose with two hedgehogs and a natterjack toad in one of them.

Do you have any idea how hard it is to get a fucking natterjack toad to sit still?

Robert actually suggested we should cable-tie it to the nearest tree branch at one point, which tells you all you need to know about the man, I suppose.

Amisha sits back in her chair. 'Ah, yes. I remember now,' she says. 'That was hell to fix, that was. Kate worked her socks off. No wonder she started drinking so much.' Amisha appears to think for a moment. 'Maybe *don't* tell Nolan you were shagging Demonic Rab for six months, eh?'

I give her a look. 'No. Perhaps not.'

'Not sure many environmental types would want to have sex with someone like him,' she points out.

The look gets a bit sharper. 'No, I'm sure they *wouldn't*.'

I thoroughly and comprehensively regret my relationship with Robert Ainslie Blake. What can I say? He swept me off my feet in such a sickeningly clichéd fashion that it makes my head hurt to even think about it nowadays. He spent so much money on me, and flattered me so much on a regular basis, that it took me several months to work out how much of an arsehole he really was.

He also did a 'thing' in bed that made my hair stand on end. You'll put up with a lot when someone can do a thing that makes your hair stand on end, let me tell you.

Amisha points at another one of my windowsill succulents. 'That one looks a bit dry, boss,' she tells me.

I let out a groan of pure dismay, and angrily spray water over the damn thing.

Putting the sorry events of my love life to one side for the moment, I still have a lot of other stuff to worry about. Namely – how I'm going to justify becoming the new Head of Client Relations.

This starts with me getting some new and exciting business for the company. A task I dearly hope I'm up to.

Hempawear have definitely come on board, thank God. I had a meeting with their CEO Kyle yesterday. He looked about twelve years old, and I kept mentally placing a skateboard under him. Nice boy, though. Very enthusiastic about making everything out of hemp.

He offered me a hemp tea, which I declined. If the damn stuff gave me a prickly vagina, I'd hate to think what it would do to my internal workings.

I came away from that meeting with a whole series of new promotional avenues for Viridian PR to explore, in order to increase Hempawear's platform – and hopefully sales. It's all enough to keep Amisha and the rest of the guys back in the office busy for the time being.

The money Kyle the twelve-year-old is sending our way isn't bad either, but it's certainly not enough to keep the company afloat for more than a couple of weeks – hence why I'm back out again today, off to a meeting with a vegan food company that Nolan has been courting for quite a while.

'This could be a big one, Ellie,' he told me. 'They've got the backing of a Ukrainian millionaire, and getting them on our books would be a massive boost. We need this account, so please make sure that you sell our services as best you can.'

No pressure, then.

Up until now, I've always been very much the *second* person in the room at meetings like this. Or perhaps even the third. I've been a lowly cog. A small piece of the puzzle. And I've been pretty happy as such.

But this is the second meeting in two days where I am the main attraction. And I don't even have anyone to back me up, as we don't have the staff to send along with me. Hempawear was easy – Nolan had already done all the groundwork, I was just there to dot the i's and cross the t's. This time it's different. This time it's all on my shoulders.

Gulp.

I hope the people who own and run Veganthropy Foods are more like the vegans I've met than the ones I've only heard about on social media . . .

Their names don't inspire much confidence, if I'm being honest. There's a chance that Petal and Mordred O'Hare are going to be down-to-earth, normal businesspeople. There's also 'a chance' I can throw on a swimsuit, stick my bum out and be mistaken for Kendall Jenner.

There's every possibility that Petal and Mordred are card-carrying members of Worriors For The Plonet, and have Bandy on speed dial.

Speaking of whom – Nolan wants me to meet with them as well, at some point. He's sure I'll have no trouble getting them to work with us, given that I am of course one of Padlo's bunch and a great friend to them all.

Sigh.

One problem at a time, I guess.

Veganthropy Foods is based on a small industrial estate a good hour's drive from the office, quite far out into the sticks. As I make my way along the gravel driveway leading to the collection of four standalone units, I see one field off to my left covered in solar panels. I'm not surprised by this in the slightest, given who I've come to see.

Veganthropy Foods is housed in the largest of the industrial units, slap bang in the centre of the estate. I can see a couple of delivery trucks parked outside it. Both are electric.

These people aren't doing this by halves, it seems. It's really quite impressive.

I am instantly ashamed of my Mercedes. Nolan is trying to secure us a Toyota Prius to use as a company car, but until then I'm stuck with my gas-guzzling German monstrosity. The clobberdy-bang may have been finally fixed, but it's still not exactly an advert for clean, green driving technology.

I park the damn thing way off to the right, with the Veganthropy delivery trucks hopefully blocking it from view.

Today, I have elected to dress down in a pair of black jeans and a blue sweater. I figured that was probably best for people called Petal and Mordred. I doubt they're ones for smart suits. I'm also wearing a pair of my most practical boots, which is just as well, as the gravel underfoot is dirty, wet and not a little uneven.

My nose is assailed by the fresh smell of cow manure as I walk around the delivery trucks, telling me in no uncertain terms – if I didn't know it already from all the B roads – that I am in the country.

There's no sign of the O'Hares as I make my way to the plain white uPVC door at the front of the unit. Above it is a small sign that says 'Veganthropy Foods', but it's not at all ostentatious. Why would it be? It's not like this place is open to the public. They'd probably have a hard time finding it, even if it was.

There's a doorbell on the left side that I dutifully press, and I wait for an answer.

When none is forthcoming, I ring the bell again.

We agreed I'd be on site at 10.30 a.m., and it's now 10.35, so I'm sure it won't be long until someone answers the d—

I have to jump out of the way as the uPVC door springs outwards and bangs against the wall. Standing in the doorway is a wizard.

OF COURSE HE'S A WIZARD. HIS NAME IS MORDRED.

'Good morning!' I say cheerfully to the middle-aged man in front of me, who is six foot five and owns the greatest beard I have ever laid eyes on.

It is a beard of consequence. A beard of enormity. A beard of such overwhelming beardness that I'm surprised there aren't other, smaller beards currently circling in its gravitational influence.

The hair is not far behind in its significance. It too is vast, flyaway, and writhes like the tentacles of Medusa in the country breeze.

Both are the greyest of greys. Both are magnificent.

Inexplicably, Mordred is not wearing a wizard's hat. That would probably be taking things a tad too far. Instead he's got a black top hat on, which is far more sensible and down to earth and normal and *who am I kidding, I'm talking to Gandalf's operatic twin brother.*

Mordred looks me up and down for a second before replying to my greeting.

'Leeks!' he snaps at me. 'What do you think about them?'

Well, this is unexpected.

In the folder I'm currently carrying under one arm, I have a long list of information about Veganthropy Foods, and a cheat sheet of answers to questions I thought I might be asked about

Viridian PR today, which I hastily put together last night at home. In it, I talk at length about the services the company can provide, the pricing structures we use, and the businesses we have worked with in the past as Stratagem.

However, I do not have any answers prepared about what vegetables I enjoy.

I simply did not think this would come up.

How stupid of me.

'I beg your pardon?' I reply.

'Leeks, girl! What do you think about leeks?'

'They're nice in a soup with potatoes?' I venture, in what I hope is an inoffensive response.

'Bah!' Mordred exclaims and throws his hands up, before disappearing back into the darkness of the unit beyond.

He is almost instantly replaced by Joanna Lumley.

'Oh, hello there!' Joanna Lumley says, with an apologetic look on her face. 'I'm sorry about Mordred. We're having a disagreement with our chief cook about some ingredients. It never puts him in a good mood.'

'Oh, okay,' I reply, still quite shocked that I'm holding a conversation with one of the biggest British TV stars in history.

My dad was always a big fan. He liked to watch the Lumley whenever possible, and certainly loved to sapphire his steel on a regular basis – especially at the weekend, when Mum was out with her sister. I bought him the complete box set of *The New Avengers* a few years ago for Christmas. I've never seen him look happier. All that Lumley, right there in his hands. It made his day.

And here she is, standing right in front of me.

I'm quite perplexed.

'You're from Nolan Reece's new company, aren't you?' Joanna Lumley says.

'Yes. Yes, I am,' I reply, snapping myself out of the surrealism of the moment and holding out a hand. 'Ellie Cooke.'

Joanna Lumley takes my hand. 'Petal O'Hare,' she introduces herself, throwing me for a loop.

She could be Joanna Lumley's twin sister. She looks like her, and sounds like her.

I'm still half convinced it *is* her, and she's just taken up a pseudonym so she can run her vegan foods business in peace, without everyone constantly asking her whether *Ab Fab* is ever coming back.

'Do come in,' incognito Joanna Lumley says to me, inviting me into the industrial unit.

'Okay,' I reply, still a bit off-kilter. Petal O'Hare is not what I was expecting *at all*. She's tall, quite glamorous, and has the kind of skin I would kill for – even though I'm a good twenty-five years younger. All that vegan food must be doing *wonders*.

I follow her in through a small entrance lobby, and out into a broad, open space that's half storage area, half industrial-sized kitchen – divided by one large wall that runs down the middle of the room. My nostrils are instantly struck by a combination of smells they may never recover from. It's not that any of them are bad, it's just that they are deeply *intense*, all thrown together like that. They are overwhelmingly vegetable in nature, which I guess makes perfect sense.

The storage area is full of bags, boxes and sacks of every kind of food ingredient that doesn't owe its direct existence to farmed animals. There's a bloke at the back offloading what looks like a sack of potatoes from another delivery truck, parked up just outside a set of flung-open double doors.

The separated kitchen area is a hive of activity. There are several people dressed in kitchen whites, all busying themselves putting together the ready meals that Veganthropy Foods are starting to become well known for. There's an awful lot of cooking going on. Things are bubbling, baking, frying and blanching at a rate of knots, and it's making me hot and sweaty just looking at it.

'Apologies for all the noise and such,' Petal O'Hare tells me as we walk past all of this. 'Busy time for us. We have a large batch going out at the end of the week.'

'Not a problem!' I tell her airily, trying to ignore the strong smell of earthy vegetables.

'In an ideal world, all of this would be better sectioned off,' Petal continues, 'but we're still a small operation, and things are a bit haphazard at the moment.' She gives me a smile. 'We're hoping to update and expand operations in the next year – which is why we've called you in, to hopefully help us get the message out.'

'Absolutely!' I reply, one eye twitching at the waft of garlic that's just gone up my nose, as we pass by what I can only assume is a pot of the stuff on a large hob.

'I'll just call Mordred over, and we can go have a conversation in our back office,' Petal says, before looking at where her husband is having what looks like a heated discussion with a man in a chef's hat. 'Mordred! It's time for the meeting!'

He turns his angry gaze to us and starts to march over, cutting the poor bloke in the chef's hat off mid-conversation.

Watching Mordred get nearer is what it must feel like to be stalked by an enraged, ambulatory hedge. Two fierce, burning eyes peek out from that wealth of grey, spiralling hair, which is bobbing and weaving all over the place now that he's removed the top hat.

That can't be sanitary around all this cooking, I think to myself. Unless Veganthropy Foods are marketing a vegan-cheese-and-hair pie, I think he should probably be wearing a hairnet.

'Leeks!' he roars as he draws ever closer.

Petal throws me another apologetic look. 'Sorry, Ms Cooke . . . Mordred does get exercised about our ingredients sometimes, and he's just discovered something online about leeks that has displeased him greatly.'

'Oh,' I respond, in a bit of a daze.

What on earth could have displeased him greatly about a *leek*? Leeks are possibly one of the most inoffensive things on the planet. It'd be hard for me to get angry about the existence of leeks, even if you threw one at my head. It'd be *you* I'd be angry at, not the leek. The leek would have become an unwilling ballistic weapon, a decision it would have had no choice in . . . being that it was a leek, and an inanimate object.

Mordred appears to have sidestepped this relaxed attitude towards leeks, as he truly looks incandescent about them when he reaches us.

'We can't have them, Petal!' he roars at his wife, before turning to me again. 'We just can't have them, Viridian PR!'

I think he just referred to me as Viridian PR. He does know that's who I work for, and not who I am, right?

'Calm down, Mordred,' his wife tells him, gently picking what looks like a small leaf out of his beard. 'If we don't want to use leeks any more, we don't have to.'

Mordred points a large and meaty finger back over at the guy in the chef's hat. 'Montrose begs to differ!'

I see Montrose roll his eyes as he turns back to the frying pan in front of him on the stove he's stood at.

'Well, Montrose will just have to recognise that leeks are now unacceptable,' Petal says, remaining calm and placid.

The angry hedge stares at me with great intent. It's deeply disconcerting. I may never be able to visit the garden section of B&Q again. 'And what say you, Viridian PR?' he asks me.

'I'm sorry?' I splutter back.

'Are leeks unacceptable?'

This is the second time he's asked me for my opinion on leeks in nearly as many minutes. I've never felt so pressured to provide an answer about any topic in my life before.

'Why would they be unacceptable?' I venture, feeling as if I require more information before I am able to accurately give him what he wants.

Mordred shakes his head sharply, causing the beard to surge and undulate in ways inconceivable to science. 'The *moths*, Viridian PR! Because of the moths!'

'The moths?'

'Yes! *Alliumaris lepidoptera!*'

'Sorry, what?'

'*Alliumaris lepidoptera!*' Mordred repeats, the beard heaving.

'Sorry? Is that a type of pot plant?'

'No, Viridian PR! It's a very special type of moth!'

'Is it?'

'Yes, of course!'

Petal steps slightly in front of her maddened husband, forcing him to move away from me a little. 'Mordred has discovered a special species of moth that feeds on leeks, and is worried that if we use them in our recipes, we might be removing its food source,' she explains.

'That's right!' Mordred agrees, before pulling out his mobile phone from his jeans pocket. He thrusts the screen in my face – upon it is a picture of the single ugliest fucking moth I've ever laid eyes on. 'Isn't it a thing of wonder and beauty?' he insists.

'Um . . .'

What do I do here?

I suppose I had better lie and agree with him. I want his business after all.

However, I'm slightly afraid that, if I do, I will be telling a lie of such great magnitude that it will create a rip in the space-time continuum, plunging me into another universe – possibly one that does not contain leeks.

Alliumaris lepidoptera is a moth of such overwhelming hideousness that it fair takes my breath away. The damn thing is all hairy bits, nodules and feelers.

It's like someone grabbed 'disgusting' and put wings on it.

'It's certainly a very interesting-looking . . . thing,' I eventually reply. I think I'm on safe ground with that.

'Hmph,' Mordred says. 'It's a wonderful creature of the earth, and we cannot take away its food source!'

Mordred is clearly delusional. Because the moth really is a truly hideous-looking thing – and regardless, I doubt very much that they're going to kill the silly thing off just by using leeks in their recipes. Any creature that looks this atrocious must be tough enough to adapt quite easily to other food sources, if needs be. And just how many leeks do Veganthropy Foods use anyway? I had a look at their website, and could only spot leek and potato pie in the list of their products.

I totally understand the concept of making food that doesn't use animal products, or ones that don't hurt them in any way, but this might just be taking things a bit too far.

What's next? Not using tomatoes because a passing earwig once fell into a bowl of soup and drowned?

Mordred and Petal O'Hare clearly take their veganism extremely seriously. To an almost ridiculous extent in Mordred's case.

I had better be careful here. The boots I'm wearing are made of leather, and I had a ham toastie for breakfast. If the angry hedge smells either on me, it may attack.

'Shall we go and have a chat about what PR services we can provide for you?' I say to them both, steering things back on to a track that does not involve leeks, or the insects that feed upon them.

'Yes!' Petal agrees, clapping her hands together.

Mordred looks almost disappointed by this. It's quite clear who is the businessperson in this relationship.

'Do come on through,' Petal tells me, walking towards a door at the rear of the industrial unit. I follow along again, with Mordred bringing up the rear. This is as unnerving as it sounds. Mordred would loom even without all that hair and beard.

Petal leads me through the door into a small room that is more lounge space than office. There's a small desk parked over in one corner with a laptop, a kettle and some cups on it, but most of the room is taken up by a couple of old, battered-looking chesterfield sofas, with an equally antique coffee table between them. On the coffee table is a small hotplate, on which rest three bowls, all covered with white cloths.

Hmmm.

'Please, sit down,' Petal bids me. 'Would you like some herbal tea?'

'Um. Is it hemp?' I ask, in a worried tone.

'No. Jasmine and chamomile.'

'Then yes, please.'

I park my bottom on one of the chesterfields, while Mordred sits on the one opposite. As Petal makes the tea I try not to look directly at the angry hedge (because that way probably lies moth-related madness), and instead look down at the coffee table, where I get a closer look at those three bowls.

I'm no Nostradamus, but I feel quite sure that the contents of the bowls are going to be a part of my very near future.

Lovely.

Petal brings over a cup of sweet-smelling tea and puts it in front of me, before squeezing herself next to her enormous husband on the other sofa.

Both of them then stare at me intently.

It's something they are extremely good at.

I take it that this is my cue to start my pitch for Viridian PR's services, and I open the folder on my knees.

'Well, first of all, thank you very much for inviting me here today,' I begin. 'I'm excited to be here, to share what excellent promotional services we can offer you.'

'That all sounds lovely, Ms Cooke. But first, it's time for the butternut,' Petal says.

'Pardon me?'

'The butternut,' she repeats.

'The butternut,' Mordred echoes.

'The butternut?' I also say, feeling a bit flummoxed. I have a whole spiel prepared here, why must I be interrupted with random vegetables?

Petal leans forward and whisks off the white cloth on the bowl to my left. Underneath, I see that the bowl is full of small brown cubes, covered in grit.

'We have traditions here, Viridian PR,' Mordred tells me, folding his arms.

Petal lightly biffs him on the shoulder with her hand. 'Her name is Ms Cooke, Mordred. Try to be nice.' Then she faces me again. 'When we were in the Amazon basin, we picked up a lovely local custom that the indigenous people have had for centuries.'

'Did you,' I reply in a flat tone.

'Yes indeed. We share our food before any conversation. As a way of welcoming you into our home and our livelihood.'

'Right.'

'So please . . . enjoy the butternut. It is replete with vitamins A and C, along with being an excellent source of fibre and potassium.'

'Yes, it is. The butternut,' Mordred again repeats, like this is some kind of religious ceremony – which, given just how vegan these two clearly are, it probably is.

Have you eaten butternut squash? It tastes like a depressed potato.

I gingerly pick out one cube of the orange squash and hold it in front of me, examining it. The cube is covered in what looks like sea salt and rosemary.

It's mid-morning, for crying out loud. I want a cup of coffee and a croissant, not a cube of lightly seasoned vegetable.

Lightly seasoned vegetables have no business existing in the morning. Unless they're baked beans, though they hardly qualify as a vegetable.

Nevertheless, I'm here to impress, so I pop the cube in my mouth and give it a chew. There's a moment where my brain and my stomach both rebel against this rude intrusion of vegetable matter on to my morning body clock, but once the shock is over, the cube of butternut doesn't taste all that bad. Okay, the texture is still relatively unpleasant, but the seasoning does make it taste pretty nice.

I swallow the squash and smile. 'Thank you.'

Both Petal and Mordred simultaneously nod at me slowly. 'You are welcome,' they both intone, like a pair of Cistercian monks.

'From looking at the slight dryness in your hair, you could probably benefit from a bit more vitamin E,' Petal adds, staring at my head.

'Really?' I reply, my hand involuntarily touching a couple of ends that I desperately hope aren't that split.

'Yes indeed. I thoroughly recommend more butternut in your life, Ms Cooke.'

'Um . . . okay,' I say, not sure if having sleeker hair is really worth having to eat any more of the depressed potato.

'Do continue with your presentation,' Petal then encourages, holding out her hand with her palm open.

So, with the rather odd aftertaste of butternut squash in my mouth, I proceed to outline – in as much detail as possible – what services we can offer Veganthropy Foods. And for a good fifteen to twenty minutes my life becomes sensible again. It's something of a relief. Petal asks me a lot of pragmatic questions that I am actually able to answer, thanks to the amount of research I've done, and I'm able to sell Viridian PR to the both of them in a way that reassures them that we are a company now dedicated to promoting environmentally friendly businesses. Petal is the one with all the technical questions, bringing up things like sales figures, marketing impact, messaging formats, and so on – while Mordred is clearly more interested in the moral and emotive aspects of the meat-free food industry.

They present quite the united and challenging front to me during the conversation, but I am more than up to that challenge, I am pleased to say.

Mordred even starts calling me by my actual name, which must be one hell of a breakthrough, given the man's personality type.

It's only when I start to talk about their new lines of food that things start to deteriorate.

'Would you like to try some of our newest recipes?' Petal asks. 'We've selected a couple for your enjoyment.'

Ah . . . the other two bowls. I've been trying to ignore them as much as possible during my spiel, but there they are, just waiting for my attention to turn back to them. Which is now happening, whether I like it or not.

'Um . . . yes, I suppose so,' I respond, affecting another one of my pleasant but entirely false smiles.

It's not that I don't want to eat vegan food per se . . . I just don't want to eat vegan food at 11.30 a.m.

Petal whips off the cloth over the middle dish. Underneath it is a bowl of crispy chicken strips.

Well, they look like crispy chicken strips, anyway – I'm sure they aren't *actually* chicken, otherwise these two have a very strange sense of what animal-friendly foods are.

'These are our new Tofu Crispies. A wonderful snack for everyone,' Petal assures me.

Oh, spectacular. *Tofu.*

I guess I wasn't going to get out of today's visit to a vegan food company without tofu at least getting a mention – but here I am about to actively engage in the consumption of it.

I've managed to avoid tofu for my entire life – a fact I am *immensely* proud of – but here it is, just waiting for me to try it, and I have no way of getting out of the experience, save for faking some kind of seizure.

I sigh internally, pluck a Tofu Crispy out of the bowl, and bite off one end of it.

After having thoughtfully chewed it for a couple of seconds, I can cheerfully say that it tastes of absolutely nothing. Literally nothing. It's quite the achievement. I might as well be chewing air. Crunchy air, it has to be said, as the crispy coating lives up to its name. However, that tastes of nothing either. This isn't food. This is the negation of food. The repudiation of everything that food stands for. It is the anti-food. If I just ate this every day, I'd be dead of starvation in a week.

How the hell are Viridian PR supposed to help promote this – as anything other than a drastic diet method, anyway?

Tofu Crispies – Eat Yourself Dead!

'Lovely!' I exclaim, as I swallow the nothing down.

'Excellent! Glad you liked it,' Petal says. 'We've been taste-testing it for a couple of weeks now, so I'm delighted to see it's come out so well.'

'Mmmmm,' I agree, picking a bit of the crispy nothingness out of one of my molars. I notice that Mordred is looking at me with narrowed eyes. The hedge has gone from being angry to deeply suspicious. He clearly knows I'm faking it.

Petal then whips off the last white cloth to reveal my third and final challenge. 'This is our brand-new beetroot, spelt and lentil chilli,' she proudly tells me as she does so.

In the bowl is indeed something that resembles chilli. It's a bit redder than I'm used to, but it doesn't look half bad at all. It sadly doesn't smell of much, so I'm expecting to now be required to eat runny nothing, after enjoying crispy nothing to its fullest.

There's a small spoon stuck in the chilli, which I pick up and use to scoop some of it. Without another thought, I pop it into my mouth and start to masticate once more, safe in the knowledge that this is vegan food and will therefore be about as potent as—

MY FACE EXPLODES.

Sorry to startle you like that. I simply have no choice in the matter.

If crispy tofu is the negation of food, then this chilli is the unequivocal reinforcement of food as a concept. This is the most food I have ever had in my mouth. My entire being is instantly consumed by it. There is now only the vegan chilli and my poor, poor taste buds in this universe, locked in a dance of death.

'Jesus Christ!' I splutter, sending chilli fragments splattering across my carefully prepared notes. While this looks embarrassing, it's a good thing, because at least it means a majority of the chilli is no longer in my mouth, where it can continue to burn like the wrath of a thousand suns.

'Hmmm . . . maybe your palate isn't quite ready for that,' opines Mordred from behind his big grey bush, as I choke to death on this evil concoction he's created.

This vegan wizard-man is not like kindly old Gandalf. He's the other one – the one played by Christopher Lee. You know who I mean . . . had a big, dark tower and a penchant for monologuing.

'Oh dear! Let me get you some tissue!' Petal cries, and she reaches under the coffee table to produce a box of tissues.

Tissues made of fucking hemp, it appears.

Oh, my days.

Still, what choice have I got?

I snatch a wodge of the tissue from the box and spit the rest of the chilli into it. I'm afraid that this probably isn't creating the best impression of my feelings about Veganthropy Foods, but right now I'm more concerned with my ability to taste food in the future. I don't want everything to taste like Tofu Crispies until the day I die, thanks to the fact that my taste buds have permanently shrivelled.

'I'm so sorry,' I intone as I ball up the tissue. 'I'm sure the chilli is lovely. It's just a bit too spicy for me.'

'Don't worry, dear,' Petal reassures me. 'Mordred was insistent on the level of chillies used . . . but I'm sure he now realises that we have to rein things in a bit.'

'Hmmph,' Mordred remarks, arms still folded.

If we do end up working with Veganthropy Foods, I will make it my job in life to ensure that Mordred is not featured in any promotional work *whatsoever*. I've only been in the man's company for an hour or so, and I want to go out and eat a raw steak just to spite him.

. . . we'll make sure Petal's plastered over everything, though. Let's face it, anyone who looks that much like Joanna Lumley will have no issues helping to sell the products. The Lumley is British brilliance distilled into one seemingly ageless celebrity. I'd buy anything from her. And so would you.

Petal actually looks quite upset at her husband's attitude. 'We must get it to work for everyone, Mordred. Our food has to appeal to as many people as possible. You know it must!'

This was the general thrust of their questions during the sensible part of the meeting. Petal and Mordred made it very clear to me that they want to sell their ready meals to as broad a cross section of the public as possible.

Mordred gives her a dark look.

Petal rolls her eyes in frustration. 'We can't just cater for the vegan market as it is,' she carries on. 'We have to convince other people to eat our foods as well. That's why we've brought Ms Cooke in to help us.'

'And help you, we most certainly can,' I say, as smoothly as possible. 'With our help, I'm sure we can broaden your customer base, and increase profits as much as possible.'

Yes, yes. That's just what business owners want to hear. Well done, Cooke. Very *smooooth*.

Petal looks at me with barely concealed horror.

Not so *smooooth*?

'We're not concerned with high profits at any cost, Ms Cooke,' she tells me. 'Our priority is to get people to eat food without animals in, to help save as many of their lives as possible.'

Like the Alliumaris lepidoptera . . . I think to myself, and have to suppress a smile at the idea of giving up bacon just to keep the moth of my worst nightmares alive and healthy.

That smile is immediately quashed when I look at Mordred, to see that there are tears in his eyes. The sudden anguish on his face is self-evident, and quite disturbing.

An angry hedge I can tolerate. A suspicious hedge, I can deal with – without too much of an issue. But a distressed, tearful hedge is another thing entirely.

This big, scary man with a beard the size of Coventry has suddenly become very vulnerable and small, right in front of my eyes. It's quite the change of demeanour.

Petal gently pats Mordred on one of his large knees. 'It's okay, sweetheart,' she tells him, before looking at me. 'Mordred tends to get a little upset when we talk about such things. He used to work in an abattoir in his previous life, and has . . . *seen things.*'

'Oh,' I reply. There isn't really much else I can say than that. The intensity of the change in the big, hairy man has struck me dumb for some reason.

Instead, I wait for a moment, and then lean forward, pick up the bowl of crunchy tofu nothingness and offer it to Mordred. 'Have a Tofu Crispy,' I tell him. 'It might help you feel a little better?'

He gives me a look. For the first time that day, there's gentleness in it.

The look goes on for a few moments, before he slowly raises a hand and plucks out a Tofu Crispy, then offers me a small smile in return.

Mordred's attitude towards me thus far today probably doesn't warrant such an act of kindness on my part, but the look of utter sadness in his eyes is impossible not to react to. What on earth has he *witnessed*? And do I really want to know?

'Well, guys, I'm sure that Viridian PR can really help you with getting more customers to buy your products,' I say, hoping to get back on track again, and move away from Mordred's obvious discomfort. 'You clearly feel strongly about it, and we do too.'

'That's good to hear . . . *Ms Cooke,*' Mordred says in an almost friendly tone, which I'm going to take as something of a breakthrough. 'You're the only PR firm available to us that's offering an ethical approach.'

I dazzle him with my biggest and broadest smile. 'We absolutely are!'

Mordred smiles with me, but there's still a darkness behind his eyes that's going to stay with me for quite some time.

I look at Petal again, because frankly it's a little easier.

'So, can I report back that you'd like to engage us as your public relations firm?' I ask, getting straight to the point. I've done everything I can to persuade them that Viridian PR is right for them. I'll just have to hope that gobbing hot chilli all over them hasn't put them off.

Petal and Mordred look at one another for a moment, apparently coming to a decision in that way that married couples can do – without a word passing between them. It's something I've never had the chance to experience myself, but hope to one day.

'I think so, yes,' Petal agrees. 'We'd still like to think over some of the specifics, but I'd definitely say you've done enough to get us on board.'

A tension I didn't know was there releases itself from my shoulders. Thank God for that. Having inadvertently set myself up as Nolan Reece's number two, I do not want to fail at it. Especially not at this early stage.

Petal reads my reaction extremely well. 'You can relax a bit now, Ms Cooke,' she says, and chuckles.

I slump back into the chesterfield a bit. 'Thanks,' I reply, and take a deep breath.

'We know what it's like when a company is new,' she tells me. 'The pressure that's on to persuade people to work with you can be very stressful.'

I pull absently at one earlobe. 'It's a . . . a difficult time,' I confess to her, which is the absolute truth. She's not wrong about feeling the pressure. I've never been under so much in my life. It's a wonder I don't squash like a butternut.

'It gets easier,' Mordred rumbles. 'When you know you're doing the right thing, it always does.'

I nod my head.

I do hope he's right. I truly do.

And I equally hope I *am* doing the right thing. That's something I'm still not sure about right now.

What I do know is that I've come through this meeting with my reputation intact – if not my taste buds. I can go back to Nolan and report that I've successfully got Veganthropy Foods to come on board.

The rest of my morning with Petal and Mordred O'Hare largely consists of more jasmine tea and some admin stuff that is as boring to talk about as it is to detail after the fact.

I leave the Veganthropy Foods industrial unit just as Mordred returns to his leek-based argument with Montrose the chef, having said a short but warm goodbye to me just outside the door to their small office.

'He likes you,' Petal confides as she escorts me back to the main door of the unit.

'Really?' I reply.

'Yes,' she says emphatically. 'Mordred is . . . not an easy man, sometimes. He keeps barriers up far more than he needs to. You were very kind when he got upset. I think that helped.'

'No problem,' I say as we reach the main door, which Petal opens for me. 'It was a pleasure to meet you both, and I look forward to working with you in the future.'

'As do I,' Petal tells me, before taking a deep breath of cool country air. 'All of this is very important to us, and we're happy to be working with people who feel the same way.'

'Excellent!' I say, and shake her hand, before walking back over to my Mercedes, which is now unfortunately in plain sight, given the fact that the delivery trucks have vanished.

I do my very hardest not to meet Petal's eye as I drive the stupid thing out of the courtyard. The car is a reminder that I am not, in fact, all that environmentally conscious. It's just an act I've been putting on for my job.

For the first time I feel a small sliver of shame about this.

Up until now, all of my efforts have been purely directed at keeping and maintaining my pay packet, and it's felt like a noble and just cause to me. But there's something about the meeting that I've just had with the owners of Veganthropy Foods that has shifted my thinking.

I can't quite put my finger on it, but as I wonder about the whole thing on the drive back to Viridian PR's offices, I keep returning to that look of anguish in Mordred O'Hare's eyes.

He is clearly as dedicated to his work as I am to mine – you can tell that from how emotional he got. But it feels like there's a very large difference between the two of us. Something fundamental that ties itself to that inexplicable sliver of shame I'm suddenly feeling . . .

No.

Don't do that, Ellie.

Today has been a *good* day. You're not going to sabotage it by thinking too much. You're going to go back, report your success to Nolan, and take this day as a win.

Because that's what's important here – earning your right to stay in the role Nolan has put you in. You are the Head of Client Relations, and doing a good job is all that matters.

I am *happy.*

I am *pleased.*

. . . so why can't I get Mordred's sad expression out of my head?

Chapter Five

CYCLEPATHIC TENDENCIES

'It's a bicycle.'

'Yes, I can see that.'

'It's made of bamboo.'

'Yes, I can also see that.'

'Bits of it, anyway.'

'Not the wheels.'

'No. Definitely not the wheels.'

'And this is a product you think we should be promoting, do you?'

'Absolutely!'

I study the excited look on Young Adrian's face with no small degree of trepidation.

Young Adrian is – as the name implies – a very youthful member of the Viridian PR team. The most youthful member, in fact. He is also a rather timid chap, who has a tendency to fade into the background, which is probably why he hasn't warranted a mention before now.

Young Adrian is the type of person who sadly doesn't warrant a mention 99 per cent of the time. This is not an insult – he's a perfectly decent, nice individual. It's just that he's also the type of guy who blends expertly into the background, like a particularly well trained ninja. If Young Adrian was a character in a novel, he most certainly would only ever be one of the bit players, and probably wouldn't even get mentioned until at least chapter five.

There was zero chance of Young Adrian losing his job in the Stratagem-to-Viridian changeover, simply because nobody would have remembered he was there. He basically has a job for life here, as long as he continues the way he's going.

It really is like some kind of superpower.

Colour me deeply surprised then, when Young Adrian approached my desk this morning, all excited and wanting to talk to me about a potential new client.

Young Adrian does not talk about potential new clients. Young Adrian does the photocopying and gets the sandwiches. He also now helps water the potted plants – as what's the point in being the second-in-command if you can't delegate a few responsibilities, eh?

'So, the bike is electric?' I ask Young Adrian, trying to get as much information before deciding on whether to take it to Nolan or not.

'Yep!'

'And the guy has built several prototypes?'

'He has!'

'And he's your uncle?'

'He is!'

'And he's funded the whole thing himself so far?'

'He has!'

'Which begs the question, Adrian . . . why aren't you working for him, instead of here?'

Adrian shakes his head. 'I'm not good with practical stuff, Ellie. Uncle Kev is the engineer in the family. The rest of us are better suited to desk jobs.' His face scrunches up. 'Besides, Uncle Kev isn't the type to work well with others. Not when he's designing, anyway.'

'Right.'

'The bike's his best idea yet, though. And he's very talented at what he does. I just thought it was worth bringing it to you, as we're all about the environmentalism these days.'

'That we are, Adrian. That we are.'

I must admit, it does have potential.

Not that much of a money-spinner, I hasten to add. We're not likely to squeeze much profit out of a one-man operation. But Nolan and I were having a conversation a few days ago that was directly relevant to a project like this.

'We need to champion good ideas,' he said to me, over a coffee (brought to us by Young Adrian). 'Fresh thinking, I mean. An entrepreneurial spirit . . . that kind of stuff.'

'Reputation-enhancers, you mean?' I replied, not realising for one second that the person who had just brought me my coffee would be putting just such a potential reputation-enhancer in my lap a mere week later.

'Exactly! Viridian PR should be seen not just as a PR firm for established business, but for new concepts,' Nolan continued. 'We need to get in on the ground floor of environmentally focused companies, and help nurture them going forward.'

'A bit risky,' I cautioned. 'You could spend a lot of time on something without much of a reward at the end.'

'Oh, I'm not suggesting we throw all our resources into those kinds of avenues. Make them side projects . . . when we have the time to do them,' he suggested, as he sipped his Young Adrian–provided coffee. 'Just a thought.'

And here – via the joys of extreme serendipity – is just such a potential side project for Viridian PR, by way of Young Adrian.

Ah, what can it hurt to run it by Nolan, eh?

'Come on then,' I tell Young Adrian. 'Let's go and have a chat with the boss, and see if he likes the idea.'

◆ ◆ ◆

Nolan more than liked the idea. He absolutely *loved* it. I have to confess I felt a little dubious about supporting a product knocked up by one man in his shed (albeit a very hi-tech shed), but Nolan had no such reservations.

He immediately got on the phone to Young Adrian's Uncle Kev to arrange a meeting. Nolan is nothing if not proactive when his interest has been piqued – I've learned that about him.

He can come across as a little lackadaisical sometimes (the frequent absences from the office are a prime example of this), but when he gets the bit between his teeth he doesn't like to hang around. There's also a boyish enthusiasm about him when he's excited about a project that's hard not to get caught up in.

. . . and did I mention that I find him very handsome, in an unconventional sort of way? I'm pretty sure I might have done, but just in case I didn't – he most definitely is.

I was a little disconcerted at first to have him take over from me so completely on this particular venture, but then I've had my hands full with Veganthropy Foods and Hempawear, so it didn't trouble me too much.

The next thing I heard, about a week later, was that Nolan had arranged for us to shoot a short promotional video for Uncle Kev's electric bicycles, as a proof of concept. This video would then be strategically posted to all the main social media sites, to gauge audience response. Joseph would be the man to do the filming, and Amisha would then upload her husband's video as soon as it was edited.

I genuinely thought I'd play no further part in proceedings.

Until today, that is – the day before the shoot.

'You want me to what?' I splutter.

'Be in the video with me and Kevin,' Nolan replies. 'I think it'll be for the best, don't you, Joseph?'

Joseph nods slowly. This is the way he tends to do everything. He's possibly the calmest human being to ever walk the face of the planet. The man is so deliberate and considered about the world, it's like someone's shown him his entire life story up to the point of his death, and he knows there are no nasty surprises coming. 'Yes, I'd say so,' he agrees.

Ellie Cooke does not say so. She does not say so *at all* – largely because she has no idea what her life story looks like, and is *terrified* of nasty surprises. Something like a bamboo prototype electric bicycle has 'nasty surprise' written all over it.

'Um, I'm not sure I'd be very good on camera,' I say, in a deeply worried tone. 'I might do something silly.'

Joseph pats me on the shoulder with one big hand. 'You'll be fine, Ellie. We won't do too much, I promise. Just some shots of you guys on the bikes, with maybe some GoPro footage of you cycling about a bit. Nothing too strenuous.' His smile is very reassuring – as if he already knows that things are going to be absolutely fine.

'Yeah, I'm sure you'll be great,' Nolan agrees. 'And really, you've got to be in the video with us. I'm hoping this will be a good calling card for Viridian PR as much as a promotional test video for these bikes. It can't just feature a scruffy bloke like me. Having my fantastic and beautiful second-in-command in it will sell us far better!'

This morning, I elected to wear quite a lot of foundation and concealer, as I'm having some issues with chin spots right now. Thank God I did, because it's harder to see that my face is flaming red with embarrassment.

Nolan just called me beautiful.

Fantastic *and* beautiful.

I'm self-aware enough to know that I am blessed with some attractive features (though, to be honest, the only thing on my face I really like are my lips – the rest of it I can take or leave), but to have someone say I am *beautiful* is a concept quite beyond me.

And the only thing I'd say about myself where I can comfortably use the word 'fantastic' in a positive manner is that I am *fantastic* at Pictionary.

Every time Christmas rolls around and I go home to my parents' house, everybody tries extremely hard to be on my team when we play it. Sean goes as far as bribing me with cold hard cash.

I always win. It's become a family tradition.

And I'm not even a good *drawer*. I got a C in Art at school. It's just that, for some reason, when you stick a timer on me, pop me in front of a whiteboard and tell me to represent a water bison, I can do it in ten seconds flat, with an accuracy that's almost scary.

I am the Rain Man of Pictionary.

What I'm not is someone who takes a compliment easily, especially when it comes from the man who pays my wages.

'Oh, well, I don't know about that,' I say, coquettishly. This is most definitely the first time in my life I've done anything that's approaching coquettish. It's making me feel light-headed. I'm not even sure I know what 'coquettish' means, but if it's got anything to do with being embarrassed and awkward in front of two men, then I'm your number-one coquettish girl.

Joseph gives Nolan a look that I'm far too shocked to decipher, before returning his gaze to me. 'So, are you happy to do it then, Ellie? Sounds like we need you in it.'

'Um. Okay,' I say, still processing.

Does . . . does Nolan *fancy* me?

Or is he just buttering me up to get me to play along?

Does he *really* think that I'm beautiful? And if so, what would that mean for our working relationship?

Hell, what would it mean for my working relationship with everyone else in the office? If Nolan starts to give off the impression that he's attracted to me, won't that have a negative impact on the way people treat me around here? Especially because he's just promoted me?

I do not want anybody to think I got this job because of anything to do with the fact that I'm a woman and he's a man. I did not get promoted via the medium of sexuality.

Okay, yes, I did flash my hemp knickers at him, but nobody else knows about that.

No . . . there was nothing underhand like that going on, at all. I did not use my feminine wiles to score a bigger pay cheque! I got the job the honourable and proper way: by lying through my teeth about being environmentally conscious.

Good grief.

There's every chance I'm just overthinking this. Nolan is probably just being nice to a senior member of his staff, to get them to cooperate with his plans.

Yes.

That sounds about right to me.

Nothing more to it than that.

Nothing.

Speaking of nothing, I have nothing appropriate to wear for cycling. The last time I got on a bicycle I was fourteen years old and 84 per cent uncoordinated limbs. I'm not that sure I'm much more coordinated now, nearly twenty years later, to be honest.

I eventually elect to wear a pair of black leggings, a grey sweater, and a pair of Adidas I bought for the gym – and have therefore only worn on three previous occasions.

I look *kind of* sporty. Sporty-ish.

Good enough for this silly video, anyway.

Let's hope it doesn't take ages to shoot. I could do with getting back to the office as soon as possible, given that Mordred O'Hare has decided the script for the Veganthropy radio advert doesn't contain enough information about how the leeks they are now using are ethically farmed, miles away from any unsuspecting *Alliumaris lepidoptera* colonies. I'm sure he's happy about that, but I'm not convinced that telling the public at large about it is necessarily the right way to get them to buy the leek, butter bean and roasted cauliflower stew.

I arrive at the park close to Viridian PR's offices, to be greeted by Nolan, Joseph, Joseph's extensive array of camera equipment, three bamboo bikes, and Uncle Kev.

Uncle Kev's full name is Kevin Flounder, and in a display of near-perfect nominative determinism, he does indeed look like a fish. One of the bug-eyed, thin ones.

He's also dressed a tiny bit like Worzel Gummidge, in a tatty pinstripe suit jacket and equally threadbare red corduroy trousers. You can tell he's the eccentric English inventor type from a thousand yards away. The hair is nowhere near as bushy or grey as Mordred's, but it could give it a run for its money in the flyaway department.

The park is largely – and thankfully – empty. We should be able to do a few nice, brief shots of us riding around the car park, and the path around the park, without drawing too much attention.

'Morning, Ellie!' Nolan says happily, as I walk over to where the three of them are standing. 'Say hello to Kevin and the Cyclocity 5000!' He indicates the bikes and their inventor, who gives me a little wave.

Hmmm.

We'll have to do something about that name. Cyclocity 5000 sounds like something out of 1950s America, not twenty-first-century Britain.

The bikes themselves are the type with small wheels and a high seat and handlebars. Kevin's obviously designed them to mimic your average foldaway commuter cycle. The small electric engine sits above the pedals in a chunky section of the frame, which is clearly made out of bamboo, as it is quite a pleasing stained light-wood colour.

For a bicycle that someone's knocked up in their own shed, the Cyclocity 5000 is quite an impressive piece of kit. To have made at least three of them already is even more impressive. There are a few small differences between each of them here and there, and if you look closely you can begin to see imperfections on all of them, but I am nevertheless amazed by Kevin's talent and skill. Looks like Young Adrian might have been on to something after all . . .

'Hello, Kevin,' I say to the inventor, shaking his hand as I do.

'It's extremely good to meet you!' he tells me enthusiastically. 'Really looking forward to seeing how you get on with the bikes!'

'Great. Us too,' I reply with a smile. 'So, how is this going to work?' I address this second part directly to Joseph, trying to get the show moving before the park fills up with locals ready, willing and able to gawp at the awkward thirty-something woman in her second-best pair of black leggings.

'We'll get you lined up first for a nice opening shot,' Joseph rumbles. 'Nolan will introduce you all and the bikes, and then I'll get you to ride around a little in here, before we try the bikes out on the road.'

'Sounds good to me,' Nolan says, and takes the middle bike by the handlebars in both hands.

I sidle over to the one on his right, while Kevin Flounder stands next to the one on the left.

With his camera rig set up, Joseph tells us he's ready to proceed. I'm exceedingly glad Nolan is doing all of the talking. He did offer me a few lines, but I figured it would be better for the company's owner to be the speaker.

This is the right decision, as Nolan is clearly a natural at talking on camera. Once Joseph presses record, Nolan drops into a perfectly timed spiel about how marvellous Kevin's green bikes are. He seems to have very much done his homework on them, as he's very knowledgeable about how they work. His confidence on camera is quite a thing to behold. He doesn't put a foot wrong with his speech. I'd have been stumbling all over the place, but he gets through it with no issues whatsoever.

By the time Nolan has finished introducing Kevin and his bikes, even I'm excited to see what they're like to ride. His sales pitch has been quite magnificent.

'Right, let's get you all riding together past me for a nice establishing shot of the bikes in action,' Joseph says to us. 'If you all start at the entrance to this car park and ride to the other side, that should do it.'

The three of us wheel our bikes the short distance over to where Joseph wants us to start. Once there, I take a breath and plonk myself down on the bike's seat, ready to get going.

When I was at school, I was told that diamond is the hardest substance on earth. Clearly my teachers never had to sit on a bicycle seat designed by Kevin Flounder.

'Fucking hell,' I gasp under my breath, as I stand back up off the seat and look down at it. It doesn't look like a giant razor blade, but it sure as hell feels like one. Kevin has elected to put quite racy-looking saddles on his bikes – long, thin and scalloped. Combine that with the fact they're apparently made out of a substance harder than the average human tooth, and I know I'm in for a bad time in the next few minutes.

I look over at Nolan, who is sat on his bike seat and is gamely trying not to look like he's being cut in half. I have no actual idea whether hard bike seats have a worse effect on men than they do on women, but Nolan's expression tells me that it certainly isn't a bowl of cherries for them any more than it is for us.

Kevin Flounder is sat there with a massive grin on his face, and is actually jigging up and down on his bike seat with excitement. I've never met anyone with concrete genitals before. I wonder if he requires any medical supervision.

'Okay!' shouts Joseph from his vantage point about fifty yards away. 'All three of you jump on, and just come riding past me, down to the other end! Then turn around and come back, just using the electric motors on your bikes! I'll give you a count of three!'

Yikes. Can I make it that far?

Only one way to find out, I suppose.

I remount the bike gingerly, and put my foot on the pedal. Pain and discomfort immediately set in around my nethers. I wore my second-best pair of black leggings because they are comfortable and hug my bottom in a pleasing manner. I clearly should have turned up today with my winter duvet wrapped around me like a giant nappy. I may not have looked quite so cute, but I would surely be better off on this bike than I currently am.

As Joseph starts his brief countdown, I look again at Nolan, whose expression is quite inscrutable. The gritted teeth may be due to pain, but could also be down to determination to get the video footage in the can.

Kevin looks like he's on holiday at the seaside. There's no way the man has any children. His scrotum must look like tenderised beef steak.

'Three, two, one, go!' Joseph cries out, and we all push forward on our bikes.

If sitting still on this saddle is bad, then riding along on it is a whole new level of horrible I can barely express.

Furthermore, the centre of gravity on this bike is *awful*. The little wheels and high handlebars make it pretty damn unwieldy. I'm wobbling around more than a bowlful of jelly in an earthquake.

Best try to get up some speed, to counteract the wobble. There's not much I can do about how painful the seat is, but maybe if I go a bit faster, I can stand up on the pedals.

I'm not that successful at either gambit, but things do improve enough for me to no longer fear that I am immediately going to fall off. Nolan and Kevin have both got ahead of me a little, so I pedal harder to catch up with them. Nolan's teeth are still gritted as we pass Joseph, and Kevin is now giggling away to himself like a madman.

I try my hardest to look happy about the whole situation as I fly past Joseph's camera – this is supposed to be for a promotional video after all, and I want Nolan to see that I'm trying to do a good job of it – but my manufactured look of enjoyment is absolutely unbelievable, as I am not a raging masochist.

All three of us reach the other end of the car park more or less together, and turn around to come back in the other direction.

In Nolan's introduction, he gave a very clear and easy-to-understand description of how the Cyclocity's electric motor works, so I have no issues flicking it into life with the small white button on the right-hand side of the handlebars. There are three separate speeds available, via a toggle switch, but I leave the bike on the lowest setting, for what should be extremely understandable and obvious reasons.

The instant I hit the button, the motor kicks into life.

Wing, wing, wing, wing, wing, wing, wing, wing, wing, wing, it goes, somewhat louder than I'd like.

Given that these three bikes are all prototypes, all three motors sound different from one another.

Wong, wong, wong, wong, wong, wong, wong, wong, wong, wong, Nolan's goes, while Kevin's is *Wang, wang, wang, wang, wang, wang, wang, wang, wang, wang.*

Not only are the bikes' motors quite noisy, they are also intermittent in power distribution. Well, mine is, anyway. One second the little motor is pushing me forward, the next it cuts out completely and my progress instantly slows.

I am therefore jerked along in painful fits and starts.

If Nolan and Kevin are having the same kind of issue, it's not immediately obvious. Maybe I've done something wrong?

Well, you got out of bed this morning and came here to ride this bike, so I'd say that's an affirmative, wouldn't you?

Again, all three bikes pass by Joseph and his camera – winging, wonging and wanging their way back to our starting positions.

When we arrive there, I breathe a vast sigh of relief and immediately jump off the bike – much to the delight of my reproductive system.

'Woo hoo!' Kevin exclaims, still sat on his saddle. 'That was so much fun! I haven't had anyone else ride the bikes with me so far!'

This does not surprise me. There can't be many people in the country with cast-iron backsides.

'Yes,' Nolan says, also looking very grateful to be off his Cyclocity 5000. 'They certainly are interesting bikes to ride!'

Interesting in the same manner than visiting Chernobyl fifteen minutes after the meltdown would have been 'interesting'.

'What did you think, Ellie?' Nolan says to me, with a slightly desperate look on his face.

Oh no. He wants me to be *positive*.

We should just hand these monstrosities back over to Kevin Flounder and beat a hasty retreat, but I've known Nolan long enough now to know that he's not that kind of man. Bless him, he *wants to make the best of this*. And he'd clearly like me to do the same.

I don't want to let him down, so I plaster on a smile and blink a couple of times.

'Yes, definitely *interesting*. A *unique* experience,' I agree, trying not to look Nolan or Kevin square in the eye.

'The e-motor works well, doesn't it?' Kevin asks, in a manner that suggests he's just incredibly happy to be out in public with other human beings.

'Er, yes. You . . . certainly know when it's working!' I tell him as I pop the bike on its kickstand.

Joseph then trots over to us, holding three cycle helmets. All three of them have GoPros strapped to the top, and I can tell from these that my day is about to get infinitely *worse*.

'Great stuff,' Joseph says as he arrives. 'That's a nice establishing shot done. Now we'll get some shots of the three of you on the road. The GoPros will cover things from your perspective – and I can cut that with the chase footage I'll get from the dashcam on the van. The streets are quiet at the moment, so we shouldn't have too many issues with traffic.'

We might not have issues with traffic, Joseph, but we'll be having issues with the continuing assault upon my private parts.

'Okay, Joseph, that sounds *great*,' Nolan replies. 'Let's get going then!' he adds, giving Kevin a broad smile.

Joseph hands me one of the three helmets. It's testament to the fact that he can see how worried I am that he gives me the biggest and most padded of the three.

I sigh as I unbuckle the helmet's strap. I didn't do much with my hair this morning, knowing that I'd be out here doing this, but helmet hair is something that I require days to recover from. I hadn't planned on washing it for at least another two days, but this will guarantee I'll be slapping on the Pantene this evening. Possibly just after I've slapped an ice pack on my undercarriage.

Yes. Just think about the ice pack. The cool, soothing ice pack. That should get you through this.

With my cycle helmet on, and the GoPro recording every moment of my Cyclocity torture trip, I remount the hideous contraption very slowly and await further orders.

'How long . . . how long do you think this will take?' Nolan asks Joseph, trying to maintain the impression of a man who is happy to be here, in this most rarefied of strange situations.

'Five, ten minutes?' Joseph replies. 'If Kevin takes the lead, and you two follow him about for a while, that should be all I need. Then I'll do lots of close-ups and beauty shots of the bikes alone. That'll give me everything I need for the raw footage.'

Nolan nods.

Five to ten minutes then.

Can I manage that?

Yes. I probably can. It's obvious that Nolan wants to finish what we've started, and do right by Kevin Flounder. This is quite admirable, even if it does mean that he's probably going to have a mashed penis for the rest of his life.

This is the first time I have ever considered Nolan Reece's penis. Which sounds not just a little like Reese's Pieces – a sweet I wholeheartedly enjoy popping into my mouth whenever I get my hands on one.

And now I'm thinking about Nolan Reece's penis in direct conjunction with things I pop into my mouth, and that, my happy friends, is NOT A PROFESSIONAL TRAIN OF THOUGHT.

I do not see Nolan in that way.

I *don't*.

Okay, as established, he is very cute – in that unconventional Adam Driver way. His unruly black hair and open smile are adorable – but he's not my type.

Definitely *not*.

And I swore to never have a relationship with anyone I work with again. Not after Robert Ainslie bloody Blake and his wilful destruction of nature reserves.

'Ellie? You ready for this?' Nolan asks me, as he mounts his Cyclocity 5000 again. It's plain I've been wool-gathering, and wool-gathering about Nolan's penis to boot. How embarrassing.

'Yes, yes!' I reply, a little too loudly, and nod my head. The weight of both cycle helmet and GoPro feels very strange and off-putting. Something else I'm going to have to cope with, along with the wobbly wheels, loud motor and rock-hard saddle. Joy of joys.

'Great,' he replies with relief. I think he's taking some strength from my willingness to carry on with this torment, and I don't know whether I'm happy about that or not. 'Okay, Kevin,' he says to the chief torturer, 'you ride out ahead and we'll follow. Just try to take it slowly and keep us away from busy streets. Maybe just go around the park a couple of times, eh?'

Kevin snaps a happy salute back at Nolan. 'Roger that!' he exclaims, and pushes his bike into motion, pointing it at the park's exit. Nolan takes up station right behind him, and I start to pedal right behind Nolan, with Joseph now in his van, bringing up the rear – a rather large and unwieldy-looking camera set up on the dashboard next to him, filming everything that goes on in front.

Five minutes. That's all. Just five more minutes . . .

To begin with, Kevin does as instructed, and keeps the pace nice and slow.

Wing . . . wing . . . wing . . . wing . . . wing . . . wing, goes my bike's motor at a sedate pace, as we pootle along the road that runs parallel to the park, with only one car passing us for its entire length.

This isn't so bad. I can cope with this.

But then we reach the T-junction at the end of the road, and instead of turning left to continue our circumnavigation of the park's perimeter, Kevin decides to turn right. As he does so, I swear I hear him shout 'Tally ho!', and definitely see him stick one arm out in front of him with his finger thrust in the direction he wants us to go.

Bloody hell. He may be having the time of his life, but I'm sure as hell not. The last thing I want to be is beholden to the movements of an overenthusiastic inventor, keen to show off his latest invention.

But such is my lot in life – as Nolan follows Kevin right, forcing me and Joseph to do the same.

On this bigger, broader road, Kevin starts to pick up the pace.

Wang, wang, wang, wang, wang, wang, wang, wang, wang, wang, his bike goes, as its speed increases.

Wong, wong, wong, wong, wong, wong, wong, wong, wong, wong, Nolan's bike echoes.

And *Wing, wing, wing, wing, wing, wing, wing, wing, wing, wing*, mine responds, as if the three of them were communicating in their own strange velocipede language.

'Jesus Christ,' I groan, feeling the saddle biting into my crotch again, this time much harder thanks to both the increase in speed and the roughness of the tarmac on this particular road.

After about a minute, we reach yet another junction, and I am dismayed to see that the road crossing ours is much, much busier. It's a bloody dual carriageway, it looks like. Will Kevin do a one-eighty and bring us back in the direction we've come from?

Will he fuck as like.

Instead, he indicates left – and out we all go on to the main road.

The dual carriageway is quite, quite terrifying. Cars zoom past me at forty miles an hour, which would be bad enough on a good bicycle, but on this wobbly silly bamboo bugger, it's a thousand times worse. I'm petrified that, at any moment, my dubious control over it is going to desert me completely, and I'm going to steer right out into the path of a passing truck.

At least I don't have to pump the pedals now. The e-motor has been charged, and I can rely on that to power me along. Even if it is a bit erratic.

Up front, Kevin is attempting to match the speed of the cars around him, and has flicked his bike into the highest gear that the electric motor can handle.

Nolan does the same, forcing me to follow suit.

I am instantly propelled forward as the motor reaches its maximum power output. An output that goes far beyond what I would have thought possible for such a small piece of machinery.

Wingwingwingwingwingwingwingwingwingwingwingwingwingwing, the fucking thing goes, at an alarming volume.

Now I'm in real danger of being smeared across two lanes of traffic.

Riding around on an e-bike may be much better for the environment, but it is not better for the state of my mental or physical health. I'd cheerfully punch a polar bear in the chops right now, if I could just be allowed to get off this hellish contraption and back into my lovely car, with its big comfy driver's seat.

Nolan's undercarriage must be red-raw. It's a wonder he hasn't crashed.

Kevin is far from crashing. He's having way too much of a good time. Is he riding along waving his legs about like a madman? You bet your nice, pain-free arse he is.

I might not be much of an advertisement for the joys of e-bicycles, but Kevin Flounder makes up for my lack of enthusiasm in leaps and bounds. I hope Joseph is concentrating his video on what Kev's up to, rather than focusing on my misery.

Oh, who am I kidding? This video will never see the light of day. The first thing I'm going to recommend to Nolan once we get back to the office is that we never, ever speak of these things again. E-bikes might well be the way of the future, in terms of protecting our planet, but it won't be ones made by Kevin Flounder – unless the entire human race turns into a bunch of sadomasochists overnight.

Just as I'm wincing against the draught of a large Highways Agency truck passing me, I see Kevin lurch off to the left, down a side road that splits from the dual carriageway. Thank God for that – at least we're leaving the heavy, fast traffic again.

And even better, it looks like the traffic lights ahead of us that lead on to a roundabout are turning red. Kevin will have to stop now, to make sure that he—

Oh no. The fucker isn't stopping. Not for anyone or anything.

Kevin flies out on to the roundabout – and I can see that Nolan is preparing to do the same!

I consider my options.

If you were to line up the entire serving British Army in front of me, all keen to play a nice, exciting game of soldiers, I would say fuck this. I would say *fuck this* in the loudest voice possible.

I slam on my Cyclocity's brakes as hard as I can.

Wingwingwingwingwingwingwingwing –
WERRRRRRNNNGGGGG, cries the motor as the brakes also squeal in protest. *WERRRRRRRGGGGGG – PLOING!*

Oh shit. I think I've broken something.

Never mind though, at least it's not my *fucking head*.

The Cyclocity screeches to a halt right on the line, just as the light above me goes red. I look up to see that poor Nolan has lost control of his bike, and is heading straight for the centre of the roundabout.

My heart flies into my throat as I watch him fly across the road. 'Nolan!' I wail ineffectually, as he rockets away from me towards inevitable disaster.

He mounts the kerb with an enormous clatter, and bounces up the grass mound, screaming for all he's worth. The e-bike's brakes do nothing on the slippery grass surface.

Nolan's hectic forward motion is eventually halted when he has the presence of mind to jump backwards off the saddle, sending him tumbling into a heap on the grass, as the Cyclocity spears straight for the small thicket of bushes and trees at the top of the roundabout.

Wongwongwongwongwongwongwongwongwong – FTWANG!

The bike hits a perfectly placed tree stump and pinwheels into the air, end over end until it crashes back to earth, hidden from view on the other side of the thicket.

I am delighted to see Nolan get unsteadily to his feet, with no apparent signs of injury. He looks over to me, and gives me a wobbly thumbs up. This helps to lower my heart rate a little.

There's no sign of Kevin fucking Flounder. He's probably reached a high-enough speed to go back in time and date the teenage version of his mother.

I sit on my bike, breathing hard for a moment, trying to digest what's just happened.

I then turn my head to look back at Joseph, who is staring out of the window, completely bug-eyed.

'Did you get all of that?!' I shout at him, in a decidedly frantic voice.

I do hope so. Nothing will sell the concept of riding an environmentally friendly bike more than watching one somersault over a roundabout in glorious slow motion, don't you think?

The Cyclocity 5000 – get on one of these things, and you'll never *ride another bike again!*

◆ ◆ ◆

Back at the park, I'm delighted to say that we've all made it through this experience more or less in one piece.

Okay, I will be sat in an ice bath for most of this evening, and Nolan will walk bow-legged like an eighteenth-century sailor for the rest of his life, but considering what we've both just been through, that's getting off quite lightly.

I find myself wanting to stand close to Nolan. He looks extremely perturbed by the whole incident, and I'm feeling quite protective of him. The horrible memory of watching him fly across that road is one that is not likely to leave me for quite some time.

Kevin Flounder remains unwholesomely happy about the entire thing, despite Nolan accidentally dismantling one of his precious prototypes by firing it into a roundabout. Bamboo might be a very strong material, but even it doesn't like being subjected to such forces.

'Not to worry!' he tells us, as Joseph pulls the mangled wreck out of his van. 'These things happen. I might need to go back and lower the overall performance of the motor. It might be a tad high at the moment.'

'Yes, just a tad,' Nolan says, blinking slowly.

'So . . . when do you guys think the video will be ready to go online?' Kevin then asks, showing a degree of misplaced confidence in his bicycles that would be quite heroic, were it not quite so delusional.

'Um . . .' Nolan begins, still blinking like an exhausted Labrador.

'We'll have to go through the footage and make sure we have everything we need,' I jump in, figuring that I'm probably better placed to placate Kevin than Nolan is right now. There's something about a near-death experience that doesn't do much for your diplomatic skills. 'But we'll definitely let you know what we're going to be doing with it once Joseph has finished the edit.'

I have a feeling that the only thing we're actually going to be doing with the record of today's events is bringing it out at office parties once at least six bottles of wine have been consumed.

'Oh,' Kevin replies, a little deflated. This is to be expected. He thinks today has gone brilliantly in every single respect, bless him. I don't want to puncture his balloon of happy optimism, but on the other hand I don't want him to leave here today thinking that Viridian PR are all that enthusiastic about the Cyclocity 5000. The look on Nolan's face tells me he's probably going to be having nightmares about it for the foreseeable future, so the chance of us championing the bike now is slim to none . . . as it somersaults over a bush.

As Joseph helps Kevin load the three bikes back on to the little flatbed truck our inventor friend arrived in, I walk with Nolan over to where both of our cars are parked. The Mercedes looks quite reprehensible next to Nolan's gleaming Tesla. I really am going to have to do something about that.

. . . I don't mean I'm buying an e-bike to replace it, I hasten to add.

'Well, that was a little . . . disappointing,' Nolan confides, as he opens his car door.

'That's something of an understatement,' I reply. 'If you hadn't jumped off that bike when you did, you would have had a disappointing forty-mile-an-hour run-in with a tree.'

Nolan winces as the recent memory flashes before his eyes. 'I'm sorry I dragged you into it.'

I wave a hand. 'It's fine. At least we had a go.'

'I really wanted those bikes to be good,' he continues. 'These kinds of things are so important going forward, and I really want us to be able to get people out of their cars. This should have been a perfect vehicle for Viridian.' He bangs the roof of his car in frustration. 'It would have sold us so bloody well to the right people!'

'Hey, look, it's *okay*,' I assure him. 'Not everything is going to be a winner. We've done well in the last few weeks to get the ball rolling. We shouldn't get despondent when something doesn't work out. It's bound to happen from time to time. It's better we pursue these things and find they're not right for us, rather than do nothing.'

Nolan smiles gratefully. 'You're right, Ellie.' He puts out a hand and gently squeezes my arm. 'I'm very glad I've got you by my side.' The hand lingers there as Nolan looks at me warmly.

Oh, boy.

I may have gone a bit light-headed.

It's been a while since a man touched me in that kind of . . . *intimate* way.

Too long, to be honest.

. . . and the last one to do it was Demonic Rab, so it doesn't exactly come with good memories attached.

There are parts of my brain and body that are reacting to this unexpected intimacy from Nolan in a way that can only be described in polite company as 'interested'.

But you can't be interested in your fucking boss, *young lady. Remember? We're never having another workplace romance! Remember Robert!*

'Well, time to get back to the office, I suppose!' I say, a little too brightly.

'Absolutely,' Nolan agrees, eventually taking his hand away and looking over at Kevin. 'We'll have to let him down easy,' he says in a sad voice.

He really is quite a lovely man.

No!

No, you stop that Ellie Cooke! You stop that *right now*!

'Right! See you back there then!' I splutter, and throw open the door to my Mercedes.

I barely give Nolan time to respond before I'm in the driver's seat and firing up the engine. I've never wanted to get away from a warm, good-natured conversation more in my entire life.

I have no idea whether I'm reading the signals from Nolan right, but I sure as hell know I shouldn't be giving him any signals in return. My life is complicated enough with this new job. I do not want to complicate it further by entertaining the wrong thoughts in my head about my employer.

Stay strictly professional, Ellie. That's the lesson of the day.

. . . actually, the lesson of the day is probably 'Don't get on an electric bike invented by a madman with concrete genitals', but it doesn't quite have the same ring to it – and isn't really something I can take practically forward in my life.

Your mileage may vary.

Chapter Six

The Cockatoo . . . of Doom!

Something rather amazing has occurred . . .

I'm *happy*.

More specifically – I'm happy at *work*.

Now, for those of you who are blessed with a job that they've always been happy with – and never had any complaints about – that might come as something of a surprise to hear.

But then, there are only *seven* of you out there who actually feel like that, so I won't worry too much that you might not get what I'm talking about.

The many months spent at Stratagem as the place continued to fall apart were a thoroughly miserable experience – so much so, I'd forgotten what it was like to be satisfied with the day-to-day experience of being a publicist.

But since becoming Head of Client Relations at the newly invigorated PR company I work for?

It's been quite *marvellous*.

My new job is going very well.

Like . . . *exceptionally* well.

The past few weeks have been fantastic.

Viridian PR has gone from strength to strength – not least because that first contract I signed with Veganthropy Foods has led to much more work from other businesses, who heard about the new relationship between our companies and wanted to get on board with us too.

Nolan has really struck on something of an ethical gold mine here. There are plenty of environmentally conscious companies who were apparently just looking for the right PR firm to represent them . . . and we've filled that niche wonderfully.

Okay, so Kevin and his e-bikes were a non-starter, but that's been just about the only thing that has been. We now have *seven* lucrative contracts under our belt – getting signed at a rate of more than one a week – with even more on the horizon. It's all been quite incredible.

The mood around the office has improved immeasurably. There's a spring in everyone's step that hasn't been there for months – if not years.

The pot plants are also looking extremely healthy and happy, thanks to Young Adrian's ministrations. It's a bloody good job he's got time to water them all, because I sure as hell haven't. I'm pretty much rushed off my feet every day. But I don't mind one bit, because all of it is so insanely positive right now.

When you stumble upon providing a morally upright and profitable service that other people are very keen to have, it makes coming to work something of a joy. Not only have I increased my pay packet, I'm also doing something worthwhile for our planet.

It's a heady combination.

To be frank, it's got to the point that I'm constantly looking around every corner for the thing that's going to ruin it all . . .

It's *not* going to be my relationship with Nolan, I can tell you that.

Oh no, no, no.

I have been *super* disciplined about maintaining a strict degree of professionalism when I'm around him – just to make sure I don't give him any ideas. I still have no clue as to whether he actually has feelings for *me*, beyond those of close employer and employee, but I'm not risking it.

Oh no, no, no.

Having said that, we have naturally grown to become friends, given how closely we've been working with one another on all of these new clients. We just seem to click with one another when it comes to how we approach Viridian PR's expanding client base – echoing each other's ideas quite a lot, and agreeing far more than we disagree.

I haven't even found it much of an issue that I'm not really an environmentalist. Nolan's enthusiasm for the subject is more than enough for the both of us, and when you get right down to it, a client is a client is a client – what particular business they happen to operate is pretty immaterial.

So what if I'm not as committed to 'the cause' as Nolan probably thinks I am?

Would it really make any difference to how I do my job?

Would it really make any difference to how we work together?

I don't think so. Not for one moment.

All I care about is that my workplace is vibrant, exciting and fun again. And I really do have Nolan to thank for that.

I'm very pleased to be working for and with him, and am more than happy to keep things on the professional level that they've been operating at so well.

Any kind of romance would be entirely unnecessary, and something I can firmly put out of my mind!

◆ ◆ ◆

'Ellie?'

'Yes, Nolan?'

'Would you like to come out to dinner with me?'

Gngh.

The pencil point snaps as I press down way too hard on my notepad.

Oh no.

Oh no, no, no.

My heart starts to hammer at roughly the same rate it did when I watched Nolan's Cyclocity spear him towards that roundabout. I'm not sure whether that was a worse situation than this is, if I'm honest. Okay, no one is risking life and limb this time – sat as we are in Nolan's office, discussing how we're going to approach Hempawear's next radio campaign. But the ramifications of what might happen next could be so much worse than crashing headlong into a roundabout on a bamboo e-bike.

Why did he have to ask me that?

Why did he have to ask me out on a date, when things have been going so *well*?

And how the hell do I respond? Given everything I've been saying about keeping things strictly professional?

'Oh, I'm sorry Ellie,' Nolan says in a hurry, when I don't answer. 'I shouldn't have asked you that. It's inappropriate of me.'

'No, no . . . it's fine, Nolan. It just took me by surprise a bit,' I tell him, voice a bit shaky with the shock.

And *how do I answer?*

What I should say is this: *No problem Nolan! It's not inappropriate at all, and I'm very flattered. But I think at this stage, I need to keep my work relationships professional. I hope you understand.*

Yes indeed. That is what I should be saying.

Right now, in fact.

Right at this very moment . . .

. . .

Well?

Go on then . . .

Say it to him.

'Um . . . where . . . where would you like to go for dinner?' I ask Nolan, finally looking up at his slightly worried-looking face.

No! That's not what you should be saying! You should be shutting him down – not extending the conversation enough to give you time to think about it!

But I *am* thinking about it.

God help me, my heart is hammering, my hands are shaking, and *I am thinking about it.*

Nolan swallows. 'Well, I thought we could maybe check out Paradise in Flight?'

'Oh? The restaurant Nadia took on for us?' I sound light and breezy, as if we were having a perfectly normal conversation about one of our clients, and not about the potential location *for a bloody date.*

'Yeah. That's the one.' Nolan doesn't sound light and breezy. He sounds like he's just swallowed a bucket of sand. 'I thought it would be nice for us to go there. On a . . . on a date?'

So that's made it very clear, then. This is not just the boss asking his employee if they'd like to support one of their clients with a strictly professional visit. This is a man asking a woman out on a proper, full-blooded date.

And I'm *still thinking about it.*

Everything sensible in me screams that I should turn Nolan down flat. He is my *boss*, for crying out loud!

But then he's also kind, generous, easy to work with, even easier to get along with, and has a smile that can be very disarming.

Not the kind of man I'm used to dating, it has to be said. I've previously gone for the chisel-jawed, big, blond and tanned look – just like Robert Ainslie Blake.

And look how that turned out.

I'm just not used to the kind of man Nolan is, *at all*.

Mind you, what I'm really used to is meals for one, too much Netflix, and a constant nagging feeling that I'm headed for my late thirties without having had a decent, long-term relationship . . .

Say no, Ellie.

You say no to a date with Nolan Reece right now, and get back to work. You remember work, don't you? The thing that's been making us so happy over the past few weeks?

Why would you want to complicate that? Why would you want to spoil it?

. . . because he's lovely, and kind, and handsome in an unconventional way . . . and because he said I was beautiful *and* fantastic, goddamn it!

'Yeah, okay,' I tell Nolan, out loud. 'That'd be nice.'

A smile lights up his face.

Oh, you bloody fool. You horny, *bloody fool. This is wrong on every single level.*

Not every level.

Not downstairs.

'Great!' Nolan says, jigging up and down a bit on his office chair. 'How would tomorrow evening be?'

'Absolutely fine. It'll give me time to pick out something to wear.'

'I'm sure . . . I'm sure you'll look lovely.'

Blimey, super-awkward Nolan is not a Nolan I'm used to. He usually has a relaxed manner about him when he's with me. Seeing him all twitchy and out of sorts is like watching a sloth breakdancing.

'Thanks,' I reply, with a smile. I want to reach across the desk and pat him on the hand to calm him down a bit, but now that there is *something between us* I can't do that without it looking way too forward.

And that's the real issue here – and the reason why I should have turned him down flat.

Having *something between us* probably won't work out for the best. It presents a whole series of potential scenarios that might not do my career any good at all. I've already broken up with one man in front of the entire staff, and I don't really want to repeat the experience.

But then, Nolan is a very, very different man from Robert. I'm very sure he'd never suggest cable-tying a natterjack toad to anything, no matter how much it annoyed him.

Who's to say things won't be fine with him? Who's to say that dating him will result in the same misery it did with Mr Ainslie Blake?

It could be *fine*. It could be *great*. It could end up making my working relationship with Nolan even *better*. You just never know.

Who's to say, eh?

. . . as hastily constructed rationales go, it might not stand up to that much scrutiny – but I guess it'll do in a pinch.

What won't do in a pinch is the red dress I picked out last night for the date. Mainly because it pinches. I don't mind a dress that's a little tight, but something that actively causes me pain can go straight in the bin.

This is just as well, as I'm not sure it sends the right signals. It is a very *sexy* dress, even if I do say so myself. One of those ones that hugs in all the right places – but unfortunately pinches in all the wrong ones, telling me I have several trips to the gym coming up in my near future.

And it's probably best I don't dress *too* sexy for tonight. I'm still on very shaky ground over this whole 'date with the boss' business, and should probably be a little more demure and practical with my outfit choice.

This leads me to my nicest, newest grey jeans, the three-quarter-length tailored denim jacket I got in the sale at M&S, the gorgeous little white top with the flower pattern on the collar, and the long gold necklace my mother gave me for my birthday.

I elect to wear my freshly washed and conditioned hair up in a high ponytail that takes me ages to get *just right*.

Pop on a pair of black high heels and I'm covering all the bases here. I could be here for some meaningful sex, or for a discussion about the state of society in the twenty-first century.

I've agreed to meet Nolan at this Paradise in Flight place – just because it feels right for a first date with your boss (*aargh*). It *is* a new client for us, after all.

Paradise in Flight is a wildlife park. Or more precisely, a bird sanctuary. Now this might seem like an odd location for dinner, but Paradise in Flight is a unique restaurant, because it comes with the chance to meet and greet a bunch of tropical birds while you eat. Built about a year ago, the restaurant is an offshoot of the Halliwell Bird Sanctuary and Wetland Reserve, and is the brainchild of Bernard Halliwell, a man who has forgotten more about birds than you or I will ever know about them.

The sanctuary hasn't been doing all that well financially in recent years, so Bernard created the restaurant in the hopes it would increase visitor numbers, as well as the sanctuary's reputation.

It's a strategy that's worked like gangbusters. So much so that Halliwell's has been in need of even more good PR to help manage its new platform – and God bless Nadia for finding out about it and getting them under our wing (pun most definitely intended).

Luckily, my date with Nolan is taking place on a Thursday evening, so Paradise in Flight is not booked solid. There seems like a healthy amount of people here, but not so much that the place will be overcrowded.

The restaurant itself is slapped on to the side of the largest netted aviary at the sanctuary, so that the birds can be brought in to see the diners by the staff, and interact with happy customers as they knock back the red wine and tuck into their meals.

The entire menu here is of course vegetarian. There's not a chicken dish in sight. It'd be a bit much to expect the parrots to put up with meeting you, if you're about to tuck into one of their cousins. I'm not a vegetarian (chicken and bacon sandwiches are my touchstone), but I'm not surprised Nolan wanted to eat here as he's been one for years now. And actually, given my recent associations with people like the O'Hares at Veganthropy Foods, I have no problem with meals that don't feature meat now. I've started doing meat-free Mondays after spending so much time working with Petal and Mordred. The big ambulatory bush has even started sending me recipes via email, bless him. I've tried a few for my Monday meals, and some have come out very well, even if I do say so myself. The fact that I generally feel pretty good on a Tuesday because of it is something I try to forget about every time I go to the fridge to pull out the bacon and the chicken.

I am not the biggest fan of birds when they are alive and well, if I'm being honest. There's something about those pecky beaks and beady eyes that puts me off a bit. However, Tripadvisor and Nadia both assure me that the food here is to die for, and the experience itself is something not to be missed.

The restaurant is certainly something that you couldn't miss, even if you tried.

They've gone all out on that big neon sign and those fake palm trees, haven't they?

I park my Mercedes at the bottom of the car park, as far away as I can get it from Nolan's gleaming Tesla, and make my way over to the garish entrance, walking inside to the sound of tropical birds piped in from somewhere unidentifiable.

'Hello,' I say to the girl on front of house, as I walk through the atrium just beyond the glass main doors. There's a rather cute bubbling fountain in the centre of it that helps give the place a nicely humid, tropical vibe. 'I'm here to meet someone. The table's booked under Reece.'

The smartly dressed girl looks down her list and finds Nolan's name. 'Ah, here we are. Your companion has already arrived. I'll take you through.'

I am then led into the restaurant proper, which really dives into the tropical theme with great abandon. There are rainforest plants everywhere. And a lot of perches for birds to sit on, close to the myriad of dining tables set out across the broad expanse of the restaurant's floor. Above my head, I can see small, gorgeously coloured tropical birds flitting about close to the domed glass ceiling, grabbing food from the feeders that are strung up everywhere. It's only when I really squint that I can see there is a fine mesh stretched right across the dome about three-quarters of the way up, that's obviously intended to stop the birds from getting too low and disturbing the customers. I have to therefore wonder what birds all those perches are for.

There's a nice, natural earthiness to the restaurant I definitely approve of. They've managed to make the whole thing feel upscale, without killing off the sense of a natural, rough-hewn charm. The dining tables are made of solid, reclaimed wood, and the tropical plants have been allowed to grow in a natural, slightly unkempt way.

It works.

Doing PR for this place should be a dream. It rather sells itself.

. . . I can tell what I'm doing here. I'm distracting my brain with work thoughts, because that's far easier than thinking about what I'm about to do. This is the first date I've been on in a long time, and it shows. My legs are a little rubbery, my mouth is dry, and my heart is beating way too fast.

Should have worn flats.

Nolan looks equally tense as the girl takes me over to him. It's incredibly strange that two people who have been completely relaxed around one another for weeks, have suddenly become so hammering *awkward*.

'Hi, Ellie,' Nolan says, rising from the table. He's wearing an extremely nice dark-grey suit and a white shirt. He's also had his hair cut.

He moves towards me with his arms slightly raised.

Oh, blimey. Is he going to go in for a kiss? He very probably will . . . it seems appropriate. A kiss on the cheek here wouldn't be out of the ordinary whatsoever. After all, we know each other well, and this is a date, after all. A cheek-kiss is to be expected.

'Hiya,' I reply, and lean in stiffly to receive the kiss.

His lips feel just as stiff against my cheek.

In fact, there's every danger we're both going to go so stiff that we instantly petrify right here on the spot, giving the birds a couple of extra perches to shit on.

And sit on.

With the awkward kiss out of the way, we both sit down at the table . . . and I relax a little.

Nolan seems to as well. Maybe it's the fact that there's now a barrier between us. One that's quite similar in size to Nolan's desk at work.

'Well . . . this feels a lot stranger than I thought it would,' he confesses, with a chuckle.

I laugh as well. 'Yeah. I know what you mean.'

He stops laughing, and his expression becomes a little more serious. 'Look, Ellie, I don't want things to be weird between us. I won't pretend that I don't . . . you know . . . *like you*. But if this is all a bit much, we can just treat this like a work meeting, and leave it at that.'

I stare at him for a moment.

He's given me the out that I need if I want it. Tonight can be nothing more than a meeting between two colleagues – possibly one that can be written off on expenses.

'No,' I reply. 'Let's not treat it like that. Let's . . . let's just see where it goes, eh?'

He nods, smiles and sits back. 'Okay, let's do that.'

Nolan seems to visibly relax even more, and I have to confess I do a little more as well. He likes me. He's just said it out loud. And God help me, I think I like him too.

Quite a lot actually.

Eeep.

A waiter arrives at the table and takes our drink orders. We're both on the softies as it's a work night. Nolan picks up a menu. 'This place is supposed to be fantastic,' he remarks, as he looks at what's on offer. 'Not just the food, but how environmental they are. The whole sanctuary has net-zero emissions. They're powered by solar, and nothing goes to landfill. I was looking over their business plan with Nadia. They're really doing a wonderful job. Bernard is absolutely committed to animal welfare and the environment. He's a great client for us. Makes Viridian look absolutely brilliant to . . . other people.' Nolan's eyes light up. 'They give a good ten per cent of their profits to the WWF and RSPB every month!'

Oh God. That's pretty damn sexy, isn't it?

141

Watching a man get this excited about a good cause?

Oh my, yes.

Alright, girl. Calm down a little. Just order some food and stop thinking about how good he looks in that suit.

I turn my attention to the menu, and it doesn't take me long to pick out what I want. I'm a sucker for Mexican food, and the tacos sound particularly tasty. I've never tried a vegetarian variant before, but am happy to give them a go tonight. The tacos appear to be a brand-new dish as well, according to the menu, and restaurants tend to make more effort with their new dishes, so I'm hoping they're going to be very good.

The waiter comes back over and takes our order, with Nolan going for a red Thai curry, and by the time he walks away, I'm salivating at the prospect of my tacos. I haven't eaten well today – the product of being nervous, I guess – so the damn things can't come quick enough.

I'm about to say as much to Nolan when a large set of doors at the side of the restaurant open, and a troop of Halliwell Bird Sanctuary staff members walk in, all wearing the same beige and brown polo shirts and carrying a selection of large, squawking tropical birds.

A tall young man presents himself in the centre of the restaurant floor, holding a fat white cockatoo – easily the biggest of the bunch.

'Good evening everybody, and welcome to Paradise in Flight. My colleagues and I will be bringing our birds over to spend a little time with you as you eat your meals. They are well trained and happy to be here, but we do ask that you don't reach out to touch them without getting our say-so.'

The young man then makes a beeline straight for our table, which initially surprises me, but then I have to remember that

Nolan is likely to be known to the management, given our new relationship with them. They're probably trying to impress.

'Good evening,' the young man says to us, as he plonks the cockatoo down on the perch next to the table. 'My name is Keiran, and this is Squawks the Cockatoo.'

'Hello, Keiran,' I reply.

'Hello, Squawks,' Nolan says with a grin.

Squawks is a very impressive-looking bird, but he looks entirely *unimpressed* with the pair of us. In fact, I don't think I've ever seen such a laid-back member of the avian species. He just sits there, paying us no heed whatsoever. Other customers might be disappointed by this, but I'm okay with it.

Looking at some of the other birds, I'd say we've done well with fat old Mr Squawks. There's a parrot a few tables away who can barely sit still – much to the delight of the young girl and her parents who are sat there.

'Squawks is very well behaved,' Keiran says. 'And is quite happy to be touched. He particularly likes to be tickled behind the ear.'

'Ah, well, if that's the case . . .' Nolan responds. 'May I?'

'Of course!' Keiran seems delighted that Nolan is keen to have a go on Squawks. 'Just reach out and have a little tickle.'

Nolan stands up and does this – and wouldn't you know it, the cockatoo does look quite happy about it.

I wonder if I can get Nolan to tickle me behind the ear at some point? If it worked for Squawks, it'd probably work for me too.

'Do you want a go?' Nolan asks me.

I put up my hands. 'No, I'm fine, thanks. I'm happy for Squawks and me to maintain a dignified distance from one another. You fill your boots though.'

And fill his boots Nolan does. Over the next few minutes I watch as man and cockatoo bond through the medium of gentle tickling. It's extremely sweet.

They seem to be getting along so well that Keiran tells us he's going to go and supervise the hectic green parrot I mentioned before, because the young girl handling it is having a bit of trouble calming it down.

'That's fine,' Nolan tells him. 'Squawks and I are getting along like a house on fire. We'll be okay with him.'

He's not wrong. The cockatoo is actually nuzzling Nolan's hand now.

. . . oh God. I think I'm a bit jealous of a cockatoo.

'Maybe I will have a small tickle after all,' I say, getting up and going over to Squawks. I'm not saying I'm doing this to deflect Nolan's attention back to me, but I'm not going to deny it either.

Squawks doesn't care. He's just being tickled behind both ears now, which is taking him to a sublime level of pleasure that he'll remember for the rest of his parroty days, I'm sure.

The tickling session comes to an end when the tacos and the Thai curry arrive. Nolan and I sit back down, leaving Squawks looking a tad disappointed. He doesn't make a move towards us though, to demand more tickling. He seems quite content to just sit on the perch and wait for us to come back to him. You get the impression this is a routine Squawks has been through many times.

Nolan and I tuck into our food, and once I take a bite of the first of my tacos, thoughts of cockatoos and tickling go out of my head. They are absolutely *delicious*. Stunningly good. Probably the best I've ever had.

I eat in silence for a few minutes, savouring my meal to the fullest. Once my initial hunger has been sated by two of the tacos, I look up to see Nolan smiling at me. 'Hungry, eh?' he says.

I go a little red in the face. 'Yeah. Haven't eaten well today. I guess I felt a bit nervous about tonight.'

You didn't have to tell him that. Why *did you tell him that?*

It's because I know him well, isn't it? It's because I've spent a lot of time in his company. Nolan is very easy to talk to. It's just that now the content of the conversation has changed.

'You and me both!' he confides. 'Actually, asking you out was the most nerve-wracking thing, though.'

'Well, I'm glad you did,' I tell him, plucking a third taco from my plate. 'And I'm glad you brought me here tonight. These things are fantastic, and I intend to enjoy each and every one of th—'

It's at this point that the taco magically disappears from my hand. One second it's there, the next it's gone. The only thing that indicates what's happened to it is a blur of white that crosses my field of vision momentarily.

'What the . . . ?' I blurt out, blinking rapidly.

'Bloody hell!' Nolan exclaims. 'Squawks!'

I jerk my head around to regard the cockatoo, who is now back on his perch, as if he had never moved. You wouldn't know what he had just done, were it not for the fact that he now has half a taco stuck in his beak.

'Squawks!' I exclaim indignantly, and rise from my chair. The cheeky little bugger!

I only have four tacos in total, and this parrot has just removed 25 per cent of them from my person. He's already eaten half of it, so I've irrevocably lost 12.5 per cent, but I'm going to attempt to get the rest of it back. Oh yes I am.

'Give me back my taco please, Squawks!' I demand, putting my hands on my hips.

Nolan laughs as he watches me do this.

Squawks looks at me for a second, before devouring the rest of my taco in one massive gulp.

I blink a couple of times and let out a chuckle of disbelief. I am *stunned*. Partly because the parrot has just openly defied me, but partly because I've just seen a cockatoo eat a taco.

Cockatoos don't eat tacos, do they? They eat fruit. And nuts. The occasional insect maybe. But not *tacos*. I'm *sure* they don't eat tacos. If they did, it would have turned up on a David Attenborough show at some point, and I've watched all of those buggers. Nary a mention was made of cockatoo-based taco consumption in any of them.

Keiran has made his way back over to our table, and can see what I'm doing. To him, it probably looks like I'm squaring up to his parrot. The evidence of the beaky thief's crime has disappeared down its gullet.

'Is everything alright?' he asks.

'No, not really. Your cockatoo ate my taco,' I tell him, pointing at the offending article – which has now gone back to looking around the place, ignoring us completely.

Keiran doesn't look like he believes a word of it.

'It's true,' Nolan adds, standing up as well. 'It swooped and took it out of Ellie's hand.'

'*Swooped?*' Keiran replies, incredulous. He gives the fat cockatoo another look. He might well sound sceptical. From looking at Squawks, it's hard to believe he's swooped on anything since he was a chick.

But swoop he did! Right on to *my* taco!

'It's true,' I say to Keiran. 'He took my taco, and I would very much like a replacement, please.'

Keiran still doesn't look too sure – and if I had no witnesses, I don't think he'd believe me – but I have Nolan to back me up. 'Okay . . . I'll ask the kitchen to prepare you some more.' He sounds very dubious about the whole thing.

'Thank you!' I say, still feeling a bit indignant.

'And I'll take Squawks away,' he adds.

'Oh,' Nolan says with disappointment. 'Will we get another one?'

'Yes. I'll bring Daisy over. She's our smallest parrot. She's not likely to . . . steal any of your food.'

He thinks we're lying! I can *tell*!

Keiran picks Squawks up and carries him away to another table. I sit back down again, still reeling a little from my run-in with the feathered taco thief. What a bizarre thing to happen.

Keiran returns with a small, rather stunned-looking blue parrot that doesn't seem much bigger than one of my lovely tacos, so I know I'm not going to get a repeat performance. If Daisy tried to wolf one down, she'd probably choke to death.

Nolan doesn't seem anywhere near as interested in our new, smaller bird. He'd obviously bonded with Squawks, and now looks a little sad that he's been taken away.

Oh lord. Now I feel a little guilty about the whole thing.

This is ridiculous, of course. After all, it was Squawks that nicked my food, not the other way around (I doubt seeds and crickets would go well with my digestive system) – but I don't want Nolan to look *sad*. Not on our first date.

My mood brightens with the fresh plate of two tacos that the waiter brings over to me a few minutes later, apologising for the inconvenience as he does so. 'We have never had a bird do that before,' he tells us. 'It may be because the tacos are fresh on the menu this evening.'

I nod. That sounds a likely reason for the issue with Squawks. Maybe he's always had a thing for tacos, but never had the chance to get hold of one here before.

There's probably a vast and complex backstory as to why Squawks has developed this love of Mexican food – and it would probably make a great children's novel, but I can't flesh out a synopsis right now, as there are two more tacos in my immediate future and I must get down to eating them without further hesitation.

As I chomp down on the first one, Nolan and I talk a little about work, because it was inevitable we would at some point, wasn't it? Happily, there's not much to discuss that isn't positive. Nolan is extremely pleased by the amount of business we're generating.

'And so much of that has been down to you, Ellie,' he tells me with a huge smile on his face. 'Your commitment to the environmental cause has been so fantastic. Making you the Head of Client Relations was the best business decision I ever made!'

Oh God.

Guilt instantly suffuses every fibre of my being. The tacos – so incredibly tasty a few moments ago – have suddenly lost all their taste.

Nolan really does think I'm just like him.

He really does believe I'm some kind of environmental rock star . . . when in reality, nothing could be further from the truth.

Hell, that's probably one of the reasons he *fancies me*. It's probably why he asked me out to dinner!

This entire date is predicated on a lie!

I crunch the tasteless taco in my mouth a few more times and try to avoid his gaze.

His lovely, soft gaze.

Oh, for fuck's sake!

Be honest!

What?

Be honest with him!

I can't do that!

Yes you bloody can!

My conscious is absolutely right. I *do* have to be honest with Nolan.

If I'm really going to think about starting something romantic with this man, I have to be honest and upfront with him about what I really think and feel. You can't start anything with someone based on lies.

I have to tell him the truth!

This starts with being honest about my initial scheme to keep my job – like turning up at the Worriors protest, and sticking those pot plants everywhere.

And then I can tell him how much I've enjoyed working by his side. How much I've enjoyed his enthusiasm for tackling climate change. How much his influence has rubbed off on me.

Yes!

That sounds good, doesn't it? That sounds like something he'd like to hear!

And tell him about Robert, too.

What?!

You have to tell him about Demonic Rab. About the relationship you had with him.

I can't do that! Nolan will probably know all about Robert Ainslie bloody Blake and his love of destroying natural habitats! It was all over the papers for weeks!

He'll find out, Ellie. If you start a relationship with Nolan, he will find out about it. Past flings have a way of rearing their ugly heads, you know *this.*

But . . . but Nolan will *hate* me!

Not if you explain it properly. Not if you make sure he knows how much you dislike Robert now, and how much you regret the relationship.

Oh God . . . okay.

Okay.

Jesus. Okay.

The blood drains out of my face as I look Nolan square in the eyes and start to speak. 'You see, the thing is, when you first came

149

along, Nolan, I was really worried about keeping my job, so I have to confess that I—'

A blur of white feathers. A hand full of taco becomes a hand devoid of taco.

'Bloody hell!' I exclaim, as I watch Squawks soar off across the restaurant with my food.

He banks sharply to the left, swings back again in a graceful arc, and comes to rest in a flurry of hectic wings back on the perch next to our table. Poor old Daisy is shoved aside like yesterday's news.

I'm gobsmacked.

Not only has Squawks repeated his bold act of larceny, he's now gloating about it right in front of us!

'Give that back!' I demand. The first time I could laugh the theft off, but this is the second time, and it's starting to feel a bit *personal.*

I tickled you behind the ear, Squawks. Is this how you repay me?

Out of the corner of my eye, I see Keiran and a couple of other members of Halliwell's staff start to make their way over to where I'm stood. 'You give me that taco back right now, mister,' I insist again, moving towards Squawks with purpose.

This will not *stand.* I was about to confess everything to Nolan, and this bloody parrot has interrupted me just as I'd worked up the courage to be honest!

'Give it back!' I repeat, and reach out to pluck the remains of my taco from Squawks's beak. This is not something I would do ordinarily. Birds' beaks tend to be sharp and nasty, and that's without considering the involvement of the clawed feet in any physical confrontation. But that's *my* taco, and I was just about to have a heartfelt conversation with a man who I have quite clearly developed feelings for! I did not want to be interrupted by a thieving parrot!

I grab hold of the taco, and yank it out of Squawks's mouth. He looks decidedly put out by this.

'Hah! Take that!' I crow triumphantly, grasping the now soggy, disintegrating mess of a taco in one hand.

Squawks takes one look at me . . . and launches himself at my head.

'Aaaarggh!' I scream, as bird and head come into hard and deeply unpleasant contact with one another. Squawks doesn't quite dig his claws right into my skull, but I can feel them scraping away up there, as he flaps around like a thing possessed.

This is escalation on a scale I wasn't prepared for in the *slightest*. Squawks clearly has psychopathic tendencies. Or at least an abiding love of tacos that turns him from being placid and laid-back into maniacal and insane at the flick of a mental switch.

'Fucking hell!' I shriek, as I start to stumble around with Squawks now caught up in my hair. If the little sod decides he wants a firmer grip on my noggin, I am in for some extremely bad times.

Can parrot claws pierce a human skull? And how the hell did I manage to get myself into a situation where that becomes a question I need an immediate and clear answer to?

With screeching cockatoo atop my head, I pinball around Paradise in Flight, banging into tables and chairs, my field of vision resolutely blocked by flailing white wings.

It therefore comes as a massive shock when I feel hands grabbing me around the waist.

Oh, fabulous – not only am I being attacked by a parrot, but someone is also attempting to molest me, in what can only be described as disgusting opportunism of the highest order.

'Please stop moving around!' I hear Keiran cry from behind me. 'We can't get him off if you keep thrashing about!'

Oh, I'm sooooo fucking sorry, Keiran. Is that not the proper pro-
tocol when you're being attacked by a maniacal bird of paradise? Is it
considered impolite and impractical to thrash around when a parrot is
about to claw your bloody eyes out?

'Get him off me!' I cry in a guttural, panicked voice.

SQUAWK SQUAWK SQUAWK, goes Squawks, in what I can
only assume is cockatoo for 'This'll teach you to nick my fucking
taco!'

'But it was *my* taco!' I actually scream out loud, as Keiran and
his friends attempt to wrestle the parrot away from me. 'Parrots
don't eat tacos!' I add, feeling my hair being yanked out of my head
as they try to pull him off.

SQUAWK SQUAWK SQUAWK, he screeches. 'Well, this fucking parrot does!' is what he is no doubt saying at this juncture.

Congratulations, Ellie, you've managed to turn a first date into
a no-holds-barred wrestling match with a fat parrot. What will you
do for an encore? Challenge a moose to some boxing? Karate with
a panda?

I let out a scream as Keiran yanks Squawks away as hard as he
can, taking a fair clump of my hair with him.

Squawks . . . well . . . *squawks* triumphantly as his handler does
so. He may have lost his taco to me, but he's taken his measure of
revenge by removing a chunk of my hair. It's a trade he probably
thinks is well worth it.

I bloody *don't*, and my hand flies to my head as I start to feel
the burning sting.

'Owww! You *mean* bloody bird!' I shout at the cockatoo, who
is still throwing the hissiest of hissy fits in Keiran's arms.

By now of course, the whole restaurant is watching what's
going on with a combination of horror and surprise. The little girl
who was so happily playing with her own parrot close to our table
is now staring over with a look of sheer terror on her face.

I have managed to turn her ornithophobic in mere seconds. Hell . . . I'm pretty sure I'm going to develop a severe fear of birds after this. My chances of visiting any tropical islands on holiday any time soon are down the toilet. I'll be permanently terrified that a lorikeet is about to rip the back of my head off to get at my Mai Tai.

'Ellie! Are you okay?' Nolan exclaims, coming towards me with a highly concerned expression on his face.

Bless him. Look at how worried he is, would you?

Given what's just transpired, I'm amazed he's not howling with laughter – but then Nolan isn't built that way, is he?

'I . . . I think I'm alright,' I tell him, seeing a tiny amount of blood on my hand as I take it away from my head. I give Nolan a dismayed, hurt look. 'I just . . . I just wanted to say . . . to say to you . . . I just wanted to be honest and . . . and . . .'

Do not cry, woman. Do not cry here and now, when—

Oh, fuck it. We've just been assaulted by a bloody parrot. You can for a bit, but don't indulge yourself.

Tears sprout at the corners of my eyes, and I see Nolan's face crumple in sympathy.

He then does something that is unexpected, but ever so right in the circumstances – he wraps his arms around me in a tight hug.

Oh God.

Oh *wow*.

Look, I'm not going to say getting attacked by Squawks was worth it for this – I haven't lost my mind completely – but if you are going to get mauled by a fat feathered maniac, then a hug like this is a magnificent way to make you feel like it wasn't such a bad ordeal after all.

Nolan breaks the hug, and looks me in the eyes. 'Are you okay?'

Kiss him.

What?

Kiss him. Right now.

In front of all these people?

Yes, in front of all of them. Kiss him.

With a parrot screaming the place down next to us?

Yes. It'll be memorable.

My scalp is bleeding. You're suggesting I kiss a man when I have a bleeding scalp, and hair that probably looks like I've been dragged through a hedge backwards?

Yes, I am. Now stop sodding about. Kiss him.

But I haven't been honest with him yet! I haven't told him all about Robert!

Fuck all of that. Just kiss him.

But you said I had to tell him!

That wasn't me. Kiss him. Do it now.

I've never really believed in that whole metaphor about the angel and the demon sat on your shoulders before, but both of the buggers have come on this date with me tonight, haven't they?

The question is, which one do I listen to?

. . . the wrong one, unfortunately.

I lean forward and slap my lips on to Nolan's with a ferocity that is quite unlike me.

For a split second I think Nolan is going to pull away, but then he starts to kiss me back . . . and the world starts spinning.

It would be some kind of glorious romantic Hollywood moment, were it not for the fact that Squawks has now decided to climb on Keiran's head and shit down the poor lad's back.

'Jesus Christ!' he screams in pain and revulsion, as Nolan and I remain lip-locked.

The crowd of restaurant guests now don't know where to look. Two people engaged in a passionate kiss is quite the thing, but then, does it really compete with a cockatoo defecating all over his handlers while screeching the place down?

Probably not.

I think Nolan and I would have to strip our clothes off and get down to it right here and now to even begin to compete with the show Squawks and Keiran are putting on.

. . . great. Now I'm horny.

There's a cockatoo systematically flaying somebody alive and spraying poo everywhere right next to me, and I'm getting turned on.

It might be best to pause this romantic interlude, until the chaos has been brought to an end.

I pull away from Nolan extremely reluctantly, and look into his eyes. 'Well,' I gasp, 'I wasn't . . . I wasn't planning on doing that.'

'I'm . . . glad you did.'

'Me too.'

'But, nice as it was . . . do you think we can pause for a while? I'm pretty sure I just felt some bird shit land on my neck.'

'Okay!'

We break our embrace and step back, as three of Halliwell's staff try to bring Squawks under some sort of control. They are failing miserably. He's having none of it.

Then, an idea presents itself that should make their attempts a lot more successful.

I go over to my plate, grab the remaining tacos, and lob them into the bundle of arms, legs, feathers and beak. Squawks instantly goes for them, allowing Keiran to finally get away from his attacker.

He gives me a look of pitiful gratitude.

'Might be a good idea to take tacos off the menu,' I suggest in a light tone – to which he nods feverishly, his eyes wild.

'I'll tell the kitchen,' he replies.

Squawks, for his part, has calmed down magnificently, and is tucking into the smashed remains of those tacos with great gusto.

Good for you, Squawks, I think to myself. *You got yours.*

I turn to look at Nolan, and the instant I do I feel a combination of excitement and dread. Excitement that I might be embarking on a new romantic relationship for the first time in what feels like a century, and dread when I think about the possible ramifications of that relationship on my career and reputation at work.

And then there's the whole matter of my true attitude towards the environment . . .

Don't worry about it. You'll be fine. You're good at your job, and that's all that matters.

Thank you, shoulder angel!

Ha! You think I'm the angel?

'I think I might need to go to the toilet and check myself over,' I say to Nolan, tentatively sending an exploratory finger up to where Squawks ripped the hair out of my head. There's not much blood there, but it's probably still best I go give it a proper look.

'Okay,' Nolan replies, and nods. 'I think I might have a chat with the maître d', and get us out of here before any other birds attack us.'

'Good idea.' I look around at the stunned and shocked looks on the faces of the other restaurant-goers. 'I think it might be a good idea to recommend to Mr Halliwell that he changes this whole set-up a bit. Dining with birds of paradise sounds like a great idea, but maybe dining with birds of paradise *that are securely sectioned off from diners by some nice stout metal fencing* might be a whole lot safer.'

A little later, after I've wrestled my hair back into some kind of shape and have dabbed away the blood enough to cover up the injury, Nolan and I end up in a bar close to town, where we order a couple of exciting cocktails. It's been that kind of evening.

Even later than that, there is more kissing. This time completely free of poo.

It's all rather marvellous.

I take my leave from Nolan eventually and reluctantly, and make my way home with my brain fizzing.

Tonight has been quite monumental. Things have irrevocably changed, and it's hard to see any way that they can go back.

And okay, yes – I didn't manage to talk to Nolan about Robert, or about how I'm not quite the green crusader he might think I am, but does it really matter?

After all, I *am* helping to spread the message of environmentalism by working at Viridian PR. I'm doing the absolute best job I possibly can. Nobody could be working harder right now. I *am* doing good in the world!

It doesn't *really* matter that I might not be motivated by the environmental cause to the same extent that Nolan is. The important thing is that Viridian PR does its best to promote those businesses that *are* motivated by it.

And there's no real reason why I have to get into the whole issue of Robert Ainslie Blake. It was a fling. A six-month mistake. Nothing more than that. He blinded me with his cash, his bold manner and his teeth. I was very silly to date him, but it ended a long time ago.

There's no reason to . . . ruin what I've started with Nolan.

I'm not doing anything wrong, I'm not hurting anyone.

Everything is perfectly fine.

. . . what's *not* perfectly fine is that, from now on, I will be unable to look at a cockatoo without feeling the overwhelming urge to scream and throw Mexican food at it.

On balance though, I'd say that this date can be put in the positive column. I really do like Nolan a lot. That much has been made evident – even if it took me nearly getting scalped by a parrot to finally realise it.

SQUAWK . . . Who's a pretty boy, then?

Chapter Seven

The Sticky Things Are Our Future

And so, we reach the 'two people running around behind everyone's backs, trying to keep things a secret' portion of this tale.

It was inevitable, I suppose. You simply can't enter into a relationship with your boss and not have to engage in clandestine trysts behind closed doors, away from prying eyes.

Both Nolan and I have agreed that the last thing we want is for our colleagues to find out about our fledgling romance. It would damage my reputation, of that there is no doubt, and it probably wouldn't do his much good either.

So, we are being *very careful*.

Careful to keep our hands to ourselves as much as possible while at work – and arrange dates at times and places that aren't likely to see us bumping into Nadia, Joseph and Amisha – or anyone else from Viridian PR.

Thus far, it's working very well.

Okay, there was that one time last week when Young Adrian came into Nolan's office a mere ten seconds or so after we'd been kissing by Nolan's new ficus, but I don't think he even registered how hectic and flushed our faces were, or that my lipstick had gone on holiday across my left cheek.

Other than that, we've managed to keep things very secret.

Speaking of secrets – no, I still haven't told him about Robert. I'm sorry. It's just not felt like the right time.

Everything is going *so well*, you see. Not only am I still very much enjoying the work I'm doing, I now have the added benefit of passionate kissing by a ficus with an unconventionally handsome man.

I've never had the excitement of a fresh new job *and* a fresh new relationship before. It's an extremely heady combination.

And I don't want to spoil any of it!

So I will keep my sordid past to myself at the moment, if that's all the same.

. . .

This doesn't mean that I don't worry about it constantly, though.

I'd like to just put Robert and my slightly disingenuous approach to Viridian's environmental cause to the back of my brain – but both keep on surfacing like half-melted icebergs.

I know I should be more honest with Nolan, but I equally know that it will just ruin things if I am.

And I still think that neither thing *really* matters all that much. Not in the grand scheme of things. Viridian PR continues to go from strength to strength – that's what matters, and why should a past relationship have any impact on a current one? We all have skeletons in our closet, after all. It's perfectly okay if I want to keep mine locked away for now.

That sounds convincing, doesn't it?

Reasonable?

Yes.

I think so.

Definitely.

'Ellie?'

I jump in my seat as Nolan's voice interrupts my extensive wool-gathering.

How long have I been sat here, thinking about all of this? Probably far too long.

'Yes!' I reply, trying to sound like I'm fully switched on to the world around me, rather than inside my own head, rummaging around in my neuroses.

'How's it going on that market research project? Both Hempawear and The Green Tangent are interested in getting their hands on it, and I'd like to be able to give them an estimate on when we might have something for them.'

'I'll be visiting the school on Monday,' I tell him, fully returning to the here and now. It's rare for Nolan to sound hurried about anything, so when it does happen it rather shocks you out of any complacency you may have fallen into.

'Great. Do you think you can have everything collated by the end of next week?'

'Yes, hopefully. Nadia is coming with me, and she'll help transcribe everything once we're back in the office. Next Friday should be doable, no problem.'

'Fantastic! Good to know you're on it.' Nolan smiles, and gets up from his desk. He comes over and gives me a gentle, encouraging squeeze of the shoulder.

This of course then leads to some more passionate kissing by the ficus.

If I ever write a fictionalised account of my office romance with Nolan, that will probably be the title of the book.

We manage to get ourselves under control after about five minutes, and both sit back down, with faces once again flushed.

Anyone coming into Nolan's office when I'm in it these days would probably think we've got the heating up way too high.

I take a moment to calm myself and drop back into work mode. Nolan does much the same thing.

In the short time we've been dating, we've already developed this uncanny ability to switch from work to romance and back again in the blink of an eye, without much effort at all. It bodes well for our ongoing relationship that neither of us has a problem with this.

'Seriously, don't worry about the market research, I've got everything planned out for the session. I'm sure we'll get some good data from them,' I say to Nolan, full of positivity.

'That's great. The data you get should be really helpful to us.'

'It absolutely *will*,' I reply, with what I hope sounds like a large degree of certainty in my voice.

It's a certainty I'm not actually sure I really feel . . . but you know how the old saying goes. Fake it until you make it.

The 'them' I've referred to are a class of schoolchildren in year six.

Or, as I like to call them, *The Sticky Things*.

Not as sticky as their younger counterparts in the years below, I grant you, but they are sticky enough, I can guarantee you that.

Now, ordinarily I would have no truck with going near Sticky Things of any age. I only enjoy the company of human beings once they can legally drive a car, and can safely join me in having a good old moan about their tax bill. But in this instance, I am willing to do it, because it might help me glean some useful information for Viridian PR.

You see, some of the companies we represent are very interested in The Sticky Things. They are interested because The Sticky Things are the consumers of the future – once they've reached the age and position where they get wages and a tax bill, that is. And for companies concerned with the environment, it's very important for *their* future that they understand what the young think about climate change and other environmental concerns. You don't want to be sending out the wrong message to your customers of the future.

Hence this hastily arranged market research session – organised with the help of my brother Sean. Once more I am leaning on him. Though this time it's a little more in-depth than just a phone call about ways I can keep my job.

He sounded more than happy to help me out with this market research project though, I'll give him that.

It's the environmental angle. That's definitely what persuaded him to help – and the reason for his eagerness. Sean is the kind of teacher that believes the children truly are our future, and he'll do anything he can to educate them into being better people. He's a massive idealist. Always has been. The idea of a session where his pupils get to talk to someone about their concerns for the environment is something he really couldn't pass up.

Okay, the fact that Nolan also promised to donate a good chunk of change to the struggling school greased the wheels with the rest of the faculty, but for Sean it's all about his pupils engaging with such an important subject.

You've got to laugh, haven't you? The idea that The Sticky Things will actually want to talk about climate change is *ludicrous*. If I was conducting research into the Kardashians, Fortnite, or Nando's, I could understand him thinking that way, but if I come out of the hour-long session with more than a few mumbled comments about the weather and greenhouses, I'll be flabbergasted.

Kids don't care about the world's environment. They care about their *own* environment – which is largely full of smartphones, peri-peri chicken and plastic toys. They are The Sticky Things, and they are wholly unconcerned with your adult fixations about sea levels and the destruction of biospheres. Hempawear and The

Green Tangent will come to realise this, once I report back with our findings.

Regardless, Monday will see me enter the domain of The Sticky Things, because I promised Nolan I would do it, and I don't want to let him down.

It will be Ellie Cooke and thirty or so children, locked together in a small room for sixty minutes.

I may have to spend the weekend blind drunk to prepare myself.

I had a couple of gin and tonics with the girls from the gym on Sunday night, but that was about it. I find the idea of drinking to feel better more appealing than the reality of it – largely because I can't ever remember a time when drinking lots of alcohol made me feel better about *anything*, other than the prospect of going teetotal.

Thus, I am bright-eyed and bushy-tailed on Monday morning, as I watch Nadia jump into my Mercedes in the car park at work. She looks a little less bright-eyed than me, but then she does have a hyperactive child at home. I doubt there will be much in the way of being bright-eyed for the next ten years or so.

'All set then?' Nadia says, as she pops her seat belt on.

'Just about. I'm glad I've got you with me. You can help me fight off The Sticky Things if they get too overexcited.'

Nadia rolls her eyes. 'I don't think I've ever met a woman in her thirties with such an aversion to children. They're really not that bad, Ellie.'

'Yeah, well, you would say that. You went and got one of them.'

'I didn't order Ayesha off Amazon, Ellie,' she says in an exasperated tone, giving me a playful slap on the arm.

Technically I am Nadia's boss, but the fact that she completely ignores this at every given opportunity is a source of great comfort to me.

'Probably just as well; you're not allowed to return things to Amazon if they get sticky.'

I have met little Ayesha on more than one occasion, and she's a gorgeous little giggly tumble of fun, if I'm being honest. But I only see her when Nadia presents her at the office – usually on her best behaviour, and after she's been well fed and watered.

I know what they're like behind closed doors. I've done my *research*.

Speaking of which . . .

'You had a chance to read through the questions I put together?' I ask Nadia, as I drive us away from the office.

'Yep. Looking forward to hearing what answers we get.'

I snort. 'Not so sure I am. I don't mention Fortnite once. Keeping them interested is going to be a *nightmare*.'

Nadia doesn't choose to answer that. I'm not surprised. People with kids don't tend to like it when I'm cynical about them, which is more than fair enough, I suppose. I'm much the same when people are dismissive of Chris Hemsworth's acting abilities.

The man is a powerhouse of both comedic and dramatic talent, goddamn it, and I will hear *nothing* to the contrary!

Anyway . . .

Sean Cooke more than makes up for his sister's cynicism about the next generation. He's dedicated to his job in a way that almost justifies the long working hours and small pay packet he has to endure.

Sean was born to be a teacher. He looked good in a corduroy jacket at a very early age. And my rather strong command of the English language is just as much down to him as it is to our parents. Sean would hand down all of his books to me to read, and would cheerfully help me with my homework when I needed it. In many ways, I was my brother's first pupil. I'm amazed he wasn't put off for life.

He's waiting for us both at the school's main entrance, with an enthusiastic smile on his face. Today's dark-green corduroy jacket goes very well with the black jumper, and I see he's got a new pair of his favourite black horn-rimmed glasses. Sean looked extremely awkward and geeky when we were teenagers, but at the age of thirty-nine, he has reached the point when his fashion sense is exactly in the right place. He pulls off 'nerd cool' in a way that makes me insanely jealous. There's something so effortless and comfortable about my brother that feels completely alien to me – as if he's absolutely known his place in the world for decades now, while I'm still floundering around, trying to figure out what the hell I'm doing.

'Hi, sis!' he calls out as we approach. It's genuinely lovely to hear him be so happy to see me. If I'm not careful, I might get a bit emotional.

'Morning, Sean,' I reply, and give him a hug. He smells of cornflakes and classrooms. Neither are unpleasant. 'This is my colleague Nadia Hall. She's going to be taking care of the recording for me, while I speak to your pupils.'

'Hello!' Nadia says, and shakes Sean's hand.

'Nice to meet you, Nadia. Thanks for coming along to help my sister out today.' He grins. 'I've seen her around large groups of children before . . . it's not a pretty sight. I'm sure she appreciates the backup.'

'Oh, very funny,' I say, rolling my eyes. 'I'm not that bad.'

Sean looks at Nadia. 'Is she still calling them The Sticky Things?'

Nadia nods solemnly. 'Yes. Yes she is.'

He looks back at me. 'Eleanor Cooke, you are incorrigible.'

'Incorrigible' is a word Sean taught me the meaning of when I was so young, I had no business knowing what it was.

'Shall we just get into your classroom?' I suggest, before he breaks out the family albums, in order to really embarrass me in front of my work colleague.

'Why not?' he replies with a smile. 'I'll get you both inside and set up, before the horde descends.' He looks at his watch. 'We've got about fifteen minutes before class is due to start. Follow me.'

Sean leads us into the school, and down a long corridor to his classroom. Once inside, we sit down in the corner, and await the onslaught.

Thus far I haven't touched anything that actually qualifies as sticky, but I'm sure that time is not far away.

I'm ashamed to say that my heart rate increases a little as Sean lets the long queue of schoolchildren into the classroom as the clock strikes 9 a.m. I think it's the way they're all looking at me – like I'm an interloper in their world. Which is exactly what I am, of course.

How the hell am I going to be able to communicate with them for an hour? They're so strange and alien to everything I know. I've never played Fortnite, can only pick maybe two or three Kardashians out of a line-up, and would rather eat the dust under my microwave than go to Nando's.

Sean has no such problems, naturally. He is as at home here as I am on the couch, wrapped in a duvet, watching old episodes of *Friends*.

'Good morning, class,' he says to them. 'Today we have some very special guests in, who have come to talk to you about a very, very important subject that I'm sure you're all very interested in chatting about.'

Lot of verys in that sentence, you'll notice. Sean is evidently trying to underline the significance of this session, so they don't all drift off into their own little worlds in the space of two minutes.

Sean's introduction earns us a whole gamut of looks from our sticky crowd. Most of them look curious, a few look downright suspicious (they'll do well in life), a couple seem a little scared, and one is picking his nose and looking out of the window.

I asked Sean not to tell the kids too much about what we're going to be asking them this morning. I want to be the one to do that, so I can say the right things in the right way. There's a dark art to effective market research that requires a pretty specific methodology when it comes to how you talk to your targets, and I want to make sure we get this as right as we possibly can. The lack of decent data I'm predicting we get must not be blamed on poor interview technique.

Sean says my name, along with Nadia's, and steps back to allow me to come forward and begin.

Eeep.

I stand up on legs that are far shakier than they should be. These are kids, for crying out loud. Why do I feel so nervous?

Perhaps because children are experts in the unvarnished truth. They've not had time to develop all of those social skills that let adults lie and dissemble their way through life, so as not to offend anyone accidentally – not unless they're on social media, that is, where everyone returns to the playground as soon as they start to write a tweet.

'Hello,' I say.

A few of them wave back and say 'hello' in return. I mark which ones they are. I'm more likely to get opinions out of the extroverts than I am the quiet ones.

I look over to Nadia, who has set up her smartphone to record everything that's said, and is also taking notes. She gives me a nod.

I look down at my question sheet at the first one on the list, which quite simply asks the children if they know what climate change is.

I am expecting four or maybe five of them to put their hands up when I ask it. By starting with such an open, straightforward question, I can immediately gauge both the knowledge base of my audience and their willingness to inform me of that knowledge with no further prompting. It's not a question I'm expecting much of a reaction to. A cold open like this rarely results in much of a useful response, but even knowing that is a valuable data point that informs the rest of the research session.

'So, I have a question for you all,' I say to them, trying to maintain a friendly smile and light tone to my voice – these things are important. 'Who knows what climate change is?'

Every. Single. Hand. Goes. Up.

Jesus Christ.

'Er . . . well, that's . . . good,' I fumble, my grip on the question sheet tightening somewhat.

I did ask them the right question, didn't I?

I mean, I did ask them if they knew what climate change is, and not what Minecraft is, didn't I?

They can't *all* know what climate change is. That's just silly.

They're *eleven*.

I glance over at Sean, who is standing with his arms crossed and a slightly smug expression on his face. He unfolds one arm and gestures for me to carry on, with a slowly waved hand. The floor is mine, whether I like it or not.

I'm flummoxed, to be honest. I had it in my head that it was going to be a struggle just to get this lot to engage with me about the environment, and had tailored my questions to that end. But the sea of hands suggests that I have read the room about as badly as I possibly could. I wasn't banking on *enthusiasm*. I have nowhere to go with *enthusiasm*.

'Um . . . well, let me just see what the best thing to ask you all about it would be . . .' I tell them, frantically searching down my list of questions to see if there's one that's appropriate.

Oh, here's one that should do the trick. It's one of the last, and I wasn't expecting any of them to know what the hell I was talking about. I threw it in more as a baseline for the end of the session, to let me know levels of ignorance.

'Hands up if you can tell me anything about the effects of climate change on biodiversity?'

That should do it. There's no way any eleven-year-old can—

Fuck me, that's at least a dozen hands up.

I have to lean back against Sean's desk.

I lift a finger, and point it at the boy who was picking his nose. 'Yes, you?'

He looks momentarily shocked that I've singled him out for special favour, but rallies magnificently and sits up to respond. 'Biodiversity is what we call all the different animals living together, and we keep doing things that make those animals go extinct,' he tells me, seemingly very confident that he's right. 'That means there's less of them, so less biodiversity.'

He's eleven. He knows what biodiversity is.

I didn't even know what *biology* was at the age of eleven.

'That's . . . that's right. What's your name?'

'Aiden.'

'Well, thank you, Aiden.'

Aiden beams at me with the smile of someone who knows he has *done good*. He's done more than that though; he's forcing me to re-evaluate this entire bloody thing, the nose-picking little horror.

I try another question – this one about CO2 levels in the Earth's atmosphere.

Yep, some of the little sods know about that too. A girl called Olivia tells me all about how she understands that CO2 is a greenhouse gas, and it heats up the planet. She does this while constantly twirling a long strand of copper hair that I find myself insanely jealous of. I'm almost as jealous of her knowledge of CO2 levels, if I'm being brutally honest.

I decide I might as well plough on with some of the more broad, open questions, given that I took ages deciding on what they should be – as, if I don't, this session will be coming to a very abrupt end. I have nothing else prepared.

They all know about plastic pollution. There's a visceral anger in some of their eyes about that one.

And the anger is replaced by sadness when I mention what's happening to animals across the planet. There's a palpable sense among these kids that something is being lost. Something very important.

One girl called Summer – who recently immigrated to the UK from Sydney – spends a good five minutes telling me all about how her family watched their next-door neighbour's house burn down in a bushfire, and how she and her mum raised four hundred and twenty-seven dollars and sixty-three cents to help take care of the poor burned koalas.

Summer's look of devastation when she talks about all of this cuts me to the quick.

One after another, each of my carefully constructed questions is responded to with more knowledge and insight than I was ever prepared for. I expected to come here to talk to a bunch of switched-off preteens who just want to be on their smartphones – and instead I'm having to handle a classroom of mini experts.

It only takes half an hour to rattle through everything I've prepared, such is the volume of knowledge they all have. I've woefully underestimated their understanding of climate change, and it fucking *shows*.

Bloody hell.

There's every possibility that, on some aspects of the subject, *they know more than I do*.

I didn't have a clue that butterflies had virtually disappeared across the whole of California – but Eric does.

Eric is an eleven-year-old boy who is called Eric in this day and age. This is probably all I need to tell you about him.

And Shelly knows that a third of the Amazon rainforest will be gone in the next couple of decades. She tells me this with wide eyes and a horrified expression.

Every one of them knows who Greta Thunberg is, in the same way I knew who Posh Spice was at their age.

It's *remarkable*.

'Er . . . okay. That's . . . all the questions I . . . I have,' I again fumble, looking at the clock with some dismay. I promised Sean I'd keep them occupied for the whole lesson, and here I am done with thirty minutes to spare.

In desperation, I look over at my brother, who has been watching all of this silently but with a permanently unsurprised expression on his face.

Not for the first time in my life – and it definitely won't be the last – I am looking to Sean to jump in and save my bacon.

He sees my hopeless look and immediately steps forward. 'Guys, why don't you all spend a few minutes thinking about what you've been talking about, and maybe come up with some questions you would like to ask Ellie?'

What?

That's not how this works!

I ask the questions. *They* answer. That's the way market research goes! Not the other way around!

But Sean has bought me a break in proceedings. I have to be grateful to him for that.

As his class drops into the silence of thought about what they might want to ask (*oh God*) my brother comes to stand next to me, as Nadia does the same.

'They're a bloody clever bunch!' she says, with some surprise.

'Yes, they are,' Sean agrees, smiling.

'Well done, bruv,' I tell him. 'You've done a great job of teaching them about the environment.' I scowl a little. 'You could have warned me though. I could have prepared my questions better.'

Sean looks baffled. 'What? You think this was *me*?'

'Yeah, of course.'

'You're kidding, aren't you? I don't have time to teach them about climate change . . . not beyond whatever basic stuff we might stumble over in the curriculum, anyway. I certainly can't get into the kinds of in-depth stuff they've been talking to you about.'

'Then how do they know all of it?'

Sean fishes into his pocket . . . and pulls out his smartphone. He waves it at me. 'They're not stupid, Ellie. They can see what's going on around them, and they can find out about it for themselves whenever they want to. All I can really do is make sure they're not just taking what they see online at face value.' He looks at the class for a moment. His expression is indecipherable. 'Sometimes, I think that's the best thing I can teach them – never believe anything you see until you've dug a little deeper.'

'That's a bit heavy for eleven-year-olds, isn't it?' Nadia replies, looking a bit disturbed.

Sean nods. 'We live in a heavy world.'

The grave look on my brother's face is almost as shocking as the depth of knowledge that's been arrayed in front of me this morning. Sean is an optimist at heart. I'm the one who's supposed to be the cynic. Hearing him talk like this is quite dismaying – especially when it's about the children he teaches, and the world we've created for them.

Sean gives his class another couple of minutes to think of some questions, before bringing their attention back to him. 'So, anyone thought of a question to ask Miss Cooke?' he says.

Once again, every hand in the room shoots up – as does my heart rate.

I'm about to be put on the spot – and I have a feeling I'm woefully inadequate for the task.

'Aiden? What would you like to ask?' Sean enquires.

Ah. The nose-picker. Surely the nose-picker will go easy on me.

'Do you think we should all stop eating meat?' he asks me, the nose remaining clear of finger throughout, thankfully.

'Well . . . um . . . I guess it's important to . . . to . . .'

What the hell do I say? Even though I'm doing meat-free Mondays, a Sunday roast is never something I turn down. But about ten minutes ago, Sadie at the back of the class – her of the neat hair and prim expression – was telling me all about how awful it is for the animals before they get killed. How do I stand here and say it's fine to eat meat, when these kids have a more-than-passable working knowledge (at eleven!) of what goes into getting that meat on to the table?

'. . . make your own decisions about it,' I eventually say, taking the coward's way out. I can almost see Mordred's beard shaking with disappointment and fury at my cop-out of an answer.

'What about petrol?' Aiden then immediately asks. You get the impression Aiden is the type of boy whose thoughts wriggle around almost as much as his finger does when it's in its favourite place.

'I'm sorry?'

'Do you think we should be driving petrol cars still? Only they do loads of damage, don't they? Especially the big ones.'

'Erm . . . that's also a difficult one, Aiden,' I flap. 'We need to get around, but we could also do with driving less. And maybe we should have more electric cars. It's bad that we still use petrol too much. But we need to . . . to get around . . . so . . . you know.'

When I say nothing else of any merit, Aiden looks extremely disappointed, and sits back, his finger starting its inexorable climb back towards its favourite frontal orifice.

'Jade? How about you? What would you like to ask?' Sean says, trying to ignore the upward trajectory of the digit.

Jade is the type of girl who will be wearing too much make-up in a couple of years, and constantly asking her friends if they have boobs yet. 'Yeah, well, what I reckon I want to know is what's the main reason we've got, you know, lots of people who want to come here from other countries? Is it because they've, like, lost their homes 'cos it's got too hot, and they haven't got enough water and stuff? And that's 'cos we've been burning lots of fossil fuels, and like, messed up their homes?'

Jade there, probably doing a better job of summing up the growing and worrying refugee and migration crisis across the globe than any dissembling politician I've heard speak for the past couple of decades.

But again . . . what the hell do I answer? What do I tell her? I've become the de-facto expert on climate change and the environment, simply by coming here today, and yet I have formed absolutely no opinion around this kind of question. These kids think I know what I'm talking about. But I don't. I really, really don't.

I just wanted to keep my job, *damn it*.

'It's . . . possible, I guess,' I tell Jade. 'There are lots of . . . factors to take into consideration, but you might be right. Could be right. Yes.'

Fuck me. What a terrible way to respond. I'm the one sounding like the dissembling politician here – but only because I have no real answers to give.

'And you, Alex? What's your question?' Sean says to another boy with his hand up, near the back of the room.

'Uh . . . yeah,' Alex says, and looks at me. 'Are we all gonna die because of viruses and stuff?' he asks bluntly.

'I'm sorry?' I splutter.

'Viruses. They happen 'cos of us, don't they? 'Cos of how bad we treat the animals. We keep destroying their habitats so their diseases spread to us more easily.'

'Er . . . yes. I suppose that's right,' I agree. 'But are we all going to die? I certainly hope not,' I tell Alex. 'I really, really hope not.'

Fuck me, I'm so *reassuring*. I should be able to say that of course we're not all going to die of a bloody pandemic – but I can't, can I?

Alex suddenly looks very sad. 'Only my nan died, and I don't want anyone else in my family to.'

Jesus Christ.

'Oh, I'm so sorry to hear that,' I tell Alex, with genuine sympathy, before I lapse back into a stupid silence when I can think of nothing else to add.

Sean goes on to pick out three more of his class, who all ask me the same kind of questions about climate change – and I am forced to give the same mealy-mouthed answers. Each time I do, I feel a little worse. Children don't hide their emotions, and their disappointment in me is self-evident.

I'm the adult. I'm the one who came here to talk to them about the environment. I should be able to tell them what they need to know. That's what the adults are supposed to do. We are the Knowing Things.

They are *The Sticky Things*, and we are supposed to be *The Knowing Things*. The ones that have the knowledge. The ones that can guide them and teach them about the world as they grow into it.

And I'm failing at that task, one thousand per cent.

'I don't . . . I don't know, Summer,' I respond to the Australian girl, after she's asked me how long it will be until the weather gets better in her country and the koalas come back again. I know nothing about what's happening out there. I know they have fires, and it's hot, and the Great Barrier Reef is in bad shape, but . . . that's it. I have no answers.

I just have *no answers*.

'Okay everyone, I think we'll leave it there for today,' Sean eventually says, as the clock gets to the hour. 'Would you all like to thank our guests for coming in today?'

The class do so, but I'm not convinced they mean it.

I wouldn't want to thank me either. I've just spent an hour first patronising them, then fobbing them off.

The bell goes, signalling the end of the lesson, and I watch as they all file past me, out of the door and towards the first break of the day. A few of them look in my direction as they go, but most don't. Most seem to want to ignore me. It feels horrible.

When the room is at last empty of children, I rub my eyes and look at Sean. 'Sorry about that. I think I misjudged things.'

Sean nods slowly. 'Maybe a little.'

'We did get some good data though, Ellie,' Nadia points out. 'We can go back to Nolan and say we've done our best to get an idea of what the customers of the future think about the environment!' She sounds chipper and upbeat, but I can tell she's trying to persuade herself it was a positive research session. She knows as well as I do what's actually just happened.

'They know far too much,' I say with a sigh. 'They shouldn't know some of that stuff. About animals being slaughtered, and refugees . . . They're kids.'

Sean folds his arms. 'It's not like they *want* to know about it, Ellie. They just have no choice. It's all around them. They see these things happening, and want to know what the hell we're doing about it.'

I try not to think of Aiden's disappointed expression, or Summer's look of worry when I couldn't tell her that the koalas will be okay.

'Did you know it would be like this?' I ask my brother.

He shrugs. 'I thought they had a good idea of what climate change is, but even I was surprised by how much they knew.'

'And what about me? Did you think I'd know a bit more? That I'd handle it better?' I sound a little peeved, but I'm feeling guilty and vulnerable after all of that, and he's my brother. Brothers are there to be peeved at. It's their job in life.

Sean looks at me with the same knowing expression he had on his face when I was seventeen and came home at eleven thirty at night, having told my parents I'd be back at ten. Sean and I crossed on the landing that evening, and I'll never forget the way he stared at me. It told me that he knew damn well I'd been out with Lloyd Davis, rather than with his sister Sian.

'I thought you'd be good at your job, Ellie. You always are. I thought you'd be well prepared, and up to the task of talking to a bunch of Sticky Things.' The look hardens on his face a little. 'But I also thought you might struggle with the subject matter. You've . . . you've never been one to worry about that kind of thing. You know . . . big-picture stuff.'

This is as close as my brother will get to saying I'm self-absorbed. He's a good man. And not one who likes to point out the faults in others.

But he's right. Goddamn it, he's as right as he was when he warned me not to keep seeing Lloyd Davis – even when I told him to fuck off and die, because I loved Lloyd.

Lloyd Davis broke my damn heart that year. He cheated on me with Carlie Owen, and told everyone at college I'd let him play with my boobs in the back of his Toyota Corolla. I did nothing of the fucking sort. I was a good girl, and it took me a long time to restore my reputation – with my big brother's help. But that's a story for another time . . .

I suddenly feel very emotional. Partly because I've just thoroughly let down a class of intelligent, engaged and worried children, and partly because I love my big brother and feel like I've let him down too.

Sean sees the look on my face, and immediately puts his arm around me. 'Look, don't worry about it too much. This whole thing is complicated, and nobody is expecting you to have all the answers.'

'I work for an environmentally conscious PR agency, Sean. I should have had more answers than I did.'

'Well, possibly. But like Nadia said, you do have a lot of great information to go back to your boss with. That's a good thing, right?'

'Yeah, I suppose so,' I agree, though a bit half-heartedly.

'There you go, then. It was a successful session for you guys. I'm very pleased.'

'Me too,' Nadia says, nodding her head.

'Mmmm,' I respond, in an extremely non-committal fashion. 'Can we get some of that lovely staffroom coffee now?' I ask Sean, in an attempt to change the subject.

He smiles. 'Of course! Though you may want to make sure your wills are up to date before drinking it.'

That's better. I much prefer Sean making bad jokes – instead of peering into my soul and showing me where my faults lie. I'd rather be drinking his terrible coffee any day of the week.

Actually, the coffee isn't that bad, and the half an hour we spend with Sean in his staff room is quite pleasant. There's something that feels ever so naughty and privileged about being in here – despite the fact that it's been nearly twenty years since I was a schoolchild.

My mood has lifted considerably by the time Nadia and I say goodbye to my brother and walk back to my car. The kids are all milling around us, going to their next classes as we do so.

As I open my car door, I look up to see Aiden staring at me from about thirty feet away. He has his finger up his nose (of course) and a deeply disappointed expression on his face.

For a moment, I can't work out why he looks like that – and then it hits me.

He can see the car I drive. He knows I have a big old petrol-guzzling Mercedes.

Instantly, I am filled with shame. The same shame I feel every time I get into this car these days, only multiplied beyond all comprehension.

I break eye contact with Aiden, climbing into the Merc as quickly as I can. By the time I work up the courage to look out of the windscreen, I can see that he is gone.

'You alright, Ellie?' Nadia asks. 'You look like you've seen a ghost.'

'I'm . . . I'm fine,' I tell her, flicking the ignition switch. The raw, horrible sound of that big, rattling three-litre engine bursts into life – and every time it does from now on, I will see Aiden's disappointment, Alex's sadness and Summer's worry.

Every single time.

Chapter Eight

THE MANSPREADER COMETH

Oooh . . .

Just look at it.

Gaze upon its magnificence – and know in your heart that *yes*, the upholstery does smell absolutely *fantastic*.

It is, if you are interested – and you had better be, otherwise we might not see eye to eye from now on – a Mercedes-AMG C-Class, in Polar White. Just under three years old, and on less than 25,000 miles, it is a thing of such amazementology that I am fully prepared to invent new words just to impress upon you how much I love it.

It's got more bells and whistles than Bell & Whistle Ltd, the world's oldest bell and whistle factory. The nice man with the cocaine sniff at the Mercedes dealership assured me that the car will park itself. This is something I never intend to trust it to do, but it's lovely to have it as some sort of option, if I ever feel daring enough, or just want to impress people.

Including you. You remain impressed, do you not?

Good.

We can proceed without further complication.

The list of features my new car has is extensive, but by far and away the best thing about it, and the main reason I bought the car, is that it is a *hybrid*. An environmentally friendly, gorgeous, Polar White hybrid, with climate control I can set remotely.

It does more than double the miles my stupid old car did. Its emissions are incredibly low. If I don't drive it like a complete wally, I will reduce my carbon footprint exponentially.

And I can't tell you how good that feels.

Because Aiden's expression has stuck with me. As has Summer's. And Jade's. And Alex's. And my brother Sean's. And mine, when I looked in the mirror that evening.

For two days I walked around in an absolute slump. A melancholic guilt hung around my shoulders like an unwanted embrace. Not just because I'd spent the last few weeks and months of my life pursuing and undertaking a job I didn't understand one little bit, thanks to my purely selfish desires – but also because my entire lifestyle up to this point hasn't been environmentally friendly in the *slightest*.

I've now managed to get rid of the car, but I can barely look in my wardrobe. The amount of fast, cheap fashion stuck in there that I've never even *worn* makes me sick to think about. And don't get me started on the pile of bags-for-life in the cupboard under the stairs, or the fact that I still don't own a proper recycling bin.

Being the type of person who will wallow in self-recrimination if I get even one-millionth of a chance, I spent yesterday evening on the internet for three hours, really delving into the issue of the climate crisis for the first time. Can you believe that? I've been working for a green PR firm for a while now, and hadn't even bothered to do much of my own research.

But when I did, I really wished I *hadn't*.

It's a bloody disaster zone. Not just the facts about climate change, but the attitudes of a worryingly large number of people in the world, who clearly don't think it's actually going on. I have never been environmentally conscious, but at least I didn't deny that it was happening. I was just lazy – and happy to wallow in ignorance. These folks seem to be wilfully ignoring all the evidence put in front of them, in what I can only assume is in a similar fashion to a man who ignores the blood in his urine every morning.

The baffling thing is, it's not hard to find real, hard evidence of climate change online. I did it in a matter of mere minutes. To be able to just dismiss it all takes a heroic amount of denial that I would have trouble mustering even if I took classes in it for three years, and graduated with a first-class honours degree in sticking my head in the sand.

No wonder Summer looked so fucking worried.

Those three hours I spent on websites like NASA, the Royal Society and the WWF scared me silly. Because of both the extent of the damage we're doing, and the complete lack of a decent response from our governments.

I deliberately avoided any organisations I couldn't verify the status and independence of, thinking that the information I got would be accurate and therefore wouldn't end up being too scary – but nope, it's carnage out there.

Oh, not necessarily for humanity. Not the rich bit of it anyway – that'll go on just fine in whatever small pockets of niceness it can create with all its money. But everything else, and everyone else, is more or less down the toilet if nothing changes. It's *horrifying*.

I almost feel like some of this stuff should be kept from the children, because it can't be doing their mental health any good – but then how do you hide it from them when it's outside their window? Summer watched it coming towards her in a sheet of angry orange flames when she was back in Australia. Alex lost a grandparent because of it.

I eventually had to shut the laptop off, and go and drink the rest of the bottle of white I had in the fridge. By the time I got to the end of it, I was just about able to sleep okay, and by the time I woke up this morning, I had a plan in my head. A plan to show the bloody world – and myself – that something fundamental had altered in my entire approach to this job.

Nolan was happy to give me the morning off, so I could drive to the nearest Mercedes forecourt and trade my 2004 clobberdy-bang piece of crap in for something new, clean, economic and better for the environment. In fact, he sounded pleased that I was going to be out of the office for the first few hours of the day. Told me to take all the time I needed to get my new car. God bless him, he's wonderful.

And here she sits – gleaming in the midday sun.

It is, of course, *just a start*. Just a symbolic representation of how my thought process has been changed and updated by all the soul-searching – and Google-searching – I've done over the past couple of days. But it is *a start*.

Which, incidentally, is keyless on this car. Did I tell you that?

I want to show my new Merc off. Not just because it is my new car, and looks absolutely gorgeous, but because it's a hybrid. I want to show off my green credentials properly for the first time, without feeling like I'm being a bit of a fraud. And there's one person above all others I want to show it off to.

I may have been pretending that I'm an environmentally conscious person to Nolan all of this time, but no more. After the session with Sean's class, I have turned one hell of a corner, and really do want to make sure Nolan knows it.

I'm going to get him to come for a drive with me, so I can show the car off, and while I'm doing that I'm going to have an honest and frank conversation with him about *everything*. I'm going to pour my heart out, and tell him just how much I've changed. And he'll have proof of that change, in the shape of the greenest, most efficient car I could buy on my current wages.

Yes. That sounds like a marvellous plan to me. It's bound to do the trick.

I proudly park the new hybrid Mercedes right next to Nolan's Tesla, and hurry towards the main entrance to our building, a bubble of excitement rising in my chest as I do so.

This is all going to work out fine.

Ellie Cooke no longer has to keep anything hidden from her boyfriend and boss. She can't wait to tell him all about the new car, and all about the new way she sees the world!

I hurry into our offices, and walk straight past everyone without giving them a look.

This will turn out to be something of a grave oversight, as if I had, I might have seen the worried, shocked looks on all their faces.

'Ellie!' Nadia calls out to me as I pass her. 'I need to speak to you!'

'Yeah, no worries, Nadia. Just let me go and chat to Nolan first. I have something important to show him!'

'I think you might want to—' Nadia starts to say, but I am already hurrying towards Nolan's office door, my mind completely focused on getting him downstairs to see the Mercedes.

'In a moment, Nadia! I promise!' I tell her, as I get to the office door and excitedly open it.

'Nolan?' I say eagerly, as I pop my head in. 'Would you like to come and see the car I've just bou—'

I stop mid-sentence.

Shock and dismay suffuse every part of my being.

Nolan is sat behind his desk. There's a look of shock on his face too, at me bursting in like this, but there's also something else there I've never seen before – a high degree of *irritation*. It doesn't sit well on his usually placid, calm features.

The source of the irritation is sat opposite him, in the chair I usually take when I'm talking over work with Nolan.

I can't manspread like its current occupant, though.

I doubt there are many men in this world who can manspread as much as this guy. He's one of those blokes who have raised it to something of an art form.

And it's a manspread I am well used to seeing. It's one of the things that irritated me the most about him, over the six months we were together.

'Robert?' I say in a cold, tight voice, as I feel the blood drain from my face.

Robert Ainslie Blake – Demonic Rab himself – is sat across from Nolan Reece, that near-permanent, languid, smug smile plastered across his face.

'Ellie! Hi there!' he replies, and snaps off a patronising salute with one hand. 'How's it going, yeah?'

Oh God . . .

That's right. He does that, doesn't he? He likes to end sentences with the word 'yeah', even when it makes no fucking sense whatsoever.

You know what else makes no fucking sense whatsoever?

Robert Ainslie Blake being sat in Nolan Reece's office.

Why is a man whose every action is complete anathema to Viridian PR's environmental message sat here, manspreading for all he's worth?

. . . and that's not because he has a large penis, let me assure you. Robert Ainslie Blake is endowed with the most aggressively average penis to ever grace the human population. He has absolutely no need to keep his legs that far apart.

Some men are compensating for having a small penis, but Robert is definitely just compensating for having a boring one. That's why he tries to make out he's the most interesting person on the planet – to compensate for the overwhelmingly nondescript thing parked between his legs. He's not interesting though, so his attempts just come across as obnoxious.

I didn't know all this when I first started dating him, of course. It took those six months for his true personality to really rub itself up against me enough times to see through the facade.

I think I managed to subconsciously ignore the type of man he really was for a long time, simply because I was enjoying all the attention he lavished on me. It's amazing how enough sun-soaked minibreaks and fancy restaurants can blind you to a person's real character, if you're willing to let them.

Then there was that thing he did in bed . . .

Seriously, if my toes had curled any further, I'd have needed some sort of corrective surgery afterwards.

But what is he fucking doing here? With my *new* boyfriend? And why is Nolan even *talking* to him?

'What are you doing here, Robert?' I demand, in a voice that would keep the Antarctic frozen solid for a millennium.

'Just came in to see the new guy!' Robert replies, pointing a finger at Nolan. 'Figured I could do with his help, yeah?'

'What kind of help?' I demand, closing the office door, so no one outside can see this horrific reunion taking place.

'Robert here wanted to have a meeting with me to talk about improving his company's green image,' Nolan tells me in a slightly strangled voice. His eyes dart over to Robert for a moment. 'He *insisted* on it, in fact. Didn't you, Mr Ainslie Blake?'

Robert sees the expression on Nolan's face, notes it carefully and smiles at me. 'Ah . . . yeah. That's it, Gorgeo. I really wanted to come in and see if your new business could help me show people how green I'm doing things these days. And after all the great ideas you had the last time I needed your help, I'd certainly like you involved this time, Gorgeo.'

Gorgeo.

I'm so, so sorry you had to hear that.

It's what Robert always liked to call me. Not gorgeous. But *Gorgeo.*

I liked it when we first started dating. I thought it was cute. But now it just makes my Gorgeo rise, threatening to deposit my breakfast all over the office floor.

And look at poor Nolan! Look how bamboozled he is!

That's the effect Robert has on people. He comes at you like a bull in a china shop, and you have no choice but to capitulate. It doesn't help that he's six foot three, and covered in the kind of muscle you can only get by staring at yourself in the gym mirror for years on end.

No wonder Nolan took the meeting – if Robert 'insisted' on it. He *insisted* on dating me for six months, and I let him do that, didn't I?

And Nolan is a polite, decent man. He probably tried to steer Robert away in a professional, calm manner – which would have worked with my ex about as well as trying to stop a hurricane with a leaf blower.

I look from Robert's nonchalant manspread in one chair, to Nolan's tight, anxious body language in the other, and know what I have to do.

I will not let my stupid ex-boyfriend bully my lovely new boyfriend into anything.

I *won't!*

I fold my arms and stare Robert Ainslie Blake down. I'm going to be the one doing the insisting today.

'Robert, I don't think there's anything we can do for you at Viridian PR,' I tell him, in no uncertain terms. 'You terminated your relationship with the company in its previous guise in a way that was highly detrimental to its continued existence. I see no reason to entrust our services to you again, for fear of the same result.'

I know I'm treading on Nolan's toes here, but I am incensed about this pig of a man thinking he can walk back in here and get us to do his bidding again.

Nolan looks quite taken aback. Robert just gives me that stupid smug smile again.

He then gets out of the chair languidly.

Robert does everything languidly.

The bastard even had sex *languidly* – something that should be completely impossible. You always kind of felt like he was doing you some kind of favour.

Robert holds out his hands. 'Hey, hey. It's fine, Gorgeo.'

'Please don't call me that.'

He rolls his eyes. 'Okay, okay . . . It's *fine*, yeah? It was a bad idea to come here, I see that, yeah?' He looks over at Nolan. 'Not the right time for it, don't you think, Reecey?'

Reecey's look of irritation has returned, not least because he's just been called *Reecey*, I shouldn't wonder. 'No. Not the right time *at all*,' he replies, also rising from his seat.

'Cool, cool,' Robert says, with a languorous nod. 'Time for me to get out of Dodge then, yeah?'

'Yeah,' I say, fixing him with a stare of purest disgust.

He sees the expression on my face and actually backs away a bit, looking a little perturbed. By the time he gets to the door, the smug smile is back though – because it always is. The fucker will probably die with that smug smile on his face, and his corpse will look languid in the box, of that I have no doubt.

'See you guys,' he tells us both, and walks nonchalantly out of the door, leaving chaos and confusion in his wake.

Once the door closes, I look back at Nolan, whose face is a picture.

Not a nice picture. It's one that screams confusion, irritation and shock in equal measure.

'I can't believe he came here,' I say to Nolan, walking over to him. 'I can't believe that bastard came here, actually thinking we'd work with him.'

Nolan nods. 'He didn't book a meeting, Ellie. He just *turned up at the door and expected to see me.*'

'Yes. That's how he operates. That's who he is.'

'I knew about him from the notes left by Peter, and all the stuff that was in the papers, but I had no idea he was . . . *that* bad.'

'No. I bet you didn't. Robert is a pretty awful human being, all round. Awful to people, awful to animals. Awful to everything but himself.'

Nolan gives me a look. There's something broken about it that will stay with me for the rest of my days.

'So, why did you *date him* then?' Nolan asks me, the look of betrayal writ large across his face.

◆ ◆ ◆

It turns out that one of the first things out of Robert's mouth was that I used to date him.

Can you imagine how hideous that was for Nolan? To know that the woman he was just starting a romance with had previously been in the clutches of an arsehole like that? To know that she actively and willingly shacked up with a person responsible for the death of at least three thousand birds and animals – all to throw up a block of flats for rich people to feel smug about living in?

I tried to explain, of course I did. I tried to tell Nolan every-thing I had planned on telling him in my lovely new hybrid Mercedes – but it all rang completely hollow, I know it did.

Oh, Nolan tried his best to understand where I was coming from. Tried his best to believe what I was saying about having turned over a new ecological leaf, after my time with the kids in Sean's class – but how can my words compete with six foot three of Robert Ainslie Blake?

He's a walking, talking, manspreading symbol of the lies I told to keep my job, and nothing I could say or do in the two-hour conversation I had with Nolan in his office after Robert had left could do much to change that. By the end of it, Nolan *seemed* to accept what I was saying, but I could tell he wasn't sure about anything any more – about my commitment to Viridian's cause, or my commitment to him.

We ended the conversation by agreeing to talk about it again the next day.

I then went home and cried.

It felt like the most appropriate thing to do.

It's all just so bloody UNFAIR.

Just as I was about to handle things. Just as I was about to calmly and sensibly speak to Nolan about everything, in my new, shiny, super-green car – along comes Demonic bloody Rab to throw a manspreading spanner in the works!

No wonder I've been reduced to a frustrated blubbering mess.

My descent into teary-eyed misery is only interrupted when I get a phone call from Nadia, checking in on how I am. My abrupt departure from the office didn't go unnoticed, and she's worried about me, bless her.

'I'm so sorry, Ellie. I should have done more to stop you going in there. I just didn't have a chance to warn you properly,' she says apologetically, after I've answered the call.

'No, no. It's not your fault at all, Nadia,' I tell her, blowing my nose on a recycled tissue. 'I was so caught up in wanting to tell Nolan about my new car that you couldn't have done anything to stop me marching in there like that.' I pause, feeling my nails bite into my palm. 'God almighty, why did that bastard come back? Did he really think we'd want to have anything more to do with him?'

'That's Robert Ainslie Blake for you,' Nadia says. 'The man permanently thinks the world owes him something.'

'A kick in the testicles?'

This makes her laugh. 'Quite probably!'

The sound of Nadia's laughter brightens my dark mood for the briefest of moments, before I remember the hurt look on Nolan's face.

'How long was he in there for, Nadia? Before I turned up?' I ask.

'About half an hour or so,' she replies, making me grimace.

That would have been more than enough time for Robert to really get into the details of his past relationship with me. It would have been exactly the type of thing he would do. For Robert, conversations with other men largely consist of him bragging about his previous conquests – whether it be in work, love or sport – and I am very sad to say that I am one of those previous conquests, no matter how much it makes my skin crawl to think about it now.

Ugh.

And to think I was partially responsible for helping to rehabilitate Robert's reputation, after he mowed down all of those poor animals and plants! I should find that poor bloody natterjack toad, and offer him my most humble of apologies for ever putting him that close to the git.

'I'm frankly amazed Nolan still wants me in the job,' I say to Nadia in a flat tone.

'Why's that?'

'Well, we're supposed to be an environmentally friendly PR firm, Nadia – and I spent six months banging a man who thinks nothing of wrecking nature reserves.'

'But that was a long time ago, Ellie. Stop being so hard on yourself.'

'I was going to tell him, as well . . . Nolan, I mean. I was going to tell him about my dirty little Demonic Rab–shaped secret, I just never . . . never got the chance.'

Thanks to a greedy fat parrot, and my own lack of gumption.

'I think you're worrying a bit too much about it,' Nadia says, trying to comfort me. 'Nolan is a sensible guy, and he can see what a great job you're doing. I'm sure he's not going to hold a previous silly relationship against you, no matter how much you think he might. He's a good boss. And a sensible bloke. I think you'll be fine.'

But he's not just my boss! I want to scream at Nadia.

For a moment, I open my mouth to confess everything about the fact that Nolan and I have been dating . . . but then I close it again. Would Nadia be as sympathetic as she's being if she knew the truth? If she knew that I was making the same mistakes I did with Robert, by mixing business with pleasure?

I'm not sure. I'm really not.

Oh, great. Another load of guilt can be added to my shoulders. Not only do I feel terrible about my attitude towards the planet in times gone by, I now feel awful about not being honest with Nadia over my relationship with Nolan.

'I really am different!' I blurt down the phone.

'What do you mean?' Nadia replies, sounding more than a little taken aback by this sudden outburst.

'About the environment, Nadia! About the world around us!'

'Oh, okay.' I can't see the look on Nadia's face, but I'm pretty sure she wasn't expecting to hear me sound so shrill or urgent.

I don't think I managed to convince Nolan that I had turned over a new leaf, but I'm sure as hell going to make sure Nadia knows it.

'I've bought a new car!' I assure her. 'A super-green one! And I did a load of research online, so I know all the stuff I should have known before . . . all that stuff they talked about in Sean's class.'

'I'm sure you do,' she says to me, trying to calm me down a bit. She thinks I'm going overboard, I know she does. But Nadia doesn't realise what's really going on with me and Nolan – that it's not just about me trying to keep my boss happy.

It's about so much *more* than that.

'Getting up to speed on all this environmental stuff isn't easy,' Nadia says, in an attempt to placate me. 'We've all struggled with it a fair bit.'

'Yeah, I know,' I reply. 'It's just all those *kids*, Nadia. All the things they said . . .'

She's quiet for a moment, before speaking again. 'It hits you hard, doesn't it?'

'Yeah. It really does.'

'And that's why you're worried about Nolan knowing that you dated Robert. You don't want him thinking you don't really care about the environment. Because of your brother's class. Because of the things they said.'

Wow. How perceptive can you get?

'Exactly!' I say. 'That's exactly it!'

'Seriously, Ellie. Don't worry so much. Actions always speak louder than words, and Nolan's had weeks working with you now. The good job you've been doing overrides anything Robert Ainslie Blake could say or do.'

'Do you really think so?'

'Absolutely!'

God, I hope she's right.

'Thanks, Nadia,' I say to her with genuine gratitude. I still don't feel particularly great about the situation, but at least my nose and eyes have stopped streaming.

'No problem. Now, why don't you tell me all about that new car of yours? You hightailed it out of the office so fast, I never got a chance to see it.'

'Yeah, okay,' I say, reaching for the owner's manual.

I then proceed to bore Nadia senseless over the next fifteen minutes.

By the time the call ends, I'm pretty sure she knows more about Mercedes hybrid cars than she ever wanted or needed to. But it was very kind of her to just sit and listen to it all. I think she knew I needed to talk about something in a positive way, after all the previous negativity.

After I've put the phone down on Nadia, I sit back on the sofa and reflect on the events of the day with a slightly calmer head on my shoulders.

Detailing how effectively the reverse-parking sensors are calibrated will do that for you. It's a little hard to remain emotionally volatile when you're describing German automotive engineering. If you ever feel yourself about to have a panic attack, I thoroughly recommend reading the owner's manual of a new Mercedes. By the time you reach the page about how the climate control functions, you'll be perfectly fine again.

Robert Ainslie Blake drove an Italian sports car, you'll be deeply unsurprised to know.

I can't remember what make it was – it wasn't one of the famous ones, like Ferrari – but I do recall that it had a very long bonnet, and big rear-wheel arches. He loved that fucking car. He certainly spent an inordinate amount of time polishing it.

I close my eyes and rub them, trying to scour the memory of the car from my mind.

. . . trying to scour the memory of Robert Ainslie Blake from it, as well.

This is of course impossible, given that Robert is many, many things, but forgettable is not one of them. Much like a really, really bad case of diarrhoea is unforgettable. Or World War Two. Or that *Cats* movie, where they made Judi Dench do all those unspeakable things.

And I doubt Nolan Reece is going to forget about him any time soon, either.

Nor is he likely to forget about all the sordid details no doubt imparted to him about my relationship with Robert, over half an hour of hardcore manspreading – which could all spell the end for any future I might have with Nolan.

Nadia is probably right about my job. I doubt that's in any real danger thanks to Robert's revelations.

But my relationship with Nolan? That's an entirely different matter.

Damn you, Robert Ainslie Blake.

Damn you, your manspreading and your penis-shaped car to hell and back!

Chapter Nine

The Tale of the Nefarious Narwhal

This morning, when I got in to work, I went straight back into Nolan's office, and started babbling at him again about how much I had truly changed, and how he could trust me going forward, and how I *was* committed to Viridian and him, more than I could ever express in words.

'Okay, Ellie,' he tells me, holding up one hand. 'You don't have to keep explaining yourself to me.'

Oh, but I do, Nolan. I have to keep explaining myself to you until I die.

'I believe what you're saying,' he continues. 'I went home and thought about it a lot last night, and I think you've been a bit hard on yourself.'

'Do you?'

'Yes. Okay, you weren't honest about things to begin with, but you were trying to keep your job.'

'Yes! Yes I was!'

'And you've done such a good job ever since. I find it hard to believe you don't care about the environment.'

'That's right!'

Nolan's face darkens a little. 'I just wish you'd mentioned your previous relationship with that . . . man.'

'I know! I know! I'm sorry, Nolan! I really am!' My knees feel like they want to buckle, just so I can get down on them and beg.

'Can you promise me you'll be honest and open with me from now on?'

'Of course!'

He nods. 'Then let's try not to worry about it any more.'

'You forgive me?'

He looks a little awkward. 'Yes. Yes, of course I do.'

'Oh God, thank you!' I say, eyes filling with tears. I take a step towards him . . . but he backs away from me as I do so. My heart sinks.

Nolan may say he has forgiven me, but I'm not entirely sure he believes it himself.

'Shall we . . . shall we get to work?' he says, going around to sit back in the chair behind his desk – subconsciously putting a large, solid barrier between us.

'Um. Yes, yes. Okay,' I reply, the taste of ashes in my mouth.

I also sit down, trying to switch my brain into work mode again. This has been an easy thing for me to do in the past, when things were going well with Nolan.

It most certainly is not easy now.

All I want to do is make things right with him again. All I want is for things to go back to the way they were.

I want to know that he forgives me *properly* . . . in a way that doesn't make him want to back away from me, and put a desk between us.

'I'd like to discuss World Action Today,' Nolan says in a matter-of-fact voice.

My shoulders slump a little.

Okay.

That's the way it is for now, then . . .

'World Action Today?' I say, trying to mirror his matter-of-factness, and probably failing miserably.

'Yes. They're holding an event tomorrow at the seafront. I've managed to book us in a meeting with their CEO just before it kicks off. I was going to go down there and speak to her myself, but I've now got another important matter to take care of, so I was hoping . . .'

'I'll do it!' I immediately reply.

I feel an overwhelming desire to do just about anything for Nolan right now. To make him happy with me again.

'Okay, thank you so much,' he replies, and actually smiles.

'No problem! No problem at all!'

I try to keep the desperate tone out of my voice – but I *am* desperate. Desperate for Nolan's full and proper forgiveness. And desperate to prove that I have turned over a new leaf, and that I am now fully on board with Viridian's ecological cause.

This visit to the World Action Today event sounds like the absolute ideal way for me to accomplish this. It's the perfect opportunity to prove my worth to Nolan. To get back in his good books . . . and to get *him* back.

Actions speak louder than words, after all. And me smooth-talking the World Action Today CEO into coming on board with us is the action that I definitely need to take.

I swear to whatever gods may be tuning in to have a laugh at my expense – I'm going to win back whatever trust Nolan may have lost in me thanks to Robert Ainslie Blake's conversation with him. I bloody well *am*.

The first step in doing that is getting to know the good people of World Action Today, and their sponsors, Bio-Plast Engineering.

WAT are a small but firmly established charity that specialise in highlighting the dangers and destruction that plastic causes to our world – most notably in the ocean. Bio-Plast Engineering are leading the way in developing biodegradable plastics. The synergy between the two is obvious.

And rest assured, I will not be using the word 'synergy' again, and I apologise for even bringing it up once. It's one of those buzz-words that make me want to tear every follicle of my hair out, and every time it spills out of my mouth I want to punch myself for it. If I ever utter the word 'holistic', you have my permission to hunt me down and do terrible things upon my person.

Regardless of that, Bio-Plast have deep enough pockets to help WAT stage a big, public event close to the sea. It will be a three-mile march along the road that parallels the seafront, undulating up and down the chalk hills that lie just behind it.

WAT want to spread the word about their cause by entertain-ing and informing the public, rather than lecturing at them, which is a refreshing and positive change from Bandy's hectoring of pass-ers-by at Whitehaven.

There's even going to be people in fancy dress, and a steel band – along with some jugglers, fire breathers and stilt walkers to bring the whole thing to life in a celebratory manner.

On Saturday morning I get to the location of where the march is starting – outside a pub called The Happy Seahorse – about an hour before it's due to kick off. I can already see lots of people lin-ing the route, so they've clearly done a good job of organising the march. The weather is typically British – grey, damp and about three weeks into a course of antidepressants – so it's testament to the effectiveness of the organisers that so many people have come along.

The CEO of World Action Today is a well presented woman in her mid-forties called Helen Carmichael. I've been told I will find

Helen ensconced in a sizeable motorhome that's been converted into an office space, with the WAT logo on the side. It's parked a few yards away from the start line of the march, which has been demarked by a large, very professionally produced banner hung over the road.

There are a lot of people engaged in frenzied activity around the start line, including lots of volunteers in WAT/Bio-Plast T-shirts, those circus acts I mentioned, the steel band, several people dressed in outlandish foam costumes made to look like plastic bottles, and one very large carnival float that has a massive tarpaulin over it, covering what's beneath.

All very interesting, and all very exciting.

I go into the motorhome, marvelling at the size and scope of today's event, and see Helen Carmichael stood in the centre, at a small desk. She's talking on the phone with a couple of volunteers buzzing around her, both wearing WAT T-shirts and one in dungarees. Looking at this busy tableau, I instantly know that Helen Carmichael is the type of woman I want to be when I grow up.

You ever met anyone that just *exudes* competence? The kind of person that walks into a room and immediately takes charge – sometimes accidentally, sometimes deliberately?

Helen Carmichael strikes me as just such a person, before I've even said one word to her.

I unconsciously smooth down the front of my business jacket as I approach. I'm pleased I decided to go semi-formal this morning. I'm not in trouser-suit territory, but the black jacket is crisp, the dark-blue cashmere roll neck is austere, businesslike and the most expensive item of clothing I own, and the jeans are sensible and smart. I even have my hair tied back in a sharp ponytail.

Compared to Helen Carmichael though, I look like I've just stepped out of the bath.

She's wearing a suit with shoulder pads so precise she must use a spirit level in the morning. The suit itself is bright red, and therefore there's no way she should be able to pull it off. If I tried, I'd look like a clown at a job interview. No such issues for Helen Carmichael, though. And the precision with which she's applied her make-up is, quite frankly, terrifying. I study her face as I walk up to her, and can see no blemishes or smudges whatsoever. Her black hair is glossy and shiny, and she has a fringe that sits just above her meticulously plucked eyebrows and is straighter than a sobered-up horizon.

I don't know why the hell this woman would even begin to consider the idea of hiring a PR firm; it's quite clear she could just order the entire country to do whatever she said, and they'd fall into line without a moment's thought.

I must impress this person. I must impress this person in ways that they have never been impressed before. Then I'll get World Action Today's business, and Nolan will see how I am truly committed to our cause.

'Good morning!' I say crisply to Helen Carmichael as she puts her phone down, having concluded the call. I thrust out a hand as well.

'Eleanor Cooke?' she replies, taking my hand and pumping it up and down – once and once only.

'Buh?'

'You're Eleanor Cooke, correct?'

'Yes, yes, that's me!' I tell her, marvelling at just how straight that fringe truly is up close.

'Thank you for coming. Can I get you a drink?'

'Um . . . yes. A tea would be lovely.'

'Very well.' Helen turns to one of the volunteers. 'Emily, please get Miss Cooke a cup of tea.' Then she addresses the other one. 'Skye – I think we'll just go with the main route. If they say the parked cars will be cleared, I believe them. If there are any problems, I'll take it up with the council afterwards.'

Both Emily and Skye nod and go about their respective tasks, moving past me to disappear from the motorhome, leaving Helen and me alone.

'So many things to organise on a day like today,' Helen says.

'It all looks like it's going well,' I assure her.

'Yes, it is,' she replies, clearly indicating that she needs my reassurance about as much as a fish needs an electric bicycle made out of bamboo.

Helen crosses her arms gracefully. 'Miss Cooke, I've agreed to this meeting because Nolan is someone I respect, but I'm not sure what service we really require from your agency.'

Nor am I any more, to be honest.

Part of me wants to just throw in my job and come work for Helen. I think I'd look good in one of those T-shirts.

'Well, thank you for seeing me at such a busy time.'

Helen raises an eyebrow. 'I would have preferred it in a quieter period, but Nolan was quite insistent. I'd say he has a lot of confidence in you, to send you down here on today of all days.'

I raise my chin slightly, and cock my head. 'And I'd say he was obviously very persuasive to get you to agree to it.'

My posture, tone and phrasing here are something of a gamble.

People like Helen Carmichael either want those around them to be compliant and easy to manage, or they enjoy challenge and conflict – as long as it's constructive. I'm betting that this woman is the latter type.

She regards me for a second, before a smile forms on her perfectly lipsticked mouth. 'Well, quite,' she finally says, with the most warmth in her voice I've detected since coming in here.

I heave a massive internal sigh of relief.

'Why don't we sit down and have a chat?' she suggests. 'I can only give you about ten minutes, but that will be time enough for you to let me know what you can do for us.'

'Oh yes, it absolutely will,' I reply, tucking myself into the seat behind the motorhome's desk, as Helen sits opposite me.

Emily the volunteer brings me my tea, and I thank her and take a small sip of it, before beginning my Viridian PR sales pitch.

The next ten minutes are intense. Helen Carmichael is forensic in her examination. Her questions are as crisp as her suit, and she never takes her eyes off me. I feel like I'm being studied – which, of course, I am.

But I hold my own, and get the pitch across in a way that I am extremely happy with, given the audience. By the time I'm done, Helen looks quite pleased with what I've had to say. I feel like I've passed an exam.

'Well, you certainly do have a very good handle on your brief, Miss Cooke. Admirably professional,' she tells me. 'And your passion for tackling the climate emergency we all face is obvious.'

'Thank you,' I reply, smiling inwardly. As part of my pitch, I made a brief mention of my time spent with Sean's class, and how profound an experience it was for me. Business pitches never hurt from a little bit of a personal touch, I always find.

'You've certainly given me food for thought,' Helen continues, 'but I'm still not sure just how much of your company's services we actually need.'

Bugger. She's still wavering. I have to do more. I have to find a way to prove both my conviction about the environmental cause and my ability to go above and beyond to push World Action Today's agenda. I cannot leave here without a successful new relationship! I need it, to make sure the one I have with Nolan is put back on track!

A potential solution to this arrives with Skye the volunteer, in a very harried state, who bursts into the motorhome and rushes up to where we're sat.

'We've got a problem, Helen!' she says, red of face and wild of hair.

'What's the matter, Skye?'

'It's Deandra . . . she's got food poisoning, and can't wear the costume on the march!'

'What?'

'Deandra went and bought a punnet of whelks from that weird old man in the shack by the pier,' Skye explains in a rush. 'We all told her not to, but she was adamant about trying the local street food. And I said, "It's not like going to Wahaca on the South Bank, Deandra" . . . but she was insistent, and now she's in the women's toilets, throwing up!'

Helen's eyebrows knot. 'Can we get somebody to replace her? We really do need to use all four of the costumes to get value for our money.'

Skye looks heavenwards. 'Well, we could take Lolly off float management, I suppose . . . or we could get Calvin to do it.'

Helen arches an eyebrow again. 'Calvin is seventeen stone, Skye. He wouldn't fit in that costume if you gave him six months on the Atkins diet.' Helen's hand thumps the table in front of her in frustration. 'How annoying. Deandra should have known better . . . and now we have to move somebody around to fill in, which will throw my personnel charts off for the appraisal.'

'I'll do it.'

Yes.

That's me speaking.

I'm as surprised about it as you are.

'I beg your pardon?' Helen says, looking at me again.

'I'll wear your costume for you,' I repeat. 'I'd be happy to.'

Because it's *perfect*, isn't it?

Helen Carmichael here has a problem – one I can help her with. Volunteering to help her out with the parade will show just how valuable I can be to her, and will surely grease the wheels even more for her coming on board with Viridian PR.

'You want to wear our single-use plastic bottle costume, and hand out leaflets to the public?' Helen says, clearly stating what it is I'm letting myself in for.

'Yes. Why not? I'd like to help out. I've attended a protest with Warriors For The Planet before, so I'm no stranger to this kind of thing.'

'You have?' Helen seems quite taken aback.

'Yes. I was one of Padlo's bunch.'

This means nothing to her of course, but I sound pretty convincing about the whole thing, which I feel is all that's required at this juncture.

Helen looks at Skye. 'What do you think?'

Skye looks me up and down. 'Er . . . the suit is quite heavy.'

I wave a hand. 'It'll be fine. I'm stronger than I look.'

Obviously I'm *not*, but that desire to impress Helen Carmichael has taken hold to such an extent that I'm happily willing to lie about my physical prowess in order to seek her favour.

This is what being a man must feel like.

I'm not sure I could cope with it full-time. It must be horrific.

Skye shrugs her shoulders. 'It'd make life easier for all of us,' she concedes. 'Means we wouldn't have to pull anyone out of the job you've assigned for them.'

Helen looks at me gravely for a second, assessing this latest development.

'Alright, we would appreciate the help,' she eventually says. 'We'll have to further discuss any future relationship between World Action Today and Viridian PR at a later date.'

And there it is. She's not committing herself yet, but she's not shutting the door on us either. It'll just have to do for right now.

'There's an empty bedroom at the end of the motorhome,' Helen tells me. 'You can leave your jacket in there. Skye, go get the costume.'

'Yes, Helen,' Skye acknowledges, and beetles her way out of the motorhome again.

'And you're sure about this?' Helen then asks me, evidently still weighing up my motives.

'Absolutely. Glad to help out. Plastic pollution is a scourge we have to stop.'

'Yes. It most certainly is,' she replies.

I nod to Helen and get up from the table, making my way down to the small bedroom at the end of the narrow corridor and letting myself in.

Inside is a tiny single bed with no sheets on it. I take off my jacket, popping it on the bed for safekeeping.

'What the hell are you doing?' I whisper under my breath as I await Skye and the costume. 'Same thing we always do,' I reply in slight exasperation. 'Throw ourselves into something without considering the bloody consequences.'

There's a knock at the door, and I open it to find the entire corridor of the motorhome filled with light-blue foam. Behind this is Skye, who pushes herself into the bedroom. I have to step back against the rear wall, such is the size of the damn thing she's holding.

'Well, here it is,' she tells me. 'It's not hard to get on. You just open it up and slip it over your head. It's brand new. No one's had it on before, so it's nice and clean.' She regards me critically. 'Do you have anything on under that roll neck?'

'Um. Yeah. My bra.'

207

'Oh, okay. You'll want to take the sweater off. These things can get bloody hot. Dulcie's in the other one, and she's had to take off her shirt.'

'Okay.'

'I'll just leave it here for you. If you get into any difficulties, let me know.'

Skye drops the costume to the ground and beats a hasty retreat.

The last thing I want to do is take off my sweater, but I guess I'd better do as she says. I don't want to get the roll neck sweaty and dirty. It cost me an endlessly stupid amount of money, and I have no desire to ruin it.

I whip it off, shivering a little in the cool of the empty bedroom.

Then I pick up the heavy foam costume and attempt to put it on. At first I have some issues, given the tight space I am occupying, but with a little wriggling and manoeuvring, I successfully get the silly thing on, poking my head out of the hole at the front, to complete the fitting.

I know how ridiculous I must look, as I saw the others dressed up like me (including this Dulcie person, no doubt) when I came over to speak to Helen Carmichael. The costume is a big blue foam representation of a single-use plastic bottle, complete with fake label on the front. My arms stick out from the sides, my legs stick out from the bottom, and my head pokes out from a hole just below the bottle cap. The damn thing is big, round and annoyingly heavy.

This had better be worth my time. This had better lead to Helen Carmichael agreeing to work with Viridian. This had better show Nolan just how different I am from the person he first met.

I fumble open the door again, to find Skye just outside waiting for me.

'Ah, good. You're all set. Well done,' she says to me. 'We'll just get you out of here and over to the start of the march. We're kicking off really soon.'

'Okay,' I reply, already feeling the heat start to ratchet up. Hopefully it'll be cooler outside.

Skye turns around and walks back up the corridor, allowing me to follow. This is quite difficult, as I have to squeeze the awkward foam along the narrow passage, keeping my head ducked so I don't keep clonking the bottle cap on the ceiling.

I get to the front door of the motorhome and look at Helen Carmichael – who, for the first time today, has a smile on her face. It's not a big one, but it's definitely there. I get the impression that this is Helen's equivalent of laughing her arse off.

'Off I go then,' I say cheerily, pushing the foam away from my chin, where it's started to get a little tight.

'Yes, indeed,' Helen says. 'Off you go.'

I let out an involuntary nervous chuckle, give her a dubious smile and push my way out into the open air.

Thank God it is quite a cold day, as I'm already starting to sweat, just from the exertion of getting out of the bloody motorhome. Christ knows what I'm going to be like on the parade.

Speaking of which, everything has moved on apace since I went in to speak to Helen. Everyone involved is now lined up in the street below that massive banner, and the crowd has grown a huge amount in both size and excitement level. This is probably because everyone's waiting to see what's under that giant tarpaulin, which has yet to be thrown off the float.

'Come on!' Skye implores me. 'It's all about to kick off, and we need to get you in place with everyone else!'

'Er . . . what exactly am I supposed to be doing?' I reply, as Skye grabs a hold of the foam just below my left arm, and starts propelling me towards the rest of the parade. This is probably a question I should have asked long before now.

'You just have to walk along, talk to the crowd and hand out leaflets,' she tells me.

'Leaflets?' I ask, trying my hardest not to fall over as Skye continues to drag me towards the start line. The bottom of the bottle costume is quite restrictive, and I can't open my legs very wide. This makes hurrying exceptionally difficult.

'Yes! Here!' she says, and yanks out a large stack of leaflets from one of her large dungaree pockets. She hands them over to me, and I take a look at the top one as we reach the start line of the parade.

STOP THE PLASTIC TIDE! it says in big bold blue letters. *All the ways YOU can help us save our oceans – in conjunction with World Action Today and Bio-Plast Engineering.*

Ah, right. This will be easy enough. Just wobble along the road, stuff some leaflets into people's hands and try not to fall over. And if I can hand enough of them out, then maybe it *could* make a difference. Maybe some people will actually read what's on them, and go away from this with their minds changed.

We can but hope, eh?

'Good!' Skye exclaims with relief. 'We've made it. Now all you have to do is follow the lead of the others in the same costumes.' She indicates the three other volunteers dressed in the same foam bottles as me. They all nod gravely at me, and I nod gravely back at them. It's like we're all members of a secret society or something. One that hasn't been going very long, and largely involves people who are also undergoing psychiatric treatment.

Over a loud and somewhat obnoxious tannoy, a voice booms out across the crowd. 'Okay! It's almost time for the parade to start!' cries a disembodied male voice. I look around to find the source, but there's just too much commotion and too many bodies around for me to see. 'But first, it's what you've all been waiting for – the grand unveiling of the narwhal!'

A roar of approval erupts from the crowd. Never have I heard so much excitement about an endangered sea creature. Not since I had to watch *Finding Nemo* with my brother's kids.

I watch as several strong-looking WAT volunteers go and take up a corner of the tarpaulin each. Skye joins them to help.

She gives them all a three-count, and to the accompaniment of Beethoven's 'Ode to Joy' blaring out from that bloody loud tannoy, the tarpaulin is pulled slowly off the float underneath, to the cheers and applause of everyone here gathered.

Except me. I'm too disorientated by recent events to do anything other than just stare. Besides, clapping might be a bit difficult in this costume, as the foam is so thick I can barely bring my hands together.

Finally, the star of the parade is revealed – a bloody enormous narwhal made out of what looks like thousands upon thousands of plastic bottles. It sits atop a long, low carnival float that is powered from the back by a grumpy-looking old man in a small cockpit-like arrangement just under and to the left of the narwhal's enormous tail.

The giant sea mammal is an incredibly impressive bit of modern sculpture, while at the same time being the most disheartening thing I think I've ever seen. That much plastic together in one place is quite stomach-churning.

The narwhal's massive front tusk protrudes out over the parade's start line, and a sign is hung on its side that reads: *Placcy the Plastic Narwhal – made from the amount of bottles that go into our oceans every second.*

Fuck off.

That can't be true.

There are *tens of thousands* of plastic bottles in that narwhal. It must weigh a *tonne*. There's no way that figure can be accurate!

The kids in Sean's class would know it's true, Ellie. So you should too.

Jesus Christ.

I'm so glad I only ever carry a reusable bottle around with me these days, otherwise the guilt would be eating me up.

'Okay, everyone! Let's start the countdown to the beginning of our fantastic parade!' the tannoy voice blares. 'All organised by the wonderful charity, World Action Today, and sponsored by Bio-Plast Engineering – *making your future the job of our present!*'

I grimace.

That's a pretty awful tagline you've got there, lads. About as catchy as a snapped fishing hook.

The tannoy voice starts a five-second countdown, as the circus acts and steel band all line up beside the narwhal, ready to get proceedings underway. I line up just behind them with my fellow foam bottle-heads. The volunteers in T-shirts surround us as we do, and I am instantly put in mind of the start of a marathon. Possibly the most garish, camp and ridiculous marathon in human history, that is.

'Five! Four! Three! Two! One!' tannoy man cries, heralding the start of our wonderful parade. The stilt walkers, fire breathers and jugglers all start moving forward, with Placcy the Narwhal just behind them, being piloted by that grumpy old man, who looks like he'd rather be anywhere else but on a cold, drizzly road adjacent to the grey beachfront to our collective left. The steel band also start playing at a tinnitus-inducing volume. I'm glad my ears are covered in all this foam.

Thankfully, the pace is as slow as you'd expect, given that the main attraction is a quarter-tonne of narwhal-shaped plastic. I am able to keep up perfectly fine, despite the restrictions on my leg movements.

The crowd are unendingly delighted that things have finally got underway, as you'd imagine.

I'm not so sure I am, as I am now forced to plaster a happy smile across my face, while thrusting leaflets into the hands of people who probably just want to enjoy the circus acts, and not be reminded that everyone is only here because we're royally fucking up our planet. But they do need to be reminded. They just do.

Regardless, it's nice to see so many people out here watching all of us go by. It really is a testament to how effective Helen Carmichael is. Getting a horde of human beings to come to one place and watch something is extremely difficult, unless your name happens to be Taylor Swift or Manchester United. Without celebrity or sporting prowess, getting the public to turn up to watch you is never a simple task. It takes a lot of planning, thought and talent.

If I'm going to get Helen to come on board with Viridian PR, I need to make sure that she knows we can offer her something more than she can accomplish herself. That starts with making the best job possible of being a big foam bottle.

But am I doing a good enough job of that right now? Okay, I am waddling along in the silly foam suit, handing out leaflets as I've been told, but I can't say I'm really doing anything to distinguish myself from the others engaged in a similar activity. I'm not really *standing out from the crowd*. Looking around, I can see that the other bottle-wearers are a lot more animated and excited than I am. But then, they probably should be, given that they've been preparing for this parade for ages, instead of being thrust into it at the last minute.

Look at them dance and caper! The bloke on the other side of the narwhal is going as far as playing with the kids he passes, ruffling their hair and singing songs at them. What a *bastard*. He's making me look deeply pedestrian and dull by comparison. I must do something to up my game here . . . otherwise my contribution will be forgettable, and that might not bode well for my chances of convincing Helen Carmichael that Viridian PR is the right company for her to work with!

. . . quite how I've reached the opinion that I need to dance around in a foam fancy-dress costume to persuade someone to go into business with me, I can't quite fathom. I have become caught up in the moment to such an extent that rationality has begun to desert me somewhat. I am so keen to prove to Nolan that I am a changed person that I am willing to do some quite ridiculous and extraordinary things to accomplish it.

I must stand out from the crowd!

But how? I can't fire breathe, juggle or walk on stilts – and I'm not sure I'm comfortable enough yet with The Sticky Things to go and interact with them.

I *have* to think of something else to get myself out in front.

Out in front.

That's it! If I can get myself out in front of the rest of the parade, then surely I'll be noticed!

Helen will be super impressed!

Not only will I have volunteered to wear the suit in a show of extreme solidarity, I will also have distinguished myself – by calling even greater attention to the evils of single-use plastic bottles by gyrating around at the head of the parade!

Hah! Take that, bloke on the other side and your stupid hair-ruffling!

There's every chance having my head squeezed through the hole in this foam has cut off the circulation to my brain. That's the only way I can justify this current train of thought.

With a plan fixed firmly in my mind, I start to bop and shuck my way towards the patch of road in front of the narwhal. As I pass the guy piloting the large plastic mammal, I can see that his misery has compounded itself even further in the half-mile or so that we've been going along the road. Poor chap. What he needs is the thrill of watching a bopping bottle.

And he's about to bloody well get it!

Increasing my pace so my little legs are motoring away under the costume, I speed past a fire breather, a couple of the steel band, and the legs of one of the stilt walkers, emerging from between them to come alongside Placcy the Narwhal's long pointy tusk.

As I do this, the float starts to power up a slight incline in the road, forcing me to puff and blow a bit to get ahead of the end of the tusk, and take up my place at the head of the march.

Once there, I look around to see that the crowd is looking at me with a degree of confusion on their faces. As well they might. A plastic bottle has just erupted from the rest of the parade like it thinks it's the star of the show. But there's nothing to distinguish it from the rest of its foamy blue brethren, so why the special attention?

I have no doubt that my fellow parade members are looking just as confused, given that this is not part of the plan. I bet Mr Hair Ruffler is particularly put out.

Shit.

What have I done?

What am I *doing*?

I didn't really think this whole thing through, and now I either have to do something big and bold enough to justify this move to front and centre, or I have to slink back to my previous position, with my tail metaphorically between my legs.

What would Helen Carmichael do?

What would Nolan Reece do?

What would a version of Ellie Cooke not desperate to impress do?

Fucked if I know.

I guess I'll just start doing the Macarena.

Whether, in the grand scheme of things, doing the Macarena dressed as a foam bottle in front of a giant plastic narwhal is the greatest strategy ever invented, I will leave you to decide. It's probably not up there with the Roman conquest of Britain. But my options are limited here, and I can't remember all the moves from the Whigfield 'Saturday Night' dance.

Also, I'm not really doing the Macarena, because that dance involves a lot of rhythmically wiggling your hips from side to side in time to the music. This is virtually impossible to accomplish in a large foam bottle suit, so I just look like I'm having a seizure – possibly brought on by an allergic reaction to the foam.

I then try to do the bit of the dance where you put your hands up on the back of your head, but I can't get my arms above shoulder height, so they just stick out in front of me. Therefore, I now look like I'm a *zombie* having a seizure.

Fucking hell. I'd better switch this up before they send in the emergency services.

Let's try the Time Warp.

This, if anything, is even harder than the Macarena in this bloody suit.

The jump to the left is difficult.

The step to the right is a chore.

Putting my hands on my hips is impossible, and have you ever tried bringing your knees in tight while trying to stay ahead of a plastic narwhal tusk?

Oh God. Here comes the pelvic thrust.

And I think I really am going insane.

As I crest the top of the long, low hill that the road rolls over, I am thrusting my hips out in front of me, like some invisible force is jerking me along the street towards oblivion.

I look like I'm trying to shag the horizon.

Do I think this will impress Helen Carmichael?

Quite possibly not.

Maybe I'll tell her and the rest of World Action Today that my dance is interpretive. That I'm trying to describe the plight of our oceans by thrusting my crotch out towards the heavens. That jumping to the left and stepping to the right are in fact my way of highlighting how our governments are sidestepping the issue of plastic waste.

Yes, that sounds convincing.

Very convincing indeed . . .

At least the crowd are having a good time.

They certainly sound like they are, anyway. What with all the laughing and pointing.

I wave back at them, momentarily halting my revival of late twentieth century novelty dances to take in the approval of my audience.

Placcy the Narwhal clearly does not approve of my dancing though, as he chooses this moment to poke me between the shoulders with his tusk.

'Oi! Bloody hell!' I exclaim, as I am pushed forward. Lucky I've got all this padding, otherwise that might have hurt!

This just makes the crowd laugh even more. I'm not laughing, though. I nearly went tumbling to the ground then.

Ignoring the temporary narwhalian interruption, I continue to Time Warp down the slight incline of the hill, now playing to the crowd for all I am worth.

Unfortunately, I think I'm losing them, as they appear to have stopped laughing at me, and are turning their attention to the bloody narwhal behind me.

Fuck it. I just can't compete with a quarter-tonne of plast—

The tusk prods me in the back again, this time a little harder. I am nearly sent flying, and my feet have to do some fancy footwork to maintain my balance.

'What the hell are you doing?!' I wail, stumbling forward, and turn around to see what the hell is going on.

The sight that greets me is one I won't forget for a very long time.

The rest of the parade are now a good twenty feet behind me. The only thing that is keeping pace with me is Placcy the Narwhal.

And when I say Placcy the Narwhal is the only thing still with me, I mean it – because when I look back past its massive plastic body, I can see that some of the jugglers, fire breathers and volunteers are all crowded around the grumpy old man who was piloting the float Placcy sits upon.

He's no longer in control of the float though, because he's lying face up on the concrete.

This means that nobody is piloting Placcy any more.

And he's on a slope going downwards. With me just in front of him, close to the business end of his tusk.

. . . and his speed is *increasing*.

I watch as the tusk comes spearing towards me with ever-growing momentum. Suddenly, I'm gripped by sheer and abject panic. This is not a surprise, as having ten thousand plastic bottles wrought into the shape of an endangered sea creature coming inexorably at you is not something the human brain is well equipped to deal with.

I can't run away in this suit! I can't run at all! I can barely do the fucking Time Warp!

The narwhal is going to get me!

I'm going to be skewered on the end of its tusk!

Aaaargh! I have to get away from it! I have to get away!

I turn away from Placcy's horrible pointy front end and start to shuffle along the road, determined not to be run through by a bunch of melted-down Evian bottles.

YES.

I know I could just run to the LEFT OR RIGHT, but I'm having a massive panic attack, and common sense has completely deserted me, okay?

When I feel the tusk once again brush my shoulders, I redouble my efforts to increase my speed. This is helped by the downward incline of the hill, but that also increases Placcy's pace as well, keeping us locked in our now-frenzied chase along the seafront.

'Stop the narwhal!' I scream to anyone who will listen. I am the first human being to scream this sentence since the last Victorian expedition to the Arctic Circle, some one hundred and thirty years ago. That was probably the last time that narwhals posed any kind of threat to humanity. Since then, it's been one-way traffic in the other direction.

Ah.

Perhaps this is the point.

Maybe Placcy is attempting to take revenge upon humanity – currently being represented by yours truly covered in foam rubber. He will chase me down relentlessly, until that tusk goes up my backside, in order to gain some sort of recompense for all of the pain and suffering we've caused his seaborne brethren.

I am to be the sacrifice that turns the tide, Placcy is no doubt thinking.

Or maybe he just can't stand the fucking Time Warp.

One or the other.

The shallow hill we're on reaches its bottom, to be replaced by level ground, which should improve my situation considerably, but I'm too far gone with panic to realise it.

'Help me!' I cry out to the crowd, desperation writ large across my face. They of course respond with nothing but befuddlement (and a few giggles from the highly entertained children), given that they know damn well I should just run off to one side to end my torment. If only one of the bastards would actually vocalise this opinion, I might stand a chance of surviving Placcy the Narwhal's implacable attack.

I should have known he'd be implacable. The clue's in the name.

But no such helpful comment transpires, so I continue to jiggle forward, fighting against both the foam around my legs and my rapidly failing strength.

Both give out about ten yards later, on the now level ground.

'Aaaargh!' I wail, as my tired legs finally get entangled in one another, and I collapse to the tarmac. This would be extremely painful, were it not for the fact that I am ensconced in a load of soft, yielding foam. Good job too, as otherwise I would have roy-ally face-planted, and probably broken my nose. I am spared this tragedy by my single-use plastic-bottle suit – my nose just lightly brushing the road's surface before bouncing away again.

And now I am a stranded turtle, waving my ineffectual arms and legs around as death bears down on me from behind. This is a far, far more convincing impression of a dying animal than I gave at the Worriors For The Plonet demonstration. I have truly upped my game.

I let out a low and exhausted wail of terror as I await my hid-eous fate. Placcy is about to run roughshod over me, and there's not a damn thing I can do about it.

I close my eyes, and await my doom.

When said doom doesn't materialise within the next twenty seconds, I open my eyes again, and roll over on to my back. With arms that will barely hold my weight, I sit myself up a little, to see that Placcy the Narwhal has ground to a halt a good ten feet behind me.

The children on the ground are in hysterics, and even some of the adults are having a good old chuckle at my expense.

I don't care. I'm not a narwhal shish kebab. That's all that matters to me.

Several volunteers have made it to Placcy's float, and are securing it to prevent further out-of-control shenanigans. One of them walks over to where I am still spreadeagled on the road. It's Skye.

'Are you alright?' she asks, looking down at me with a half-concerned, half-bemused expression on her face.

I gaze back up at her for a moment, trying to think of the most appropriate thing to say.

Am I alright?

I'm not physically harmed, that much is true – but I have been mentally traumatised by a narwhal, and I'm so knackered I can barely raise my head.

'Been better, Skye,' I confess. 'Been worse.'

That about covers it.

Skye looks around at the crowd, who are all looking somewhat disappointed that the show has apparently come to an end. They were vastly enjoying the woman in the rubber suit being pursued by the narwhal, it's plain to see. And why not? It truly is 'something you don't see every day'.

Or every century for that matter. Not since the one that featured Victorians on jollies up to the North Pole at regular intervals.

◆ ◆ ◆

Helen Carmichael's expression is extremely hard to read.

This is probably the case most of the time, but especially applies in circumstances such as this. When presented with a woman who has just partially ruined your parade by doing the Macarena while dressed as a plastic bottle, it's probably best advised to remain inscrutable.

I should probably say something.

'Is the man who was driving the float going to be okay?'

Helen takes a breath. 'Yes,' she replies blandly. 'He's been taken to hospital, but it appears he just fainted.'

'Aah . . . that's good.'

'The narwhal is undamaged.'

'Aah . . . also good.' I give Helen a shy but heartfelt thumbs up. It's probably the least I can do.

The parade went on without me. In fact, it's probably still going on as we speak. We all felt it best that I wasn't involved any more. Partly because I was too tired to wear the costume, but partly because nobody wants to see me attempt a fucking moonwalk – me included.

So I find myself back in the motorhome, back in my own clothes, and back under the gaze of Helen Carmichael.

Gulp.

'And you are . . . *okay?*' Helen asks me. There's a lot going on in that slight pause.

'Yes. I'm fine. A little tired, and a little embarrassed, but fine otherwise.'

'Well, you certainly . . . threw yourself into it, didn't you?' Her eyebrow doesn't quite arch, but it wants to. It can barely resist the temptation.

'I did.' I contrive to look apologetic. 'I'm sorry for it not quite going to plan.'

And there goes the eyebrow. It just couldn't help itself.

'One wonders what the plan *was*, Miss Cooke,' the woman under the eyebrow replies. 'I'm told you were . . . *enthusiastic* about being at the front of the parade.'

'Um . . . yes. I really wanted to do my part.'

If her eyebrow arches any more, it will leave her forehead and go off to live an independent life somewhere on the ceiling of this motorhome.

'Indeed.' Helen sits up straight. I get the impression that my time with her is coming rapidly to an end. 'Well, I certainly can't fault your enthusiasm, or your passion,' she tells me.

I nod a bit meekly. I don't want to do this, but Helen Carmichael brings out the meek in me, what can I say.

'Look, Miss Cooke,' she continues, 'I can see you're very keen, and willing to go to a great deal of effort if something is important to you . . . I admire that. And despite what happened with your . . . er . . . performance out there today, I am not suggesting I do not see the benefits of working with a company like Viridian PR. Your pitch was very good. But I have to think carefully about who we get into business with here at World Action Today. I'm sure you understand.'

'I do. I really do,' I say, somewhat taken aback. I'm pretty sure there was a compliment in there somewhere.

'Good. Then we'll part on good terms, and I will be in touch shortly with a decision.'

Helen immediately stands and offers me a hand to shake. The meeting is most definitely over.

I take her hand, and then take my leave.

Outside, I stand for a moment in front of the motorhome and take a very, very deep breath. What a very peculiar morning.

But! That sounded positive, didn't it? At least a bit?

Maybe my enthusiasm did get through. Maybe – despite my run-in with Placcy the Narwhal – I did just about enough to convince her that she can work with us. Maybe this will all work itself out.

And we would be a good place for her to come for her public relations. Viridian PR is *perfect* for her cause. She wants to save all the real Placcys of the world, and so do we!

I think back on the sign on Placcy the Plastic Narwhal that told me how many plastic bottles get dumped in the ocean every second, and my blood runs a little cold.

Yes. Viridian PR is the place she should come – despite my strange shenanigans today. I'm sure she'll realise that, being the intelligent, brilliant woman she quite clearly is.

I actually have something of a spring in my step as I go back to the car, which is unbelievable, given how tired my legs still are.

Yes. Things will be alright. We will get the business of World Action Today.

I will have done my job.

Helen Carmichael will say yes, and Nolan will be convinced that I really am totally committed to the environmental cause. I will win his approval back.

I've just tried to do the Macarena in front of hundreds of people, dressed in a foam bottle costume, and I did it *willingly*. How could I fucking *not be committed to it*?

Three days later, Helen Carmichael said no.

The tale of the nefarious narwhal therefore ends in abject defeat.

. . . and with you probably humming 'The Time Warp'.

Chapter Ten

37 Seconds

My first failure for Viridian PR, then. The first time I've truly let Nolan Reece and the rest of the gang down.

None of them are particularly upset with me, it appears. In fact, when I told them all about how I managed to screw up getting Helen Carmichael's business, they didn't look upset at all. Most of them were trying not to laugh.

Nadia Macarena-ed her way around the office like a thing possessed when I told her about it. Then Joseph found 'The Time Warp' on Apple Music, and everybody joined in. We had to clear the desks out of the way.

I say 'we' because I did it too. I've learned in life that when you cock something up good and proper, it's probably best just to own it. Trying to run away from it just stresses you out even more.

But just because the rest of Viridian PR aren't that bothered with my failure, it doesn't mean *I'm* okay with it.

Alright, I couldn't have predicted being chased down the road by a giant plastic narwhal, but I didn't exactly display the best judgement in the lead-up, did I?

My desire to impress overrode my good sense, and look where it got me.

Nolan, bless him, wasn't angry. This almost made it *worse*. I think I would have liked a good, hard dressing-down. It might have made me feel a bit better, and would have got me to ease up on the self-recrimination a little.

As it stands though, I feel quite awful about the whole thing.

My attempt to get back into Nolan's good books has failed, and I'm having trouble dealing with that.

It's all so *frustrating*.

On the surface Nolan seems fine with me, but I can tell that he still has his doubts.

We've only seen each other at work. He hasn't once suggested we meet up socially. That is not a good sign for the ongoing health of a relationship, I'm sure you'll agree.

But he really has nothing to worry about . . . absolutely *nothing*.

I *am* the person I say I am now. The old Eleanor Cooke – the kind of girl who'd date a bastard like Robert Ainslie Blake, and wouldn't remember to take her bag-for-life shopping with her – is completely *gone*.

My conversion to the environmental cause has been all-encompassing. When once it was an abstract thing – a means to an end, rather than a goal in itself – it is now a vital and important part of my life.

The work I do, the people I meet – all of these things have changed my outlook on the world to such an extent that it's a wonder I ever felt differently.

Because how could you not be converted to the cause, when you are constantly exposed to all of the information there is about the climate crisis?

. . . proper information, I mean. Not stuff on Facebook or Twitter.

It's a little hard to deny something is going on when you have actual science types showing you actual independently verified data – rather than just trusting in a few memes, the opinions of politicians, and what @KevinTheSprout says in his Twitter feed about a vast conspiracy to destabilise the fossil fuel industry by the Israel lobby.

Kevin is neither an expert on climate change, nor a sprout. He should not be listened to.

But a lot of the clients we work with should be. They are universally in the businesses they are in because they've seen all that hard scientific and first-hand evidence. And it all rubs off on you, let me tell you.

It rubs off *hard*.

My flat now contains only ultra-low-energy LED light bulbs, which are never on when I'm not in the room. When I pop to Sainsbury's I use three hemp shopping bags, which I never forget to take with me – and I never buy anything wrapped in plastic when I get there. I'm not quite a full vegetarian just yet, but I'm almost at that point. I've put a stop to all paper-based communications from every utility company and service I have. I've started looking around second-hand clothes shops and on eBay, instead of heading to the high street. And I drive my hybrid Mercedes as carefully as I can, to keep any emissions I might still be making as low as possible.

I know I could do even more, but I think I've made one hell of a start.

At work, things continue apace.

The conversion I've undergone has made me even better at communicating with our client base. Despite the failure to get Helen

Carmichael's business, I am still motoring along quite nicely with the portfolios we have already – my work with the O'Hares at Veganthropy, Bandy and co. at Worriors For The Plonet, and Twelve-Year-Old Kyle from Hempawear is fun, exciting and extremely fulfilling.

Unfortunately, I have also become a right pain in the arse around the office because of my new-found environmentalism. I've severely restricted the use of paper, for instance. You can imagine how well that's gone down with a bunch of people who have to do a lot of admin.

I've also put in strict new regulations about leaving PCs and monitors on. They use a dreadful amount of energy, and making sure they're turned off at night is of paramount importance to me.

The fucking pot plants have never looked healthier. I've basically turned Young Adrian into a one-man watering machine. I'm actually thinking of getting an entire living wall installed down one side of the office, if I can work out how to afford it. It'll be like working in the middle of the Amazon rainforest. Just think of how *healthy* the air will be!

My work colleagues are taking this all with good grace, by and large. Partly because I'm their boss, and partly because they know what I'm like.

There was a tight incident with Nadia last week, when I had a moan about her buying a new top on ASOS. I pontificated to her about how much better it is for the environment to get second-hand stuff on eBay, rather than buying disposal first-hand fashion. She then reminded me that I used to spend half my wages on clothes in the ASOS sale, and I went away suitably chastened.

I made it up to her by buying her a voucher for eBay. I *think* she was pleased. It was a bit hard to tell.

By and large though, I do think all of my work colleagues have also become far more aware of the environment since we became Viridian PR.

Like I say . . . it rubs off *hard*.

Joseph and Amisha at first rolled their eyes when I berated them for leaving their monitors on at night, but now everything at their combined desk is switched off before they go out the door.

In fact, everyone is doing their bit now. I haven't really had to chivvy them along at all. And God bless them all for it. They really are a good bunch, and I am very proud to be part of this team.

So, the only real problem I have right now is my faltering relationship with Nolan.

To tell the truth, I think the problem is more the fact that I initially lied to him about my environmental credentials than it is about how green I am now. You'd be hard-pressed to think I was anything other than environmentally conscious, given how I've reshaped the office.

But I've lost Nolan's trust, and it's going to take a lot more effort on my part to get it back.

And I *do* want it back.

I like Nolan a hell of a lot – that much is obvious – and I don't want to think that one stupid meeting with Robert Ainslie Blake may have ruined our burgeoning relationship before it really had time to get going.

Actually, Nolan is not the only problem I have, of course. I also have to deal with the existential dread that the human race is slowly but inexorably destroying our entire planet out of greed and ignorance, but . . . one thing at a time, eh?

Also, there's Belgium to think about.

. . . sorry, the change of subject there was probably enough to give you whiplash. I have a tube of ibuprofen gel somewhere, if you need it.

But there *is* Belgium to think about, whether we like it or not.

More specifically, there's a *meeting* in Belgium to think about – one that's been planned for a couple of weeks now.

'So, you're okay with the travel arrangements for tomorrow, then? You're happy to take the train?' Nolan asks me, as he joins me by the ficus in his office. Previously, this has been the location of much passionate kissing. Not today though, unfortunately. And maybe not ever again, if I don't sort this silly situation out.

'Yeah, of course,' I tell him. 'It'd be bloody stupid for a company like ours to travel by plane. Especially when it's so easy to use more environmentally friendly transport.'

'I'm sorry I can't come with you,' Nolan says apologetically, as I examine the ficus for leaf mould.

Leaf mould can be a real problem, if you're not very careful about how you treat your pot plants. I have impressed this upon Young Adrian, in terms that brook no argument.

I'm feeling a little awkward in Nolan's company, for obvious reasons, so the ficus examination is saving me my blushes.

'I have some leads here I'd really like to chase up, which can't wait,' Nolan finishes, still looking remorseful about the sudden change of plans. 'Hope you're not mad with me.'

I wave a hand, to indicate that I'm not bothered in the slightest.

How could I possibly be *mad* at him? After everything that's happened?

And besides . . . I'm more than used to Nolan being out and about on his own, chasing up leads. Sometimes it feels like he's out of the office more than he's in it.

'It's fine, Nolan,' I tell him. 'Honestly. The meeting will be *easy*. Viridian's reputation already exceeds the other companies who will be there, in my opinion. I'm sure I can wangle the account all by myself. And a nice train ride across the European countryside? I'll love it.'

He nods and relaxes a little. 'Okay. That's good to hear,' he says, and smiles at me.

'Do you think . . . do you think when I get back, we could maybe go for a drink?' I ask, in a tentative voice. 'I've . . . I've missed you.'

'Ah . . . yeah. That'd be . . . that'd be nice,' he replies, but I wouldn't exactly say he looks overwhelmed with joy at the prospect. 'Let's have a chat about it when you get back, eh?'

'Okay, let's talk about it then.'

I instantly return to my examination of the non-existent ficus leaf mould. It's easier than looking into Nolan's eyes.

It will take me about four hours to reach the location of my meeting in the centre of Brussels. A swift taxi drive from the city's main train station will find me at the offices of Hergebruikt Ltd – a company that specialises in the recycling of old electronic components. They have just been blessed with a large grant from the EU, and are on the lookout for a new PR company.

Enter Eleanor Cooke, her smartest black suit, the most professional ponytail you've ever seen, a black suitcase full of winning arguments, and a look of confidence on her face that you could bottle and sell to the permanently anxious.

Things didn't go well with Helen Carmichael and World Action Today, but there is no fucking way in hell they are not going to go well with Hergebruikt Ltd.

I will be one of four PR companies pitching their talents and skills to the board of Hergebruikt, and I'm lucky enough to be the last one to speak, at 3 p.m. This means I can send them out with a pitch so brilliant, it will cast all others from their minds completely. I'll have half an hour to do my work – and that's more than enough time, as far as I'm concerned.

My first train of the day is late, but never mind – I have given myself ample time to reach my destination. I intend to arrive a good two hours early, so I can grab some lunch and do some last-minute preparation in a rather lovely-looking coffee shop I've identified on Google, close to Hergebruikt Ltd.

A few delays here and there have been fully planned for. I have contingency. Lots and lots of lovely, stress-relieving contingency.

That doesn't stop a small worm of stress burrowing its way into my mind as I stand on the platform awaiting the now twenty-minute-late train that will take me to London, from where the Eurostar will whisk me to the Continent in two shakes of a lamb's tail.

Who needs a plane?

The journey time may be a fair bit longer doing it this way, but at least I won't have to go through all the bother of negotiating a busy airport, and the security is far less onerous when you take the train. Also, none of that ear-popping stuff, or having to sit in other people's farts.

No, the benefits of staying on the ground (or under it, in the case of the Channel Tunnel) are many – and that's before we talk about how much better it is for the environment. I looked up the Eurostar's emission figures, and when compared to flying, I might as well be spending my day planting an entire deciduous forest while simultaneously hand-feeding a baby seal.

The train to London arrives, which calms that stress-worm down magnificently. I've still got more than enough time to reach the Eurostar before it leaves. I am somewhat dismayed to find that the thing is packed more solid than a tin of sardines, but I'm on board now, and on my way.

I push through the carriage, searching for a seat. As I do, the reaction of my fellow passengers breaks down thusly: 87 per cent don't look at me at all – as is right and proper on British public transport; 6 per cent of them give me a look of pity, because I am unable to find anywhere to sit; 2 per cent look guilty, which is an equally British response to seeing someone in such a situation; 3 per cent try to contain their smugness that they are seated and I am not; and the final 2 per cent look terrified that I'm about to try to throw them out of their hard-won seating.

All pretty much par for the course, then.

The only space I am able to find is outside the toilet, leaning against the window.

'Why is it so busy?' I ask a portly-looking man with a beard, whose thousand-yard stare isn't as fixed as everybody else's.

'They cancelled two services this morning,' he replies. 'Something to do with electrical problems.'

'Oh no,' I respond, hoping that this train does not suffer from the same issue at any point.

The next hour or so of my life is not what you could call pleasant.

Unless of course you enjoy the waft of excrement assailing your nostrils every time the toilet door opens and closes. If you do, I suggest seeking some kind of help at your earliest convenience – no pun intended.

You inadvertently learn a lot about the toilet habits of the great British public when you are forced to stand stock-still in front of a busy toilet for sixty minutes. The amount of people who take a shit in public is quite phenomenal. I couldn't do it if you paid me, especially not if the only thing between me and twenty other people was an automatic sliding door with a locking mechanism that is dubious in its efficiency, to say the least.

One poor lady discovers this about forty minutes into the journey, when she neglects to lock the door properly and is exposed to everyone else just as she is about to park her bottom on the toilet seat.

You see, the sliding doors on British trains are very precisely timed to open again just as you are parking your bottom on the toilet seat, if you don't lock them properly. Thousands of man-hours went into providing this very important service in the cause of public humiliation. There are only two objects in this world that keep absolute, perfect time – that atomic clock in Greenwich, and the sliding doors on British trains when they aren't locked properly.

By the time we approach London, my legs are killing me and my nose has gone on strike. I've also drained far too much of my phone's battery idly flicking through Facebook and Twitter, just to while away the uncomfortable journey.

But at least we're at Waterloo. I just have to jump on a second short train to St Pancras, and then the journey can begin proper.

Then, as we're literally about a hundred yards away from the platform, the sodding train stops. For no apparent reason.

Here we sit for ten minutes. For no apparent reason.

Nobody comes on the tannoy to tell us why this is. For no apparent reason.

They should just remarket the rail network with that as the new slogan: *Network Rail – For No Apparent Reason*. It'd be the most accurate and descriptive company slogan ever invented.

The stress-worm that has been wriggling about a bit thanks to all of the standing around, smelling other people's farts (which I was supposed to avoid by not taking a plane!), is now starting to thrash about like it's been caught on a hook.

If this bloody train doesn't get into the station soon, I will be in danger of not making the Eurostar. I still have forty minutes to get there, but this is really starting to cut it fine.

The chorus of tutting coming from the entire train has now reached audible levels.

This is the equivalent of all-out rioting in any other country. If someone starts actively swearing out loud about the delay, it will be akin to rabid cannibalism.

Eventually the train does move into the station proper, still with no reason given for the delay. Then begins the struggle to get off.

Usually, I'm the type who's happy to wait for other people – but not today, pal. Today, I'm Captain Elbows. That Eurostar is not leaving without me!

The portly bloke with the beard is a bit put out as I elbow my way past him, but other than that, most people can tell when someone is running late, so the passengers do their best to accommodate me as I push past with a frantic expression on my face.

At the ticket barrier, the machines aren't working. Of course they're not. Why would they be? That would be far too easy.

Would you like to know why they're not working? Then please refer to my new Network Rail slogan.

Now I'm seriously up against it.

I get past the barriers, having had to wait for the slowest train guard in history to get through looking at my ticket. I'm surprised he didn't want to set fire to it and render it down to its constituent parts, so he could analyse its carbon levels before allowing me through.

Now I have to run – and I do mean *run* – across Waterloo to get the train to St Pancras. This is not easy in black high heels, on legs that have already stood on a packed train for over an hour.

When I reach the barrier for the right platform, I'm pleased to say that these ones are working – after a fashion. It takes me five swipes of the ticket across the sensor before it finally lets me through. I swear a little louder with each attempt. If anyone tries to stop me now, I'm likely to take a chunk out of their shoulder.

I jump aboard the connecting train literally as the doors are closing.

. . . and find myself stood right next to the toilet in a packed carriage.

Unbelievable.

Is fucking *everybody* catching the Eurostar today? And have they all developed severe bowel problems?

It certainly seems that way, as the twenty-five minutes it takes the train to get to St Pancras is punctuated by farts, the smell of pee, more farts, and a toilet door that this time opens on the delightful vision of the hairiest bottom I have ever seen in my life. I can see the guy's backside because he has inexplicably *dropped his trousers to have a wee.*

Is this a thing? Do men do this on a regular basis? Just strip themselves naked from the waist down when urinating? Surely not. The dry-cleaning bills alone would bankrupt the country.

The hairy-arsed man is of course aghast when he realises that the toilet door has swung open, exposing him to all of us. He handles it a little better than the poor woman in the last train, by shouting, 'Sorry folks! I'll keep my cock away from you!' as he leans over to bash the close button repeatedly. How considerate of him. I don't think my soul could take seeing a stranger's penis at this stage in my day. I want my overriding memory of this trip to be a successfully gained client contract, not the sight of a winky nestled in what must be a magnificent thatch of pubes, if the hair on the backside is anything to go by.

When the train pulls into the station (this time with no inexplicable delay), I am again first off. I am now Field Marshal Elbows, having been repeatedly promoted in battle for the excellent use of the boniest part of my anatomy.

Originally, I had a good hour to get through Eurostar security and passport control. I now have thirteen minutes.

The stress-worm is now a snake, coiling its way from the top of my brain, down my spine and into my rapidly tiring legs.

Unbidden, thoughts of being thirty thousand feet in the air with a gin and tonic in my hand appear in my mind, as I'm shuffling forward with my passport and ticket actually grasped in it instead.

No.

Don't do that.

You've just been a little delayed is all. You still have time.

This is still better.

It is.

In the first bit of good luck I've had today, the queues at the security checkpoints are minimal. Everybody else is already on the Eurostar, ready to leave. But I'm still on the verge of total panic as one of the female security guards directs me over for a manual pat-down. I could scream. I really, really could.

Not at her, though. I don't need a night in a jail cell. So I hold my frustration in with a bitten lip as she checks I'm not carrying any offensive weapons or explosives.

I can't miss this train. I just *can't*.

There won't be another one for two hours, and that'll be way too late to get me to the meeting on time.

The pat-down finishes, and I snatch up my briefcase from the X-ray machine's conveyor belt. I have two minutes. Two minutes to get on board the Eurostar.

There are actual grunts and moans of stress and tension erupting from my lips as I rush headlong through the departure lounge and towards the platform. The seconds are counting down, and I'm deathly afraid I'm going to be late.

I'm going to miss the train! I'm going to miss the bloody tra—

Oh, it's going to leave thirty minutes late.

Of course it sodding well is.

I could have sauntered through security. Fucking *sauntered*.

I don't know why this damn train is going to leave so late – but the slogan is already taken by Network Rail, so the Eurostar company will just have to think of something else.

Eurostar – Pour Aucune Raison Apparente Non Plus, possibly.

Regardless, I have made it on time. I can climb aboard, in the safe and secure knowledge that I will make the meeting at Hergebruikt.

And I can barely contain my gratitude when I see that I will not have to spend the whole journey watching people go to the toilet. There's something very wrong with the British transport system that this is a thing you have to be grateful about, but there you have it.

No, on the Eurostar I have my very own seat. In fact, I have a seat with *nobody sat next to me*. Can you imagine such a thing? To have room to put my briefcase down, and to be able to stretch my legs out? All without having to look at any arses?

Joy unconfined.

I can now take the next couple of hours to recover from the ordeal of getting here, relax a little, and maybe even have an alcoholic beverage.

Lovely stuff.

As the Eurostar eventually pulls away from the platform, I have to reflect that it's probably a good job I'm on my own. Nolan is many things, but he's not the kind of guy who would cope well with toilet views and a hot, cramped train carriage. He has many,

many great characteristics, but I'm not sure resilience is one of them, bless him.

No, it's far better he's off chasing leads for Viridian, rather than coming along with me. That's where his talents quite obviously lie.

I can handle this meeting on my own – of that I have no doubt.

And the trip should be plain sailing from now on. No more delays for Ellie Cooke now we're headed towards the Continent, I'm sure.

I'm an *idiot*.

Why did I jinx myself?

The Eurostar journey was fine until we hit the outskirts of Paris, where the train came to a grinding halt thanks to signalling issues in the city.

The Eurostar's progress through to Belgium isn't going to be halted completely by the problem, but it will delay us. Right outside Paris, to be exact, while they try to get everything sorted out at the Gare du Nord. The French countryside is always beautiful, but I could really do without having to look at it today.

The stress-snake – which has uncoiled nicely thanks to the smooth ride under the Channel, and the two gin and tonics I've downed – starts to wind itself up again. I still have a lot of contingency time in hand, but this delay is really going to start eating into it, if we don't get moving soon.

We do not get moving soon, however. We don't get moving at all for nearly *half an hour* – and when we do, it's at a much-reduced rate, thanks to the fact that the poor buggers working for the French rail service are having to negotiate every train in and out of Paris without the full use of their complicated signalling system.

Gnawing.

That's what I'm doing.

Gnawing on my fingernails like an overexcited squirrel.

Perhaps I'm just hungry.

I had planned on sitting in that lovely coffee shop around the corner from Hergebruikt to grab a bite to eat, but time is ticking away, so I'd better grab some food on the train instead. At least then I can chew on something constructive, instead of my own fingers.

I purchase a large cheese pastry thing. This is quite tasty, but I find that I am only able to eat about half of it, thanks to the fact that the stress-snake is now coiled tightly around my stomach.

The rural scenery slowly gives way to the city as we approach Paris. The Eurostar will go straight through, so I don't have to change trains, but at this rate of progress it might be quicker to get out and hire a cab. Or a bicycle. Or walk. Or shuffle along on my butt cheeks.

We eventually do get across and out of Paris, but we're easily running an hour late by this time, and my contingency is rapidly disappearing into the ether. I still have to catch a taxi when I get to Brussels Midi station, so I hope to God there's plenty of them sat outside waiting for customers. These are the kinds of things that don't cross your mind when you think you've got plenty of time, but become acute when that time rapidly diminishes into nothing.

I am again forced to think about how my journey may have gone if I'd taken a plane – and I have to immediately stop that train of thought before it stresses me out even further.

You'd be there by now.

Shut up.

You would though, wouldn't you?

Shut up. Shut up!

When we pull into Brussels Midi, I am a bundle of nerves. I now have less than thirty minutes to get across the city to the meeting. I had originally planned to have two hours. I'm still likely to get there on time, but I'm not going to be the cool, calm and collected operator I wanted to be. Instead I'm going to be exactly what I am – a woman who's now been travelling for over five hours, has only eaten half a cheese pastry thing, has smelled more than her fair share of farts and sweat, and is only keeping her stress at bay through the medium of gin.

For the third time today, I leap off a train with my heart in my chest. My anxiety levels are way beyond what they should be. I do still have time to do this – I don't need to panic so much. But when your stress levels are as high as mine are now, it's quite hard to act rationally, take a deep breath and see a situation for what it really is. As far as my anxious brain is concerned, I have to rush, rush, rush – otherwise I will be late. I've turned into the White Rabbit from *Alice in Wonderland*, only without the ability to look good in a waistcoat.

I *must* make the meeting. I cannot lose out again. Not after Helen Carmichael.

Nolan is *depending on me*.

And I must prove that it's perfectly fine to take more environmentally friendly methods of transport. That I don't need to take a plane.

I *must*.

The platform at Brussels Midi feels about seventeen miles long, but at least the ticket machines here are working fine.

Now it's just a case of getting out of this building and flagging down one of the many taxis that are no doubt sat outside, just waiting to ferry me to my—

Where are all the fucking *taxis*?

They should be here! All lined up and ready to go!

But there's no sign of any. Not one single black cab is in evidence as I walk frantically along the front of the station, my eyes darting about like a mayfly.

'Excuse me?' I say to a passing man in a long coat. 'Do you know where I can get a taxi from?' I wouldn't normally accost someone like this on the street – especially not in a foreign country – but the stress-snake is now a boa constrictor.

'Zer are no taxis,' he tells me matter-of-factly.

'I'm sorry?'

'Zey are on strike.'

'On strike?!'

'Oui. It is about ze Uber, I believe.'

'Uber?'

'Yes. Zey are unhappy wiz ze Uber people.'

'Oh. Okay. Thank you.'

'Pleasure,' the man replies, and carries on his way.

No taxis.

No taxis to take me to my meeting.

I am fucked.

Royally, comprehensively *fucked*.

I have never used Uber, so I have no idea how to order one. This is a massive and glaring oversight on my part, but I live in a part of the world where Uber isn't much of a thing yet, and I have that lovely hybrid Mercedes to use, so why would I need bloody Uber in the first place?

If you'd driven it all the way here, you'd probably be there by now.

Fuck off, brain! You're not helping!

What the hell do I do now?

I'll have to download the Uber app and use it.

242

There's no way I have the time to try to negotiate the Brussels public transport system. I can barely use the one in my own country. Four years ago, I had a nightmare getting across Manchester on the bus. And that was somewhere I spoke the language.

My hands are visibly shaking as I pull out my mobile phone and spend about three hundred quid downloading the Uber app using my roaming charges.

A good five or so minutes go by while I put in all of my information and get the account verified.

Eventually I work out how to book the car – which is actually very easy once you get past the signing-up part of the process – and I order one to come pick me up as soon as possible.

This takes a further five minutes to arrive. I now have fifteen minutes to get to Hergebruikt. A quarter of an hour to do a journey that Uber tells me will take twenty minutes. I am most definitely going to be late for the start of the meeting.

Never mind! I'll be on time for my pitch session! That's all that matters!

When the Uber arrives, it's being driven by a Belgian man who must be in his eighties. The app tells me his name is Alphonse. It does not tell me what actions I need to take when Alphonse suffers a heart attack, which he looks like he is about to do the entire time I'm in the car with him.

Alphonse is not the fastest driver in the world, but then the traffic doesn't really allow him to drive that quickly anyway. This is possibly just as well, as I think if he had to go quicker than thirty miles an hour it would rupture his left ventricle.

Time ticks by . . . faster and *faster*. The minutes dwindle. The boa constrictor wraps itself around my neck.

And then, when we hit a massive load of roadworks about a mile away from the building I'm going to, it jumps down my throat and starts to snack on my vital organs.

The road ahead looks jam-packed with cars. None of them are moving. I can see two men in fluorescent vests arguing with one another over a set of traffic lights that are drunkenly leaning to one side.

'I am zorry for zis,' Alphonse says, coughing as he does so. 'Traffic 'az been very bad today, and now ve 'ave zis.' He's gone red-faced. Whether this is with anger at the traffic conditions, or embarrassment about the transport infrastructure of his great nation, I do not know.

All I do know is that I'd better get out of this car and start running, before I'm too late to do my pitch, and before Alphonse keels over his dashboard.

'Thanks! I'm going to go the rest of the way on foot!' I tell my Uber driver, and leap out of the car before he has a chance to say anything. At least I've prepaid the fare. Poor old Alphonse won't go without his heart medication this week.

So now I'm running again – this time along the streets of Brussels. I have my iPhone clasped in one sweaty hand, using it to negotiate my way around. It tells me I have half a mile more on this traffic-choked road, before I can turn off and go down the street Hergebruikt are on.

Excellent.

Nearly there.

So very nearly there.

But also, so very, very late now.

I run around the corner and see that lovely coffee shop just in front of me, that I will never see the inside of thanks to my awful journey here.

Never mind. Just keep running. We're nearly there!

This is when the heel on my right shoe decides to snap.

No!

Oh God no! This can't be happening!

But it is.

It's all that leaping, you see. You can't leap in a pair of high heels off trains and out of Uber cars without it taking a massive toll on your footwear. These shoes are meant for boardrooms, not cross-town sprints.

And I'm not sprinting any more. Now I'm *falling*. The broken heel has thrown me off my stride completely, and turned a head-long sprint that I had some sort of control over into a headlong *stumble* I have no control over whatsoever. My briefcase goes flying from my hand.

And I'm falling right towards that lovely coffee shop – or more precisely, a table and chairs set up outside of it.

And even more precisely, I'm falling at the young couple sat at the table, who are engaged in an animated and happy conversation about something very Belgian and interesting.

'Waaaaah!' I cry, as my forward momentum takes me straight at them, like a guided missile. Given that they are young and quick off the mark – probably because their brains haven't been turned to sludge yet by the vagaries of the world around them – they have the presence of mind to whisk their coffee cups off the table before I slam into it.

I'm only prevented from flying right over the glass tabletop by my hips crashing painfully into its metal rim.

'Ow! Fuck!' I scream, as the pain jolts up and down my body. For the briefest of moments it looks like this disaster is going to turn into a catastrophe, as the table starts to tip forward, unbalanced by my weight. Thankfully, gravity reasserts itself before this can happen, and I topple back again, falling off the table as the reversed momentum sends me crashing to the pavement.

'Jesus Christ!' I scream, as my backside hits the deck.

'*Est-ce que ça va?*' the young man exclaims with concern, reaching out a hand to help me up.

'*Fais attention! On dirait une folle!*' the girl adds. She must be as worried for my welfare as her partner is.

'I'm okay! I'm okay!' I say, taking the young man's hand and getting back to my feet. I'm not sure I am okay, you know. I have a ring of pain around my entire midriff that is going to need more than just a couple of painkillers to get rid of. 'I'm so sorry!' I tell them, dusting myself off.

'Do you . . . do you need zome 'elp?' the young man says. 'You need . . . an ambulance?'

'No, no! Don't worry!' I say, waving a hand. 'I'm sure I'll be fine.'

'*Sois prudent! Il se peut qu'elle essaye de nous voler.*'

Oh, bless her. Look how concerned she is for me. These Belgians really are lovely people.

. . . and there's a roomful of them waiting for me down the street!

I go over to where my briefcase has landed in the gutter and pick it up, wincing as I do. Not only have I bashed both my hips and my bottom, but my right ankle feels like it's twisted as well, thanks to the broken heel.

But I can't let that stop me.

'Thank you! I must go! I have a meeting!' I say to the couple, affecting an air of British politeness that my mind and body are in no fit state to keep up for any length of time.

'*Partez, pauvre folle!*' the girl says.

'You're very kind!' I tell her, before scuttling off down the street again, in a bent-legged, awkward hobble.

Nearly there . . . nearly there . . .

I know I'm late. I know it's gone three o'clock. But I can still *do it*. I can still get the pitch across. I can still win the contract!

Hergebruikt's offices are in a tall, gleaming glass building that sits a little incongruously among the more classic European architecture that surrounds it.

I hobble like a drunken pirate across the flagstone plaza in front of the building, and push my way through the revolving doors, emerging in a quiet, cool foyer, devoid of people other than a receptionist behind a long, black desk.

'Hergebruikt!' I bark at him as I stagger over.

'*Excusez-moi?*' he replies, a little taken aback.

'Hergebruikt! What floor is Hergebruikt on?'

'Oh . . . tenth floor, *madame*,' he says, effortlessly switching into English.

'Thank you! I mean, *merci!*' I say, and make my way over to the row of elevators next to the desk.

'Oh! I am sorry, *madame*! Ze elevators are not working!' the receptionist tells me.

I freeze on the spot, and stare at him with the fury of a thousand blazing supernovas. '*What* did you say?'

He takes a step back. 'Ze elevators are not working, I am afraid. Some zort of electrical problem.'

I'm fucking jinxed.

Truly, truly fucking *jinxed*.

'Where are the stairs?' I ask, between gritted teeth.

He points just beyond the row of elevator doors.

'Thank you,' I mutter, and move right along. I don't trust myself to say anything else to this poor man. He doesn't deserve me right now.

Grunting – actual proper *grunting* now, like a backfiring pig – I clatter through the door to the stairwell, and begin my long and painful climb.

'Hergebruikt, Hergebruikt, Hergebruikt,' I repeat over and over under my breath as I make my way up each flight of stairs.

Something may have broken inside my brain.

'Gotta get the Hergebruikt . . . It's the Hergebruikt or nothing!'

Yep, something's definitely gone twang.

It was the out-of-order elevators that did it. That was the last straw.

'Hergebruikt, hergebrokt, hergybricked,' I ramble, as I reach the eighth floor on legs that are so shaky, it's a wonder I can still stand.

My strange, incomprehensible mantra continues as I pull myself up towards the tenth floor. 'Hergybergy, Hergobroko, Hergé's Adventures of Tintin,' I mumble, as I finally reach my destination.

Pull yourself together, you madwoman.

I take a deep and shuddering breath, before pulling open the door that leads to the tenth floor. Going through, I find myself in another foyer area that leads past all of those broken elevators, to the glass doors of Hergebruikt's offices.

I still have time.

I still have time.

I. Still. Have. Time.

Stumbling through the doors, I happen upon a smartly dressed woman in a charcoal suit, coming the other way. She is carrying a briefcase, and has a satisfied look on her face.

That's me.

That's me if I'd come by plane . . .

Fuck off!

No!

Fuck off!

I will not think that way! *I still have time!*

Hobbling down the hallway, I don't even bother to stop and ask anyone where I'm going, such is my extreme state of painful distress. The only thing I care about is finding a room full of people having a meeting.

Any meeting. Don't care what it's about any more.

And lo and behold . . . there they are: a room full of dapper gentlemen and elegant women, all sat around a dark oak boardroom table. One man is standing at the head of the table, looking at his watch. That must be Hergebruikt.

Yes, yes! That is Hergebruikt! Captain Hergebruikt of the good ship *Hergebruikt*!

I must *impress* Hergebruikt! Hergebruikt is who I am here to see! He is the man! The man who will give me Hergebruikt!

I've totally lost it now.

My blood sugar is in the toilet, my hips are throbbing like mad, my ankle is swelling, and my brain has been utterly broken into small pieces by a day of travelling that I will have nightmares about until I die.

'Hergebruikt!' I actively say out loud as I reach the oak double doors leading to the boardroom.

I throw them open and let those within bask in my radiant glory.

'Hergebruikt!' I exclaim, as if it's my own personal catchphrase that I scream aloud to the world whenever I enter a room.

The poor people of Hergebruikt regard me as you might regard a strange wild animal that has suddenly burst into your tent at three in the morning.

They look stunned at my appearance. And well they might. They've been waiting on a businesswoman who has made her way here today on public transport from the UK. But what they've got is a businesswoman who has clearly been through a war zone backwards, while being constantly attacked by an enraged gorilla.

'Miss Cooke?' the man I have identified as Mr Hergebruikt says to me.

'Yes! That's me, Mr Hergebruikt!' I exclaim.

His brow furrows. 'My name is Pieters.'

Of course his name isn't Mr Hergebruikt. The word *hergebruikt* means 'recycled' in Dutch. His name would literally be *Mr Recycled.* That would be a level of nominative determinism that would put Kevin Flounder completely in the shade.

'Sorry!' I tell Mr Pieters. 'Sorry I'm late! Do I still have time?'

'It's . . . it's three thirty, Miss Cooke,' he tells me. 'The pitch meeting is over, I'm afraid. We must move on to other things.'

I stare up at a clock on the wall to my left-hand side.

He lies!

It's not 3.30 p.m. yet!

It's 3.29!

I still have time!

'Please, please, just let me tell you all about Viridian PR,' I entreat, as I hobble over to the boardroom table, slamming my briefcase down when I get there.

'But we must move o—'

'No!'

No, Mr Pieters Hergebruikt! It is not 3.30 yet! I have . . . I have . . .

Thirty-seven seconds!

Thirty-seven seconds to tell you all about Viridian PR! And that is all I need!

I wrench open the briefcase and yank out the top sheet, on which I've typed my opening speech. As I do, most of the other contents of the briefcase go flying – including what's left of my Eurostar cheese pastry thing. This lands in the lap of one of the elegantly dressed Hergebruikt women, who pushes her chair away from the desk with an exclamation of horror.

I pay her no attention. I have thirty-seven seconds to go!

'Viridianprisanewenvironmentallyconsciouspublic-relationsfirmthathasalreadyestablisheditselfasamarketleaderinprovid-

ingthehighestqualitypromotionandmarketingtosomeoftheuksmostex-citingenviromentallyconsciousfirms,' I begin, at a speed and volume that should really make a straitjacket magically appear. The spittle flies from my lips as I rush through my prepared statement, rendering it completely incomprehensible to anyone other than a passing hummingbird.

'Weareacompanythathastheskillsexperienceandtalent-toprovideyouwithwhateverpublicrelationsyourequiregoingforwardandIcanguaranteethatwithusyouwillseebothyourbusinessandyourreputationgrowalreadywehaveseentheclientsonourbooksincreasetheirprofitmarginsandtheirstandinginourlocalcommunitiesgofromstrengthtostrengththankstotheuniquelyenviromentallyconsciousprthatwecanprovide—'

'Please stop!' Mr Pieters cries.

I stare up at him. 'But I'm not finished yet, and I have' – I glance at the clock – 'three seconds left. No, two seconds. No, one second. No – oh, damn it.'

Silence descends. A horrible, awkward, terrified silence. The kind of silence that just wants to forget it was ever brought into existence. The kind of silence that will probably develop a serious drinking problem at some point, in a vain attempt to dull the pain and misery of its agonising life.

I sniff a couple of times, before slowly gathering up my scattered papers and placing them back in my briefcase. I do this as the room of Hergebruikt's finest watch me with aghast horror. They dare not speak. Possibly because my high-speed rant has just sucked most of the oxygen out of the room.

With all the papers gathered back into the briefcase, I turn to the woman with my pastry in her lap and pick it up, placing it on top of my failed speech like a revered artefact placed upon a velvet cushion. I then close the briefcase slowly and look back up at the table of people, a bland expression on my face.

'Thank you very much for seeing me,' I say, mustering as much dignity in my voice as I can. 'I hope you will consider Viridian PR for your public-relations needs.'

I then pick up my briefcase, turn very, *very* slowly on the heel that isn't broken, and hobble my way back out of the conference room, closing the doors behind me silently as I do so.

I stayed the night in a nearby hotel.

The minibar didn't stand a chance.

Chapter Eleven

Four Normal Lightbulbs

'You could do with a holiday.'

I look into Nolan's concerned eyes, and feel some (not much, but some) of the rage dribble out of me.

'Yes. I probably could,' I concede. 'But I'm not going to get one. We're just too busy.'

'That's my point. Everything is very . . . intense right now. It's probably making us all a little crazy, and a bit of time away from it would be the best thing for us.'

'*Me*, Nolan. You're talking about *me*. I don't see anyone else around here ranting at a bunch of terrified Europeans.'

'You were trying your best.'

'I was having an *episode*, Nolan. I'm self-aware enough to know that. A stress-induced episode, brought on by one of the single worst days of my adult life.'

'Well, I thought you did very well to even get to the meeting before it was completely over. And . . . you know . . . you had a go.'

'I threw a cheesy pastry at someone. If that's what happens when I have a go, it's probably best I don't.'

You can't fault him for trying to make me feel better, but his words are falling on deaf ears. I made a right idiot of myself in Brussels, and there's nothing anyone can do to make me feel better about it.

I am embarrassed and angry. Embarrassed at myself for letting the trials and tribulations of that day turn me into some sort of raving, insane woman – and mad at the rest of the bloody world for allowing me to get into that state.

It should not be that fucking *difficult* to get across such a small section of continent without having a nervous breakdown. Not without having to resort to something with wings, anyway.

How the hell are we meant to fly less when the alternative is tight crowds, smelly farts, hairy arses, ballistic cheese pastries, strikes, delays, broken heels, broken elevators and broken trains?

Not to mention broken minds, after having to negotiate that lot.

I have been incandescent with rage at the unfairness of it all since I got back to the UK this afternoon – having had to endure another elongated journey back from Brussels, thanks to the fact that those signalling issues were still going on the next day. At least I had the luxury of not having an important appointment to keep, though. I could eat my falafel wrap (I'm never eating anything that combines pastry with cheese again in my life) in relative peace, and watch the world go by – very slowly – in the safe and secure knowledge that I was under no time constraint whatsoever.

If we could all just travel like that, then there'd be no need to pollute the atmosphere with all of those planes. The aviation industry probably only really exists because we all have to get everywhere as fast as possible. I doubt anyone actually likes doing it. Not if they're being honest with themselves, anyway.

And I have to be honest with myself as well – I'm allowing my new-found sense of urgency about the climate to turn me into a stressed-out, frustration-filled fool. The kind of person who others probably avoid at dinner parties.

But I don't know what to do about it. Everywhere I look I see nothing constructive being done. Everywhere I look I see people with their heads in the sand.

Aaaargh!

'I know. It's frustrating,' Nolan says, when I've told him all of this. 'But there's no point in letting it ruin your life. Anger won't help.'

'No? I think a bit more anger from enough people might just do the trick,' I argue, not willing to just let the whole thing slide off me.

'Well, you've got to try,' Nolan tells me, 'otherwise it'll just drive you mad.' He sits back in his chair. 'Which is why I'm recommending you take a few days off. Not a whole week – you're right, we don't have the time for that – but Friday through Monday should do it. A nice long weekend . . . we can go somewhere pleasant. Unwind a bit.'

'We?' I say, blinking a couple of times.

Nolan smiles a little shyly. 'Yes. I'd like to come with you, if that's . . . that's okay?'

'Okay?' I say, suddenly feeling quite emotional. 'I'd *love it*, Nolan.' I pause, and take a deep breath. 'But I thought . . . thought what with everything that's happened . . . the stuff about how I pretended . . . and that whole thing with Robert Ainslie Blake . . .'

Nolan takes my hand, squeezing it in a gentle and comforting manner. 'It's fine, Ellie. Honestly. I've been thinking about it a lot, and none of that matters. Okay, you didn't start off on the right foot with the job, but I know you've changed. The lengths you went through to get to that meeting without jumping on a plane prove that. You're different now, from the way you were back then.'

'I am! I really am!'

'And I can't really be upset with you just because you dated a man . . . a man like that.' He grins. 'I once went out with a girl who liked to fart on my head.'

I can't help but burst out laughing.

Nolan chuckles too. 'She did. She would wait until I was comfortable on the couch, and then she would stick her arse in my face and let rip.' His brow furrows. 'She was actually surprised when I ended the relationship, can you believe that?'

I'm laughing so hard now, I think I'm going to start crying.

'So, we're . . . okay?' I eventually say.

Nolan nods. 'Yeah. I really do like you a lot, Ellie . . . more than just like you, in fact. And nothing you've done in the past has changed that. It's the Ellie Cooke of the present and the future I care about. Can we just forget about it all, move on, and go away for a few days together?'

'Oh God, *yes!*' I cry happily, and throw my arms around him, to give him the biggest hug possible.

It's fucking wonderful on every level.

And *he's* wonderful on every level, isn't he?

Robert Ainslie Blake was the biggest mistake of my entire love life, but Nolan Reece just might be the complete opposite of that.

I finally feel like I can put the sorry business of both Robert and my dishonesty behind me, and move forward again, into a brighter future.

. . . which starts with a great deal of *Passionate Kissing by the Ficus* (available soon on Kindle and in paperback).

In fact, if I'm not very careful, and don't get myself under control, there will be much more going on against the ficus than just passionate kissing, and I don't think the poor thing needs to be subjected to that.

I reluctantly pull myself away from Nolan, so we can both regain some sort of composure. After all, Young Adrian could walk in again at any moment.

'That's settled it then. We're off on a break!' Nolan says happily. 'Nadia can hold the fort, and get in touch if anything really serious happens. I have no meetings booked in until Tuesday, and neither do you. It's the perfect time to get away.'

I have to admit, the idea of going off somewhere nice for a long weekend does appeal greatly. We could visit the Italian lakes, or maybe somewhere in the south of France—

'Oh, fuck me,' I say out loud, with mock despair.

'What's the matter?'

'We'd have to *fly*,' I say, feeling my heart sink.

'Fly where?'

'To anywhere *nice*, Nolan. For our long weekend.' I look slightly aghast at the prospect. 'I can't get on a train across Europe again, I just *can't*. And everywhere else is too far away for just four days.'

He looks at me for a moment, letting this sink in.

He knows I'm right. To travel anywhere decent in such a short space of time, we'd have to fly. That's the way it always was with Robert. He always used to make a point of saying how fast we could get to southern Italy for some sun. It seemed like not a week would go by when he wasn't keen to jet off somewhere with wall-to-wall blue sky and cheap alcohol if it could be reached in less than three hours.

You see? We all have to get everywhere *quickly*. We're all the White Rabbit from *Alice in Wonderland*, when you get right down to it, and we're killing our planet because of it.

No. No, Ellie. Just *stop*. You're starting to sound like someone who climbs on top of a tall building dressed as Spider-Man and holding a banner proclaiming the world is dead.

His face brightens. 'Staycation.'

'What?'

'We'll do a staycation.' He smiles. 'We don't need to go abroad for a nice time.'

'We don't?'

'No! Of course not. Haven't you ever done a staycation before?'

'Yes, Nolan. I have. It involved a *caravan*.' My face darkens. 'Nothing good – and I do mean *nothing* – has ever come from anything that involved a caravan.'

Nolan looks a little wistful. 'I've never stayed in a caravan before.'

'That probably explains why you seem so well adjusted.' I roll my eyes. 'I *have* stayed in a caravan before, Nolan – and let me tell you that they are where hope goes to die. They are despair on two wheels. They bring the rain, and the thunder. And the dog poo, Nolan.'

'What?'

'The dog poo. The only times I have ever rolled in dog poo were on caravanning holidays.'

'Possibly just a coincidence?'

'No, Nolan. That's just what they *want* you to think. But with caravans come poo. And rain. And heartache. And distress.'

'They're very environmentally friendly.'

'I don't care if they bring endangered species back to life, Nolan. I am not spending four days in a caravan.'

He pauses for a second, thinking. 'Why don't you just let me surprise you?'

'Surprise me?'

'Yes. I'll find somewhere nice for us to go. Trust me, you'll enjoy it.'

My eyes narrow. 'No caravans?'

'No.'

I give him a speculative look. 'Alright. I trust you.'

'Great!'

I *do* trust him. I really do.

I'm sure he'll find us somewhere nice to stay. If you can run your own PR company successfully, finding a getaway for a long weekend should be a piece of cake.

And a few days away would be *very* nice. As long as they don't involve a caravan, I'll be quite happy with whatever he comes up with. Just the chance to spend some time with him, now we've made up, will be quite, quite *wonderful*.

'Welcome to the Cotswolds!' Nolan says expansively, as we drive past a large sign that's been partially obscured by a slightly out-of-control bush.

I smile back, and relax into the passenger seat of his Tesla a little more. There's something about passing a sign which says you have reached your destination that has a profound psychological effect on you. Especially when that destination promises a week-end of leisure and relaxation – two things I've almost forgotten existed.

This really, really was a good idea. I'm glad Nolan thought of it.

And I'm glad I left the organising to him as well, because he's done a bang-up job. He found us a B&B in the charmingly named village of Withy-on-the-Wold. A B&B that purports to be *eco-friendly*, no less. It's one of the first things you read in their Tripadvisor blurb.

Withy Views is nestled right by a small but exquisitely picturesque river, and couldn't look more quaint if you pumped it full of the early-nineteenth century and told Constable to paint it with wattle and daub.

A few days here should help me unwind magnificently.

Okay, the weather is being typically British again – it's currently overcast, cold for the time of year, and spitting with rain – but as long as it's cosy inside, I'll be happy. If there's any chance of a crackling fire in my near future, then that'd be marvellous.

It had better have a big, comfy bed as well, because . . . well, you know.

I am fully prepared to have my wild spirits soothed – all in the comfort of a B&B that apparently does its bit for the environment.

Lovely stuff.

It takes about an hour for us to reach Withy Views, which I have no problem with, as the countryside we drive through is quite glorious.

By the time we arrive at the B&B I have seen more hedgerows, trailing ivy and waving conifers than I can shake a stick of willow at. And all of it is *gorgeous*.

How does anyone get anything done in the Cotswolds? If I lived here, I'd spend my entire time watching babbling brooks and fluttering butterflies. I'd be unemployed in weeks. Which would mean I wouldn't be able to afford to live here any more, because the place is slightly more expensive than Elton John's taste in menswear.

'Here we are then,' Nolan announces, as we pull off the B3241 on to a small unsealed road that leads down to Withy Views. The place looks even better in real life than it did in the picture, because real life brings with it the smell of flowers, and the sound of a happy, fast-flowing river.

'Oh my,' I say quite breathily, as I climb out of the car.

'Lovely, isn't it?' Nolan says, as he gets our cases out of the boot.

'That's putting it mildly,' I reply.

'Hello! Hello!' a voice calls to us from the porch of the large thatched cottage we've come to stay in.

'Hello?' Nolan replies.

From the relative gloom appears a woman in her late sixties who could only ever be the owner of a B&B in the English countryside. She was probably *born* owning a B&B in the English countryside. And she obviously takes her sartorial cues from the Queen. There's a lot of extremely sensible, hard-wearing fabric going on here, all dyed in earthy tones. If this woman doesn't wear a headscarf when she's out and about, I'd be amazed.

'Good afternoon!' she says in a matronly voice, as she approaches the Tesla.

'Good afternoon to you too,' Nolan says to her.

'Hello,' I add, resisting the urge to curtsey.

'You are the Reeces, aren't you?'

My face goes a little red.

'Er . . . yes,' Nolan replies, avoiding my gaze. I could point out that we're not actually married, but what harm does it do to maintain a pleasant little fiction, eh?

'Good, good. Well, please do come on in. Here. Let me take that.' The woman grabs my case from Nolan. I put my hands out to warn her that it's very heavy – I couldn't travel light if you put a gun to my head – but before I get the chance she's already bustling back towards the cottage, carrying it like it's full of polystyrene and feathers.

'Follow me!' she commands, and we fall immediately into line. You can't say no to the Queen, can you?

We go into the cottage, through a large entrance lobby, past several rooms and a staircase, and emerge into a large country kitchen with a massive oak table slap-bang in the centre of it.

'I'll show you the room presently,' our host says, 'but first a cup of tea and some proper introductions.' She thrusts out a hand. 'Irene McClapperty.'

I blink a couple of times.

Is that her name? I guess it must be, otherwise why would she have said it?

But *Irene McClapperty*? This woman, who screams of an upper-middle-class upbringing where Daddy bought her at least two ponies, is called *Irene McClapperty*?

I take her hand. 'Ellie. Very pleased to meet you, Mrs . . . Mrs McClapperty.'

'Oh, please, it's Irene,' she says, and shakes Nolan's hand as well as he introduces himself. 'Now for some tea!'

Irene McClapperty (I may have to use her full name throughout here, just because it sounds so *monumentally* out of place . . . I need to bed it in properly) goes over to one of the enormous worktops that ring the entire kitchen, and pops the kettle on.

'It's a lovely place you have here,' Nolan says, looking around the kitchen with an approving expression on his face.

'Thank you! We do try to maintain a good home for our guests.'

'It's lovely you're concerned with being environmentally friendly,' I add, keen to ask her about it. It's one of the main selling points of this trip for us, so it's worth finding out a bit more before we go any further.

'Oh . . . oh yes,' Irene McClapperty responds as she pops a couple of teabags into a pot. 'We are trying our best to be kinder to the creatures of God's green earth.'

'What kind of measures have you taken?' I enquire in a serious tone, trying to ignore Nolan's slightly uncomfortable expression. Doesn't he want to know? 'What efforts are you making to be greener?'

'Oh, you know. Lots of things,' Irene McClapperty tells me, looking a little awkward. 'The bins. Bulbs. Composting. That kind of thing.'

'That sounds lovely,' Nolan says. 'Nice to see folks making an effort. How long have you owned this gorgeous cottage?'

Well, that's moved the subject on, hasn't it? It's clear Nolan doesn't want to question Irene McClapperty further about her B&B's green credentials. I wonder why?

The next few minutes are taken up with idle small talk as we drink our cups of tea, and then Irene McClapperty shows us to our room – which is enormous, gorgeous, and comes with a roll-top bath and a bed you could lose at least six puppies in.

I should be ecstatic about all of this, but instead I feel a little perturbed.

'Why didn't you let me ask her more about how green the B&B is?' I ask Nolan, after Irene McClapperty has left us to settle in.

'Because there's plenty of time for us to find out about all of that stuff. It doesn't need to be the first thing we ask about.'

I think on what he's just said for a moment, and sigh. 'Yeah. You're right. It doesn't.' I pinch the bridge of my nose. 'I think I'm becoming a little *obsessed*.'

Nolan comes over and wraps his arms around me. The hug is long, lovely and entirely what the doctor ordered.

'Look,' he says, continuing the hug, 'just don't worry about it for the next few days. We're here to unwind. You don't have to be on an environmental crusade every minute.'

'Okay,' I agree, nestling my face in his neck. It smells *divine*. 'I'll try to be a bit more . . . a bit more relaxed.'

Nolan ends the hug with a long, lingering kiss – and wouldn't you know it, my concerns about how kind Irene McClapperty is to the polar bears go right out of my head.

I'm more concerned with puppies right now. Or rather, that bed that you could lose six of the cute little buggers in.

Nolan's right.

I have to unwind.

I've got myself so passionate and committed to my job and the cause it champions that it's turned me into a stress-filled frustration monster. That isn't good for anyone – including me.

A few days of not thinking about it – and not thinking about work at all – will be good for me.

And that starts with seeing just how comfortable that bed truly is . . .

Very comfortable, as it turns out.

And that's all the detail you're getting.

Later that afternoon, Nolan and I drove a couple of miles to a pub restaurant that Irene McClapperty recommended to us.

The Lamb's Tail was delightful, and the food was delicious.

By the time I'd consumed my salted caramel pudding, I truly was feeling relaxed for the first time in weeks. Neither of us mentioned work once during the meal, which made a massive change. Usually it's the main topic of conversation in any chats we might have. I get the feeling that Nolan is deliberately not bringing it up, which is fine by me, as I don't want to either. I don't want anything to ruin my chilled-out mood, and talking about how The Green Tangent are still a bit unhappy with the new logo designs would certainly do that.

No. I am a chilled-out Ellie Cooke, and I intend to stay that way for the rest of the weekend.

If only . . .

If only those bulbs were all low energy.

Those ones.

Up there.

In the lounge light fitting at Withy Views B&B.

But they're not, are they?

They're *normal* bulbs. Normal, sixty-watt bulbs. Big, bulbous, normal, sixty-watt bulbs that I can't stop looking at as Nolan stokes the fire, and I sip on my third red wine of the evening.

I noticed them about five minutes after we came in here to relax, after getting back from The Lamb's Tail. Nolan suggested we spend a little time in the expansive cottage living room on one of the comfy sofas, and there was nobody else about, so it seemed like a great idea.

But now I see those bulbs, I can't relax. Not properly.

Because *why* are they there?

If Irene McClapperty runs an environmentally friendly B&B, then why does she have normal bulbs in here? I haven't seen them anywhere else. All the other lights seem to be fitted with low-energy LED bulbs.

The ones I've seen, that is. There are plenty of places around the B&B I haven't visited. Are there more normal bulbs here? And what does that say about Irene McClapperty's true commitment to reducing her carbon footprint?

I should never have had that conversation last week with Donald from Earth's Future Lighting. He's one of our newer clients, who came into the office to talk to Amisha about the layout for his company's website. Donald told me how bad normal light bulbs are for the environment. I knew they weren't great, but I had no idea just how much energy they use until he gave me a very detailed rundown of the damage they cause both to your electricity bill and the world around you.

And there's four of them right above my head, right now . . . and I can't relax.

Neither can I express my opinion about the four light bulbs to Nolan, without ruining the laid-back vibe we've had all day.

'Let's go up to bed,' I say, trying to sound as chilled out as Nolan looks.

It's utterly ridiculous that four light bulbs are forcing me out of a room, but I can't help it.

'Really? I was just getting comfortable,' he says, looking a little disappointed.

'Oh, I can make you comfortable, mister,' I purr in his ear. 'Very comfortable indeed.'

You can get a man out of any room in the world, if you purr in his ear like that.

I'd like to say I don't feel a slight wave of relief come over me as we leave the lounge and its normal light bulbs, but I'd be lying.

What has become of me?

◆ ◆ ◆

'Toast?' Irene McClapperty asks, as she pours me a filter coffee the next morning.

'Yes please,' I reply, continuing my appraisal of the massive kitchen as I do.

Is that one of those big range cookers I can see over there? Because I've heard they can be really bad for the environment.

Surely someone who claims to run a green B&B wouldn't have something like that in her kitchen?

I've already clocked the utility room that lies just off the kitchen. That's probably where she keeps the kitchen bins. Whether they are recycling ones or not, I just don't know. And I really do need to take a look in Irene McClapperty's cleaning cupboard to see if she's using the right kinds of products or not. If I see any disposable wet wipes, I may need to lodge a formal complaint.

Irene McClapperty brings over my toast, and with it a pat of butter in a dish. 'Here you are, Ellie,' she says, as she puts it down in front of me. 'Only natural butter here. None of that fake stuff with the palm oil in it.'

She's obviously keen to point out what efforts she's making to be green, after my questions yesterday.

'That's lovely,' I reply with a smile. And it is.

If only there weren't those four normal light bulbs to worry about.

I manage to finish my breakfast without saying anything more. I don't want to upset Nolan – or the two other guests currently at the B&B, for that matter. Maggie and Charles are here on their twenty-fifth wedding anniversary, and they really don't need me harping on about whether Irene McClapperty uses bleach when she cleans the toilets while they try to eat their breakfast at the other end of the long table.

'I read all about what the palm oil is doing to the poor orangutans,' Irene McClapperty continues, looking at me solemnly. 'Poor orange things.'

I affect a half-hearted smile. 'Yes, it is a tragedy.'

It was Mordred O'Hare who convinced me of such. There's only so long you can be talked at by an animated bush with tears in his eyes, before you start to feel real sympathy for the apes he's telling you about.

I'm glad Irene McClapperty knows all about the evils of palm oil, and is doing her bit to combat it.

But she also has four normal light bulbs in her living room, so I don't say anything else to her as I bite down on my buttery toast and try to ignore that feeling of tension that just won't leave the space between my shoulders.

'We're all finished,' remarks Charles to Irene McClapperty, as he slurps the last of his morning tea. 'Time for us to get up and about. It's a lovely day!'

'It is!' our host agrees, starting to clear up their used crockery. 'Any plans, you two?'

'Oh, we'll probably just go for a walk along the river,' Charles replies, smiling indulgently at his wife. 'At our age, nothing quite beats a lovely long walk somewhere beautiful.'

'No indeed!' Irene McClapperty says, trying her best to balance a couple of nearly empty plates, a teapot, two cups, and several used paper napkins. I wonder where she'll be dumping the food residue. Does she have proper recycling facilities in that utility room or not?

Only one way to find out.

'Let me help you!' I exclaim, rising from my seat and bustling over to where Irene McClapperty is still trying to juggle all of that breakfast detritus.

'No, no! I'm fine!' she insists.

'It's no bother!' I reply, with a brittle good humour in my voice.

I'm going to get to the bottom of how green you are, Mrs Irene McClapperty, and there's nothing you can do to stop me.

I pluck away the two plates, along with the napkins. 'I'll just take these over to the bins, shall I?'

'Oh . . . er, yes please.' Poor Irene McClapperty looks quite distressed at my sudden insistence on helping her clean up. It's probably not something that happens too often in her B&B. Most people are content to let her get on with it, given how much money they've paid to stay here.

'Your bins are out in the utility room, yes?'

'Um . . . yes dear, they are.'

'Thanks.'

And with that, I beetle over to the utility with triumph in my eyes.

Time to see just how green Irene McClapperty really is!

There are two large black bins out here, hidden behind a white wooden partition so the guests don't have to look at them. But this guest is going to give them a good going-over, of that there is no doubt.

One is clearly an ordinary refuse bin. The other is green-topped and must be for the recycling.

But where is the bin for the waste food, eh?

Clara from Protocol Waste Management told me that all homes should have three bins. One for non-recyclable waste, one for recyclable items, and one for food waste!

But Irene McClapperty only has *two*.

I grumble to myself as I scrape the remnants of Charles's beans and Maggie's fried egg into the black bin, and deposit the napkins in the recycling bin – which is only a quarter full. How much recycling is Irene McClapperty actually *doing*?

I plonk the plates on the kitchen counter near the sink and return to the table, where Nolan is giving me an indecipherable look.

'You . . . you did put the napkins in the recycling bin, didn't you?' Irene McClapperty asks me.

'Oh yes. I most certainly *did*,' I tell her.

'Oh, well, thank you.'

'What do you do with it?'

'I beg your pardon?'

'With the recyclable waste? Where does it go?'

Irene McClapperty looks a little perturbed. I'm not surprised. I'm now fixing her with an expression that would have been familiar to anyone undergoing questioning by the Wehrmacht about eighty years ago.

'We have a composting system out the back,' she tells me. 'My son put it in.'

My eyes narrow.

Hmmm.

Believable, or not?

Would anyone with four normal light bulbs and no food waste bin have a composting system out the back?

'Ah . . . that's good . . . that's good to know,' I tell Irene McClapperty. I'm not sure whether I believe a word of what she's saying, but I can hardly question her further right here and now, can I?

I will need to investigate this claim of hers about the composting system before I can say anything more . . .

'I think a walk might be a lovely idea too, don't you Nolan?' I say to my boyfriend, who up until now has just been sat silently, watching me with an incredulous look on his face.

'What?'

'A *walk*, Nolan. Like Charles and Maggie are doing.' I point at the couple with a finger that's probably just a little bit too firm. 'A walk would be nice. Very nice . . . *indeed.*'

'Er . . . okay, Ellie,' Nolan says, nodding slowly.

'Excellent. That's all sorted then. We'll finish up here, and go for a lovely walk. We'll start in the cottage garden. If that's alright with you, Irene McClapperty?'

Oh God.

It's one thing to mentally say her full name over and over, just because it's so incredibly incongruous with her demeanour and look – but it's quite another to say it *out loud*.

'Yes, yes. The cottage is freely available for guests to enjoy.'

'Excellent! Excellent, excellent,' I say, sipping at my now-cool cup of coffee. I *will* find out whether Irene McClapperty is telling me the truth about her composting system, or my name's not Montgomery Burns.

Sorry, I mean *or my name's not Ellie Cooke*.

It *is* a lovely day outside. Charles was right. The sun, which has been entirely absent from this trip so far, has come out to play – although there are some large dark clouds off to the south that look like they might be ruining the party before long.

Time enough for that walk though.

Or should I say . . . *investigation*.

'What is wrong with you?' Nolan asks me, as we walk down the side of the cottage and out into the centre of the massive, mature garden. The damn thing is filled with so many flower-covered terraces, pergolas, gazebos and trellises that finding this composting system is going to be a job and a half.

'Nothing! I'm perfectly fine, Nolan. How about a game of hide-and-seek?'

'What?!'

'A game of hide-and-seek. This garden looks like it's perfect for a game of hide-and-seek, don't you think?'

Well, how else am I supposed to get rid of Nolan while I look for Irene McClapperty's composting system?

'I don't think—'

'Come on, Nolan. Where's your sense of childhood adventure?'

'Er, back in my childhood?'

I give him a playful punch on the arm.

'Ow!'

'Oh, come on, that was just a playful punch. The kind you gave when you were a kid.'

Nolan rubs his arm and looks at me with an expression that is rapidly descending from mild befuddlement into full-blown concern. He knows something is most definitely up with me, but is probably too scared to bring it up.

That's fine, Nolan.

You just go along with my ridiculous suggestion to play hide-and-seek, so I can catch Irene McClapperty out, and I'll be okay for the rest of our minibreak. No worries at all.

'Go on, you go off and hide,' I demand, 'and I'll come and look for you after the count of fifty.'

Nolan has zero interest in playing hide-and-seek, but he can also see the expression on my face, so he does as he's told.

I give him a few moments to disappear behind one of the ivy-covered trellises, and then nod in a satisfied manner. That's got rid of him. Now I just have to find the composting system – if it exists!

One problem, though – what the hell does a composting system *look like*?

I know what a compost heap is, but a composting *system*? That sounds techy. And something that's probably made out of biodegradable plastics.

It probably looks like a big green dalek, doesn't it? Oh yes. That's the type of look a composting system would have, and no mistake.

Let's have a look around the corner here.

Nope. Not there.

Behind that trellis?

Nope.

Underneath that hyacinth-thronged gazebo?

Not there either.

Behind that lovely wooden bench and miniature fountain?

Certainly not.

Damn.

I'm not thinking this through properly.

A composting system would be nearer the house, wouldn't it? Because you'd need it to be to get to it easily. Yes. Nearer the cottage. That's where I'll look next. Nolan went off in the opposite direction, so I won't have to worry about him.

I search along the south wall of the cottage to no avail, pricking myself on a couple of rose bushes as I do so.

I then have a go at searching along the west wall – and wouldn't you know it, I find the bloody composting system!

Only, it doesn't look like a big green dalek. It's just a slightly raised, square metal hatch, sitting in the middle of a neatly cropped patch of grass, enclosed by some brown, wicker fence panels.

Nevertheless, this must be it.

I'm almost disappointed.

I really wanted to catch Irene McClapperty out, but here we are – at her composting system. She was telling the truth.

Aha! But does she *use* it? That recycling bin in the utility room was nearly empty. Who's to say Irene McClapperty actually puts this to any better use?!

I'll have to open it up and have a look.

The metal hatch is only about a foot and a bit wide, but it's also pretty damn heavy. Far heavier than I was expecting, and it takes all of my strength to pull it up and slide it off on to the grass.

A slightly unpleasant whiff hits my nostrils as I look down into the darkened guts of the composting system. I can barely see anything down there, so I employ the torch on my iPhone to get a better look.

About two feet below the hatch cover is a layer of greenish brown sludge.

Hmmm.

That certainly looks like compost, doesn't it?

Perhaps I'll just give it a poke to check.

Please be quiet.

I know. I just *know*, alright?

I reach down into the composting system, but can't quite touch the surface of the sludge. I strain a little more to reach it . . . then a little more . . . and just a little more . . .

My balance then gives up the ghost, and my head disappears down the hatch with the top half of my body right behind it, wedging itself in the square hole. At exactly the same time, my hand plunges right into the sludge.

Only it's not really a sludge.

It's a *crust*.

And what's inside is not compost, my friends. At least not the kind produced by plants.

The second my hand breaks through the thick crust, a stench so enormous it should have a harness on it erupts right into my face.

I want to pull back from it, but I'm wedged in the bloody hole, with nothing to use as leverage.

The colossal smell fills every orifice in my head. My hair now dangles in the disgusting dark mass hidden underneath the thick crust. My hand is covered in it, like I'm wearing a filthy brown glove.

There's nothing I can do except vomit.

Which just makes things smell even worse, so I vomit some more.

'Help!' I then scream, into what can only be described as the worst thing I've ever seen – and I sat through all of season eight of *Game of Thrones* in one ill-advised binge session.

I actually feel like I'm going to black out.

There's no two ways about it, I am definitely about to black—

I feel arms around my waist, and I am yanked backwards out of the hole to emerge into the light – and more importantly, the fresh air.

'Aaaargh!' I screech, as I sit down hard on the grass, carried by the momentum generated by those arms. As I do this, my wet hair slaps against my face.

With horror, revulsion and another high-pitched scream that verges on the insane, I hold up my dirty hand and examine what's on it.

I want to *die*.

'What the hell were you doing?!' Nolan exclaims from where he's also come crashing down on to the neatly clipped grass.

'I was . . . I was looking for the composting system!' I wail, now holding my hand as far away from me as possible. If I could chop it off, I fucking would.

'Is everything okay?' I hear Irene McClapperty say in an extremely worried voice, as she appears from between the wicker fence panels. 'I heard screaming and I—' A hand flies to her face. 'Oh my lord! What's happened?!'

I look up at her, and try to think of a good excuse for this sorry sight. 'We were . . . we were playing hide-and-seek!'

She recoils. 'And you thought you'd hide in the *septic tank*?'

Yep.

We all knew what it was anyway, didn't we? But Irene McClapperty has confirmed it for us.

I didn't find the composting system, full of dead plants and useful nutrients – I found the cottage's septic tank, full of shit and piss.

I am covered in shit and piss.

Some of it probably my own.

In my overwhelming and over-the-top obsession with the environmental credentials of Withy Views B&B, I have managed to immerse my hand up to the elbow in faeces.

It's in my hair too. And all over my face.

I want to die.

'I need . . . I need a shower,' I weep, pulling a wet strand of hair away from my forehead. I'm just going to think of it as 'wet' and nothing else, because if I don't, I'm likely to lose my mind.

Nolan leaps to his feet. 'I'll go run it for you!' he says, and sprints off in the direction of our room.

Irene McClapperty gives me a look. It's one I will never forget. 'You must . . . you must really like winning at hide-and-seek,' she says.

I have no answer.

I am covered in faeces and urine because I have turned into some kind of environmental maniac, who just couldn't forget about four normal bloody light bulbs – and I really have no answer.

It turned out Nolan was hiding behind the composting system.

Because of course he bloody was.

276

The rest of the weekend is spent avoiding Irene McClapperty like the plague. I took my breakfast in our room, feigning illness brought on by my visit to the inner recesses of her septic tank.

I have had a lot of thinking to do.

A lot of thinking about what I have become.

Which – in case you hadn't already come to this conclusion – is a raving environmentalist loon.

There's nothing like plunging your hand through a thick crust of dried-over poo to make you really look at your choices in life – and my recent choices have been driven by several months of working in a job that has turned me into an obsessive.

Poor old Irene McClapperty didn't deserve all of that.

And she certainly didn't need to be judged unworthy by the likes of me, just because she had four normal light bulbs.

She wasn't lying about the composting system. In fact, she wasn't lying about Withy Views being environmentally friendly. It turns out that the whole cottage is run on solar power, from panels on the roof – they're just hidden on the other side, away from view when you arrive at the cottage.

If I'd taken a breath, and bothered to actually look into things a bit more closely, I would have discovered them, and avoided having to dig poo out from under my nails.

Irene McClapperty wasn't lying. Not at all.

I wasn't deceived. Not for one second.

The poor woman is trying her best to do her bit for the environment, and I'd decided she was unworthy thanks to her light bulbs.

Good grief.

And I embarrassed Nolan. I know I did. He's been awkward around me, the other guests at the B&B, and Irene McClapperty the entire rest of the time we've been here.

I suppose I can't blame him for feeling that way.

I was rude, weird and judgemental. Who wants to spend time with somebody like that, eh?

Ellie Cooke from a few months ago certainly wouldn't.

But then, the Ellie Cooke from this weekend would probably punch the Ellie Cooke from a few months ago for driving around in that clobberdy-banging, gas-guzzling Mercedes.

I really thought that my job at Viridian PR had made me a better person – that my new-found desire to save the planet had improved me.

But I'm now forced to admit that in some ways I've become *worse*.

And I might have *once again* soured things with Nolan. We'd only just restored the happy dynamic of our relationship, and yet here I am – acting like a right wally and jeopardising it once more!

The fact that the problem which might ruin our romance *this* time around is how insanely environmentally conscious I've become, is an irony that is not lost on me. I couldn't bloody lose it if I were at the bottom of the Mariana Trench, in a camouflaged submarine.

Hell's bloody teeth.

I just need to get home now. Get home, and try my best to come down off this bizarre, frenzied plateau I've stuck myself on.

And that starts with maybe taking a bit of a step back at work. Not from the job itself, but from some of the client relationships I've developed. It's just not healthy to be constantly talking with – and following the advice of – a large selection of green crusaders. You can't be bombarded with that much information, passion and righteous indignation without being heavily affected by it.

I'll also try to prove to Nolan that I am not as insane as I have seemed on this trip down to the Cotswolds.

Quite how I'm going to do it, I don't know. But I'd better think of something fast, otherwise I really am going to lose him properly this time.

. . . if seeing me – and smelling me – covered in his own waste matter hasn't done that already, of course.

Chapter Twelve

An Extremely Inconvenient Truth

I sit at my desk, drumming my nails on its wooden surface, in a rapid staccato fashion that perfectly echoes the turmoil going on in my head.

I can't think straight.

And I certainly can't get any work done.

I've been like this for days now, ever since we got back from Withy Views.

Nolan has been avoiding me *again* – I know that for a fact. We were supposed to spend the night together last night, but he called to cancel, telling me he had too much paperwork to catch up on. It's an excuse that would have been more believable if I didn't know exactly what Nolan's workload was like at the moment. He doesn't have any paperwork to do right now.

I can't even go speak to him today, because he's off on another one of his regular scouting-for-business missions. I have no idea where he's gone.

I just have to sit here and drum my fingernails on my desk, letting my brain stew in its own half-guilty, half-frustrated juices.

'Everything alright?' Nadia says.

'I'm sorry?'

'I said . . . is everything alright? Only you've been doing that for so long, you're starting to wear holes in the wood.'

I look down at my drumming fingers and will them to stop. 'Sorry. Bit preoccupied.'

'With what?'

I open my mouth to spill my guts . . . but of course I can't do that, can I? Because Nadia – like the rest of Viridian PR – still has no idea I'm dating our boss.

Bollocks.

'Nothing important,' I eventually tell her. 'Just some work-related stuff.'

'Anything you can discuss with me?'

'No. Not really, I'm afraid.'

'Ah . . . well, then maybe you should have a chat with Nolan? Maybe he could help.'

My face darkens. If only she knew.

'He's out of the office today,' I tell her. 'Off touting for business again somewhere.'

Nadia looks a little confused. 'He told me he was working from home today. Catching up on paperwork. It's in his diary on the intranet.'

Oh, *great*. So now he's lying to me about what he's doing with his work days.

. . . I'd better go see him.

I'd better get this sorted out. I'd better apologise – *again* – and hope that he's as forgiving as he has been before.

My heart leaps into my throat. The idea of just turning up unannounced at his door fills me with dread, but if I call ahead to say I'm coming, he'll likely just give me an excuse to avoid seeing me.

No. I have to go round there and talk it out with him. Pin him down, and try to convince him I'm not the maniac from the weekend that he thinks I am.

'Right,' I say, out loud.

'Right what?' Nadia asks.

'I will go speak to him, Nadia. That's good advice.'

'Thanks,' she replies, as she watches me rise purposefully from my office chair. 'And remind him we're meeting with the guys from Barks & Larks tomorrow. They want to talk through the ideas we had for their radio campaign.'

'Will do,' I tell her – hoping that I actually get a chance to do so.

With a decision made, and some kind of plan in place, I feel galvanised for the first time in a few days. I've been listless and out of sorts – disappearing down a septic tank will do that to you – but now I feel motivated to sort this mini crisis out, before it can get any worse.

And that begins with the twenty-minute drive to Nolan's large Victorian terraced house.

It feels slightly strange to be making the journey on my own. Every other time I've been this way, I've been with him. Going over to his place without him knowing I'm coming feels extremely strange – but then I guess it would. It's not like we've been together all that long, and we've certainly had our ups and downs. We're not in each other's pockets just yet.

Not that we ever will be if I don't do some fast, convincing talking when I get there.

On the drive over, I formulate what I'm going to say in my head – and it largely consists of me telling Nolan about my thought process over the past few days. I know I have more apologies to make, but I also think I have some pretty good mitigating circumstances for my behaviour.

I'm just the type of person that can get way too caught up in something if I'm given half the chance. My recent strangeness has only come about with the best of intentions – and I need Nolan to know that.

Surely if he sees that I have developed this odd, judgemental attitude only because I am now dedicated to the same cause as him, it'll smooth things over? He can surely appreciate that, can't he? My heart's in the right place, even if my brain possibly hasn't been.

Yes.

That sounds about right to me.

My justifications are convincing. It should all be fine.

So why do my hands get very cold and sweaty as I turn into Nolan's road?

Just take some deep breaths.

The only parking space I can find is about twenty yards away from Nolan's house. As I squeeze my hybrid Mercedes into the space between two parked cars that I would never get into were it not for the super-duper park-assist technology that the car comes with, I look in the rear-view mirror to see someone coming out of Nolan's front door.

My hackles immediately go up, as this person is dressed in an extremely shifty manner. He's wearing a black baseball cap, sunglasses and a dark-blue hooded top, with the hood up over the cap. As he walks down the three steps that lead to Nolan's front door, he looks in both directions up and down the street.

Burglar.

That's who this person is!

Someone has burgled poor Nolan and is making off with his valuables—

Wait a minute.

That's not a burglar doing Nolan's pad over.

That *is* Nolan.

He's just briefly taken off the sunglasses to give them a wipe as he crosses the street, and I'd know those kind, easy-going grey eyes anywhere!

What is he doing?

Why is he dressed like that? And why is he acting in such a furtive manner?

Part of me wants to jump out of the car and go over to him to confront him, and see what he's up to . . . but there's another part of me that just wants to sit here and see what happens.

It's a very primal part of my personality. Something that I'm sure is a holdover from one of my distant ancestors, who knew that discretion was the better part of valour sometimes – especially when it came to observing that massive sabre-toothed tiger in the grass over there.

Okay, I don't think Nolan poses any real kind of threat to me just because he's dressed like that, but something very strange is going on, and alarm bells are ringing in my head.

I hunker down in my seat a little and turn to look through the rear windscreen as Nolan walks straight past his neat little Tesla – and goes straight towards a frankly enormous bright-green BMW M3.

I've noticed that gaudy fucker a couple of times when I've come down this street in Nolan's car, and have blanched at it every time. It must be hideously bad for the environment. The fact that the bonnet bulges outwards must mean the engine underneath is gigantic.

Maybe Nolan is going over to vandalise it?

That's why he's wearing those odd clothes and looking so suspicious?

Oh God.

I have to stop him. Being dedicated to an environmental cause is one thing, but committing criminal damage to someone's property is quite another! I must stop him before he—

Hang on a bloody minute . . .

He's not vandalising the stupid green BMW – he's *climbing into it*!

Nolan Reece is getting into an overblown German muscle car, and is starting the engine.

What the hell is going on?!

I can hear the loud, guttural roar coming from the BMW very easily, despite the fact that I am in my own hermetically sealed Mercedes car cabin. The sound of it must echo around the street like a jet aircraft taking off.

My jaw goes slack as I watch Nolan pull out of the parking space in the brutish sports car and drive past me. Instinct tells me I need to duck my head so he doesn't see me.

I have to see what Nolan is up to, and I won't get to do that if I am discovered . . .

As Nolan reaches the end of the street, I fire up my own nearly silent car, and follow along behind him, keeping enough distance to stop him from noticing that he now has a tail.

Bloody hell.

I came here this morning to make my apologies and make amends. I didn't expect to find myself thrust into an impromptu spy thriller!

As I turn on to the main road, and continue to follow my furtive boyfriend, my mind starts to race with the implications of what I'm seeing.

Why is Nolan acting so suspiciously? And why is he driving such a different car?

Then it hits me.

The bastard!

The bastard is having an affair with another fucking *woman*!

That must be it!

He's carrying on with another woman behind my back – and is behaving this strangely because he doesn't want to get caught!

That must be it.

Not only is he conducting a relationship with me behind the backs of all our staff at Viridian PR, he's also conducting *another* relationship with *someone else* behind *my* back . . . as well as everybody at Viridian PR.

Cheatception.

And today – when he's supposed to be working from home, or out and about touting for business, depending on whether Nadia was right about his activities or not – he's going off to see his fancy woman dressed like a member of a particularly bad boy band from the 1990s.

My hands grip the steering wheel so tightly they go white.

After everything!

After all that's happened!

After everything I've done to stay in his good books!

After all the bloody *forgiveness* I've sought!

After all the apologies I've made, and was *going* to make!

I'm going to catch him in the act. I'm going to see who this bitch is, and I'm going to make her pay!

All thoughts of apologies and amends-making have gone completely out of the window. I am now incandescent with rage about being cheated on (despite the fact that I have absolutely *no* evidence of this, beyond Nolan's impression of Justin Timberlake, and a sickly green sports car).

I can feel my breath starting to come in long, slow exhalations that end with a slight grunt. My eyes are fixed on Nolan's disgusting green car, as he weaves his way between the traffic.

Where is he going?

Is he going to *her place*? Are they meeting for some hot, hard morning sex? I bet that's it! I just bet it is!

If that *is* the case, Nolan is obviously buying some contraceptives, because he's just parked outside a convenience store.

I pull in, several car lengths back, and wait for him to come back out again.

On impulse, I pull out my mobile phone, and bring up the camera. I have the overwhelming desire to record what Nolan's up to. Maybe it's because I feel like I've suddenly entered a bad spy novel, or maybe it's just that I want to make sure I have proof of his infidelity when I do confront him.

Nolan emerges from the convenience store – but it's not condoms he's come out with.

It's *cigarettes*.

Standing right in front of his horrible green BMW, he unwinds the cellophane around the packet, opens it, pulls out a cigarette, and lights it with a box of matches.

What the actual, *actual*, ACTUAL fuck?

Nolan doesn't *smoke*! I've *never* seen him smoke!

Is his fancy woman a weirdo who likes the smell of tobacco on a man? I guess she must be, otherwise why would he be sparking up like this? Maybe she also loves the stench of petrol, hence the stupid gas guzzler.

But why would environmental crusader Nolan Reece want to be around a woman *like that*?

I am utterly confused, horrified and distressed as Nolan gets back into his BMW and starts it up again.

I then proceed to follow him around the streets, still keeping my distance so as not to be noticed.

In my ongoing desire to capture everything that Nolan is doing, I put my car's dashcam on continuous record, so that I have proof of all of his movements as we drive along.

OH MY GOD.

He just flicked a cigarette butt out of the window!

Nolan just *LITTERED*.

I blink a couple of times at the enormity of it. I can't believe my eyes. I'll have to look back at the footage on the dashcam later to make sure it actually happened.

And where is he going now?

KFC?

He's turning into the drive-through at KF *motherfucking* C?

I have to park the Mercedes across the road, in an industrial unit's car park, because my legs have started to shake so much I can't control the accelerator pedal properly.

Is this woman *insane*? She wants her man to stink of fags, petrol and fried chicken?

And how good must she be in bed for Nolan to go along with all of this?

I watch – with my phone camera *and* my dashcam recording – as my soon-to-be very ex-boyfriend gives his order at the drive-through window, grabs his purchase as soon as it's ready, and parks the big green monstrosity in the KFC main car park. There he proceeds to devour several pieces of KFC's finest fried chicken, and guzzles an enormous milkshake.

He then sparks up another cigarette, and sits back in his car seat with a very contented look on his face.

I am at the opposite end of contented.

I am so far away from contented that I may never be able to feel contented ever again in my natural life, without swallowing a bucket of diazepam.

And I'm starting to think I might have read this entire situation wrong . . .

These are not the actions of a man about to go and have sex with a secret lover.

I don't really know what kind of man these are the actions of, but I'm pretty sure no man on Earth would think covering himself in chicken grease and cigarette smoke is the best way of getting a woman in the mood for love.

So, this begs the question . . . what is Nolan up to?

I have to let out an audible gasp when I watch him drop his brown KFC paper bag out of the window.

I can see a rubbish bin not ten yards away from where he's sat!

Nolan then pulls out of the car park in his loud, stupid car, and proceeds to roar away at a great rate of knots, forcing me to get going as quickly as I can so I don't lose him.

The spy thriller then moves into an action chase sequence, as Nolan decides to open the taps on his awful BMW along the motorway. It's a good job the fucking thing is the garish shade of green that it is, otherwise I would lose him, given the speed he's going. It also helps that he keeps revving the engine, which produces a loud bark of exhaust noise that is hard to fucking miss.

I repeatedly check that my dashcam is pointing in the right direction, to make sure I capture all of this reckless, wasteful driving for posterity.

Several miles down the road, Nolan takes the slipway off the motorway, and drives down into Whitehaven Shopping Centre.

I haven't been here since that day with the Worriors For The Plonet.

In my time at Viridian PR, I've come to learn just how environmentally unsound the kinds of clothes that are sold in places like this are. Nolan himself once lectured me about the evils of disposable fashion. How the clothes are made in sweatshops, by unscrupulous manufacturers, using production techniques that send tonnes of chemicals into rivers and lakes every year.

So this is my first time back to Whitehaven, and I'm doing it in the strangest and most awful circumstances I can possibly think of.

My lovely boyfriend Nolan Reece – my lovely *boss* Nolan Reece – is acting so completely out of character that he might as well be another man. And it scares me to death, to be honest. Who have I been seeing all this time?

I'll tell you who:

A man who has just bought a shitload of clothes in Primark!

Fucking PRIMARK, everybody.

The absolute *king* of throwaway, disposable fashion!

I've just spent the last fifteen minutes creeping around behind Nolan with my iPhone grasped in one shaking hand – trying to remain concealed behind the mountains of sweatpants and onesies – watching him grab a whole pile of cheaply made clothes. This includes several pairs of plain black boxer shorts. The same kind of boxer shorts I've seen him wearing before. And the same kind of boxer shorts he told me were organically produced by bloody Hempawear!

They're not Hempawear! They're fucking *Primark*!

He must've just cut the bloody labels out!

Incandescent with rage doesn't even begin to cover it now. I am fucking NUCLEAR with it. It's taking every ounce of my being not to leap out from behind this stack of £10 skinny jeans and confront him right here and now on the shop floor.

I gaze on in horror through the screen of my iPhone as I record him paying for his pile of offensive clothing and walking back out of the store with a stuffed Primark bag.

'Is he cheating on you?' a voice says from just beside me.

I whirl round to see a woman in her mid-forties holding a pair of jeans and regarding me with a solemn expression.

'I'm sorry?'

'Is he cheating on you? I had that same look on my face when I hunted Derek around Tesco on Valentine's Day,' she explains. 'He was buying *her* a box of Ferrero Rocher and a bunch of flowers. I got a cheap card and a Creme Egg.'

'No . . . no, I don't think he's cheating on me. It's even worse.'

'Oh, really?'

'Yes. I think he's cheating on the *planet*.'

I don't give Jeans Lady time to respond, as I want to make sure I keep up with Nolan for the next stage of his secret sojourn into the life of a wasteful prick.

There's a sticky moment in Whitehaven car park when he nearly sees me, but I manage to duck behind a Veganthropy Foods delivery van before he does.

Oh, what would Mordred O'Hare think of Nolan's actions today? What would *he* do?

Place some sort of curse on him, involving toads and a sprig of heather, possibly. I don't have access to such pagan magic though, so I'll just have to think of something else.

. . . and what would *Robert Ainslie Blake* think about Nolan's actions, for that matter? Why, he'd probably think he was looking into a fucking *mirror*. The seats in that stupid muscle car look like they're more than wide enough for a bit of hardcore manspreading.

Nolan actually heads for home now, still driving the muscle car like a complete bellend. If he revs that engine much harder, he's likely to develop a clobberdy-bang of epic proportions.

Thanks to the speed he insists on going, we arrive back at his street in no time at all.

I watch Nolan park up and get out of the vomit-green BMW with his bag of Primark nastiness – again with that furtive look on his face – and make his way back across the street to his house.

Right. That's quite enough of all of this malarkey. It's time to confront Nolan and find out what the hell is going on!

It's very important I do this while he's holding the evidence of his crimes.

My efforts at subterfuge now gratefully set aside, I pull the Mercedes up right in front of his house, jump out, and attempt to dramatically slam the car door to alert him to my presence. Annoyingly, the hybrid has a special soft-close system that means the door shuts with barely a clunk, no matter how hard I try to slam it.

Damn me and my sensible car choices!

I'll just have to scuttle over without the dramatic introduction, I guess.

Actually, I'm done scuttling. I'm going to fucking *stomp*, and there's not a damn thing anyone can do to stop me.

Nolan still doesn't appear to notice me however – given that he has his head down and that stupid hoodie up over his face – so he's putting the keys in the front door before I reach him.

But when I do, he sure as hell knows I'm there, because I slap him hard on his left shoulder.

'Waaaa!' he exclaims in shock, dropping the bag of Primark goodies (baddies?) on the doorstep. He swings around wildly, forcing me back down the steps. I start to lose my balance and pinwheel my arms to try to maintain it.

This is not the look I wanted to present. I wanted to be standing there with my hands on my hips like an irate Wonder Woman – not flailing around like I'm in an amateur dramatics production of *Wuthering Heights*.

I manage to steady myself on the pavement enough to look up at Nolan with towering indignation. I'd ideally like to have the high ground here, but this will just have to do. I'm pretty sure I have the moral high ground regardless.

'Ellie?!' Nolan blurts out, the blood draining from his face.

'Yes! *Ellie!*' I roar back at him. 'What the hell do you think you're doing, Nolan?!'

Of course, this is not the way one should talk to one's boss. Under any circumstances. It's a guaranteed one-way ticket to unemployment town. But of course, I'm not talking to my boss now, am I? That relationship has been superseded by *the other one*.

'What do you mean?'

Oh!

Look at that guilt! Just *look at it*!

'You know exactly what I mean!' I point at the Primark bag. 'You! Yooooouuuuu!' I howl accusingly, stabbing my finger down at it again.

Nolan yanks the hoodie off his head and takes off the sunglasses. The jig is up, and he knows it. 'It's not what it looks like!' he entreats.

'Not what it looks like?!'

'No!'

'You mean to say you haven't spent the entire day driving around in that fucking green thing over there, smoking cigarettes, eating fried chicken, littering everywhere . . . and buying Primark pants?!' For some reason, it's the last thing that really gets my free-range goat. 'Primark pants, Nolan!' I point at his crotch. 'You wear Primark pants!'

He also looks down at his crotch with mounting horror. I hope it's because he realises he's not getting anywhere near *my* pants again (genuine Hempawear, I should add – I still have to use creams every now and then), unless he comes up with a decent explanation for his behaviour pretty fucking quickly.

'You've been *following* me?' he eventually says, looking back up at me.

'Yes, Nolan! I have been following you! And I've seen what you've been doing!'

'No! No! It's really not what it looks like! I've been . . . *role playing*. Yes, role playing.' His expression changes to the thoughtful one he always gets when he's had an idea for Viridian PR and is bouncing it off me. 'I wanted to spend a day in the shoes of an ordinary person, you know? Get inside their head and try to—'

'Don't you even bother!' I interrupt. 'There's no way you'd do something like that! At least, there's no way the Nolan I thought I knew would do something like that! Tell me the truth! What's going on? Why are you acting like this?'

For a moment Nolan's face contorts like it's being pinched by invisible hands. He's obviously weighing up the situation and trying to devise an excuse that I might believe.

My face, however, tells him in no uncertain terms that there is nothing he can tell me right now that will sate my rage. He might as well come clean. I have him bang to rights and *he knows it*.

'I can't *take it any more*!' he eventually screams, his voice echoing around the street. 'I thought I could live like a greenie for as long as I needed to. For as long as it took to really establish Viridian PR.' His face crumples. 'But it's *impossible*! If I have to look at another fucking tofu stir fry again, I'll kill myself!'

'What do you mean, *live like a greenie*?'

He waves a hand. 'You know . . . like *one of them*. The vegan types. The climate-change weirdos. The beardy weirdies.'

'The beardy weirdies?'

'Yeah! The beardy weirdies. All of that bunch.'

I am utterly astounded, and not a little devastated. 'Are you telling me . . . are you telling me, Nolan, that you've been *faking it this entire time*?'

He shrugs his shoulders. 'Of course I have.'

If I clench my fists any tighter, my nails are going to draw blood. And I'm not necessarily talking about mine.

'WHY?' I screech like an enraged fishwife.

He plasters himself against the front door. 'Because . . . because I wanted to make Viridian PR profitable!'

'What?!'

'There's a lot of money in environmental stuff, Ellie,' he attempts to explain. 'You know that. And they don't have that many people fighting their corner, so I thought it'd be a good idea to target them. Get them all on board with a company that *understands* them. Get the business really going, before—'

He stops himself, his eyes suddenly going very wide.

'Before *what?*' I demand.

'Nothing!'

My eyes flash. 'You'd better say what you were going to, Nolan, otherwise I'm likely to start doing things to your person that we will both regret.'

He gulps.

'Talk!' I demand.

He gulps again, but does indeed speak. 'Before I . . . before I sell it off.'

'Sell it off?!'

'Yes! That's the endgame with these things! Get a company up and running, get loads of clients, and then sell both to the highest bidder once you've earned a good reputation. There's millions to be had.' He gives me an imploring look. 'And I've tried my hardest to keep up the environmental lifestyle, but it just gets too much. I have to go off and . . . you know . . . let off some steam every now and again.'

Oh *Christ*.

That's where he's been going on his little sojourns out of the office! I thought he was touting for business, but he's really been cramming his face with fast food and polluting the atmosphere like an absolute arsehole! He hasn't been avoiding me because of what happened at Irene McClapperty's!

I'm speechless.

My blood has run cold.

I can feel the edges of my vision starting to blur.

I think I'm about to have a panic attack.

No you bloody don't, missus. You didn't have a panic attack with your head stuck in other people's shit and piss, and you're not going to have one now.

I bite my lip painfully hard, to bring myself out of it.

It works, but now I've tasted blood, I want more of it.

'You lied! You lied *to me*!' I screech.

I hope the neighbours are all out at work, otherwise they're going to have their afternoon ruined by all of this shouting.

Who cares though? I am clearly *never coming back here again*, so I am going to go to bloody town on Nolan Reece – in a golden carriage pulled by fucking horses.

'You lied to *everyone*!' I continue, scarcely able to believe what I'm saying.

My entire relationship with Nolan Reece has been built on a massive falsehood. Both as a boss and a lover, everything about him has been a lie. Everything I knew about the person I may well have been falling for has been completely manufactured, just in the pursuit of financial gain!

You did the same thing though, Ellie. Remember?

No!

No! I am not having that!

I was just trying to save my job! Save my skin! I wasn't trying to manipulate dozens of people just to sell them down the river when the time was right!

And besides . . . I'm *not* that person any more. I've had my eyes opened, *goddamn it.*

Unfortunately, all of that started with this lying charlatan standing in front of me, and that's why I'm so bloody *angry*.

Nolan contrives to look apologetic. 'I was going to share it all with you though, Ellie! I was going to tell you everything!'

'Rubbish! I don't believe you!'

'I was! Once Viridian was in the right position, I was going to sit down with you, and go through the next stages. You would have been instrumental in helping me sell the business off!'

'Oh, would I?!'

'Yes! Especially if someone like Mr Ainslie Blake was keen on buying it. You could have sweet-talked him for me, given . . . you know . . .'

Instantly, all of the warmth in the whole universe is sucked into an inescapable oblivion.

'Robert?' I hiss.

Nolan actually looks terrified. 'Yes. He . . . he could have been a buyer. He wanted to improve his property development company's image – and diversify his portfolio. What better way to do that than owning your own PR firm? And, you know, because you dated him, you might have been able to . . . to . . .'

I feel faint.

Taking a deep breath, I force myself to look into Nolan's eyes. 'That's why he was in your office that day, wasn't it? The *real* fucking reason?'

He doesn't say anything. This is probably for the best, because I think you get about twenty-five years for murder, don't you?

I hold one finger up and point it at Nolan's face. I can't stop it shaking. 'And I thought . . . I thought he *bullied* you into seeing him. I thought you were upset he was there. I thought you were upset with *me*!'

'Well, I was.'

'What?!'

Nolan shrugs. 'You came in just as we were starting to talk numbers. He got put off when you appeared, and—'

'Shut the fuck up, you fucking fuck *fuck*!' I scream, my ability to swear effectively having deserted me completely in my all-encompassing rage.

I was so *sorry*!

I was so *guilty*!

I went around thinking I'd betrayed Nolan by not being honest with him!

And all the time, *he* was the one lying through his teeth! He wasn't scared of Robert, or disgusted with him being in his office. He was the one that probably *organised the meeting in the first place*!

Aaargghh!

What an absolute fucking fuck fuck!

'You wanted *me*,' I spit, 'to help *you* sell Viridian PR to Robert Ainslie Blake?'

'Yeah, probably.'

Jesus Christ. He really means it. He would have actually tried to make me do that.

'It's a bloody good job it didn't get that far,' I hiss. 'Because I would have told you where to fucking stick it!'

Now, for the first time, I see something in Nolan Reece's eyes I really, really don't like. He sneers at me. 'Really? Well that would have been bloody stupid of you, wouldn't it?'

'No! No, it bloody wouldn't!' I stab a finger at him. 'And I'm not going to let you get away with this!'

The sneer gets bigger. 'Ha! What are you going to do about it? I'm your fucking *boss*, Ellie. Remember?'

The total change of demeanour knocks the stuffing out of me. This is a different man standing in front of me. This isn't Nolan Reece.

Of course it is – you're just meeting the real Nolan Reece for the first time. A man who actually manages to make Robert Ainslie Blake seem like a nice chap.

But what are you going to do about it?

I think I'll hit him.

Yes.

That's what I'm going to do.

But I'm not going to punch him. No. I need something more appropriate to whack him with than my fist. I'm just as likely to hurt myself as I am him if I do that.

I know. That Primark bag is good and heavy, isn't it?

Yes.

That'll do nicely.

I bend forward, forcing Nolan to pin himself against his front door again. Then I pick up the large Primark bag and swing it up over my head with all the power I can muster. When I bring it back down again, it is borne upon the winds of unholy anger.

As the bag connects with Nolan's face, I let out a scream of such primal rage, it will leave me with a sore throat for days.

But it's oh so bloody *satisfying*.

To batter this stupid, lying bastard with a bagload of cheap pants is the greatest feeling in the world.

'Aaaargh!' Nolan squeals, as I thwack him, sending his cheaply made clothing flying in all directions.

'Yes! You squeal!' I cry to the heavens. 'You squeal as I belt you with pants! You scream as I assault you with knickers! You cry as I box you with boxers, you lying . . . worthless . . . little shit!'

The Primark bag splits asunder, cascading the rest of its contents across Nolan's entire doorstep in a glorious explosion of cotton and polyester.

'You're bloody mad!' he exclaims, arms held up protectively in front of him.

'You're damn fucking right I am!' I draw myself up to my full height and stab my finger right at his chest. 'I *doted* on you!' I roar at him, probably revealing more in my anger and frustration than I should. 'I *admired* you! I . . . I . . . changed my life because of you!'

He actually tries to smile, and shrugs his shoulders. 'Well . . . that's *good* then, isn't it? I must have had a positive effect on you! I've done you *good!*'

This comment is so unendingly awful and self-serving that I am momentarily struck both dumb and immobile by it. For a second, all I can do is stare at Nolan. Stare at this man – who has so convincingly pulled the wool over my eyes for so long, that I don't know how I'll ever be able to trust anyone ever again.

Then I pick up a pair of Primark boxers and start to thrash him with them.

Have you ever tried to thrash someone with a small piece of thin material? It's not easy. But I am, in my heightened state, giving it a good bloody go.

'Meeargh!' Nolan wails, as I flick the boxers around his head and neck, like I'm trying to kill a particularly large and fast mosquito.

I look like an enraged morris dancer.

'I can't believe I trusted you!' I scream, as I take another swing. 'I can't believe I took your advice!' *Whack.* 'I can't believe I thought you were committed to making the world a better place!' *Thwack.* 'I can't believe I felt so guilty about not being honest with you!' *Thwack.* 'I can't believe . . . I can't believe *I had sex with you!*'

'Stop hitting me!' he spits, trying to dodge the thwacking boxer shorts as best he can.

It's a good job Nolan Reece has never come across as much of an alpha male. I would be in some danger of getting hit in retaliation if he were a different man, but as it is, I'm pretty sure I could stand here all day assaulting him with pants, and not get smacked in return. He's just not that type of bloke.

What type of man is he, though?

This type, apparently . . .

'I'll sack you!' he screams. 'I'll sack you right here and now if you don't stop doing that!' Nolan threatens, as one of the plastic buttons on the fly of the boxer shorts leaves a satisfying red mark on his forehead.

'Sack me?!' I scream indignantly. 'How the hell are you going to sack me, Nolan, when I fucking QUIT!'

A few months ago, the idea of screaming at my boss that I was going to quit my job would have filled me with horror. After all, you're talking about a person who was so scared of being out of a job that she faked an entire lifestyle just to keep it.

But now, it feels like the most natural thing I've ever done. I absolutely know it's the right thing to do, and – even in the midst of my enraged boxer-shorts assault – there's a small part of my brain that realises becoming environmentally conscious isn't the only change that working for Viridian PR has brought about in me.

I am a different person in more ways than I thought.

I may know how dangerous palm oil, light bulbs and plastic pollution are, but I'm also . . . *braver*, I think. I'm also *stronger*. In my newly discovered desire to make the world a better place, I've inadvertently made myself a *better person*.

It's because of all the things I've done. All the crazy, crazy things I've been through in pursuit of doing a better job for me, and then doing a better job for the environment. The taking part in protests, the dressing up in a foam bottle costume, the sticking my head down a septic tank.

. . . okay, maybe not that last one, but you get the point.

I've gone from someone very passive to someone entirely active – perhaps a little *too* active, in some respects.

But all in all, I *am* better. I am more than I used to be.

I am now the kind of person who can bellow that they quit in their weasel boss's face, and not regret it for a moment.

This revelation stops my assault on Nolan's person as quickly as it started. This is just as well, as the Primark boxers aren't holding up under the battering, and have already torn themselves to bits.

I don't need to be doing this.

I don't need to be standing here, making a spectacle of myself in public like this.

I need to leave.

I need to get away from this horrible individual and *think*.

Think about what I'm going to do next, now that I have the truth laid out in front of me.

I drop the boxer shorts and give Nolan the most derisory look I can possibly muster.

'You're a sad little greedy troll, Nolan Reece,' I tell him. 'And I don't want to work for somebody like that. *Ever*.'

'Oh, piss off, love,' he sneers at me. 'You've had it *great* working for me. And you could have had so much more, if you'd just gone along with it a little bit longer.'

'I don't think so,' I tell him in a low voice. 'I'm not going to pretend I'm something I'm not just to keep a bloody job. Not any more.' I fix him with a stare. 'I'm not like you.'

The sneer now turns into a full-blown look of hate. 'No . . . you're *not*. You'll never be a success like me, because you don't have the *killer instinct*. I didn't get where I am today being all righteous and up my own arse. I got where I am today by – FUCK ME!'

I've just picked up a new pair of boxers and have started thrashing him again. It was either that or listen to him monologue. I don't want to listen to him monologue – he's only going to say a lot of things I already know.

I only stop again because my arm grows too tired to continue. It really is time to leave.

'Yeah! Go on! Piss off!' Nolan spits at me, as I begin to walk away. 'I don't need *you*, Ellie! I can run that company fine without *you*!' And then he says the first thing I've heard all day that makes me genuinely fearful. 'Nobody will believe you, you know! They'll all believe me! I'm Nolan Reece!'

He's *right*.

He's absolutely right.

I may have exposed Nolan's real personality and his real intentions today, but that doesn't mean anybody else will turn away from him. He's the *boss*. He's the great Nolan Reece – PR genius, and all-round good guy.

What can I possibly do to—

. . . ah, but of course.

I pop a hand in my pocket, and feel the reassuring cool metal of my iPhone . . . with its lovely video camera and large hard drive full of recently recorded clips.

And as I climb into my equally lovely Mercedes hybrid, I look up at the dashcam – which I put on constant record earlier, didn't I? And its hard drive that can hold up to three hours of footage. I distinctly remember my cocaine-happy car salesman telling me that when I bought the car.

There are three hours of me following Nolan Reece around in his vomit-green BMW on that dashcam. All in glorious high-definition vision and audio.

What a clever girl I am.

What a clever and decidedly *lucky* girl I am.

From through the windscreen I give Nolan Reece a smile. It is a shark-like smile, laced with such a huge degree of intent, that it can't help but make him physically balk, right there on his doorstep.

I've got you, you little toad. I've got you.

Still with the shark's grin on my face, I reverse the car, pull back out into the road, and stamp on the accelerator.

I have things to do.

I have plans to make.

Plans that are already formulating in my mind around this central hypothesis:

How can I both expose Nolan Reece for the deceitful wretch that he is, and ensure that my future is not equally damaged by today's events?

In short – how can I screw him, and at the same time, save myself?

By the time I get back to the offices of Viridian PR, I think I know how I'm going to do it.

And it's going to involve *theft*.

Grand-scale theft – the likes of which I don't know if I have the courage, or the capacity, to accomplish.

But I'm going to give it a bloody good go . . . because I'm brave now. I'm brave, and perhaps more importantly – I'm *motivated*. Motivated to save myself, and this bloody planet while I'm at it.

'Ellie? Ellie? Are you alright?' Nadia asks me when I get back to my desk and start to pack my stuff into a small brown box.

What the hell do I say? Do I tell her what's just happened?

No.

Not yet . . .

This has to be done *right*.

'I'm . . . I'm fine, Nadia,' I tell her, and I walk over to briefly put a comforting hand on her shoulder, before going back to my desk. 'Look, things are about to happen that are going to seem horrible, but they will work themselves out, I promise.'

The blood drains from her face.

We are joined by Amisha and Joseph, who both look as understandably perturbed as Nadia.

'What's going on?' Amisha exclaims. 'Why are you putting your stuff in that box?' She recoils. 'Are you *leaving*?'

'Yes. I'm done here at Viridian.' I look up at everyone in the office – most of them have also clocked what I'm doing. 'But I'm not *done*, Amisha. Not by a fucking long shot.'

From my desk, I pick up my sweet little succulent pot plant, and pop it into the box. I bought that thing in an effort to keep this bloody job – it's only right I take the plant with me now I'm leaving it.

I wait for the bloom of fear and doubt to suffuse my entire being.

When it doesn't happen, I smile to myself.

Everyone is staring at me now. They know something fundamental is happening.

It only feels right to say something.

'Guys . . . this is my last day here at Viridian PR.' There are a few gasps. Not much of a surprise, really. 'But I just wanted you all to know, it's been great working with you.' I steel myself. 'And I hope . . . I hope that you'll all want to work with me again very soon.'

'What do you mean?' Nadia asks, rising from her seat.

I smile at her. There's steel in it. 'You'll see, Nadia. Very soon, I promise.'

I pick up my box and walk past a sea of confused and worried faces.

Oh boy. That looks familiar.

I am transported back all those months to when Stratagem PR was in deep, deep trouble – until it was saved by a man I *thought* was decent and good.

And now Viridian PR is in as much trouble, even though my colleagues don't know it yet. Nolan will sell them all down the river as soon as he thinks he can make enough cash from the deal.

And I have to stop that. I have to stop it for them, and for me.

That begins with walking out of the door, and starting to act out the plan I came up with on the way over here.

This whole thing started with me trying to impress my new boss.

It's going to end with me trying to *become one*.

Time to get to work.

Chapter Thirteen

Two Stops And A Start

'Are you okay, sis?' Sean asks me.

'Yes, Sean. I'm absolutely fine.'

'Do you . . . do you need some help?'

I give my brother a fond look.

That's Sean. The sensible one. Always there to lend a helping hand. Always there to offer advice. Always there to lead his little sister down the path away from destruction and regret.

Not any more though. Not after all this.

I shake my head. 'No, Sean. I'm fine, thanks. I can handle this all on my own.'

I get up from my seat and go to stand in front of his class.

'Hello, guys,' I say to The Sticky Things, smiling as I do so. The last time I stood here in front of them I was shaken, unsure of myself, and deeply perturbed by everything they knew about climate change.

This time, the smile is genuine, and I'm standing tall. Because I know as much as they do now.

I get a chorus of hellos in return. Some even sound quite pleased to see me. Summer has a bright smile on her face, at least. Children can be very forgiving, if you give them half a chance.

'Now,' I continue, 'if you remember the last time I came in, we had a chat about the climate, didn't we?'

This earns me lots of nods.

'And I didn't really say much that made you feel better about the whole thing, did I? In fact, you might have felt worse after I left.'

A lot of the class look a little stunned at this. They're not used to adults admitting their mistakes or flaws. That is not meant to be the dynamic between children and adults *at all.*

I smile again. 'Well, I wanted to come back and talk to you all about the new thing I'm going to do that will help the environment. And I'm hoping that you'll want to give me a bit of help with it.'

'What is it?' Aiden asks, finger hovering in its eternal place just below one nostril.

'Something I hope will help make the world around us a bit better, Aiden,' I tell him. 'Something that I'm quite scared about starting, but really want to, because it could be *great.*' I look fondly around the whole class, at the sea of faces that fundamentally shifted my outlook on the world all those weeks ago. 'And I need you guys to help me give it a *name*,' I tell them, pulling out my recycled notepad and pen.

◆ ◆ ◆

The offices of R.A.B. Developments are as swish and modern as you'd expect for a company that specialises in building luxurious flats and houses.

I grimace as I walk in through the sliding glass doors and up to the reception. There's no pot plants anywhere, and I can see the amount of paper wastage that goes on just behind the semicircular reception desk in front of me.

This place is *anathema*.

'Hello,' I say to the guy behind the counter, who must be struggling to breathe, given how tight that tie and collar look.

'Can I help you, madam?' he replies, affecting his no doubt well practised welcoming smile.

'I want to see your boss Robert,' I reply, a little curtly. I don't want to be here. I don't want to be here at all, but I have a question that needs answering. 'Is he in his office?'

'Yes, but I'm not sure he's available for a meeting right now. You'll have to make an appointment.'

I smile. It's not a warm one. 'Well, Robert's never been one to worry about silly things like appointments, has he?' I tell the receptionist. 'So I'll just pop through and go speak to him. His office still the big one at the back, is it?'

I don't wait for a reply. Instead, I stride right on to the office floor that spreads away to the left of the reception, and make a beeline for what I remember to be Robert Ainslie Blake's sumptuous office.

The receptionist tries to stop me, but by the time he reaches me, insisting that I withdraw, I'm already banging his boss's door open.

'Morning, Robert!' I say brightly. 'You and I need to have a *chat*.'

Robert Ainslie Blake is sat with his feet up on the desk, playing with his iPhone.

Having a busy day, then . . .

'Ellie!' he squawks, nearly tipping himself back off the luxurious leather seat he's parked his manspreading arse on.

'I'm sorry, Mr Ainslie Blake! She just barged her way in here!' the receptionist cries.

I nod. 'That I did.' I give the guy a cheeky grin. 'Don't worry though, your boss is well used to doing this kind of thing, so I'm sure he won't mind.'

'It's okay, Troy, yeah?' Robert tells him, as I cross the floor of his office to stand right at his desk. 'She's a friend.'

I shake my head and cross my arms. 'Oh, I don't think so, Robert.' My eyes narrow. 'It gives me no joy to come and speak to you . . . but I have a question to ask.'

Robert rolls his eyes.

Another little woman getting all hot under the collar, he's probably thinking. *Probably on her period, or something.*

'Okay, Gorgeo. It's fine. Calm yourself down . . . and ask away.'

'How much?' I snap, as the receptionist wisely withdraws.

'What?'

'How much money did you offer Nolan Reece for Viridian PR?'

'Well, I don't think that's any business of yours, Ellie,' Robert blusters. 'I mean, it's a private thing, between two men, and I don't—'

'Robert, you either tell me how much you offered Nolan, or I'm going to post that naked picture of you I took in Sicily all over social media. I still have it.' I smile slyly. 'You know the one. After you'd got out of that plunge pool? That *cold* plunge pool?'

I don't still have the picture at all. I deleted it the day I split up with him, but he doesn't know that, does he?

'A million!' Robert squeals, knowing just how bad what I'm threatening to do could be for his reputation.

My jaw clenches.

So, there you have it. That's how much it costs to sell people right down the river. I had to know. I just *had to*.

'Thank you,' I tell Robert, looking at him like he's a bug under a microscope. 'You might want to rethink that offer, though. Nolan's company is about to become worthless.'

Robert's brow furrows. 'What do you mean?'

'Don't worry, Robert. You'll find out very soon.'

I turn on one heel and head back to the door. Before I reach it though, something occurs to me, and I turn to face Robert Ainslie Blake for the last time in my life.

'You know, I do owe you an apology,' I tell him.

'Do you, Gorgeo?'

My turn to roll my eyes. I breathe deeply. 'Yes. I do. Because I made you the *villain*, Robert. I made you the big bad guy. But that's not what you are, is it? You're not evil. You're not a monster. You're just a reckless, stupid man who wants to manspread himself about as much as possible, to make up for his inadequacies – and you don't care who or what you destroy in the process. Up to and including any wildlife sanctuaries that might be nearby.' I heave a leaden sigh. 'And God help us – the world's full of people like you, isn't it?'

'Here, I don't think you can come in here and say all that to me, yeah?'

'I think I just *did*,' I say in a weary voice, opening his door. 'You're not the villain here, Robert. But I fucking know who *is*, and you might want to pay attention to what I'm about to do next . . . just in case you get any ideas in the future.'

I go through the door and slam it behind me, never to see Robert Ainslie Blake again.

◆ ◆ ◆

The arms of Nolan Reece's office chair have been worn smooth by his hands.

He has a habit of running them up and down the threadbare cloth when he's thinking about something. I've seen it happen many times, during long conversations about how we can make the world a better place by providing ethical, environmentally friendly public relations to companies trying to make the planet greener and more sustainable.

At the time, I thought he was as committed to this cause as I have become, but now I know the truth. Now I have all the facts.

You know who else has all the facts?

. . . oh my. You're about to find out, and it's going to be *glorious*.

Nadia let me in to the offices of Viridian PR this morning. She – along with Joseph and Amisha – has been an absolute *rock* over the past couple of weeks. As soon as I'd told them all what Nolan had been up to – and showed them the footage I'd captured of his double life – they were all 100 per cent behind what I had planned, both for him and for them.

Without all three working with me, I wouldn't have known that Nolan was coming into the office late this morning due to a 'meeting'. I put the word in quotation marks here, because for all I know he's actually choffing down an Egg McMuffin some-where, while simultaneously kicking a polar bear in the testicles. The bastard.

Knowing his movements in and around Viridian PR has allowed me to set up today's entertainment. I'm probably verging on the melodramatic here (hell, there's no *probably* about it), but I feel this entire situation needs wrapping up with something osten-tatious and memorable – if only to keep Nolan Reece off guard long enough so I can get him to do what I want.

Besides . . . the man has humiliated me for the past few months without me even knowing about it. Payback is due.

Which is why I'm sat here, at this desk, waiting for Nolan to come in.

According to the watch that sits just above my shaking left hand, this will be in about a minute or so.

Through the glass door that leads to Nolan's private office I can see the whole of the main office floor, including the glass double doors that lead in from the elevator foyer. I will have a clear view of my ex-boss and ex-boyfriend as he comes through it and walks towards me.

The pot plants are looking a little limp, it has to be said. I'll have to take them with me.

This will be the first time I have seen Nolan since that day on his doorstep, when I thrashed him with his underpants. He hasn't attempted to communicate with me, which has probably been wise.

I did receive an email from Young Adrian, regarding when I'd be getting my last pay cheque, but that's been the only contact I've had from Viridian PR in any official capacity.

Unofficially, things have been very different, though. Oh my, yes.

Unofficially, there has been a *lot* of communication between Ellie Cooke and the staff of Viridian PR – everyone except Nolan Reece. My lovely Mercedes hybrid has been toing and froing between the homes of everyone I know from work with remarkable frequency. It's a good job the car is so green to run.

I've had a lot of fast-talking and a lot of convincing to do, you see.

All of this activity might explain why just about everyone out there in the office is looking directly at the main doors to Viridian PR, with expressions on their faces ranging from barely concealed disgust to outright anger.

I have set the stage, my friends.

Now we just need the star of the show to come in.

The door flies open, and in walks a dishevelled Nolan Reece.

My . . . that's very interesting, isn't it?

313

He looks like a man on the edge.

Could that possibly be because of the way people's attitudes have subtly – and in some cases not so subtly – changed towards him in the past couple of weeks?

I do think that might be the case.

I've asked them all to stay silent until today, but I'm sure a man as smart as Nolan Reece can pick up on the fact that *something* is wrong.

His demeanour today suggests that this is very much the case.

My hands involuntarily grip the arms of the chair as the nerves try to take hold. I am instantly transported back to that day in this very office, when I sat in the chair opposite, gripping the arms as tightly as I am now, because I thought Nolan Reece was about to fire me from my job.

The day he actually offered me a *better* job, because he thought I was environmentally conscious. Little did he know I was lying through my teeth back then. And little did I know *he* was lying through *his*.

Maybe he actually knew damn well I wasn't being honest with him, and saw a kindred spirit.

Blimey. That might be exactly what happened!

There I was thinking I'd been so clever to pull the wool over Nolan's eyes, when maybe he knew all along what I was up to, and the only wool-pulling going on was resolutely over my stupid head.

Nolan was a lot smarter than me, back then. I hope to Christ he isn't now.

I take a very deep breath, and allow my grip to loosen a bit on the arms of the chair. I'm not the one who should be nervous here today. *He is.*

I continue to watch as Nolan attempts to say good morning to his staff as he passes them – in much the same way he has done every other morning (or afternoon, depending on what secretive bullshit he's been up to that day). He doesn't get much of a response – and the ones that he does get are cold in the extreme.

As he gets closer and closer to the tinted glass door that leads to his private office, I feel my pulse quicken. The moment is nearly here.

The moment I've prepared for over the past fortnight.

The moment I laid awake in bed thinking about until the early hours of this morning.

I've planned everything down to within an inch of its life, but that plan playing out successfully now depends on how Nolan Reece reacts to what I've done.

He's reached the door.

Here we go then. In for a penny, in for a pound.

'Nadia? Can you get Adrian to make me a coffee, please?' Nolan barks at my colleague, as he pauses with his hand against the door. If he peered in here through the tinted glass he'd easily see who was inside – but he's clearly quite stressed and off kilter. *Good.* That's exactly how I want him to be. 'I've barely slept,' he continues, pushing the door open, 'and need something to wake me – *oh bloody hell*!'

Yes!

That's more or less the reaction I was hoping for.

'What the hell are all of you doing in my fucking *office*?!' he exclaims.

'Waiting for you, you lying pig's scrotum!'

That wasn't me.

I wouldn't use the phrase 'pig's scrotum' if you paid me.

Mordred O'Hare would though.

In fact, he just has. And for Mordred O'Hare to start naming the parts of animals in his insults, you know he must be in a bad mood. Usually he'd avoid anything to do with pig parts. That's kind of his raison d'être.

Nolan stares at Mordred in horror. 'Why are you here?'

'Because Ellie asked us to be!' Petal O'Hare says, from where she's stood next to her ambulatory bush of a husband. When you're confronting someone the way I am today, it's great to have a woman who channels Joanna Lumley so effectively right beside you. It's very comforting.

'Why?' The blood is draining from Nolan's face. He might be a lying bastard, but he's also clearly a *smart* bastard.

He's probably putting two and two together right now, and coming up with *fucked*.

'Because she's told us – and *shown us* – what's really been going on around here!' says Bandy, my best friend from Worriors For The Plonet.

See?

I have been busy, haven't I?

In fact, you can barely *move* for the Viridian PR clients I've persuaded to come down here this morning to confront the owner of the business.

There's Mordred and Petal on my left, with Sierra from The Green Tangent on theirs. On my right is Bandy, along with Kyle the twelve-year-old CEO from Hempawear, Clara from Protocol Waste Management, and Donald from Earth's Future Lighting.

These are the only clients I could get here at such short notice, but I've been in touch with *all* of Viridian's now-extensive list over the past two weeks.

I did a very good job as Head of Client Relations – keeping communication channels open as much as possible, and staying friendly with each and every one of the people running the businesses we represent.

Every client was pleased to hear from me, even though I am no longer at Viridian PR, and has been happy to listen to everything I had to tell them. And *show* them.

They've all had a good look at what Nolan Reece gets up to on his days off. I put together a lovely video package with Joseph and Amisha's help – featuring all of that iPhone footage I captured, along with highlights of the three hours that my car's dashcam caught.

Most of Viridian's clients were very surprised at the audio quality of the dashcam footage. They couldn't quite *believe* that it managed to pick up every word exchanged between Nolan and me on his doorstep. Especially all that stuff about Nolan selling the company off. They were *extremely* interested in that part of the video.

How do you think it went down with them all?

'You're gonna sell us all off, are you?!' Kyle from Hempawear exclaims. He looks so full of frustration and dismay he could almost pass for an adult.

'What? I . . . what?' Nolan splutters.

'I don't appreciate having my company used as a tool just to earn *you* a big fat payout!' Donald remarks in a cold voice, looking about as incandescent as one of his most popular products.

'I'm sorry? I don't know what you're all talking about. I have no clue why you'd all . . . why you'd all . . .' Nolan says, before grinding to a halt and fixing me with a stare of pure hatred.

He takes a deep breath, gaining back some of his composure. You can see the cogs whirring away up there in his brain, trying to think of a way out of this. 'I don't know what Miss Cooke has been telling you,' he says, addressing everyone in the room but me, 'but I would advise you that I've had to let her go from Viridian PR, due to some unfortunate incidents of sexual harassment she's been guilty of towards me.'

. . .

. . .

You hear that?

You hear that sound, do you?

That's the sound of every atom in the universe collectively wincing at the lowest thing anyone has ever said or done since the dawn of time.

The entire snake population of our planet is positively *airborne* in comparison to how low Nolan Reece has just sunk.

'It's a real pity that she's stooped to such a petty act like this,' Nolan carries on, resolutely ignoring me and concentrating completely on them. You can feel the force of his persuasive personality in full effect now. It's quite a thing to behold.

A crying shame that it will do him no good *whatsoever* – and in this particular case, is making things even *worse* for him.

'Ellie is a very troubled girl, so please don't believe anything she may have told you about me or Viridian PR,' Nolan says, sporting the most ingratiating smile he can. 'I can assure you that your businesses are in safe hands with us moving forward.'

'Ahem,' I cough lightly into one hand, placing the other atop the laptop on Nolan's desk. I swivel it around so that the screen faces him. I then look up, straight into Nolan's eyes, and press the enter key.

On the screen, the video footage from my dashcam appears. I've got the volume turned up nice and loud.

'There's a lot of money in environmental stuff, Ellie. You know that. And they don't have that many people fighting their corner, so I thought it'd be a good idea to target them. Get them all on board with a company that understands them. Get the business really going, before—'

'Before what?'

'Nothing!'

'You'd better say what you were going to, Nolan, otherwise I'm likely to start doing things to your person that we will both regret. Talk!'

'Before I . . . before I sell it off.'

'Sell it off?!'

'Yes! That's the endgame with these things! Get a company up and running, get loads of clients, and then sell both to the highest bidder once you've earned a good reputation. There's millions to be had!'

The video freeze-frames on this moment, and zooms in on Nolan's face. As it does, cartoon horns sprout from Nolan's forehead and the entire screen is washed in a red colour.

Then, in a horrible slow-motion voice, dripping with electronically engineered malice, Nolan repeats, 'There's millions to be had . . . millions to be had . . . millions . . . millions . . .'

I roll my eyes. I knew I should have stopped Joseph playing about with the video too much. It's rather undercut the impact.

Mind you, it's obviously had the desired effect on Nolan. He looks like someone's just inserted something unfortunate into him.

He clearly doesn't need to see any more. My point has been made. I close the laptop, cutting off his slow-motion drawl as it repeats the word 'millions' over and over again.

Nolan goes to open his mouth to make up another excuse – but immediately closes it again, as soon as he gets a good look at everyone's faces.

'I think the phrase you're looking for is "done up like a Christmas turkey",' I tell him.

'Ellie,' Mordred chides from beside me.

'Sorry, Mordred,' I reply, forgetting how the mention of prepared meat tends to make him quite upset. I turn my attention back to Nolan. 'Now. Here is what is going to happen,' I tell him, sitting a little more upright in the chair. I feel like I'm channelling Helen Carmichael as I speak.

No.

To hell with that.

The only person I'm channelling here is Ellie Cooke, and that's all I bloody *need*.

'You are going to release all of these fine people from their deals with Viridian PR,' I inform Nolan in the steeliest of voices. 'I've looked into their contracts, and the clauses state it can easily be done.'

Nolan shakes his head vigorously. 'Not a chance in hell!'

I smile. 'I thought you might say that. That's why I took the liberty of consulting with a very nice lawyer at a firm who specialise in representing ethical companies. Clara here put me on to him.' The woman in question looks at Nolan smugly. 'They have told me that my friends beside me have grounds to sue you for every penny you've got, thanks to your false representation of both the services Viridian PR provides and the company's future remit.'

I'm pretty sure I got all that right. I certainly rehearsed saying it in the mirror enough this morning.

'But . . . but . . .' Nolan chokes.

'No, Nolan. I'm talking. You *listen*,' I reply, the steel having turned into diamond. 'You have a choice. Either release all of Viridian's clients from their contracts right *now*, or face a lawsuit you will lose – and lose extremely *hard*.'

Nolan sneers at me. 'And if I do release them, what are they going to do, eh? Where are they going to go? Nobody is dumb enough to run a PR company like this. Not for very long, anyway. Most people just don't care enough about the environment.'

I sit back in the chair. 'All of Viridian PR's clients have agreed to become clients of What We Can PR.'

'Who the hell are What We Can PR?'

I slowly raise one hand, extend my index finger and point it at my chest.

The kids in Sean's class came up with the name, in a brainstorming session that took half an hour and descended into giggles on more than one occasion. They said I should call my business something that anyone can understand . . . something nice and

320

simple. Something that says what I want to do for the planet. What everyone should be doing.

They told me, and I listened.

Nolan laughs. The bastard actually *laughs* at me. '*You?* You're going to start your own company?'

'Yes.'

'Ha! And where are you going to get the staff to do that?!'

I fold my arms. 'They're standing right behind you.'

Nolan quickly turns to see every member of Viridian PR's team crowded around the office door, staring daggers at him.

Nadia, Amisha and Joseph are right there at the front.

My three musketeers. My colleagues. My friends.

Perfect.

Nolan turns back slowly, and regards me with a look that is . . . quite unexpected, actually.

I think . . . I think it's *grudging admiration.*

'Well, well,' he says hoarsely. 'Looks like you've strung me up like a fucking kipper.'

Mordred makes a strangled noise from beside me.

I nod though. It feels like the perfect analogy. 'Yes. It does appear that way.'

He offers me a tight, knowing smile. 'You think you're oh-so-clever right now, Ellie. But doing this kind of thing? It's nowhere near as easy as you think it is.'

'Possibly not.'

'You'll *fail*, you know. I've seen it happen time and time again.'

'Maybe.' I rise from the chair. 'And maybe not. But however it goes, Nolan, I'll know one thing.'

'What's that?'

'I'll be doing it for the right reasons.'

He barks with laughter. 'Oh my God. You're *delusional!* You've got no chance!'

'She's just taken your entire business away from you in less than a fortnight,' Petal O'Hare points out. 'I'd say her chances are much better than you think.'

Nolan Reece has no answer for that.

That's okay, though. I'm kind of done listening to what he has to say, anyway.

'Shall we leave, folks?' I ask my companions. 'Nolan here has some contracts to release.'

I walk around the desk, very glad to be getting out of there. While this confrontation has gone about as well as could be expected, I don't particularly want it going on longer than is necessary.

'Good luck, Ellie,' Nolan sneers at me. He's very good at sneering, now all his make-believe, nice-guy bullshit has been laid aside. 'You're going to need it. Especially when I get back on my feet.'

Oh . . . a threat. How *nice*.

I give him a tight grin. 'I look forward to it, Nolan. I truly do.'

I resist the urge to pat him on the cheek, as I really don't want to touch him again. Ever.

The impromptu round of applause led by Nadia as I emerge from the office is probably a *little much* to be honest, but then I guess I am about to become her boss, along with everybody else at Viridian – sorry, at What We Can PR.

Just as well Mordred and Petal are going to let me rent out the nicest of the side buildings on Veganthropy's estate. I'm going to need the space.

Oh . . .

There's that flutter of anxiety in my chest.

I've been feeling it quite a lot over the past few days. Every time I've contemplated what I'm about to do, which is go into business for myself. Actually do the thing that Nolan Reece was *pretending* to do – run an ethical, environmentally friendly public relations

322

company. One I have no intention of ever selling off to the highest, manspreading bidder.

It should be something I can handle.

I've been second-in-command here for the past few months and have done a pretty decent job of it (foam bottles, thirty-seven seconds, and septic tanks notwithstanding). Why shouldn't I be able to take it one step further and run the whole damn thing myself?

Because he's right, Ellie. You might fail.

Yes, I might – horrible little voice in my head that I could really do without at times like this – but alternatively, I might *not* fail. I might *succeed*.

And even if I don't . . .

Even if Nolan Reece is right, and it all comes crashing down around me – at least I will know that I *tried*. Tried to make the world a little better, by helping people who believe that climate change is a real and gigantic threat to our whole planet.

Because that's what's important here . . .

Trying.

Not necessarily worrying about the end result – but being on the *journey itself*.

That's what convinced me I could start my own PR company – and take on all of these disparate clients, and a group of hard-working staff members.

I don't *have* to succeed; I just have to give it my best.

I can't do everything. I can't win every battle. I can't solve every problem.

But I can sure as hell *do what I can*.

That's why I went with the name for the company that Sean's class came up with, because that's absolutely the philosophy behind it.

We're going to do *What We Can* to make the world a better place. We're going to do *What We Can* to stop climate change and the destruction of our planet.

Just like Irene McClapperty and her composting system.

Okay, she may have had four normal light bulbs in her cottage living room, but in so many other important ways she's doing *what she can*.

None of us are perfect. None of us have all the answers, and very few of us can make massive, sweeping changes to our lives. But we can do *What We Can*.

That's both the name and the mission statement for my new company.

All of Viridian PR's ex-clients love it. I should hope they do, given that without them – without their example – I wouldn't be in a position to name anything. They have irrevocably changed me as a person. Each and every one of them . . . because they're doing what they can.

And I'm going to keep paying them back for that, by doing the best job that I'm capable of, by providing the best service I can, for as long as I can.

The same goes for my new staff – who are all equally as excited about the prospect of working for What We Can PR as my new clients are about working with us.

I'm not the only one here who has been profoundly affected by the direction Nolan Reece led us in when he took over from Pierre and Peter Rothman. He may have done it for all the wrong reasons, but that doesn't mean his contribution to our lives has been any less important.

That's why I've taken his business away from him, instead of getting his clients to sue – and potentially ruin him for life. And that's why I only thrashed him around the head with a harmless pair of Primark boxer shorts, instead of kicking him square in the testicles. I went soft on him, believe it or not.

Nolan *will* be back, of that I'm sure. He's that type. And I may have run-ins with him again. But I'll be prepared for them when they do come along, of that I'm sure.

However, none of that is a concern *right now*.

Because I have work to do, with all of these fine people – who are now following me out of the offices of Viridian PR and into a brand-new world.

I just hope I can help make sure that world is around for as long as possible. Because there's Summer to think about. And Alex. And Jade. And Aiden too – with his finger up his nose, and his brain afire with worry about what the adults are doing to stop the disastrous climate change going on around him.

I'll do what I can, because that's what they've asked me to do.

That's all I'm capable of.

. . . but that might just be enough.

I hope you feel the same way.

Do what you can. The rest will come in time.

ACKNOWLEDGMENTS

This book-writing business never gets any easier, let me assure you of that. Without the help of a great many good and kind people, I would probably have collapsed into a pile of neuroses a long time ago.

Therefore, my thanks go to: everyone at Amazon Publishing, for continuing to give me money in exchange for the contents of my brain. My agent Ariella, for making sure those contents make at least some sort of sense. My mother Judy, for – you know – just being my mum. All of my close friends, especially the ones who read these books of mine. And finally, as always, my wife Gemma – the world around us may be in a bit of a state, but *my* world will always be amazing, as long as she's in it.

. . . oh yes, and you lot. Don't worry. I haven't forgotten about you – my fabulous readers. Thank you for continuing to buy my books. I remain entirely honoured that you choose to do it.

ABOUT THE AUTHOR

Photo © 2017 Chloe Waters

Nick Spalding is the bestselling author of fifteen novels, two novellas and two memoirs. Nick worked in media and marketing for most of his life before turning his energy to his genre-spanning humorous writing. He lives in the south of England with his wife.